A Wanderer
on the Earth

A Wanderer on the Earth

The Birken Saga—Book 2

Harald Lutz Bruckner

A Wanderer on the Earth

Copyright © 2019 Harald Lutz Bruckner. All rights reserved. No part of this book may be reproduced or retransmitted in any form or by any means without the written permission of the publisher.

Published by Hideaway Park Press
Green Valley, AZ

ISBN: 978-0-578-54287-4 (paperback)
ISBN: 978-0-578-54288-1 (ebook)
LCCN: 2019909591

Books by Harald Lutz Bruckner

The Blue Sapphire Amulet

The Birken Saga
A Trilogy

Book 1 *Escape on the Astral Express*
Book 2 *A Wanderer on the Earth*
Book 3 *The Born-Again Phoenix*

For Paul, Ethel, Bernie, Marlene,
and Harry

When you till the ground,
it shall no longer yield to you its strength;
you shall be a fugitive and
a wanderer on the earth.
—Genesis 4:12

A Wanderer on the Earth

1948 to 1952

Chapter I

AT the end of the school year, Hektor scheduled a conference with Rektor Nagelmann, his principal and teacher at the Kupferschule. The outcome would ultimately shape the rest of Hektor's life. His mentor looked forward to the meeting since he was very much interested in helping Hektor find answers to the many questions concerning the boy's education.

"What do you intend to do with your life? Where do you see yourself going when you leave this school a year down the road? You have excellent skills in English and have mastered our German language far beyond your age."

Hektor had known these questions would be asked of him one day. A decision had to be made on how to proceed with his education. And so he blurted it out: "What I really would like to do when I finish here is to attend the *Folkwangschule* and study acting."

Rektor Nagelmann peered over his wire-rimmed glasses and was all ears. He seemed totally surprised, his face spelling all sorts of questions. "Have you discussed this with your family?"

"No, I haven't. I'm sure they'll be shocked to learn of my intentions; and I am positive there will be a lot of opposition."

Hektor had made up his mind to confront his family at the next opportunity. His parents had invited Hektor's grandparents for Sunday dinner. He walked into the family dining room. At the head of the table sat his grandfather, dominating the conversation. Reflections from the chandelier bounced off the old man's bald head. His strange-looking eyeglasses clasped the bridge of his bulbous nose and appeared to be slipping off the dominant facial appendage. Grandfather's beady eyes were fixed on his fourteen-year-old grandson. Hektor needed to pinch himself not to laugh at the sight of the fat jowls drooping off the much-feared man's face. When his grandfather finally spoke, Hektor knew he was in for a confrontation with his nemesis.

"Your brother is doing well in the second year of his apprenticeship. I hear nothing but praise from his master butcher. Do I dare ask what trade you would like to learn?"

"I don't wish to be apprenticed in any trade; my visions for my life are very different from yours. After my next school year, I am entering the *Folkwangschule* to study acting." Hektor didn't blink an eye, glaring at his grandfather. His stance conveyed what the expected reaction would be.

Grandfather cupped his ear. "Did I understand you correctly? Did you say acting?" He picked up his stein and took a healthy swig from the vessel. It was obvious he wanted to wash the bad taste from his mouth. Hektor nearly burst out laughing, contemplating his grandfather's foam-covered mustache, almost Hitleresque in shape. The old man stared at Hektor and his father. "You must be joking!" His eyes bulged as he slammed the *Bier Stein* on the highly polished surface. Beer spilled all over.

Hektor's mother covered her mouth as she beheld the ugly scar left on the precious dining room table that survived the war without a scratch.

Hektor looked his grandfather straight in the eyes. "As a matter of fact, joking is the furthest thing from my mind. I've never been more serious about anything!"

"Who the hell in damnation do you think you are talking to?"

"Sorry to disappoint you and to be disrespectful, Grandfather, but you are the one who set the tone for this discussion. I may or may not become an actor, but one damn thing is for sure: I will never be a butcher. There are already enough in this family!" Hektor stayed out of striking distance, knowing the old geezer might have struck him with one of his crutches. He realized his fate was sealed.

"There will be no dilettantes in this family." Grandpa Krämer glared at Hektor and faced his son-in-law as he struck the dining room table repeatedly with his balled fist. "Alex, I want you to remove this boy immediately from that school where such crazy ideas seem to be hatched and planted in his head. You apprentice him post-haste in a respectable trade. No grandson of mine will ever stand on any stage making an ass of himself." He reached for the crutches and pushed himself out of his chair; his arthritic hips were giving him fits. "When I come back from taking a piss, I expect to hear an acceptable answer to my demands."

Stumbling back onto the scene, Grandpa caught everyone looking at him in shock. His pants were still unzipped; he had obviously pissed all over himself and soiled his pants to boot. Hektor's mother walked over to her aging father and guided him back to the bathroom. Embarrassed, Grandma and daughter Helena undressed and cleaned up the old man. One of Alex's robes would have to do the trick. He was still fuming at Hektor when he finally emerged from the WC.

"This is all your fault; it was your crazy scheme that caused me to have the accident. If I could stand alone on my two feet, I would horsewhip your ass like I used to do years ago, you bastard."

"I always knew you enjoyed whipping us. I hate saying it, but it doesn't bother me, seeing you humiliated. You seem to thrive on doing it to others and especially me. What just happened to you is exactly what you deserved—and I should feel sorry for you?"

"How dare you speak to your grandfather that way?" screamed his mother.

"And why not? He threatened me and called me a bastard. Last I knew, it was Dad who fathered me, not the milkman." Hektor wanted to walk out of the room, but his father grabbed his arm and stopped him.

"You better forget about this acting idea. Who do you think would pay for you to attend the *Folkwangschule?*"

"Frankly, I thought you and Mom would, since my entire education was screwed up by the damn war. Because of lacking more than two years of schooling, I can't even consider enrollment at a *Hochschule* [German high school]. I'm just sick of running into roadblocks everywhere."

His father understood Hektor's dilemma. "When you were a little boy, you used to say you wanted to become a pastry chef. Maybe I should speak to Herr Nudelmann at his bakery. Becoming a baker might be an honorable and acceptable trade for you to learn. It might appease your grandfather."

"Why do I need to appease him? It's my life we are talking about. Personally, I don't give a damn what he thinks of me!" Hektor had to have the last word in this argument.

⋈

His father and Herr Nudelmann executed the contract. Hektor began his three-year apprenticeship the next week. The following Sunday, sitting in his piss-soaked chair, the old man grinned with pleasure when Hektor was forced to tell him what had transpired.

"As you wished, my father took me out of school and enslaved me to this lousy bakery apprenticeship. I hope you are happy now that you have once again imposed your will on me. But let me assure you the last word hasn't been spoken on this matter."

"Where did you learn to speak in that way? Count your blessings that I'm handicapped by my physical ailments. If I could, I'd give you the whipping of your life!"

Hektor was tempted to spit into the old man's face but opted to just walk out of the room and sought his grandmother in the kitchen. He liked having one of her cookies, but he found little else to talk about. His grandmother knew how hurt he was by his grandfather's bullheadedness. Hektor was glad when he could escape.

He didn't know where he got the gumption, but on the Saturday concluding the sixth and final week of his probationary period, he stepped into Baker Nudelmann's office. The desk was covered with all sorts of papers, slightly dusted with flour.

"Sir, I won't be back on Monday. I've hated every second of being under your roof. This isn't the life I envisioned for myself. It's my grandfather who forced my father's hand to apprentice me to you. It's not what I want. I realize my educational dreams were destroyed by the war, but I will not be sacrificed on the altar of tradition. I will never be a baker, a tradesman, or anything that would please my mother's father. I hate the man and am convinced he has had no use for me from the day I was born."

Herr Nudelmann sat behind his desk, his mouth agape. Hektor thought he might have given the man a heart attack.

"Are you OK, Herr Nudelmann? I didn't mean to shock you!"

"That you did! But I'm OK. I'm glad you spoke up and regret that you feel the way you do about your grandfather. That said, I wouldn't want someone working for me for three years, hating every moment. More power to you; you'll do OK in life." He got out of his chair and reached for Hektor's contract in the safe. Tearing it to pieces, he handed it to the astonished boy. "You'll catch hell from your folks, but I'm proud of you for speaking up." He shook Hektor's hand and wished him well.

Hektor couldn't wait to get home and have dinner with his family. When the last person around the table was finished eating, he felt emboldened enough to share his news with the family. "I'm going back to school on Monday. I'm all done with my trials at the bakery." He threw the torn contract on the table. "Herr Nudelmann was happy to let me out of it when I told him I was forced into slave labor and didn't want any part of it. I told him it was Grandpa's wish and not mine to become a baker."

The expected pandemonium broke out; he was prepared for Papa Alex's choleric outbursts, but in the end, Hektor returned to school for one more year. When his grandfather learned the following weekend what Hektor had done, he was furious with him for opposing his wishes.

"How dare you back out of a contract your father signed! What will people say about our honorable name?"

"Frankly, Grandfather, I don't give a rip!" He was tempted to use a gesture but decided he had done enough to convey to the old man that he was standing his ground.

⋊⋉

When Hektor started to work at the bakery, his classmates were in recess. They just started their final year at the *Volksschule* [basic school].

No one was more shocked to see Hektor grace the frame of the classroom door than Rektor Nagelmann. There was a frown of uncertainty on his face; he didn't trust his eyes. "What are you doing here? Why aren't you at work at the bakery?"

"I hate to surprise you. I'm done with that episode in my life and am here to stay. Don't look so astounded! If you remember, I told you I wouldn't let myself be railroaded into a world I couldn't face for the rest of my life." Right after class, he cornered Rektor Nagelmann, who was eager to get back to his office. "When may I have an appointment with you to discuss my immediate future?"

"How about tomorrow afternoon at four? My calendar is clear, and we can chat as long as you wish."

"Great! I have a thousand questions."

Arriving at his mentor's office the next afternoon, he was put at ease by the teacher who had become more than an educator to him; he was his ally and friend.

"Well, young man, what's on your mind today?"

"I know I can stay here for another year, but I want you to show me the way beyond this school year. Since an acting career seems to be clearly out of the question, I would like to pursue a teaching career. A classroom could become my stage."

"Are you suggesting that I am acting in class?"

"No and yes; you seem to enjoy dramatizing the points you try to make. You are not a buffoon, but you have a way of acting things out that make learning fun. I could see myself doing that in front of a class. Becoming a teacher would certainly be more acceptable to the whole clan than being on stage."

"Now that you put it this way, I have to agree with you. I do enjoy being in front of the class. However, I hate to put a damper on your aspirations because it will be next to impossible for you to pursue that educational track at this time. To follow an academic career, you should have been enrolled in a *Hochschule* at age ten, although that couldn't be done because of the war."

"Why couldn't I go to a *Hochschule* now?"

"Hektor, no pedagogue in his right mind would put a fourteen-year-old in a classroom with ten-year-old children. You are a young man with developed ideas. Psychologically, you have a different mind-set than a child aged ten. It just wouldn't be done. However, I am not an autocrat; I will set up appointments for you with a couple of high school principals. Knowing your interests, I am inclined to get in touch with the rectors at two *Humanistic Gymnasiums*. Don't be too disappointed when they reiterate what I have tried to explain to you."

At the first school, Hektor did not even get past the rector's secretary. After asking Hektor why he was there, she simply opened the door to her boss's office and whispered the reason for his appointment.

The man raised his eyebrows and yelled loud enough for Hektor to hear what he had to say. "I am too busy to waste my time on such a nonsensical idea. Tell him to learn a trade. Not everyone is fit for higher education!"

Hektor was out of the office so fast he didn't know what hit him. He couldn't say that Rektor Nagelmann hadn't warned him.

The second contact was somewhat more positive. While the same negative explanation was put to him with reference to starting way back with ten-year-olds, Hektor was let down more gently. Rather than aiming to obtain his *Abitur* [equivalent to an Associate's degree], the suggestion was he apply to the *Handelsschule* [School of Commerce] and pursue a degree and career in business. At first, that seemed like a cop-out. However, when he related the suggestion to his trusted mentor, his reaction was positive, and his comments encouraging as well as guarded.

"You realize there will be an entrance exam. They are highly selective in terms of their admissions, although I am not concerned about that. The other negative element is that you will have to commute by train. The school in Essen was destroyed during the war and is now housed in an old cloister in Steele. Train travel will add to the cost of your schooling, and of course, your parents will have to pay tuition. It is not a free educational ride."

Hektor didn't jump to any conclusions; he mulled over the suggestions the rector at the *Gymnasium* [preparatory high school] and

Herr Nagelmann had made. Finally, he wanted to discuss the issue with his mother. Helena was definitely the better choice. She had a pretty good idea what Hektor was going through.

Her own educational aspirations fell victim to the aftermath of World War I; of course, her father was of the opinion women should never pursue advanced studies. Hektor could never understand why his mother venerated her father the way she did; he was a tyrant and always enjoyed imposing his will on others. Helena was deprived of postsecondary schooling by design. Hektor knew he had an ally in his mother.

"How would you feel about sending me to the Handelsschule in Steele for two years?"

His mother was perplexed. "How will you get there? By train from Essen-West and changing trains at the *Hauptbahnhof* [main railroad station]? Do you realize how long a day this will be for you? Classes will start at eight o'clock in the morning, and you will be there until three or four o'clock in the afternoon. During the long winter months, you won't come home until well after dark. And then there will be studying in the evening. And how much is the tuition?" The pragmatist had finally spoken.

"Mother, by the time I start attending the Handelsschule, I will be fifteen years old. What's the big deal with taking a local train? You sent Albert and me halfway across the country in the middle of a war when we were nine and eleven. Didn't you think that was pretty gutsy? The first thing that will have to happen is my passing the entrance exam. The tuition is another issue." That probably should have been the first of all questions raised with his parents and was the real clincher. Hektor knew that anything that cost money might cause a major catastrophe in the Birken household.

"Let me discuss it with your father. I might be more persuasive in loosening his tight purse strings." When she broached the subject after the evening meal, Alex became thoughtful.

"Who knows? By the time 1949 rolls around, things will be

better. I expect our business to pick up and make a greater profit one of these days. Let's look at the future more positively. Hektor's educational aspirations were thwarted often enough. We should make every effort to support him."

Hektor was dumbfounded. Had he heard his father correctly?

For a moment, he shed any inhibitions and gave his dad a bear hug. No words were spoken; none were needed. At that moment, they fully understood each other.

Chapter 2

TIME passed all too swiftly. The entrance exams at the School of Commerce came and went; Hektor did well. On the first Monday after Easter 1949, Hektor Birken found himself walking toward the railway station in Essen-West. He had to catch the early train to Essen *Hauptbahnhof*, where he transferred to the Essen-Steele train.

Hektor took the many steps from the train platform down to the street level two at a time. He was anxious to get to the school presently housed in the old cloister nearby. He was out of breath when he walked into the old building. It was dark and dingy and showed significant signs of neglect and damage from the war. This was an all-boys school. The headmaster, Herr Wagemann, marched into the classroom. Twenty-six pairs of eyes were watching him. He was of average height and looked plain grumpy. His mean appearance was underscored by the punctuating noises he made with the cane he carried.

Hektor had seated himself in the front row of the class to the far left. He had the best view of the whole class over his right shoulder. Directly behind him sat Nicklaus Beerenbaum, whose partner in crime was Heinrich Ruppelkist. Little did Hektor know on that first day of school how their lives would intertwine.

Herr Wagemann mumbled something before spitting out his last name, introducing himself as the classroom teacher. "I shall read your names. Please stand as your name is called. Stand until you are asked to take your seat."

Hektor got it—the old crab wanted to get a good look at each student before moving on to the next. Wagemann coughed and walked over to a brass spittoon to relieve himself. He had pretty good aim, but the sound was ghastly. Most boys in the classroom thought they weren't seeing correctly. Once they all passed muster, he proceeded.

"Business management, German, and English will be taught by me. Mathematics, accounting, and bookkeeping will be taught by Herr Korsch; he is your other teacher. You will meet him at eleven o'clock."

The students referred to their teachers strictly by their surnames when they were speaking among themselves. This precedent was established by their teachers; they also called the students only by their last names.

The class couldn't wait to lay eyes on Korsch. If they thought Wagemann was an old grump, they were not prepared for Herr Korsch. He was tall and imposing. Korsch was impeccably dressed and sported an old-fashioned bowler hat when he entered the classroom. Wagemann at least cracked a stolen smile now and then. Korsch never had a change of heart; he always was the stern taskmaster, which was as he wanted to be known.

When Hektor and several of his classmates walked back to the railway station, their new teachers were the talk of the group.

"Can you imagine we have to put up with those characters for the next two years? I don't know who is worse, Wagemann or Korsch," said Ruppelkist.

"What do you think, Birken?" inquired Beerenbaum.

"I think Korsch is far more untouchable than Wagemann, whose meanness is just veneer. Korsch is mean through and through. I think he will delight in being a real bastard. I still can't get over that spitting bit by Wagemann!"

With those pronouncements, they hopped on the train to Essen Hauptbahnhof.

In the fall, the class went on a week-long retreat to the youth hostel in Langenberg. The event was designed to foster and improve relationships among the student body and between students and faculty in a less-academic atmosphere. The class worked on a play that involved all twenty-six students in some fashion. The high point of the retreat was the presentation of a comedy to parents and invited guests of the student body.

Hektor played the part of an audacious maid with bravura. The Beerenbaums, parents of Nicklaus, sat in the front row of the auditorium and were among the first to congratulate Hektor on a successful performance. They extended an invitation for dinner the following weekend.

Nicklaus's family lived in the fashionable residential neighborhood of Bredeney, not too far from the exclusive Villa Hügel, the former residence of the Krupp family. There was one distinct difference: Villa Hügel was spared in the war. The home and business of Greta Beerenbaum's parents on Weidenweg was leveled during one of the last bomb attacks.

Kurt Beerenbaum was in the process of reconstructing his own business at the former site of his in-laws' property. The Beerenbaums were in the whipping cream business. The lower level of the complex was built to the latest standards in hygiene and refrigeration. It gleamed with its ceramic tiling and stainless steel.

A single-story structure would house the family living quarters when completed; a large terrace separated the Beerenbaums from her parents' apartment and the business offices. Greta Beerenbaum's parents, the Hutlingers, were once the proud owners of the restaurant and inn that stood on Weidenweg. Now, in their old age, they were thankful their son-in-law was willing to build a new business on their land. He provided them with a comfortable place to live, albeit not resembling their former home.

)(

Hektor took the streetcar from Essen-West to Weidenweg. *I better buy some flowers for the lady of the house. I'm sure they'll have something in the shop on the corner.* He stopped at the florist on Bredeneyerstrasse to select a bouquet of flowers.

Fifteen Japanese star chrysanthemums of the purest white and attractive greens were fashioned into a splendid floral arrangement. As he walked up the hilly, tree-lined road for the first time, he had no idea what would await him. Little did he know how profoundly this first visit would change his life.

Arriving at the Beerenbaums' home, he remembered. *I better remove the wrapping carefully before I ring the doorbell. I want to be certain to present these flowers properly to my hostess.*

Greta Beerenbaum opened the door. She was a woman in her early forties, an attractive blonde, sporting a fashionable hairstyle. One might not have called her beautiful, but she was all charm. Her excellent figure was draped in a silk dress, a print of impressionistic flowers in vivid colors that suited her perfectly. Her smile was infectious. There was a certain twinkle in her eyes. She beamed as she looked at Hektor, standing there holding his fancy bouquet of mums.

"Come in, Hektor." With that, she freed him of the gift of flowers he had selected for her. "Thank you; these are lovely. Now, what are you going to do with the wrapping paper? I always thought it was the silliest thing to have to unwrap flowers before handing them to the recipient. You men always just stand there not knowing what to do with the refuse. Please let me have it. I know what to do with it, and please step inside. The whole family has been looking forward to this evening. All of us so enjoyed the performance in Langenberg. We are most anxious to learn more about you and your family. We were so sorry your parents could not be there that evening."

Interesting that they noticed. It was par for the course for me. Helena and Alex Birken have never, ever managed to get away from their business affairs to attend any of our school functions. He smiled at Greta Beerenbaum. "Thank you for the compliment. The play was a lot of fun. We learned much about each other and our families. Best yet, it also gave us an opportunity to see a different side of our teachers."

"We thought all of you boys did a great job. It looked like you enjoyed doing the play."

"Yes, we did, and I was sorry none of my family could be there. Being in the meat business, their busiest times of the week are Friday nights and Saturdays. I guess business is business, and business always comes first."

Hektor opted not to say more. It was prudent not to criticize one's own parents to essentially total strangers. However, they didn't treat him like a stranger. He was welcomed with open arms. Introductions were not necessary; Hektor had met most of Nick's family at the retreat. He shook hands with the Hutlingers first, in deference to their age; next a firm handshake with Kurt Beerenbaum was in order; finally, he greeted his school chum, Nicklaus, and his sister, Judith. She was a surprise and fourteen years younger than her brother.

As everyone took their seat at the large ebony dinner table, Hektor noted one too many places were set. Greta could tell Hektor was wondering who was missing.

"We are expecting one other dinner guest. It's a lifelong friend of my parents. Aunt Laura is now living with us. We have refurbished the former gardener's quarters for her. She will be here momentarily."

With that, the dining room door opened, and a large woman with a short, mannish haircut hobbled on the scene. She was supporting herself with a cane when she was introduced to Hektor. He had gotten up from his seat, as did all the males present at the dinner party. Greta steadied the elderly lady as they approached Hektor.

"We'd like you to meet Laura Norderney. All of us call her Aunt Laura. I am sure she won't object if you call her Aunt Laura as well."

The woman stuck out her right hand, wishing to shake Hektor's. Her fingers were sausage-like appendages that were swollen and quite red. Similarly, her face seemed flushed and reddish. Her eyes were bright and shiny. Hektor wasn't sure what to make of this strange-looking but extremely friendly face before him.

Once all were seated, Kurt poured wine for everyone except Judith; she enjoyed the customary apple juice *gespritzt* with a shot of soda water. Kurt presented a toast to the "star" of the school play, and all joined in the celebration.

After the sumptuous meal, they all retired to the living area. Old but comfortable chairs were the order for now. Hektor could barely make out the scratchy sound coming from a Victrola that survived the war.

"Is that Zarah Leander singing?"

"Yes, it is. She was always one of my favorites in the thirties and throughout the war," said Greta. "I still can hear her singing, 'Davon geht die Welt nicht unter!'" ["The world will not end because of this!"] She started to hum the tune, and Hektor remembered his mother singing the song when she was down in the dumps. Of course, Helena didn't sound quite like Zarah Leander.

Kurt spoke up. The conversation largely centered on the decorative changes that would happen during the coming months. "You just wait and see. The next time we entertain you, you won't recognize our home."

Hektor hadn't even thought about being asked to visit again.

Walking toward the tram that would take Hektor home to Kup-ferstrasse, he couldn't help himself. *Whoa! What a difference in atmosphere and attitude. These people know how to live.* The conversation did not center around money and the importance of making it, having it, or spending it. Money was just a means of allowing them to live every day as best they could.

In early November, Nicklaus extended another invitation.

"What are you doing on Sunday? My folks are having a little celebration for Saint Martin's Day. My mother was wondering if you could join us for dinner."

Hektor accepted and inquired about what time he should arrive.

"Why don't you plan on three thirty in the afternoon? Most of the Sunday deliveries will be completed, and the family usually has *Kaffeeklatsch* at that hour. My mother specifically asked me to tell you not to waste your money on flowers. Your company is all my parents wish."

When Hektor arrived at the appointed hour, two of the drivers and Kurt and Greta were standing in the large courtyard, still clad in their sparkling white coats. Business was good. Despite the lateness in the season, many citizens paid a visit to local cafés and consumed several pieces of cakes and tortes heaped with Beerenbaum's marvelous whipped cream.

Germans spoke of different "waves" inundating the country. The first was the *Fresswelle* [eating wave or wave of gluttony], describing the number-one need for satisfying their appetites for delectable foods. They had been starved for so long.

The Fresswelle was followed by the *Anzugswelle* [clothing wave], which was followed by the *Möbelwelle* [furniture wave]. First, they ate; then, they clothed themselves; and finally, they decorated their homes with new and modern furnishings. The priorities were the same for most Germans; those of means simply arrived at the last wave sooner than others.

Greta and Kurt asked Hektor to step inside. As they walked up to the front door, Hektor noticed new Florentine lace curtains draped across the expanse of the huge living room windows. He took one look at the floor and bent to kick off his shoes, as might have been expected by his mother. She had a fetish about people carrying in undesired elements from the outside world. Hektor always thought it was such a joke.

"Oh no, Hektor. You need not do that here and certainly not with those shoes, the way they are polished," mused Greta.

"Is this parquet floor new, or did you have it refinished?"

"The flooring was of such good quality that we chose to have it restored. Didn't it turn out beautifully?"

"Absolutely. I like the splash of color added by the Oriental runner. And that coat rack and mirror reflecting the gleaming chandelier are something else. Did Nick get a new record player?"

"Yes, we got it for his birthday. He loves all the current new records. Like all you kids, he's in love with the big-band imports from America. That's Harry James playing; he's one of Nick's favorites."

They stepped into the living room. Hektor held his breath. "I can't believe what I'm seeing. You've done wonders with this room. What did you do with the old chairs?" he asked Kurt.

"Sandmann, one of our drivers, was more than happy to have them. Greta fell in love with that curved and comfortable sofa. Try sitting in one of those matching chairs."

Hektor sat down. "Nice, very nice. I like the height of the elegant marble coffee table. Also, your choice of colors and fabrics is quite tasteful. That deep rose velour on the sofa, two of the chairs, and the drapes framing the Florentine curtains is a nice touch. I like it all. The third chair in the tapestry pattern and the Oriental in those glorious shades of reds, blues, and beige add to the picture. Where did you ever find that Velazquez painting of the *Infanta*?"

"Of course, you realize it's a reproduction. But we like it and think the carved gilded frame helps to make quite a statement."

"Whoa! What a change! I can't believe you achieved all this since I last saw you. What a tour de force!"

Kurt and Greta showed off their perfectly appointed home with pride. Hektor noticed the large brass chandeliers in both the living and dining rooms. The dining room table was refinished and was joined by a large buffet and china cabinet, also fashioned from carved ebony. As they walked into the dining room, Hektor saw a large oil painting hung across from the buffet. "I like that idyllic alpine scene. Why do we flatlanders have such a love affair with mountains?"

"You're right; they always call to me," responded Kurt.

"This Oriental is gorgeous! I love the lighter colors and the value change from the deep rose tones in the living room."

"Well, young man, the tour is almost over."

Kurt led the way into the bedrooms, baths, and the kitchen. He was clearly proud to show off the marvels of the super-modern bathrooms and Greta's domain, a fabulous kitchen.

Hektor couldn't help asking, "Why do you have two toilets side by side in the same room?"

"Have you not seen a bidet before?" Kurt wanted to know.

"No, I haven't. What's it for?"

"It's a convenient and easy way to wash your whole bottom without taking a shower or a bath. Let's leave it there for now. You'll learn more about it later. Take a look at Greta's kitchen."

While Greta liked to officiate in the kitchen, much of the work was done by others. The days of sleep-in maids were gone, but Greta always had adequate household help.

"Well, what do you think?"

"You have left me speechless with the wonderful job of assembling a tastefully decorated home."

The thought of having to face his parents' home later gave him pause to reflect. He could not help making comparisons. *Here, everything is new and elegant and positive. At home, a negative atmosphere is pervasive in every way. Attitudes are somber and argumentative; some of the furnishings still suffer from damages inflicted by the marauding and invading troops four years ago. And the main topic is always money—or the lack of it.*

When they sat down to a fashionably late dinner, they were joined again by Greta's parents and Aunt Laura. On this evening, Hektor noticed the aunt was less steady on her feet. No one seemed to make anything of it.

Later, he learned Aunt Laura was wont to consume at least a liter of some kind of spirits every single day. She took to the bottle to drown her sorrows over losing everything during the war, not just all her belongings but also every relative in her immediate family. She suffered from diabetes and arthritis and refused to take any medications.

She cured and pickled herself with her daily regimen of alcohol. Aunt Laura learned to tolerate unbelievable quantities of booze. She had a terrific sense of humor, was never obnoxious, and clearly was a lady with worldly attitudes. Hektor learned to treasure her and her profound desire to live every moment of her remaining days to the fullest.

After dinner, another friend of Greta's joined the gathering. Ginger Pratt was divorced from her husband, Anton. She and Aunt Laura had similar likes, except Ginger would become pathetic after a few drinks. Often, she would trip over her own feet and sometimes knock things down.

"Sorry, I shouldn't drink so much"—was her only excuse.

It soon became evident to Hektor that Greta and Kurt's home was always open to any of their friends, including those who had lost their way in the aftermath of the terrible war experience.

Despite the next day being a school day, Hektor didn't want to leave. Finally, Kurt took the initiative.

"We better get you home; it won't take long with the car." He was dying for Hektor to see his coup de grace, a Mercedes convertible. It was too cool to put down the top, but he would have loved to present his newest toy in its best light. Nicklaus joined them on the ride. Kurt had a proposition he wanted to present to both young men.

"How would you feel about spending a few hours with us and Nicklaus each weekend? We could use a competent person at the telephone, taking orders. On Sunday afternoons, you could help us with getting the bank deposits ready. It will be good practical experience. What do you say?"

"Of course! I will plan on seeing you next Saturday and Sunday."

Hektor was taken aback by the proposition and their investing him with so much trust and responsibility. *How can they do that after spending just a couple of evenings with me?*

Chapter 3

At first, Hektor's parents saw no harm in his regular weekend excursions. Eventually, objections were raised here and there. There was nothing wrong with Hektor getting some professional experience, but he couldn't help occasionally commenting on the differences between his home environment and that of the Beerenbaums.

He became aware of his mother's blatant manifestations of jealousy and needed to defend his absences from home more and more. When he was not in school or working on school projects, he spent time with Nicklaus and his friends or at the Beerenbaum business and residence.

Eventually, he became a "periodic guest" in his parents' home. He saw less and less of his entire family. What he didn't miss at all were the regular Sunday visits with his grandparents, especially not the taxing interactions with Grandpa.

Hardly a year had passed before he was treated like a second son, brother, and grandson by the Beerenbaums and Hutlingers. *My God! I still can't get over the trust they've invested in me. Thousands of marks are dumped on my desk by the drivers on any given weekend. My job is to count and bundle the money, getting it ready for deposit at the bank on Monday morning. What a joy to help them in their business.*

Hektor met many of their customers firsthand when Kurt and Greta took their young associates out to dinner at some of the most fashionable restaurants and cafés in town. Kurt expected the young men to do their jobs well. He, in turn, was most generous with his rewards. To pay Nicklaus and Hektor would have been insulting. Instead, he opened doors for them in the business and social worlds they never would have discovered on their own, especially not Hektor. Greta delighted in finding *le dernier cri* in neckwear, shirts, or sweaters for her young men. Hektor was never forgotten on his birthday and Christmas.

In early May 1950, Hektor had a major confrontation with his mother. She pounced on him with fury, pointing her finger at him. Momentarily, Hektor had visions of a cat-o'-nine-tails.

"I know you are very much taken and impressed by the Beerenbaums and feel obliged to help with their weekend business. Nevertheless, I expect you to make every possible effort to visit with your grandparents during the week. Your grandmother is very ill and probably won't live much longer."

No one dared to say she was dying of *Krebs* [cancer]. It was a disease nobody wanted to speak about.

While Hektor continued not seeing his grandparents on weekends, he made an effort to visit with his grandmother every Monday night on his way home from school. It was a little detour since he had to get off the train at the Hauptbahnhof and then take the streetcar to Rüttenscheid. He didn't mind as long as he could avoid any unwanted interactions with his grandfather. Whenever

Hektor visited his grandparents, he could tell that Grandmother Waltraute was fading rapidly.

On Monday, October 2, 1950, he wrote in his diary:

When I arrived at Grandma's, I was greeted by my mother and Aunt Georgine. Mother had been crying. Her red eyes spoke of the anguish she was suffering. I could tell immediately that I was in for a challenging evening. My grandfather was sitting by himself in the living room, smoking his cigar. He was not in a talkative mood, which was exactly what I had hoped for. After my perfunctory greeting, I walked straight through to the bedroom in the company of Mother and Aunt Georgine. I became immediately aware of the aura of "death in waiting" within the room. After I kissed my grandmother on both cheeks, I stood at the foot of the large oak bed. My mother hovered to my left. She was stifling her crying with one of her large handkerchiefs heavily trimmed in lace. Grandmother was holding Aunt Georgine's hands. Grandma's knuckles had turned ghostly white. She was squeezing the hands of her youngest child with all the strength left in her. When she spoke softly and hesitantly, she pleaded with my aunt. "Promise me you will, at least once in your life, say the Lord's Prayer." Aunt Georgine never did make that promise. Mother moved in to wipe Grandma's brow, which was heavy with perspiration.

Suddenly, Grandma began to cough violently. For a split second, she raised her body off the thick down pillows. As she did, she retched and then expelled a very large ball of a gray, slimy substance. It looked like a giant tumor. The ugly lump struck the inside of the foot of the bed. My immediate reaction was to jump back. I didn't want to be hit by what Grandmother spat out. When she fell back, I could hear the death rattle in her throat. Instinctively, I knew she was going. Soon mother realized that Grandmother was dead. She drew down Grandma's eyelids and then knelt by the bed and recited the Lord's Prayer and the Twenty-Third Psalm. It was the first time in my life I actually saw a person die. I was shaken to the core.

A few weeks after Grandma's funeral, Hektor was witness to what ultimately became the beginning of the decline of the Krämer family. Like King Lear, Friedrich faced his three daughters, who were present to divide Grandma's jewels. He asked Helena, his eldest daughter, to remove a painting that was hiding his built-in safe in the living room. Grandpa turned around in his adjustable swivel chair. He reached in his pocket for the key and deftly unlocked the hidden shrine, pulling out a huge old cigar box that held most of Grandma's valuable jewels.

"Mother always wanted me to have the bracelet with the 1888 gold coins," Georgine enlightened her sisters.

"That cannot be true. That bracelet with all the gold coins from the *Dreikaiserjahr* was supposed to be mine," said Elsa. The bracelet was particularly valuable because all the coins had been issued in 1888, the year when three different Kaisers ruled in Germany: Wilhelm I, Friedrich III, and Wilhelm II.

"Those diamond earrings and that diamond brooch are supposed to be mine," intoned Elsa.

Helena didn't ask for anything. The bickering between Helena's two younger sisters for certain pieces of jewelry continued for quite a while. Helena finally spoke up and asked her father if she could have her mother's garnet jewelry—nothing too valuable.

Grandpa Friedrich and Hektor just sat there and watched. Friedrich puffed away on his cigar, taking in the whole scene without saying a word. Hektor could tell the old man was becoming utterly disgusted with his daughters.

At last, he had heard enough. Grandfather extended his right arm and, with a single sweep, returned all pieces to the cigar box. A few pieces fell to the floor. Hektor bent down and handed them to his grandfather. Turning around in his chair, Friedrich literally tossed the box into the safe and slammed the door, underscoring his anger with his daughters as he faced them. There was no question he was bitterly disappointed with the behavior of his two younger daughters.

"Your mother is probably turning over in her grave. You are acting worse than vultures. For now, get the hell out of here, all of you. When you can find it in your hearts to come back and act like adults in a civil manner, we may or may not revisit the distribution of your mother's jewels."

Helena and Hektor left the apartment, as did Georgine and Elsa. None of the Krämer sisters spoke to each other as they were leaving. Worse yet, they didn't speak to each other for the next ten years.

⋈

Nicklaus and Hektor graduated from the School of Commerce in the spring of 1951. Nick assumed a position in his father's business. Hektor graduated with highest honors. He had excellent credentials and recommendations and passed an entrance exam with ease at the most prominent retail establishment in town. He was one of thirty-two accepted from more than four hundred who applied to the firm. It was the only business in Essen that Hektor had considered.

When he entered the "hallowed" building, Hektor had no idea he apprenticed himself for three years to a slave mill. The realization came on his first day on the job. Like all new apprentices, he took his turn working behind the scenes in the Receiving Department. Herr Lantz, the head buyer and Hektor's immediate boss, delighted in being the meanest, most impersonal character Hektor ever had encountered.

"Birken, these bolts of suiting material were not properly rolled by the machines in the factory. Unroll them completely, and roll them until they meet with my approval!"

"Yes, Herr Lantz. I will try my best."

Before the day was over, he had rolled many of the bolts twice and three times before the miserable man gave his approval. Hektor never had been so humiliated in his life. When he came home that night, Alex couldn't wait to ask his son, "Well, how was your first day on the job?"

"I am prisoner number 684! That's the number affixed to my time card."

Hektor obviously tried to respond like a smart-ass to his dad. He wished not to go any further. No way would he own up to the fact he wasn't happy with the company he had personally chosen.

His escapes were his Sundays with the Beerenbaum family. It was the single event during the week to which he looked forward. Kurt and Greta knew his employer, Fritz Loren, well and were fully aware of his reputation as an insufferable tyrant. Those in the know, however, would only speak of the endless opportunities afforded to those who could tolerate and survive the daily onslaught of mental and physical anguish and challenges.

After three months in the "dungeon," Hektor was transferred to the first floor, working under Herr Gallstein in fine fabrics for gentlemen. Hektor's area of responsibility was directly in front of the offices of Herr Lantz. He had much difficulty producing a somewhat acceptable greeting as "that man" would make his entrance every morning.

His thoughts as he said *"Guten Morgen, Herr Lantz"* ["Good morning, Mr. Lantz"] fell into the domain of German expletives. An occasional *Arschloch* [asshole] would quietly escape his lips. He hoped there were no lip-readers among his colleagues. Nevertheless, he survived that evil with Herr Gallstein's and his colleagues' assistance.

He also learned quickly that the proprietor of the store was assigned a secret warning code by the staff. As the boss would get off an elevator or escalator, those who spotted him first would whisper, "Seventeen," in the direction of his movement, announcing his imminent presence.

God help the clerk who didn't spot a customer who possibly wanted some attention. "The boss" would roar like a lion by simply opening his gigantic mouth and producing an animal-like utterance. His reddish-blond mane gave him a lion-like appearance. He was anything but a gentleman, even though he was one of the most successful and respected businessmen in Germany. He had a national reputation, and owners of similar establishments vied to expose their sons to his business savvy and training.

1952–1954

Chapter 4

IT was a Monday morning in the fall of 1952. Hektor looked at the large clock hanging in the foyer as he rushed in. He barely smiled at the gatekeeper as he grabbed his time card, realizing he just made it in time. He hurried up to his department, taking two steps at a time. He did not want to start the week engendering a run-in with Herr Lantz.

Hektor had learned to hate the man from the first day he laid eyes on him. Lantz was short and rather corpulent and wore expensive tailor-made suits for no other reason than to hide his massive gut. His receding hair was combed back severely and always looked like it was dripping with pomade. Most of the time, his hair looked downright dirty. At times, Hektor detected body odor. The man never smiled and basically gave Hektor the willies.

Walking onto the floor, Hektor saw as tall a man as he had ever seen. He was young and very slender. One couldn't miss him. His hair was fashionably cut short and slicked back, giving him that military look. His suit was cut from deep French-blue worsted and was double-breasted, featuring wide lapels. The latest in neckwear complemented the suit. The young man spotted Hektor walking into the department of fine woolens for men and stepped right up to him.

"Hi, I'm Peter Weldenfeldt. I'm supposed to start working in this department. My first job assignment is with Herr Lantz! Can you point me toward his office?"

"Guten Morgen, I'm Hektor Birken." He pointed at Lantz's office with his right middle finger. "You'll find him behind this door. He's probably blessing his hair with another layer of grease." Hektor was practically standing in front of the guy's door. He made a face that conveyed he felt sorry for Peter. "Good luck with this first-class jerk," he whispered. Hektor almost called him an asshole. "You'll see what I mean the minute you lay eyes on the man. He's as mean as they make 'em. Talk about arrogant and self-impressed."

"Thanks for the warning. Not to be presumptuous, but would you care to have lunch later? I'd like to get to know you and a few people around here. I'm new in town. My parents are in the retail business in Worms. My father arranged my stint at this store with the owner. The old man thought this would be a good place for me to test my wings." As he talked to Hektor, Peter fingered some of the fine fabrics. "Pretty nice quality," was his assessment.

Hektor looked at his watch. "How about twelve thirty in front of the cafeteria on the sixth floor? I have an hour for lunch. Would love to get to know you, Peter. See you later."

"Great, Hektor. I'll see you upstairs."

Just then, Herr Lantz emerged from his office. Fritz Loren got off the escalator two hundred feet away. He saw the tall young man standing not too far from Herr Lantz's office. Loren recognized Peter instantly and stuck out his hand as he approached him.

"Good to see you, Peter. How are your folks?" He completely ignored Herr Lantz.

"They are just fine, Fritz. Thanks for arranging with my dad for me to be under your tutelage for a couple of years."

"Don't mention it, Peter. Glad to have you on board. Oops! By the way, this is your first mentor, Herr Lantz. You'll be his assistant for three months. We'll make sure you'll have some other interesting experiences while you are with us."

"Nice to meet you, Herr Lantz. I'm Peter Weldenfeldt."

Peter chose to be deferential and formal and shook hands. He wanted to reach for his handkerchief and wipe his hand after shaking Lantz's clammy right appendage.

Hektor could read Peter's face like a book. The expression conveyed how disgusting the experience was.

"Likewise, Herr Weldenfeldt," said the schlemiel. He didn't dream of calling him Peter.

Hektor stood there watching Lantz's face. When Peter had addressed the owner by his first name, Lantz looked as if he was about to go in his pants. Hektor could see those ugly wheels turning, as if the man was thinking, *The audacity to ignore me, be on a first-name basis with this young whippersnapper, and let me stand here like I was snow from yesterday.*

Loren shook Peter's hand and welcomed him once again to the store. "See you around, young man. I'm off to a meeting with our personnel director, Herr Dr. Wiesenstorch."

One could tell Loren had little respect for his underlings, Herr Lantz and Dr. Wiesenstorch. In Loren's opinion, they were both social climbers. Of course, anyone who knew Fritz Loren well enough was aware that he was an impossible and ruthless monster, known for his habit of walking away from "corpses" left in his trail.

Peter and Hektor walked into the cafeteria and grabbed a nice lunch off the assembly line. Actually, it was pretty good chow and reasonably priced.

"This doesn't look too bad, Hektor. You'll discover I can eat enormous portions and never gain a pound. My folks have tried for years to fatten this beanpole without luck."

"Where are you living, Peter?"

"My parents were able to find a studio apartment for me after greasing a few palms. You know what it's like to find housing in this town. Even seven years after the war, there are still thousands of people looking for a place to hang their hats. I'm in a little place practically under the roof. It's called a *Mansardenzimmer*. There's no elevator. All those steps to the fifth floor are keeping me trim and fit. The place is in one of those old houses in Rüttenscheid that managed to survive the war. It is located on Isabellastrasse."

"Oh, I know that neighborhood very well. My grandparents own a house on Rosalindenstrasse. Only half of theirs survived the war. It was their first house and was built in 1906. The retirement villa they moved into in 1938 was completely destroyed."

"Where do your folks live? Are they anywhere near the inner city?" Peter asked.

"My parents have a butcher shop in Essen-West. I take tram number eighteen to work. It's about a ten-minute ride. How about planning to have dinner with us tonight? My mom loves to cook and feed lost sheep."

"Are you sure that's OK? I'd love to have a home-cooked meal. I've tried a few restaurants in Rüttenscheid. They weren't too bad, and I can well afford it. My per diem from my father isn't too shabby. I just miss talking to people. At home in Worms, there are always at least five of us around the table. I have two younger brothers. My mom plans the meals, but we have a great cook among the staff who work at the house."

Hektor got the message. *Things are a bit different at the Weldenfeldt home than ours. It sounds like shades of the Beerenbaums.*

"Just plan on riding home with me on the tram tonight. There's always enough food on the table to feed an army. My mom loves nothing better than meeting my friends over a friendly meal."

When the young men arrived about six o'clock that evening, Helena Birken was delighted to make Peter's acquaintance.

"Make yourselves comfortable. Hektor, offer your friend something to drink. Your father is getting himself cleaned up. He'll join you in a beer or a glass of wine when he's finished. Dinner will be on the table shortly after seven. Kläre, my household help, has been cooking all afternoon. She's trying to learn how I make *Spaetzle*. I prepared the *Sauerbraten*, red cabbage, and applesauce days ago. I know it's one of Hektor's favorite meals."

"That sounds great, Frau Birken. I can smell the *Sauerbraten*. Can't wait to sample it."

Before Hektor's father came to the table, Hektor broached another subject. He leaned toward Peter and spoke quietly. "I usually spend my weekends with dear friends, the Beerenbaums, in Bredeney. Their son, Nick, and I were school chums. His folks have become surrogate parents of mine, so to speak. I love them, and they love me like I'm their second son. I would like you to meet Nick and his family. You'll fit right in. From what you said about your folks, it sounds like they have a lot in common with the Beerenbaums. I'm positive you'll like them."

"Would it be possible for me to meet them this Friday night? My dad and our chauffeur are picking me up on Saturday after the store closes. I've an idea my dad wants to check on my place and then head straight home to Worms. It's about a three-hour drive."

"Let's talk about it tomorrow at the store, rather than discussing it while my parents are around. My mom is a bit jealous of the Beerenbaums. She believes they stole my heart."

"My mother wasn't so sure about my spending two years on my own in Essen. I'm twenty-one and my own man. But Mom and Dad like to keep tabs on this free spirit. I'm just a bit different than the rest of the family. As the oldest, I've always been monitored more than my younger brothers. My youngest brother has his own issues; he gets away with murder. I'm sure the old man will show up as planned on Saturday."

Peter had a delightful time at dinner. The food hit the spot, and he enjoyed talking to Hektor's mother and father. When he took his leave, close to ten o'clock, Mother Birken had convinced him to have at least two meals a week with Hektor and his family. Peter called for a cab rather than dealing with two tram rides.

Over lunch on Tuesday, Hektor discussed his plans for the week. "I've got Thursdays free. What about you, Peter? Did Loren, Wiesenstorch, or Lantz offer you a day off? Everyone on the staff has a free day between Monday and Friday since all have to work every Saturday; it's the busiest day of the week."

"Actually, Herr Lantz told me yesterday afternoon that Thursday would be my regular day off, unless there were some special circumstances."

Hektor remembered that he had plans to see Nick in Düsseldorf on Thursday. "How about joining Nick Beerenbaum and me in Düsseldorf this week? He and I love this restaurant; it's called Zum Csikós. It's just a little dive run by a couple of Hungarian guys who know how to cook goulash. You've never tasted Hungarian goulash unless you've had it at Zum Csikós. The guy who owns the joint is a hoot. I love to listen to him when he talks. What do you say, Peter? It'll be a great way to meet Nick."

"Sounds OK. Let's plan on it."

On Thursday afternoon, the trio took the train to Düsseldorf. Nick met Hektor and Peter at the Hauptbahnhof in Essen. The guys shook hands and were on their way. They headed for the *Altstadt* [old town] and had a few beers. It wasn't too long before Peter wanted to know when he could check out that goulash at Zum Csikós. His stomach was in need of some hearty food.

Nick primed Peter. "I don't know what Hektor told you, but you'll love the Hungarian chef's specialty. It's to die for, especially after a few beers. You've never had Hungarian goulash any better."

"That's what Hektor said!"

The three musketeers walked into the place. Csikós recognized Hektor and Nicklaus from previous visits.

"Come in, come in. Goot to see you again. What'll you ev to drink? The oosual?" He yelled at Andras Virile, his business partner, "One round of Dreher for these yentlemen! The goulash eez a-perfect as a-ever. How 'bout a little sample for your new friend? Maybe he like; maybe he not like. Eet eez acquired taste."

Csikós's German wasn't so hot, but he sure knew how to cook; he was hot in that kitchen of his. Peter loved the goulash that Hektor and Nicklaus had been bragging about. It added a bit of zest to their lives. Drinking the famous Dreher Hungarian brew was just what their palates needed.

Their eyes adjusted to the dim atmosphere in the joint. They spotted a table way in the back. Three attractive young ladies were enjoying Csikós's cuisine as well. They were engaged in lively conversation.

The guys couldn't help getting a closer look at the three women as they passed their table on the way to the men's room.

Standing by the urinals, Hektor spoke up. "You want to talk to those girls? They look about our age. That tall, skinny one intrigues me. Did you catch that sparkle in her eyes when she smiled at us? Or was she smiling at me? I broke off my affair with Giselda. She works in kitchen fabrics. Two weeks ago, I apparently got a little too friendly with her. She told me she didn't want to get laid until she was married. That was the end of that. I told myself to calm down and walked away."

"You sure know how to pick 'em." Nicklaus zipped up his fly.

Peter was still at it. He'd had a few more beers than Hektor and Nicklaus. Peter turned to Nick. "I could use a little female attention. Nothing serious. At this stage in my life, I enjoy being footloose and fancy-free. I didn't have anything going for me in Worms before I landed in Essen a few days ago. I'm game to converse with the three dames out there. Why not? Who knows?"

Nicklaus stepped ahead. "Mind if we join you? You look like you could use a little attention from three lonesome guys."

"Sure, why not? Pull up some chairs. It's a round table. No problem accommodating six. My name is Andrea. This is Mathilde, and that's Doretta. Who are you?"

"I'm Nick. This is Hektor and his friend Peter. Where you from?"

"All of us live in Essen," Andrea answered for the ladies.

"Oh, small world. We are also from Essen. Just needed a little diversion. Nick and I love coming to Csikós. The goulash and the Dreher are the best in town," Hektor responded.

Nick searched for Andras Virile. "Please bring us another round of Dreher. It's on me."

Nicklaus was the one with the deep pockets. Peter's weren't too bad either. Hektor needed to watch what he was spending. His pocket money at home wasn't too generous. His earnings during his apprenticeship weren't anything to rave about either, but he managed OK.

Hektor chose to sit closest to Doretta. Somehow, those long slender arms and her elongated overall appearance got to him. Nicklaus focused on Mathilde. Peter had no problem carrying on a conversation with Andrea. She appeared to be several years older than her friends. Nick brought up a ski trip to Oberstdorf and caught Doretta's ear.

"That sounds like a wonderful vacation and a great way of escaping the gray and dull days in the heart of winter in this region. Who is going to Oberstdorf?"

Hektor detected Doretta's interest in the adventure. "Actually, it's Nick's dad, Nick, and I. Some friends of Nick's dad have been skiing in Oberstdorf for years and recommended the place. Nick's mom doesn't much care about winter sports. She's a summer girl."

Doretta smiled but didn't say much. She was clearly thinking about the winter vacation.

By nine o'clock, they'd settled their bill with Andras Virile and were headed for the train station. The six of them made quite a splash walking down the Königsallee, arm in arm, singing at the top of their lungs. Other pedestrians were pissed, having this garland of boisterous young people coming straight at them. The young folks weren't about to break up their act. None of them was exactly sober. They got on the train.

Hektor was with it enough and got up his nerve. "Doretta, would you mind giving me your phone number? I'd like to call you tomorrow."

She wrinkled her brow and reluctantly wrote the number down on the slip of paper Hektor had handed her.

Peter and Nicklaus grabbed a cab at the Hauptbahnhof; Hektor got on the number eighteen tram and headed home. He unlocked the apartment door. He could hear voices coming from the living room parlor. He was startled and stopped dead in his tracks. This late at night, he expected his parents to have gone to bed hours earlier. Friday was always one of the busiest days in the butcher shop.

Hektor hadn't heard his parents laugh like that in a long time. Curiosity got the better of him. Normally, he would have just turned in without saying good night. Their relationship had become strained since he was spending most of his free time with Nick and his family.

Approaching the living room door, he could barely see three figures through the smoky glass panel. They were seated around the cocktail table. Glasses clinked as they toasted each other. Hektor walked in. He immediately recognized the guest his parents were so generously entertaining. Hektor gasped. He thought there had to be something wrong with his vision. There wasn't.

The laughter ceased instantly when he stepped into the room. The guest focused on Hektor's eyes. The miserable bastard hadn't changed much. Lothar's head still looked as polished as a billiard ball. His wire-rimmed glasses looked new and fashionable. He was sporting a dark tan. Hektor envisioned him lying on the nude beaches of Sylt, getting his kicks while working on his tan. That smirk on his face convinced Hektor that prick was fantasizing about him. He probably came back to check out what had happened to little Hektor's dick.

Hektor let loose. "What in heaven's name is he doing here? Are you two out of your fucking minds? Have you experienced a sudden memory loss?" Hektor glared at his parents and then at Lothar Zend. "Seven years ago, that bastard sodomized me. He made me suck his miserable prick and unloaded himself into my unsuspecting throat. I don't believe what I'm seeing—you sitting here with this pedophile, drinking the night away. Couldn't you find some other entertainment? You must really be desperate for friends."

Hektor turned away and walked out. He slammed the door so hard everyone thought the tempered glass gracing the new door would smash to bits. That was exactly what Hektor had hoped would happen. It would have punctuated how he felt about his discovery. Seeing the predator who abused him at age eleven enjoying joviality in the company of his parents almost made him lose his last meal.

Alex got up and followed Hektor to his bedroom. "Son, we are sorry. Lothar stopped by this afternoon. He was so lonesome. He still is a vagabond and looking for help from his friends. Listening to his tales of woe, Mother and I were shocked to learn how he lives these days. Before the war, we were good friends. We thought you were grown up and more adult about what happened. We believed you could forgive Lothar his little indiscretion."

"Little indiscretion? You're shitting me! That bastard friend of yours tried to rip my ass with his dick. I was an innocent kid. At the time, you were pissed. Did you think I forgot after seven lousy years what that scum did to me? Obviously, you and Mother have struck that episode from your memories. I don't know how often I think back to those nights when he affronted me. Are you telling me, now that I'm a young man, you have forgiven this asshole? How can you forget what that guy did to me? I don't give a crap that he is your friend from the distant past.

"And don't feed me that shit about Lothar being a vagabond and destitute. Just look at him. He wears expensive glasses and stylish, tight pants, and he's been lying on some beach, soaking up the rays, while checking out his next victims. This shmok is feeding you a line. Take another really good look at him. He's fantasizing about a repeat performance since you promised to put him, once again, in the bed next to mine. He likes males of any age. You must be out of your living gourd."

"Actually, we thought you might not remember what happened. We asked Lothar to stay and spend a few nights, sharing your bedroom with him, since your brother is no longer staying here."

"You must be joking about my having forgotten what that bastard did to me. Whose idea was this? Yours or Mother's? You two are out of your frigging minds! No way will I have that man lying next to me. I know all about the birds and the bees. I certainly don't need a refresher course by that pervert. If he stays, I'm out of here!"

Helena couldn't help hearing what went on between Alex and Hektor. "He's an older man now. He won't touch you. He promised us."

Hektor looked at his mother in total disbelief and laughed hysterically. "He won't touch me? You bet your sweet ass he won't touch me again. He promised you? This is absolutely unbelievable! Sounds to me like you even had a discussion with Lothar regarding his little indiscretion, did you? Not in my wildest imagination can I visualize what you are trying to do to me. The nerve to invite Lothar back into my bedroom where he raped me. What were you thinking? Just because you haven't had any sex with Dad for the last eleven years doesn't mean Lothar has turned off his need for attacking unsuspecting boys and men. What makes you think you are an expert on human sexuality all of a sudden? I've got to get out of here before I do something I might regret."

He reached for the phone and called Greta Beerenbaum. "Greta, I have a problem at home. I cannot stay here for a few days. May I bunk with Nick for a couple of nights? You don't want to hear what's going on at the home front."

"You want Kurt to come and get you? He wouldn't mind. He's just listening to the news. I would send Nick, but he had too much to drink at your party in Düsseldorf. He went straight to bed when he got home. You sound pretty sober. I know all about that place you boys like to frequent. I'm glad you had such a good time. I want to hear all about the girls you guys met. Nick mentioned meeting your buddy, Peter Weldenfeldt. We look forward to getting to know the young man. And you don't have to bunk with Nick. I'll turn down the bed in the guest room."

"Thanks for offering to have Kurt fetch me. And you are right. I am extremely sober after what I encountered when I came home. You'll never believe it. I'll just take a change of clothes, a pair of pajamas, and my toiletries. That will do me for now. Thanks again. I'll wait for Kurt outside. I've got to get out of this bawdy house."

Greta hung up. She couldn't believe what she was detecting in Hektor's voice. As long as she'd known him, she'd never known him to be this angry and upset.

Chapter 5

HEKTOR was glad to be standing outside, catching some fresh air. He still couldn't believe what just happened. *How could my parents allow that man to enter our home again? Never mind entering our home and having a hi-ho time with Lothar, but worse, putting that scum practically in bed with me after all he did.* Hektor shivered; he could almost feel those clammy, fleshy hands touching him and the offensive mouth pressing its disgusting tongue into every possible orifice of his body. *How could they forget?* Hektor certainly couldn't. *My God, are those two showing signs of early onset dementia?*

He was glad when he detected the bright car lights approaching. It was after eleven o'clock when Nick's father pulled up at Kupferstrasse. Hektor tossed his stuff in the back seat and jumped into the car.

Kurt shook his hand. "What's going on? You look terribly upset."

Hektor looked at Nick's dad. "I never thought I would discuss anything like this with you. When I was about eleven, an old friend of my parents showed up. He supposedly was destitute. My brother Albert was gone—he had started his apprenticeship with the butchery on Karstrasse. 'Uncle Lothar' was asked to share my bedroom with me."

"Don't tell me that uncle abused you? Did he rape you?"

"How the heck did you figure that one out?"

"Hektor, I've been around. That sort of thing isn't as uncommon as some people may think. Older, strange men or "uncles" don't belong in bed next to young boys."

"When it happened, my father blew his top and kicked the guy out of the house. We never heard from him again. Tonight, when I arrived home from our outing at Zum Csikós, I surprised my folks. They were having a great old time of joviality with my former predator. They actually invited him to stay with us for a while. He duped them into believing he was still destitute but reformed. I could just tell by his smug expression that he couldn't wait to get into the sack with some fresh, young meat. Thanks for rescuing me. I'm eternally grateful to you and Greta. I need time to sort out all of this. My parents know how furious I am about this latest development. They'll probably house this prick for a number of days. When they realize I won't be coming home, they'll show him the gate. In the meantime, I am happy to stay with you. Thanks again for putting me up."

"Any time, young man. You know you are always welcome at Weidenweg."

Greta was still up. The guest bedroom was waiting for him. "Come in. What's all this about?"

Hektor told her the whole story.

"I cannot believe that your parents would welcome a man like that back into their lives. We've often been forgiving to some of our lost souls. Just think of Aunt Laura and Ginger Pratt and their drinking problems. But this is different. That man abused you. You stay with us as long as it takes. I hope to God your parents will see the light." She kept shaking her head. "To invite that pervert back into your bedroom! Unbelievable!" She gave Hektor a quick hug. "Sleep well, young man. Don't give it another thought. You are safe with us."

At breakfast, Greta wanted to hear more about Peter Weldenfeldt and the young ladies the boys had met at Zum Csikós in Düsseldorf.

Hektor bragged, "At least I was sober enough to get a telephone number from one of the girls. Her name is Doretta Osram. I'm sure she knew the other two girls well enough. Nick was taken by this girl called Mathilde. I'm not sure about Peter and Andrea. When Nick brought up the ski trip, I thought Doretta was keen on the idea. Who knows? She might consider joining us. I certainly plan to further discuss it with her. I can't remember exactly, but I swear I overheard her whispering to Mathilde that she would have the time and the money to join us. Wouldn't that be fun?"

Kurt concurred with Hektor's assessment. "Just let me know as soon as you're certain she wants to go. I'm sure I'll have no trouble getting her a room at the Maria Theresia. You young men need to start thinking about getting the right kind of boots and clothes for the trip. While it will be sunny, with all that snow, you will have to be dressed properly. I'm sure the sports house will have a lot of stuff you need on sale right after the Christmas holidays. It's too bad your company doesn't sell ski clothing. Your discount would come in handy."

Greta spoke up. "Don't bother looking for sweaters and jackets. That goes for both of you. I'm certain Mrs. Claus has done some early shopping. She never likes to wait until the last minute." A broad smile flashed across Greta's face. She winked at Kurt and then at Nick and Hektor.

Hektor got up from the breakfast table. "I've got to get going. I need to be at the store by eight forty-five. If I punch in one minute after nine, personnel will dock my pay by one hour. It's a rotten shame. I can't wait to have these three years behind me and get out of that prison. I don't know what possessed me to take a job with that outfit. It was supposed to be the best. Could have fooled me. That owner and his ilk are a royal pain in the butt."

During his lunch hour, he called Doretta from the phone outside the employees' cafeteria. He was certain to have enough twenty-pfennig coins with him. He made up his mind; he'd skip the formality and address her as Doretta rather than Ms. Osram.

"Hi, Doretta. It's Hektor Birken, the guy you talked to yesterday at Csikós. Was that your first time there?"

"Yes, it was. A friend told us about Zum Csikós and the great Hungarian goulash."

"Did you like it?"

"My friends and I loved it. It's so different from typical German restaurants. We liked everything about the place, especially the way the three of you introduced yourselves to us. The evening turned out different than the typical hen party."

"Glad to hear that. Did I detect a certain interest in joining us on that ski vacation in Oberstdorf in February, or was that just my vivid imagination?"

"You got it right. How long do I have before you must know about Oberstdorf? I'm not in the habit of making those kinds of commitments overnight. Let's face it; I don't know very much about you or your friends. I would like to see you again, talk, and get to know more about you. Are you getting what I'm trying to say?"

"Check! I don't know what the hell I was expecting. You are absolutely right, Doretta. Talk about impetuous. What are you doing tomorrow night? Would you care to see the comedy at the Lichtburg—*Das Haus in Montevideo*? It's supposed to be hilarious. Right now, I could use funny very much."

Doretta didn't hesitate. "I'd love it. How about if we meet in front of the old opera house? That's an easy landmark—what's left of it. I remember you told me you work in that vicinity. Did you say you get out at five o'clock?"

"Yes. And I do work right around the corner from the opera house."

"I'll meet you at five fifteen. It's not difficult for me to get there. You don't need to worry about picking me up at the house. My folks have no problem with my meeting you in the city in broad daylight. Let's grab a bite at the Weinstuben. That's right next door to the Lichtburg. We'll catch the early movie at eight o'clock. If we feel like it, we could dance a bit afterward. They have a great combo. The parquet floor is always in super shape. I know you mentioned you like to dance. Me too!"

He could sense a smile in her voice. Hektor was familiar with the restaurant. "I am good with the Weinstuben. I've been a guest of the Beerenbaums at the place several times. Also, it's one of my godmother's favorite haunts. She took me there to break in my dancing shoes—fun memories, fun times. I'm looking forward to our date. See you tomorrow at five fifteen or so." He was thankful for the serendipitous meeting at Zum Csikós. Peter arrived at the cafeteria just as Hektor finished talking with Doretta. "Guess what? I just made a date for tomorrow night."

"You mean with one of the girls we met yesterday in Düsseldorf? What was the name of the tall and slender girl who caught your fancy? Doretta something?"

"You got it. I'm taking her to the Weinstuben for a bite before we take in a movie at the Lichtburg. We might even dance after the show."

"Boy, you are good at this."

"Thanks! By the way, Greta and Kurt Beerenbaum want us to join them at their home for cocktails tonight. I haven't told you what happened when I got home yesterday. The shit hit the fan. For the time being, I'm staying with the Beerenbaums. I'll tell you about the whole lousy deal on our way to Bredeney tonight. I don't want to talk about it in the store. There are always too many anxious ears lurking in the background."

"That sounds intriguing. Did you say you are staying at the Beerenbaums' home right now?"

"Right. It's a long story. Let's have a bite of lunch. As I said, I'll fill you in later. Let's head up to Weidenweg on the number-three tram right after we get out of the store."

Walking to the tram station, Hektor related to Peter what had happened at home and why he was overnighting at the Beerenbaums'.

Peter couldn't believe his ears. "Smart move on your part."

They stopped at the florist. Peter insisted on taking Greta some flowers.

She welcomed Nick's friends in her inimitable way. "How nice to meet you, Peter. Nick filled us in a bit earlier today. Sounds like you guys had a good time in Düsseldorf. I can always count on Hektor to have champagne or wine with me. Nick is having a beer. What would you like, Peter?"

"I'll have a brew with Nick."

The party was on. It was a joyful occasion. Hektor told Greta and Kurt about his upcoming date with Doretta on Saturday night. Peter looked forward to future invitations at the Beerenbaums'.

"I'll be heading home to Worms with my father and his driver right after the store closes tomorrow. Of course, Hektor will be entertaining Doretta. I look forward to seeing you again. It's been a delightful evening. Thank you for welcoming me into your circle." He bowed and shook hands as he and Hektor were leaving.

Saturday was a cool but sunny day. Hektor chose to wear a medium-gray suit and sported a colorful four-in-hand tie. As he approached the bombed-out opera house, he couldn't help reading the marquee that announced the opera that had played before the place was totally destroyed. It read *"Götterdämmerung"* ["Twilight of the Gods"]. *How appropriate!*

He spotted Doretta right away; she was standing in front of the ruined edifice, tall and slender in an elegant gray wool suit. She was wearing a bright orange scarf fashionably twisted at her long neck. Everything about Doretta struck him as stretched. She was different from other young women he had known. She was striking but not what some would call beautiful or even cute. Doretta had personality and charm. There always seemed to be joy in her eyes.

"You are on time. I like that in a man. Let's head for the Weinstuben. I'm starved. I purposely ate little at lunchtime."

"Great! I like it when girls have a healthy appetite. Not this 'I don't like this' or 'I don't eat that.'"

He noticed she wasn't sporting the highest of heels. Otherwise, she might have appeared taller than Hektor. It wouldn't have bothered him. He was comfortable in the way he saw himself. He turned to Doretta. "I hear that movie is super-funny. A wonderful story. Curt Goetz is in rare form. He wrote the original play. I've always loved him. He's original and hilarious but not slapsticky. You know what I mean, don't you?"

"Oh yes, I sure do. But what's bothering you that you felt you needed 'funny' tonight? Did anything unusual happen ?"

At first, Hektor wasn't certain whether he wanted to share his experience with someone he barely knew, yet he was in such emotional turmoil that he needed to vent some of his feelings. Reluctantly, he shared with her the entire deplorable story from beginning to end. He wasn't sure how she would handle his account of what happened to him seven years as well as two nights ago.

Doretta sat there with her eyes wide open. She thought she was listening to a gory movie plot. "Let's order a glass of wine, or would you like something more potent? That's an unbelievable tale! How insensitive of your parents! How terrible you must have felt all these years since that guy first abused you! And then to invite him back into your bedroom, expecting you to have forgotten such trauma." She reached for Hektor's hands and kissed them softly on the back.

He could sense she cared for him. Her eyes were glistening in sheer empathy. Hektor agreed. "Wine is a good idea. That's what they are known for besides the good chef in the kitchen."

They selected from the menu and toasted each other.

"Let's talk about more pleasant things. I'm well taken care of for now. I'm staying for a few days with the Beerenbaums—longer, if need be. They have made me so welcome. It's Kurt, Nick's dad, who has planned this fabulous trip to Oberstdorf. If you want to join us, you'll fall in love with the family. They are in a class all their own. Through them, I have discovered how to enjoy life. Greta is quite the lady! Talk about charming."

"I'd love to meet them. You think that might be possible?"

"How about tomorrow? I spend every Sunday with them and have done so for more than three years. It's my second home. They've vested so much trust in me. I absolutely adore Greta. We'll ride the tram up to Weidenweg. Anyway, Greta was curious about the young ladies we met on Thursday at Zum Csikós. She'll be thrilled to get to know you. Well, let's celebrate with this delectable food before it gets cold. And we certainly don't want to miss the opening of that movie. I've been told it's a stitch from the very beginning."

The movie was extremely entertaining. They laughed a lot. Walking out, Hektor and Doretta held hands. He was still humming Adele's famous laughing aria from *Die Fledermaus*. He knew right there and then he wasn't letting go of Doretta.

"Let's have another glass of wine and dance for a while. I'll make sure you'll get home safely."

She hadn't expected otherwise. Before she turned the key in the front door, Hektor kissed her softly. She smiled as they said good night.

Hektor reminded her, "See you tomorrow at the Hauptbahnhof. We'll ride up to the Beerenbaums together."

Chapter 6

HEKTOR greeted Doretta as she got off the tram. He kissed her lightly and guided her across to the next platform. They caught the number-three tram to Bredeney. Getting off at Weidenweg, Hektor stopped at the florist on the corner. White mums and greens were professionally arranged.

"Greta likes white flowers. They don't conflict with any décor in the house."

Doretta approved. The five-minute walk up the street had them just smiling at each other. Neither said very much.

Greta welcomed them into the Beerenbaum home, smiling as always. "Come in, Fräulein Osram, or may I call you Doretta?"

"Of course, Frau Beerenbaum. Doretta is just fine."

"Oh, my dear, it's a two-way street. Make it Greta and Kurt. We are delighted that you wanted to come with Hektor and meet us. We are proud of our young man. He's been a great addition to our family. Come in. Hektor told us about meeting you on Thursday at Zum Csikós. Aren't chance meetings wonderful?"

"They certainly are, Greta. What a lovely home you have."

"Thanks for the beautiful flowers. Hektor knows what I like. In spring, it's white lilacs; in fall and winter, it's often white mums.

He's gotten daring on occasion. For Christmas I've gotten white lilacs and red poinsettias. It's a beautiful arrangement at that time of year. Now, what may I serve you as a refreshment? How about some champagne? This is a festive occasion. Our young men discovering some nice young ladies—that's worth celebrating."

"Thanks, Greta. I'd love some champagne; it's one of my favorites."

They sat down in the living room. Doretta kept looking at the Velázquez reproduction hanging over the plush, curved sofa. She was taken by the elegance of the entire room.

Kurt walked in and greeted Doretta. "Nice to meet you, young lady. I understand you might like to join our little troupe on the trip to Oberstdorf in February. Have you skied before? If not, you are in for a lot of fun."

"I have not. It sounds like it might be a different kind of vacation. From what I understand, the weather is a most pleasant change from our typical gray-on-gray climate in this part of Germany in February. Are you sure you want me to come along? We just met. You don't know anything about me."

"I've always been one to go by first impressions. What about you, Hektor?" Kurt smiled at Doretta and Hektor. "Seldom have I been wrong. Of course, sometimes you do step into it." He laughed. So did everyone else.

Hektor glanced at Doretta. "I'd love it if you joined us on the trip."

Greta walked back into the room. "Well, here is the promised champagne. Nick just got back from his last delivery. He'll join us momentarily." All lifted their glasses. "Here's to a great trip!" Everyone nodded in agreement.

When Nick entered the room, he smiled at Hektor. "That was quick work, buddy." He shook Hektor's hand. "You meet this nice young lady a few days ago, and today she's planning to join us on our first ski vacation. I'd call that getting a jump on things." Nick grinned from ear to ear. "Love it, Hektor. You are some operator." He quickly finished his glass of champagne. "Mom, you mind if I switch to a Löwenbräu? One of these does it for me!"

By the time dinner was served, Kurt had been in touch with the Haus Maria Theresia. He had no difficulty booking a room for Doretta. They could relax and enjoy the glow of anticipation. It was a most enjoyable evening for both Doretta and Hektor. He was pleased that the Beerenbaums had taken to Doretta as quickly as he had.

When it was time for Hektor to accompany Doretta home, Kurt offered to drive them. When they arrived at her parents' apartment, Hektor helped her out of the car and walked Doretta to the side entrance of the building. He kissed her good night and held her firmly for a moment.

"I'll call you after work tomorrow. Sleep well."

"Thanks. I had a wonderful time. I like your friends. Talk more tomorrow. I get goose bumps just thinking about the trip. Happy dreams." She was gone.

Kurt grinned when Hektor got in the car. "Nice girl. She'll be fun to have along. Glad you can stay with us while your folks come to their senses. If things don't improve, you might consider staying with us until you can make some other arrangements. We love having you."

"Thanks, that's very generous of you. I'll call my parents in a few days and see if my nemesis is still under their roof. No way will I go home if he's still there."

When they got back to Weidenweg, it was time to retire after a fun day. All had an early start on Monday morning. It had been one heck of a week.

Chapter 7

HEKTOR rang his parents at the end of the week. His mother answered the phone. He decided to confront her, totally lacking in diplomacy.

"What's the situation there? Are you and Dad still accommodating Lothar? There's no problem with my staying with the Beerenbaums. They cannot understand how you could even consider such an arrangement after what that man did to me."

"He only stayed one night. We asked him to leave when we realized how you continue to feel about the encounter you had with him so many years ago. I still feel obliged to Lothar because of his longtime friendship with Alphons von Bickel."

"What do you mean by 'so many years ago'? You make it sound like it is ancient history. Mother, it only happened seven years ago. What makes you think I'd forget about that awful affair? I was at an impressionable age. And believe me, that bastard tried his hardest to impress me. Do I need to draw pictures? If you ever as much as mention his name again in my presence, I'm out of there. Do you understand what I am saying to you?"

"Yes, son. Your father and I are sorry you feel this way. We realize we made a terrible mistake by inviting Lothar back into our home. Please come home soon."

Hektor slammed down the phone hard. He was hoping that would be the end of that sordid experience. Kurt drove him home on Sunday night.

Peter Weldenfeldt was the oldest of three sons. His family owned and operated the Weldenfeldt Haus der Mode [House of Fashion] in Worms and a group of upscale and exclusive department stores in the Rhineland. Headquarters and the family residence were in the ancient city of Worms.

Peter was pleased that Hektor had introduced him to his circle of friends at the Beerenbaums' home. Everyone loved Peter. The senior Weldenfeldt was quite aware of his eldest son's love for life. During Peter's first month in Essen, the family chauffeur had picked up the young man promptly at five o'clock on Saturdays. The three hundred-something Mercedes was a spotless vision in chrome-and-black elegance.

The first time Thomas pulled up at the store, Herr Lantz was steamed. He walked into his tiny office. Hektor couldn't help hearing Lantz mutter, "Damn asshole." It was obvious he detested his young assistant. Lantz punctuated his disgust by shutting his office door as hard as he could. Everyone knew he was pissed. They all thought Lantz was calling the kettle black. He was the biggest asshole himself.

On the fifth Saturday, Herr Weldenfeldt Sr. came along one more time. While he had discovered where Peter hung his hat after his earlier visit to Essen, he wanted to meet the people with whom his son associated. Peter introduced his father and Thomas, their chauffeur, to Hektor. Thomas removed his chauffeur's cap and shook Hektor's hand. "Nice to meet you, Herr Birken."

"Pleased to make your acquaintance, Thomas. You may call me Hektor, if that is OK, Herr Weldenfeldt."

"By all means. Let's get going before the traffic gets too bad."

They were off, moving with ease through the Saturday-night traffic. The first stop was at the Birkens'. Helena set an impromptu evening repast for the surprise visitors. Helena loved what was happening. Right away, she couldn't resist schmoozing with Peter's father.

"Is it OK if we ask your chauffeur to join us?"

Mr. Weldenfeldt had no problem with it, and Peter went to get Thomas.

"I can see why Peter likes to come here; we didn't think eating out every night helped him put on the extra pounds he needed so desperately with his height!" Herr Weldenfeldt smiled and was all eyes, watching Helena. Peter was well above six feet tall. Helena's meals must have finally done the trick.

Herr Weldenfeldt came from a humble farm family in Westphalia. He was a self-made businessman and proud of the fact. As Hektor learned later, Mrs. Weldenfeldt's background was distinctly different. She was the epitome of class and elegance and never dressed in anything but the latest in haute couture. Peter's father was certain Mrs. Weldenfeldt would be concerned if they weren't back in Worms by eleven o'clock.

"My wife knew I wanted to meet you, since Peter talked about nothing but the great meals he's enjoyed with you, Frau Birken. Of course, I did not expect to sample your cooking myself. I don't know when I'll be able to come back. I'm pretty busy at our stores. We'll catch up sometime in the future. However, I would like to meet the Beerenbaums as well while I am in town."

Hektor was watching his mother; the corners of her mouth were curved down in distaste. She hadn't expected that turn of events.

"We hate to eat and run. During a future visit, we can continue our conversation. By the way, Mrs. Weldenfeldt asked me to extend an invitation to Hektor for a visit in two weeks. Thomas will pick up the young men on Saturday evening and return them in time for their duties at the store Monday morning."

Helena had no problem with the invitation; she could already see all the advantages and doors that might open for her son. Hektor's mother was forever the pragmatist.

The stop at the Beerenbaums' was rather perfunctory. Weldenfeldt Senior was well satisfied with the social circles in which his son moved. For once, he was pleased with Peter's choice of friends. That had not always been the case. He was delighted to report his positive impressions to an anxiously waiting Mrs. Weldenfeldt.

"I believe it was a wise decision for Peter to work under Fritz's supervision for a couple of years. He has excellent exposure and will come away well trained. I am pleased with his friends. As you asked me, I have invited Hektor Birken to spend the weekend with us in two weeks. He has never been in Worms, so let's make sure we show him a good time."

It was barely daylight when Thomas pulled into the driveway at the house in Worms two weeks later. A curved stairway of flagstones stretched along a beautifully landscaped front yard and entrance. Peter's mother warmly greeted her son and his friend, extending her exquisitely manicured and jeweled hand.

"Welcome to Worms, Hektor, if I may call you that."

"Of course, and thank you for inviting me."

Walking into the house, he noted the foyer was agleam with marble and mirrors. Oriental rugs lent touches of color to the entire home. Exquisite art graced the walls. The T-shaped house provided the space for the entrance, guest quarters, and kitchen along the shorter dimension. Peter walked Hektor to his room.

"I hope you'll be comfortable in here. It's nice and quiet, unless

Marta is whipping up something special for breakfast early in the morning. She does have a tendency to be a bit boisterous. Set down your bag. I'll give you a little tour of the house. The western half of the house includes four bedrooms, three baths, and a sitting parlor, which separates the master bedroom from mine and those of my brothers. You'll meet Alfred later. My youngest brother, Horst, is away at school.

"And this is the living room and adjacent dining room. Mom loves this part of the house, which affords unobstructed views of the landscaped garden with eastern exposure. The Aubusson rugs were created to fit these areas."

"I can see why she likes the gardens. Whoever did this did a fantastic job. It's a perfect house, and one most people can only dream about at this point in time. Don't forget; it's only seven years since Germany lay largely in ashes." Hektor couldn't help himself. *I just wasn't careful enough in the choice of my parents.* That thought had also crossed his mind when the Beerenbaums had befriended him.

They met Peter's mom in the hallway. Hektor and Peter were considered adults, and the Weldenfeldts had nothing but the highest expectations of them. Mrs. Weldenfeldt shooed them in the direction of their respective bedrooms.

"Please freshen up for dinner. I have made reservations for eight thirty at the Alter Kachelofen [Old Clay-Tile Oven] Restaurant. As soon as your father is finished dressing, Thomas will drive us there."

Both Peter and Hektor knew what that meant: *Take a quick shower and be dressed in a dark suit and appropriate tie in no time flat.* The old man did not like to be kept waiting.

Mr. and Mrs. Weldenfeldt could not have been more gracious to Hektor. The young men sat across from the Weldenfeldts in their limousine and discussed the latest in market trends. Peter's parents had just returned from fashion shows in Paris and Berlin. It was a perfect evening for Mrs. Weldenfeldt to sport a French-blue suit tailored from lightweight bouclé. Both the jacket and a matching hat were trimmed in some exotic fur.

Thomas dropped them off at the Alter Kachelofen. Hektor and Peter needed to use the men's room. Standing by the urinals, Hektor turned to Peter.

"What's that beautiful fur on your mom's outfit? I've never seen anything like it."

"My mom loves chinchilla. It's so soft."

"I was drawn to that beautiful fur and had to restrain myself, wanting to touch it. Of course, I knew better than committing such a faux pas."

They were ushered into the restaurant and fawned over by the maître d'.

"Madame Weldenfeldt, your usual table? Please follow me."

After they were seated, a waiter brought the wine list and the menus for their perusal. There were more formally clad males flitting about their table than Hektor had seen in one place since his visit to the Baden-Baden casino when he was barely ten years old.

Mrs. Weldenfeldt liked all the attention. Her husband made an aside that led Hektor to believe that less formality would be more to his liking. Nevertheless, he always was the perfect gentleman and knew how to please his spouse. After a splendid dinner, Thomas drove them home, where they had a brandy before they all retired.

Although Hektor was reared in the Protestant faith, he joined them the next morning for mass at the Saint Peter's Dom. Thomas was waiting by one of the side doors when the Weldenfeldt family emerged from the Worms cathedral. He pulled up to the front as they were properly dismissed by the monsignor, who looked resplendent in his purple-trimmed black cassock with a matching sash and a head covering of deep purple.

Lunch was at the Landhaus Worms, a fashionable country estate known for its charm and superb food. It was as much of an experience as the restaurant the night before, without the glitz of marble and crystal chandeliers or the waiters in tails. Herr Weldenfeldt was far more at home in the rustic setting.

He leaned toward Hektor. "This is one of my favorite places to eat. The food is excellent with a bit less folderol."

Hektor just smiled and looked at the menu. He was impressed with the separate menu featuring nothing but white asparagus with various sauces and meats. His choice was medallions of venison and new potatoes, along with the delectable asparagus drowned in melted butter. It was a feast for the gods.

Coffee and dessert, as well as a light evening repast, were served at the Weldenfeldts' home. The conversation centered on their boys' and Hektor's futures in the business world. The second son, Alfred, was clearly groomed to follow in his father's and Peter's footsteps. The future of the youngest son had not been determined.

When Peter and Hektor made their farewells the next morning, Peter's mom impressed on their visitor that this was hopefully only the first of many visits with them. As the Mercedes pulled away from the house, Hektor let his imagination run wild as he sat quietly next to his friend.

⋊⋉

Coming home, his mother confronted Hektor. He knew she would give him the third degree.

"Well, what was it like? Tell us all about the house. What was Frau Weldenfeldt wearing? Is she a nice person?" Thus started the inquisition that Monday night.

"The visit was everything I expected—perhaps even more." Hektor described the layout of the home and the wonderful experiences to which he was exposed.

"You mean to say you attended church with them at the Catholic cathedral?" Helena attacked Hektor. "Do you realize that was the church where Martin Luther was tried and declared a heretic in 1521?"

"Yes, I did, and I knew of the event. And why wouldn't I attend church with my hosts? My father is Catholic and still professes it to be his faith. I am around Catholics at the Beerenbaums' as well. As far as I am concerned, I don't care what people's beliefs are, as long as they are decent human beings. I like to agree with the person who said, 'Whether Christian, Jew, or Hottentot, we all believe in just one God.' I find it absolutely fascinating how you can insist on Dad's marching in the Corpus Christy parades with our Catholic neighbors because it's good for business but find fault with Catholicism otherwise. Sorry; I can't be that much of a hypocrite."

Helena was stunned by Hektor's pronouncement. "How dare you call me a hypocrite? I simply have a strong belief in the religion in which I was raised and cannot and will not accept Catholic doctrine and its followers. Why can't you accept that?"

"I just can't, Mother. I refuse to be that narrow-minded. I'm surprised that you accept the practices and persons of the Jewish faith."

"There is no problem. In my way of thinking, the faith of the Jews is in line with the Old Testament. Catholicism represents an abhorrent deviation from the New Testament. I cannot accept the pope representing God and bleeding humankind dry so he and his ilk can live in unimaginable comfort and riches in papal palaces in Rome and all over the world. I have always been thrilled that Martin Luther broke with tradition and promoted the Reformation. I realize I'm talking in vain and don't wish to discuss the issue any further since we obviously feel distinctly different about the matter."

Hektor decided not to pursue his arguments any further; he knew he had reached an impasse on the subject.

Peter Weldenfeldt, Nicklaus Beerenbaum, and Hektor Birken became an inseparable trio. Peter didn't make the trip back to Worms with Thomas as often as in the beginning, although his parents insisted on monthly visits to the home front. Mother Birken kept tabs on the young men by feeding them dinner twice a week. The weekends were spent at the Beerenbaums'.

The three couples had started dancing school and were looking forward to their formal ball in late December. Doretta conspired with Greta. For one of the Sundays during Advent, they arranged a little Kaffeeklatsch. Greta asked Doretta to invite her friends Mathilde and Andrea to a surprise party. When Nick, Hektor, and Peter arrived on the scene, they were totally undone by the young ladies waiting for them.

"How could you keep this little soirée a secret, Doretta?"asked Hektor.

"It was Greta's idea, and we three girls thought it was wonderful that she wanted to have us all together in her festive home at this time of year. Glad you are enjoying the surprise."

Pretty soon, Oberstdorf became the topic of choice. Peter and his family usually went to Davos, Switzerland, for the month of February. He would accompany his family for just two weeks. Greta and five-year-old Judith would remain in Essen. Greta enjoyed taking Judith to the beaches of Sylt or Norderney for a month during the dog days of August. The happy quartet—Kurt, Nick, Hektor, and Doretta—were dreaming of tons of powder snow and schussing down the slopes in the Alps.

⋈

Once the hectic weeks of the post-Christmas business had passed, Hektor made up his mind that it was high time to introduce Doretta to his parents. They learned that she was in the group of his friends who were taking dancing lessons at the Dartmund School of Dance. More important, she was joining the Beerenbaums and Hektor for the ski vacation in February. Helena wasn't so sure if this girl was right for her son. She always could find fault with women interested in either of her sons. If it wasn't their looks, parental pocketbooks, or education, then it was their religion. Hektor had gotten used to the perennial litany of concerns his mother would recite.

A week before their departure to Oberstdorf, a strange visitor appeared at the doorstep of the Birken home. It was an old flame of Helena's. Werner von Unselm had left Germany in the 1920s and had lived in the United States for some thirty years. Helena had lost all contact with him.

Before long, schnapps, beer, and wine were on the table; the conversation became livelier by the moment. Finally, at eight o'clock, Hektor's mother thought it was high time to put some food before her guests and family. Hektor and Doretta were seated next to Mr. von Unselm.

"What are your plans when you finish with your apprenticeship next spring?" Werner wanted to know.

"More likely than not, I will leave the company. I have a tentative offer with a firm in Worms. The eldest son of the proprietors is a close friend of mine. And if not there, I have other irons in the fire."

"Have you ever thought about visiting the United States?"

That certainly was a bombshell.

Helena's ears turned full antennae in the direction of her friend. *Friends like him I can live without,* she thought. "Don't go any further with such crazy ideas. My son is not following in your footsteps. We will not allow him to travel across the big pond." Helena's face had turned scarlet red. Inhaling deeply, she looked like a chicken in heat with its feathers all plumed and puffy.

Doretta watched Hektor's facial expressions. Both shrugged their shoulders.

"Why not?" said Hektor and turned to respond to Werner.

"Actually, I have been fascinated with the US for years, ever since I started studying English. I love listening to radio programs describing the country. My paternal grandfather and great-grandfather traveled in the US extensively. I also have some distant relatives in Saint Louis. The thought of visiting the States has crossed my mind on occasion. Perhaps someday when I am established in my profession in Germany, I will plan a trip."

"Why wait until you are established here? There are so many opportunities in America for young people who are willing to work hard and have something to offer the country."

Helena was ready to show Herr von Unselm the door. For once, she watched herself and kept her domineering behavior under control. Her inner voice reminded her: *This will all just go away after Werner leaves tonight. It's a good thing Hektor is going on this vacation next week. He will forget all about it. I'm glad he met Doretta; she wouldn't want to leave her family behind.*

Helena didn't know what to make of her son. She was hoping he had forgotten all about that Lothar Zend faux pas that she and Alex had committed not long ago.

Von Unselm insisted on Hektor's calling him Werner; he had assimilated the American way of informality.

"Here's my business card. Let me write down our new home address. We recently moved to Birchtown, New York."

Hektor shook Werner's hand, letting him know he would be in touch. When that would be, he didn't say.

※

The Beerenbaums and friends arrived in the tiny mountain village of Oberstdorf on a bright sunny morning. The charming town was decked out in a heavy blanket of new snow. What else could they ask for? They had blue skies, warm sunshine, and splendid snow conditions. Haus Maria Theresia was everything the brochure promised. After stomping the snow off their feet, they were greeted by a roaring fire. The smell of freshly baked bread wafted through the house.

Dressed in their baggy gabardine ski pants, they clumped around in their ski boots. It was not exactly attire they were used to wearing. Fashionable sweaters and anoraks lent splashes of color to their outfits. They had their first lessons in downhill skiing by one in the afternoon. There was a total of ten individuals in the group. The instructor was British and conducted the class in English. Aside from the Beerenbaum group, there were some Brits, a Dutch girl, and a couple from South America.

Schussing down the mountain, they had many a good laugh. Hoards of skiers were wearing carnival costumes. There were princes, cowboys, pirates, witches, and all sorts of other colorful creatures competing with them against the background of the pristine-white winter wonderland.

"Remember when you go down the hill, in the knees, please!" The ski instructor's constant phrase kept haunting Hektor, even in his sleep! What plagued him even more were the seeds planted in his mind by Werner von Unselm.

Stopping mid-hill, he talked to Doretta. "You probably won't believe this. I'm having a ball while I'm out here with you and the gang, but my nights have been something else. I keep dreaming about that guy, Werner, and his talk about visiting the US. Last night, I almost snuck into your bed. I wanted to hear what you thought of the crazy idea."

"You want my honest opinion? I don't think it's a crazy idea at all. It might be a perfect opportunity for you to get away from your family and start a new life. Lord knows they have tried to control and shape your life, from what you've told me. I might be dating an actor instead of a merchant, had it not been for your family. It's too bad you were never allowed to do what you desired so deeply. I find it disgusting. Why don't you slip into my room after everyone has retired? I'd like to hold you close when discussing the possibility of a future together or being so distantly apart."

Continuing down the hill, Hektor's mind was still on crossing the Atlantic and a future in America. Hektor thrived on the international atmosphere. The new sport was challenging but fun. The setting near the Nebelhorn was spectacular. Again and again, his thoughts turned to Werner's invitation. *It would be a great adventure. Travel abroad, firsthand exposure to English—and work experience in New York would look great on my résumé.* He was glad the snow was deep and so soft; he managed to have several spills from not concentrating on skiing.

That evening after dinner, everyone believed they were too tired from skiing to go out dancing. The comforts of the plump featherbeds were too alluring. For once, everyone turned in early. Hektor went to his room and looked for Werner's business card. He slipped into his pajamas and threw on a silk robe. He sat at the little desk in his room and penned the fateful letter to Werner von Unselm and his wife, Hannah.

He approached Doretta's room, the letter concealed in the pocket of his robe. He tried the knob on Doretta's door. It wasn't locked. He knocked and then walked in. She had been expecting him. Hektor locked the door behind him. Doretta was wearing a colorful robe. She was combing her still-wet hair. She had just gotten out of the shower.

"Come here. Give me one of those wonderful soft kisses of yours. I'm glad we're having this time to share, especially if you're leaving for the States one of these days. Before you get too excited, I should tell you: I've never been with a man before. I don't know what it was, but when you called me after we first met at Zum Csikós, I felt something stirring within me. What about you?"

She pulled him down to her side, sitting on the bed. He dropped his robe on the floor. Doretta could tell Hektor wanted to make love to her. He undressed Doretta and pulled the fluffy duvet off the bed.

They held each other, surrounded by down pillows. Hektor began kissing Doretta. He read the enjoyment of foreplay on her face. Knowing that she was a virgin, he proceeded with care.

"Don't stifle your cries of enjoyment. Just let yourself go. It's all part of the experience. Don't worry about others. They are all sound asleep or working in other parts of the house. No one is paying any attention to us. It's a pretty sound building." He pleasured Doretta and could tell she enjoyed his lovemaking. She beheld his eyes and touched his face with her hands.

"Thank you for sharing yourself with me. You didn't hurt me at all. I loved the gentle yet strong manner in which you freed me of my virginity. I don't know how I will do without you should you go through with this trip to America."

They took a shower and finally discussed his original reason for slipping into her room.

"After talking with you earlier on the hill, I wrote to Werner and his wife. Let's just see what it is all about. I don't want to say anything to anyone else. You agree?"

"Absolutely. It will be our secret for the time being. Let me see what you wrote." She read his letter and approved how he couched his inquiry.

"We'll take it to the mailbox first thing in the morning," added Hektor.

She looked at Hektor with those mesmerizing eyes. "Are you up to an encore?"

He was only too happy to oblige. They fell asleep in each other's arms.

There was only the slightest hesitation before he threw the envelope into the mailbox at the Oberstdorf post office. *What the heck? The worst that can happen is they will write back and say Werner didn't*

really mean what he said. It wouldn't be the end of the world. There are so many other opportunities. But wouldn't it be great to sail away and start a brand-new life across the "Big Lake"? It was done. They smiled at each other. They stuck to their pact; they didn't share their secret with anyone for several weeks.

Now, they could concentrate on skiing and the splendor of winter that surrounded them. Hektor and Doretta relished the days of fun, frolicking in the snow, and being with their friends. They loved the evenings and nights of intimacy, which allowed them to explore their young bodies to the fullest. It was truly a time to remember.

⋈

In late March, a typical airmail letter arrived from the United States. It was not addressed to Helena but to her son, Hektor. For a split second, Helena thought about opening it, perhaps even destroying it before her son's eyes could ever glimpse the contents. She didn't. Reluctantly and with a heavy heart, she handed the letter to Hektor that evening. Somehow, Helena knew what news it had brought.

Hektor read through the letter quickly. *Yes, yes, they are willing to be my sponsors. All I have to do is write to the American consulate in Frankfurt and get the process started.*

"Well, what did they say? Don't keep me in the dark."

"They are willing to be my sponsors and will do anything to make my visit possible."

Helena turned away and began to sob. She wiped her face with the apron she was wearing.

Hektor called Hapag Lloyd to get the address in Frankfurt and composed his letter of inquiry to the embassy. Three weeks later, a hefty brown envelope arrived containing endlessly long questionnaires and instructions on how to proceed. There were forms to be sent and completed by Werner and Hannah, as his sponsors.

"Don't we need to complete any forms? Mustn't you have our permission to immigrate to the United States?" Hektor's parents wanted to know.

He showed them the papers. "No, it clearly states that I can act strictly on my own behalf since I am nineteen."

That was a devastating blow to Helena and Alex. They felt helpless.

Helena voiced her latest. "Perhaps if Weldenfeldts make you an offer, you will forget all about this foolishness." And, of course, the old standby came into play: "I can't think about it today; after all tomorrow is another day!"

The application for a permanent visa was sent to Frankfurt. There were a few more formalities, and then came the long wait. Although patience was never one of Hektor's strong suits, his apprenticeship and his social life kept him too busy to worry about the outcome.

Hektor and Doretta became inventive in finding time and places for their secret rendezvous. Occasionally, his folks would spend the evening with a longtime friend of his mother. He knew he and Doretta could meet at his home for a few hours. On these occasions, he would sneak Doretta into his bed. The first time Doretta saw his bedroom, she gasped.

"Is this the very room where Lothar abused you?"

"Damn right. He slept in Albert's bed on my right. I'm using the term 'slept' loosely; it was the bed where he raped me. Come here. Let's forget about that bastard. I've been waiting for you."

They took every chance to be with each other. They learned to make love whenever opportunities presented themselves at different venues. Neither of them was willing or able to afford trysts in hotel rooms.

The second week in December, a notification arrived from the American consulate. Hektor's application had been successfully processed. INS approved of the von Unselms. All Hektor needed to do was to pass the physical exam in early January. Hektor lied when he told his parents he needed to stay overnight in Frankfurt. He wanted to spend the night with Doretta.

They took the train from Essen Hauptbahnhof to Frankfurt. The exams took a couple of hours. All processed, he received his permanent visa, allowing him to make arrangements to travel by boat to the United States as soon as was convenient. Doretta looked at the documents. She smiled through her tears.

Hektor couldn't wait to tell her. "They examined me carefully. I was probed and prodded by two young American doctors. One stuck his hand up my ass, checking my prostate. The other examined my dick closely. He wanted to know why it was rather red. He kept pulling my foreskin back and forth until I finally responded to his unwanted treatment. He started making some sounds and said, 'Hm, this is quite the dick. Have you been getting some lately?' I told him, 'How about all of last night?' That made him shut up. When they were all done checking between my toes and fingers and what not, they told me the only thing I needed to do was to have a periodic chest x-ray. There was evidence that I was exposed to people with TB sometime in my life. Of course, that was easy. Mother had TB when she was thirteen."

Hektor was overjoyed, looking at the morning paper. "Did you see what movie is playing? I've been waiting to see this one for years. *Gone with the Wind* is being shown for the first time in Frankfurt, Munich, and Hamburg. We can't pass up this opportunity. It's early enough. We'll catch the first showing and then have a nice dinner before we retire. No one needs to be the wiser. We need to celebrate the occasion in more ways than one."

They loved the movie. It was everything and more than Hektor had expected. Doretta hadn't read the book yet. Dinner was just OK. Their minds weren't on food. They couldn't wait to get naked and enjoy their bodies with abandon.

After they hit the heights once again, Doretta whispered in his ear, "You have no idea how much I am enjoying this. I had no inkling it could be so wonderful. The event of losing one's virginity is highly overrated and blown out of proportion. You never hurt me. I love having you that close to me. I will miss you terribly. I wonder what your mother would say if she knew what we are doing this very minute."

"'Frankly, my dear, I don't give a damn.' Didn't you just love that line? It just rolls right off my tongue. Speaking of my tongue, it wants to do some more work."

She loved it. They finally fell into an exhausted sleep. The hotel bill was worth every last *Pfennig*.

After they showered, Doretta used a makeup pen on Hektor to hide some of the love bites on his neck. The rest she didn't worry about. His mother wouldn't give him the thorough checkup the doctors had.

⋇

When Hektor arrived home the next day, his parents were waiting anxiously. They hoped he hadn't received the dreaded visa.

"Did you get permission to immigrate to the United States?" his father asked.

Grinning from ear to ear, Hektor flashed his papers in front of his father's eyes.

"Yes, this is my permanent visa. I passed all the tests; there were no health problems. And guess what? You won't believe this, Mother. We got to see *Gone with the Wind*."

His mother almost lost it. "I am jealous. I have been dying to see that movie. Unlike you, I don't care much for the cinema, but this is one I won't miss." Helena had to wait two years for it to come to Essen.

His father thought he held the trump card. "Now that you have this visa, how do you expect to pay for your passage? What do you have in mind?"

"Actually, I thought you would, but if you are not so inclined, I will write to Werner and Hannah. I have an idea they will advance me the money. I have already inquired with Hapag Lloyd. Tourist fares for most crossings from Hamburg to New York start at about two hundred dollars. Don't look so surprised. What's so startling about my getting the information? I knew you would try anything and everything to prevent me from leaving.

"Look at it positively—you'll have the damn place all to yourselves. You can even invite your despicable friend back for an extended stay. Of course, he would have to play with himself. Maybe that wouldn't be so much fun. Perhaps you should invite Alphons von Bickel as well. They could screw each other for old time's sake. I know Lothar told you Alphons isn't gay, but I also recall Lothar telling Dad how much he had enjoyed seeing Alphons at his place in Düsseldorf in 1943, before his house was bombed. I'm not so sure about those two any longer. I can't imagine Lothar sleeping in the same bed with Alphons for all those years without seducing him. He loves it too much."

His parents stood there in silence. Helena and Alex were shocked by what Hektor had to say. For the first time, they realized the extent of harm they had done to their younger son. It had never occurred to them how the boy must have suffered, reliving the experiences with Lothar that they had made possible. They had invited evil with open arms into their home. They had put the pedophile into bed with their innocent boy. Now they were paying the price. Helena pondered. *Why were we so cavalier as to invite Lothar once again after all that transpired seven years ago?*

Hektor was dead set and determined to leave all that ugliness behind him. He didn't know it then, but Lothar Zend would continue to haunt him in his dreams for years to come.

Finally, Helena regained her composure. "Sorry, Hektor, we will not pay for your passage to America, no matter how persuasive your arguments are for leaving us. You are on your own."

Hektor lifted the receiver off its cradle and called Doretta.

"You should have heard my discussion with the folks after I came home. Would you believe they were praying I wouldn't get the damn visa? The arguments following my announcement almost blew their minds. I hope I set them straight for once. If it wasn't for you and my close friends, I would say, 'I can't wait to get the hell out of this damn place. I'm done. I need to breathe some new and fresh air.' Of course, I knew all along my parents wouldn't pay for my ticket to the States. It's not that they don't have it to give; they just don't want me to take this journey. I have no other choice but to write to Werner and Hannah."

Within two weeks, he was contacted by Hapag Lloyd. His mother held her breath as Hektor read. "Hannah von Unselm purchased my ticket. I'm sailing out of Hamburg on April 24."

Helena and Alex were at a total loss.

Hektor called Doretta. "When may I see you? I need to be close to you. I dread leaving you behind."

"Mom and my brother and sister are going to a party. They'll be gone until late tonight. Please come over. I need you here!"

They spent the late afternoon and early evening together. When Hektor told her the sailing date, Doretta counted the days before Hektor would have to leave. Between making love and enjoying each other's closeness, they cried on each other's shoulders. They left all their passion behind in Doretta's room.

The next day, Hektor contacted the personnel director at the store. Herr Dr. Wiesenstorch was another of Hektor's "favorites" with the company.

"What can I do for you, Herr Birken? I realize you are almost finished with your apprenticeship. We are looking forward to a continuing working relationship with you after you have completed all your exams and fulfilled your contract."

Hektor almost barfed, reacting to the insincere syrup just poured upon him. "Yes, that is why I asked for this appointment. I am sorry to disappoint you, but I am giving you my notice. I will not remain with the company after March 31. I am leaving for New York on April 24." Hektor couldn't take his eyes off Herr Dr. Wiesenstorch. He relished every nuance of shock reflected on that arrogant face.

When Wiesenstorch finally found his voice and composure, he responded, "Well, that is a surprise on which we had not counted. The chief will be perplexed by your news. Thank you for letting us know as early as you did."

As Hektor was quietly withdrawing from the personnel office, he heard Wiesenstorch gushing the news all over the secretarial pool.

Having dropped his bomb at the store allowed him to turn his thoughts to more pleasant but also sadder moments in advance of his departure. The Beerenbaums and Weldenfeldts were crushed to hear of his impending trip to New York. However, it was just for a short while. He would be back; one had to look on the bright side of this adventure.

He celebrated his twentieth birthday with his friends. Numerous farewell parties were held in Bredeney and in Worms. There was a tinge of sadness in attending the bon voyage parties with those who were closest to him. Leaving his family behind was his least concern. While Doretta and he knew it was for the better and was his choice to make the drastic change, they both realized in their hearts how hard their separation would be. They took every opportunity to be together. Helena had no clue how much Doretta and Hektor were enjoying themselves. If she had, she probably would have soiled her panties.

The weeks flew by. Soon it was time to make final goodbyes. Hektor looked back on his years in Germany. While the time in the little village of Köndringen was the happiest of his childhood, without question the last five years were the best of his youth. His departure for the United States marked the end of a chapter in his life he would always treasure. None of them realized what the future held, but life, as they knew it, would never be the same.

Chapter 8

THE express train left Essen Hauptbahnhof on the morning of April 21, 1954, with its destination, the city of Hamburg. As the coal-fired engine puffed its black, sooty smoke into the crisp morning air, handkerchiefs were waved furiously. Some cried openly; others made every effort to hide their tears. The train made a wide swing as soon as it left the station. Those who had come to bid Hektor farewell disappeared in the fog the steam locomotive worked so hard to create.

Hektor took his seat and faced his mother and Doretta. The two women had chosen to accompany him to the final point of departure. Mother Birken saw Doretta as her secret weapon. Ultimately, Doretta would lure her son back home from that damnable country. Of course, Helena didn't realize Hektor would have much preferred to kiss his mother goodbye in Essen and have Doretta all to himself for the next few days. Sitting across from her in the first-class compartment, he envisioned making passionate love to her. He had a hard time concealing the effect of the visions of pleasure he hoped to experience with Doretta.

Mother Birken had her own plans; she spared no expense for the occasion. There was the first-class travel on the train, and the accommodations at the Hotel Reichshof in Hamburg were plush. Helena made the reservations for three adjacent rooms. She could have saved herself a small fortune, had she known Hektor only used the WC, showered, shaved, and got dressed in his room.

Hektor wondered what prompted his mother to give him such a lavish send-off. None of it made any sense. *Why didn't they just pay for my voyage to the United States? Are they trying to impress Doretta? Do they want to show me that they can do as much as the Beerenbaums and Weldenfeldts? Of course, that would have taken more than spending money excessively.* He wished they had used some of this foolishly spent money to update his former bedroom; it still was in a total shambles, dating back to war times.

Most of Hektor's luggage was sent in advance. The large steamer trunk, which at one time held Helena's dowry, was deemed seaworthy. Two other large suitcases were retrieved from a storage room; the luggage clearly showed its age and frequent use. Helena carefully packed each piece herself. Hektor acquired a new pigskin-leather suitcase, which he packed and carried with him.

His mother engaged in a lively conversation with Doretta, while Hektor's mind began its own wanderings. When not contemplating making love to Doretta, his mind turned back to the last conversations with his brother, Albert; his grandfather; his father; the Weldenfeldts; and the Beerenbaums.

Hektor and Albert had never been very close. Being the younger, he always sensed that Albert was the obvious favorite of most of their uncles and aunts and especially their grandparents. As the boys grew into manhood, they went their separate ways and traveled in entirely different circles. Albert was hardworking and practical, in the Krämer mold, always aspiring to make lots of money. Hektor treasured intellectual pursuits, the arts, and profound friendships. His departure for the United States was a nonevent for his brother. He figured Hektor would be back soon.

Grandpa Krämer viewed the trip as just another folly of his second grandson. He thought the separation from friends and family would be good for him. Grandpa's opinions were typical.

"It's about time the young man stands on his own two feet. He has been getting his way far too often. Let's see how well he will do on his own."

Hektor knew his grandfather resented his not showing up for the weekly command performances since he was sixteen. He did not hide his feelings for his grandfather. In not so subtle terms, he got the message across he was very much aware of the attitude toward him and his friends.

To be blunt, Hektor didn't give a rat's ass what the old miser thought. He was responsible for the career changes imposed on Hektor all those years ago. *Lord knows, I might have been standing on some stage in Hamburg or Düsseldorf, had it not been for that narrow-minded old fart.*

Hektor's father was crushed. "I cannot believe you can bring yourself to leave all of us behind. I realize we have not always given you all the things you deserved, but we tried our best. I hope you won't be hurt and sorry you decided to leave your home." With that, Alex put his arms around Hektor and kissed him farewell on his forehead and cheeks. Tears streamed down his jowly face. There was no pretense; he was hurting, and he let Hektor know he was truly loved.

Hektor felt sorry for his father and wished he'd let him know that he shared his pain. Much later, he would regret never having told his father that he loved him.

In his father's mind, Hektor sought the adventure of visiting a faraway country. For that matter, most of his friends thought so too. What Hektor never shared with most people was his desire to start a new life in the New World. His mind was cluttered with all that he wanted to leave behind. He intended to succeed on his own terms. Above all, Hektor needed to get away from his family, due to the constant bickering over money, the alienation between his parents' siblings, the dysfunctional atmosphere, and the ever-present discord.

He needed to put distance between him and that haunting experience with Lothar Zend. Hektor cherished the physical pleasures he had enjoyed with Doretta. He discovered better ways of living during the last five years, while spending as much time as possible in the Beerenbaums' home.

Hektor had often read that the streets of America weren't paved with gold, but it still was the land of unlimited possibilities for those who were willing to explore them. He was determined to accomplish what he set out to do. Hektor had no idea what was awaiting him.

The train cut across several tracks. Within moments, the relatively smooth ride became bumpy, jarring Hektor into reality. His mind returned to his surroundings and his travel companions. He glanced out the window. His eyes took in images of cities that still lay largely in ruins. However, there was a multitude of sites, revealing the indomitable spirit of the German people. They were toiling at rebuilding what was destroyed by the ravages of war.

"Where have you been?" asked his mother.

"No place special. I was just thinking about certain events—kind of taking inventory of all that has impacted my life in recent years." He didn't share with her the joys he had experienced with Doretta since they met in the fall of the previous year.

The train continued to race north as Hektor's thoughts turned to the Weldenfeldts. He recalled the words Peter's father had spoken: "I believe this visit to the United States will be a great experience for you. If you can apply your English skills in the proper profession, you will be able to enlarge your knowledge and your business acumen. It will serve you well when you return to Germany. And you know, young man, there will always be a position open to you if and when you opt to come back."

Frau Weldenfeldt nodded, agreeing with her husband, as they made their goodbyes. In Hektor's mind, those reassuring words were comforting. He didn't think he was making a mistake. But just in case, it was great to know he hadn't burned any bridges in the haste of his departure.

Kurt Beerenbaum was not an emotional man. He was a "man's man" who learned in life to skillfully hide behind a noncommittal visage. Kurt came from humble circumstances. His parents were poor and uneducated. He had made his name in the sport of weight-lifting and participated in the 1928 Summer Olympics. It was Greta who had opened doors to wealth and grandeur for Kurt. Now, he shook Hektor's hand firmly.

Hektor knew Kurt Beerenbaum stood behind him all the way. What neither of them realized in that very moment was that it would be their final farewell.

Greta, Nicklaus, and Judith Beerenbaum were at the railway station. Hektor's mother was surprised to see them, and even more so, when Greta stepped right in front of Hektor. She hugged him firmly and then kissed him on both cheeks. The last thing she did was remove a chain with a sterling-silver medallion of the Madonna and child from her neck and hung it around Hektor's.

She tucked the medallion under his shirt and whispered, "She'll protect you and keep you out of trouble."

Hektor thought his mother was becoming ill.

Helena didn't say anything in front of Greta, but she was shocked that the woman had dared to hang her special gift around Hektor's neck. She watched him kiss little Judith and give Nick a brotherly hug before they shook hands. And he was off.

⋈

Hektor's thoughts returned to the present. It was time to go to the dining car. He could tell his mother was upset with him, contemplating the puzzled expression on her face. Helena spoke at last.

"What are you thinking about? Why aren't you paying more

attention to Doretta and me? Are you still thinking about that Catholic medallion Frau Beerenbaum had the nerve to hang from your neck? I thought that was pretty gutsy of her to do so in front of me. I'm sure by now she knows how I feel about anything Catholic. Are you planning on wearing that damn thing? It's just a medallion of the Madonna on a silver chain."

"You don't get it, Mother, do you? Be assured that Greta's silver Madonna will stay with me for now and the rest of my days."

They were off to a good start. Helena wasn't done yet.

"You have your money and your important papers in your breast pocket, I presume? None of us has any idea what kind of people you may encounter on a journey such as this. Just the thought of your sharing a cabin with three total strangers gives me shivers. I don't understand why the von Unselms didn't book a better cabin for you."

That was just the opening he had been waiting for. "That is simple, Mother. I asked Hannah and Werner to buy me a ticket for the most reasonable accommodations they could find. Remember, they were advancing the money to me since you and Dad were not willing to pay for the trip. Furthermore, stop treating me like some dumb little boy. I don't need you to keep track of my papers and my money, such as it is. What makes you think keeping things in my breast pocket is such a good idea? That's one of the easiest places for an experienced thief to pick. Keeping money under your heel inside a boot or inside your skivvies is much safer. Besides that, how much German money did you think I was taking with me? It won't be any good in the States."

Those little zingers did not sit well with his mother. He smiled and winked at Doretta, who was intently listening to the exchange of harsh words between Hektor and his mother. Mother Birken didn't realize that Doretta was privy to everything personal that concerned Hektor and his travels. She would have been totally dismayed had she known that Doretta paid for a brand-new Leica. She and Hektor knew what a marketable commodity the camera represented. Doretta and Hektor kept this purchase at Kühlenberg's Photo Shoppe a secret. Hektor knew his mother did not understand why he insisted on packing his carry-on bag himself; there were things he considered to be none of her damn business.

His mother realized Hektor was getting more irritated with her by the minute. Doretta just winked at him and smiled. She knew all about "Sergeant Major Birken." *General* would have been a better rank and title to bestow on his mother at times. Suddenly, her dual-personality sweetness emerged.

"Well, let's not argue or stress ourselves in these last few hours we have together. I want to enjoy our dinner and the stay at the Hotel Reichshof. I stayed there in early 1938, when I accompanied a close Jewish friend who was leaving Germany for Casablanca with her family. I never liked large ships from that day forward. It's no longer a question of disliking them; now I hate them."

"Mother, it is not the end of the world. I'm just adventuring for six months or a year at most. You used to brag about your parents leaving their families in Swabia to start their own business in North Rhine–Westphalia. What's so different?"

"I'll tell you what's so different. You will be in another world, with an ocean separating us. My parents were a day's trip by train away from their loved ones. There is no bridge between America and *Deutschland*. Just the thought of seeing you leave on that ship makes me crazy with fear."

Hektor selected a wine from the list presented to him by the dining-car steward. "Let us have some menus promptly. It will keep some of us happy to be otherwise occupied." He winked at the waiter, motioning toward Helena.

She perused the menu promptly and seemed satisfied with the choices presented. As she lifted her glass in a toast to Doretta and Hektor's future, she ran her left hand approvingly over the starched snow-white linens before her. Perhaps she recalled the days when she and Alex had owned their hotel in Düsseldorf. She had always taken pride in the linens and silver used in their establishment.

She smiled at Hektor and Doretta, although her expression was neither convincing nor genuine. His mother could not hide the sadness invading her heart and soul. There was no question she had been close to and protective of her younger son during his early years. She was fully aware of the poor treatment he received from his grandfather. In Helena's opinion, that special relationship between them deteriorated only when Hektor discovered another milieu in the Beerenbaum world five years earlier.

The train pulled into the Hamburg main railway depot late in the afternoon. Everything looked more pleasant in bright sunshine; a strong breeze echoed in the leaves of the giant oak trees surrounding the railway station. A porter carried their luggage to the taxi stand. They had discussed on the train that they would have dinner at the Reichshof that night.

As they crossed the lobby, they viewed the opulent dining room and nodded their mutual approval of their earlier resolve. Soon, they were ensconced in their respective rooms. There was plenty of time for a short nap and a bath or shower before dressing for dinner.

Hektor's room was next to his mother's. Doretta got the message from his body language. *Let's get together in your room; she won't have a clue what's happening.*

※

Mother Birken was the first to retire after the elegant dinner. Hektor and Doretta went along with the charade. He had ordered champagne to be brought to Doretta's room later. For now, they had a nightcap at the bar. Hektor beheld Doretta.

"Didn't you think my mother's reaction to Greta was once again classic Helena? There are times when her jealous behavior drives me right out of my mind."

"I thought you handled it well. It makes no sense getting into a fight with her. Just let her rant all she wants. She'll get over it. Let's enjoy ourselves in these last hours we have."

Hektor took a sip from his drink and led Doretta to the dance floor. He thought the smooth parquet needed to be tested. He held her firmly in his arms, leading her in a classic foxtrot.

"Mother is sound asleep. I'm sure she had a strong drink before she hit that pillow. Let's enjoy ourselves for the few days we have. She'll never know. As much as I would like to make love to you au naturel, we can't take that chance. I don't want to leave you behind with child. Who knows when we'll be together again?" Doretta wrapped her long, slender arms around his neck and kissed him deeply. She was more than ready and willing to have these last nights with Hektor before he left for the New World.

⋈

After dinner on the second night in Hamburg, Doretta and Hektor took a cab to Sankt Pauli, Germany's notorious and widely known red-light district, innocuously camouflaged as an entertainment center. Hektor couldn't stop laughing.

"Look at some of the getups on those hookers. Never mind the getups; look at the breasts those broads are flinging at us, sitting in those well-lit windows. Gosh, can you imagine having Mother with us? She would have a hemorrhage seeing the prurient displays of human depravity. I am glad to know she's in her room, consuming a couple of snifters of brandy. I know you've wondered if she's a closet alcoholic. I'm certain Mother simply prefers a good drink to taking sleeping pills."

Taking it all in, Doretta just stood there, not believing what she was seeing and hearing.

"I want to get back to the hotel. I've been sufficiently inspired. Haven't you?" she asked as she touched Hektor lightly with an elbow, pointing to a waiting cab.

Hektor got the hint. He helped her into the car. "Hotel Reichshof, please."

They were settled in Doretta's room fifteen minutes later. He popped the champagne.

"Hm, this is nice. It has just the right amount of brut," mused Doretta as she took a sip.

"I thought you would like it. It's what Greta often served. Here's a toast to Greta. Aside from you, I'll miss her the most. She became a very special person in my life for the last five years. I don't know how I would have survived my family, had it not been for the chance meeting with the Beerenbaums."

"Speaking of chance meetings, what about meeting me?" Doretta was right; theirs was a serendipitous encounter, as would happen so often in Hektor's unwieldy life. He sat close to her on the sofa.

"Let's forget about the world out there and concentrate on us. We only have these few nights. I keep wondering how this next chapter in my life will play out. There are so many unknowns. I guess I'll deal with them one day at a time. I don't know very much about Werner and even less about my benefactress, Hannah, who paid for my travels."

"Yeah, I found that interesting. It makes me wonder if he had any regrets about having invited you. Well, if worse comes to worse, you can sell the Leica and come back to me on the next available ship."

He got up and turned down the bed. "Come on; let's celebrate."

They didn't sleep much. Passionate lovemaking and talk were the order of the night.

Keeping busy was Mother Birken's intent. She arranged a tour of the city through the concierge at the hotel. Doretta and Hektor were treated to many of the landmarks of Germany's second-largest city. Helena insisted on seeing the zoo and doing a harbor tour in the afternoon. The latter was a big mistake. Rather than distracting her, the tour guide succeeded in annoying her.

"That large white vessel moored at the pier over there is the MS *Italia*; she will be departing Hamburg tomorrow afternoon."

That was all his mother needed to hear. "I will get to see it soon enough. I did not plan on previewing my nemesis." This was one happening she had not banked on in her carefully conceived plan.

Hektor's mother was glad to get back to the hotel. She had arranged for a special table that evening. She was not in a celebratory mood; nevertheless, she wanted this last meal in Germany to be memorable for Hektor and Doretta.

"Look at those beautiful vegetables surrounding the Chateaubriand!" said Helena as the waiter skillfully set the platter before them. Hektor couldn't wait for the meat to be presented. It was lusciously pink but not bloody—just perfect and the way all at the table liked it. The recommended Cabernet was excellent, and they finished the evening with a bottle of Sekt [German sparkling wine].

When they retired, all were totally relaxed. It was exactly the state Mother Birken had desired. Hektor kissed his mother and Doretta good night. Doretta smiled mysteriously; she recalled the last two nights. She anticipated the finality of it all with trepidation.

Hektor was certain his mother had gone to sleep. A few minutes later, he was in Doretta's arms. They were fully undressed and enjoyed another glass of champagne. He toasted Doretta.

"I don't want to talk about anything but us tonight. What comes, comes. We'll both deal with it as things happen." There was a loud knock at Doretta's door. He jumped out of bed, momentarily forgetting he was stark naked. "Who is it?" He yanked a bath towel off the rod and slung it around his waist. His "friend" had come down a notch or two.

"It's your mother. I wanted to speak with you. You didn't answer my knocking on your door. Is Doretta with you?"

Hektor determined this was as good a time as ever for her to find out that he and Doretta were more than casual acquaintances. He opened the door. Helena gasped, looking at her son and then at Doretta, sitting in bed, the duvet pulled up to cover her naked breasts.

"Wha…wha…what are you doing?"

"What do you think we are doing? I'm enjoying Doretta, and we are having a great time doing it. It's a lot better than doing it with Lothar, if you know what I mean. Now, what can we do for you? We thought you cuddled up with your snifter of brandy and were sound asleep!"

"Sorry; I had no idea you were this intimate! I'll talk with you tomorrow, when you are not as preoccupied." She walked away, shaking her head; her shoulders were drooping.

Hektor slammed the door. He couldn't believe what had just happened but treated his mother's appearance as if nothing earth-shaking had taken place.

"Now, where were we? I believe I was about to tell you sweet nothings and make passionate love to you. Sorry for the untimely interruption. I believe our mutual friend is in recovery. Shall we give him another chance?"

"How can you be so nonchalant about what just happened? Your mother must be furious with me."

"Don't let her get to you. I will not allow her to spoil these final moments. As I have told you, she has some weird notions about sex. For now, let's do it my way!"

"By all means! I'm looking forward to an encore performance."

They truly enjoyed each other. Neither wanted to think about this being their last shared time. Morning came all too soon.

To say the conversation at the breakfast table was stilted would have been an understatement. Even a stranger would have known that Hektor's mother was disgusted. Her facial expressions didn't lie; she looked as mean as Ivan the Terrible. Hektor finally decided to break the ice.

"Mother, what you discovered last night was nothing unusual. Doretta and I are practically engaged. This is what young people do. There is nothing wrong with enjoying healthy, normal sex. It's better than getting acne all over one's face and body. Most people don't view sex as something obligatory or even dirty. That's your opinion. Don't try to force your ideas on us. Just forget about what you had to discover, and let's move on. Doretta isn't a bad girl just because she wanted to be with me. She was a virgin until I deflowered her in Oberstdorf a year or so ago, if that makes you feel any better. Sorry, Doretta. It had to be said. Now, let's all take a deep breath and enjoy this wonderful breakfast. Personally, I'm starved. All that healthy sex will do that to a young man."

He was all smiles. His mother had picked up her plate with her right hand. For a moment, Hektor thought she was ready to slap it—gravy, grease, and all—in his face. He looked across the table at Doretta and winked at her.

)(

The luggage was checked with the concierge. His mother wanted to do some shopping in the vicinity of the hotel. They had lunch in an ancient bar before returning to the Reichshof. Doretta and Hektor loved the intimate atmosphere, while Helena did nothing but bitch about the lack of bright lights. She always remarked that she needed to see what she was eating. At two in the afternoon, Mother Birken had to face the inevitable taxi ride to the dreaded pier and the confrontation with the vessel taking her son across the endless water.

The cabby dropped them off near the landing quay, where the MS

Italia was moored. There were hundreds of people milling around, hugging and crying. They couldn't help picking up snippets of people's conversations—"I will see you in New York in a few months. Hopefully, by then I will have a job. Then you and the children will be able to follow."

Entire families—mothers, fathers, and children of all ages and sizes—hugged each other. Many were clad in simple and some-times downright shabby clothing and traveling gear. The majority of voyagers were headed for tourist accommodations.

The announcement came over the speaker: "Passengers and visitors may now board the vessel. You may check into your cabins."

Helena had no intention of viewing Hektor's. Doretta wanted to see for herself and followed Hektor on board. They found their way to the D deck and his domicile, number 411. He was assigned berth A, a lower bunk in the relatively tiny cabin.

"This is really small. I didn't picture it as quite this humble," was Doretta's assessment.

"What do you expect for less than two hundred dollars? It's OK; I wasn't planning on buying the ship and will only be in my cabin to sleep. I'll leave my suitcase here. Looks like some of my cabin mates were here earlier. Well, I'll meet them later. Let's get back and find Mother. It will be bedlam once they ask all visitors to go ashore."

They wound their way back to the pier. Hektor's mother stood at the bottom of the landing stage, frantically searching for Hektor and Doretta among the throng of people. She began to cry as soon as she spotted them.

"I wondered how you could leave me standing here without saying goodbye. I thought I was not going to see you again. The whole experience is too overwhelming for me!"

"Mother, no question about it; after your surprise visit to Doret-ta's room last night, you were on the very top of my favorite list. However, I wouldn't get on that ship without properly saying my goodbyes. I do have a good idea what it must be like to send me off into the big wide world. I know I'm your baby. But I've grown up and need to fulfill my destiny. And this is it. I won't be gone forever."

He took her in his arms and hugged her firmly. He gave her kisses on her cheeks and her forehead. Tears ran down her face as she sobbed uncontrollably.

As Hektor predicted, repeated blasts from the horn near the two funnels of the ship were followed by the announcement—it was time for all visitors to leave the vessel and for passengers to be on board. He took Doretta in his arms and held her for as long as he could. He kissed her passionately and brushed away her tears. He had a hard time controlling his own emotions. Saying goodbye to his beloved was harder than he had envisioned. But he had said A, and now he needed to say B.

Hektor bent down to whisper in her ear. "I love you very much and will miss you terribly. You have made it much more difficult for me to leave. I'll come back to you. Be brave." He had to let go of her. He jumped on the last gangway; the crew were ready to pull it up.

Hektor swiftly walked up the long runner. He found a space near the railing, allowing him to keep an eye on Doretta and his mother. They could hear the engines churning as the crew hauled in the last of the mooring cables. Ever so slowly, the ship began to move.

Hektor wasn't sure if the sound originated from the MS *Italia* or the pier; a band was playing the German national anthem, the final touch tearing away at people's emotions. He reached up to his chest; he needed to feel Greta's silver Madonna. As the tugboats guided the ship along the Elbe, those at the pier became a kaleidoscope of little dots against the shoreline of the city of Hamburg. His eyes filled with the tears he had not dared to shed when facing his mother and Doretta.

Chapter 9

IT was high time for Hektor to meet his cabin mates. As it turned out, one of the passengers assigned to cabin 411 was missing. The other two travel companions were busily unpacking some of their stuff. They introduced themselves right away.

"I'm Delbert, and this is Ulrich. We are friends. Welcome to this cozy arrangement," said Delbert, looking up at Hektor as he was zipping up his fly.

"Hi, I am Hektor Birken." He stuck out his hand to greet them in typical German fashion. Their handshakes were firm. Hektor thought the fellows looked agreeable.

He certainly thought they could manage for eleven days in the tight quarters. He didn't believe there would be any surprises. *Friends? Did they just meet on the ship, or did they know each other prior to sailing away? Is there a certain resemblance between them?* He looked from one to the other. Delbert sported a full mustache; Ulrich was clean-shaven. Well, he could ask them later. They would be together for the eleven-day voyage.

Dinner was served from six to eight in the evening, and he was anxious to meet his dining companions. He changed into a navy-blue suit; a light-gray tone-on-tone tie finished the semiformal appearance. There was little privacy in the tiny cabin. He felt like he was being intently watched while changing his clothes. It couldn't be helped. *Perhaps Mother was right about the cheap accommodations and being with total strangers in such close quarters.*

As he approached his table, he noted two young ladies and a middle-aged gentleman. When he introduced himself, he learned the lady seated across from him was Mrs. Hiltrud Engel, who was to meet her husband in New York. Miss Irmhild Unbehaun was engaged to be married in New York as well. The gentleman was Ferdinand Traeg, returning to Canada after visiting family in Germany. They seemed a congenial group; Hektor was the youngest among the four.

The seas were calm during the night. There was some fog as Hektor peered out the porthole the next morning. When they entered the English Channel, the waters became noticeably rougher. Herr Traeg was a seasoned traveler; he thought it was an act of kindness to enlighten his table mates about the possibility of experiencing seasickness. Herr Traeg began his lecture.

"Because of the relatively narrow and confined body of water in the channel, most ships tend to pitch and roll. It makes for rather uncomfortable motions, and people often become seasick." He put his hands together, forming the shape of a ship and gave his demonstration of *pitch and roll.*

"Whatever you do, don't look out windows or portholes. Don't look at the ship as it moves up and down, relative to the horizon. It's the feedback from the ocular nerve that causes you to become nauseated. If we encounter any bad weather, always eat hearty meals—food that has substance. Have a few stiff drinks, dance, and spend a goodly portion of time outside in the fresh air. Just don't think about becoming seasick! I'm convinced it's all in one's head!"

The others at the table looked at each other. Their faces spelled disbelief.

"Are you sure about that?" Hektor asked. "You mean to say you can make yourself seasick by just thinking about it? Come on now; you must be joking."

"Well, I've tested my hypothesis and found it to be true. You do as you please. Just remember I warned you." He got up from the table and walked away, still shaking his head at the nonbelievers he left behind.

They all had patiently listened to his *spiel* and made up their minds to humor the man by tentatively practicing what he preached. He did have considerable experience crossing the Atlantic, they had to admit, while they were testing their fortitude for the first time. When they reached Southampton on the morning of April 26, everyone at the table, except Herr Traeg, had weathered their first taste of mild seasickness. He admonished them and suggested they become serious about dealing with any discomforts.

The skies cleared as the MS *Italia* plowed through the waters of the channel toward Le Havre, France, where they would pick up the last of the 1,149 passengers for the Atlantic crossing.

The departure from Le Havre was almost more emotional for Hektor than leaving Hamburg. There was a certain finality in the act of leaving the last European port; it was the break with the Old World. For the next seven days, they would be at sea before touching the New World in Halifax.

Hektor stood on the stern of the ship, snapping photos. A mass of seagulls cried their final salute to the voyagers leaving the European continent. After an hour or so, there was just the gentle lapping of the Atlantic waves against the white hull of the MS *Italia*. With the appearance of the sun, deck chairs became the spot to be while waiting for the next meal to be served. After dinner, they tried Herr Traeg's suggestion of sipping whiskey and dancing the night away. It worked. No one gave another thought to being seasick.

They enjoyed sunny days and calm seas for most of their crossing. On the third day after leaving Le Havre, a formal dance was held in the evening. After dancing and drinking for a few hours, Hektor opted to turn in shortly after two in the morning. He felt tipsy and held firmly onto the rail while walking back to his cabin.

He turned the key as carefully as he was able. He got an eyeful when he walked in. All the lights were on. Delbert and Ulrich were in the lower bunk next to Hektor's. They were sound asleep. Their uncovered, naked bodies were firmly linked and told the whole story. Hektor drew a deep breath. *I'll be damned. How lucky can I be? Friends? Bullshit. "Bosom buddies" says it better.*

He tore off every stitch of clothes and stumbled as he tried to get into his pajamas. When he hit the floor, Delbert awakened and saw Hektor lying next to him, naked. He grabbed for Hektor, trying to pull him into their bunk. Hektor was tipsy, but he wasn't drunk enough to get into bed for a ménage à trois with his cabin mates. He pushed Delbert back.

"Sorry bu…bu…buddy; I have been there."

Delbert let go of him and pulled sheet and blanket over himself and Ulrich, who never knew what transpired.

At last, Hektor got to his feet. Uncharacteristically, he didn't bother to pick up his discarded garments and was pleased when he succeeded in getting his pajama pants on. He stretched out on his bed. His ass was sore from hitting the cabin floor hard, and he hurt where Delbert had tried to grab him. *I'll be damned if I'll get out of this bunk and look for aspirin.*

He heard some kind of announcement repeated on the speaker in the gangway. *What the hell are they saying? It sounded like "Fire on board." It was something "on board."* He was too far gone and too darn tired to make out what they were saying. He quietly mouthed to himself, "I sure know how to step into things. Screw it! I can't understand what they are saying. Certainly, the cabin steward will knock us out of bed if it's something serious." He was sound asleep in seconds.

Morning came all too soon. His eyes were touched by the rays of the sun brightly shining through the tiny porthole. When he finally opened his eyes, rubbed away the sleep, and stretched, he discovered that his cabin mates were gone. He took a quick shower, enjoying his privacy for once. On his way to the dining room, he overheard people talking. Everyone was buzzing about the events of the previous night.

"What events of the night?" Hektor asked.

"Didn't you hear the announcement and what happened after that?"

Hektor could not recall anything unusual.

"They were hollering 'man over board' again and again. The ship's engines were cut. The crew searched for one of their own for several hours. Apparently, one of the sailors tried to get lucky with one of the passengers. She rejected his overtures, and in his drunken stupor, he jumped overboard. After four hours of searching in vain, the captain assumed the jilted lover had met his demise in the blades of the rudder. And you mean to tell us you slept through all of these happenings?"

"Yes, I must have," Hektor confessed. "When I arrived at my cabin, I wasn't feeling any pain. True, I vaguely heard some announcement, but when I couldn't make out what they were yelling, I must have passed out."

The event was the topic of conversation at most dining tables throughout the day. Of course, he made no mention of the discoveries and experiences with his two cabin mates.

A couple of afternoons later, Hektor went to retrieve his camera from the cabin. As he inserted the key, he heard one of the guys say, "Oh shit, here comes Hektor." He walked in; Delbert was humping Ulrich. Hektor couldn't believe what he saw. He slammed the door shut and walked away, forgetting about his camera.

On the morning of May 3, the MS *Italia* blasted its way through pea-soup fog into the Halifax harbor. Ferdinand Traeg was among several hundred passengers leaving the ship. Most of the New York–bound passengers were happy when the vessel resumed its voyage south.

"I'm glad that damn foghorn has stopped blasting in our ears," said Delbert, standing next to Hektor at the railing. "Boy, that fresh air feels good."

"Sure does." Hektor was about to walk away when he decided to question Delbert. "How long have you and Ulrich known each other? You didn't just meet on the ship, did you?" Hektor glanced sideways at Delbert.

"Don't be shocked; we've known each other since birth. We are twin brothers and decided we were queer when we were thirteen years old. We've enjoyed each other ever since. You think you can keep that under your hat?"

Hektor swallowed hard and took his leave. His head rocked side to side. He had heard it all.

The MS *Italia* sailed into New York Harbor on May 5, 1954. It was a brisk and sunny morning. The ship's flags snapped in the strong wind. The passengers were full of anticipation and looking forward to their first glimpse of the Statue of Liberty and the skyscrapers of Manhattan, the greeting committee of a new world for most travelers on board. It was one thing to have seen these landmarks in photographs or in movies; it was quite a different experience to see them with one's own eyes for the first time.

1954–1956

Chapter 10

THE MS *Italia* slowly entered the harbor waters of New York. It was indeed a glorious morning. From a distance, the passengers on board could make out the faded green of the Statue of Liberty. Its distinguished figure with the arm raised high, holding the torch, became more impressive from one moment to the next. Hektor pinched his left arm, reminding himself it was reality he was experiencing. He turned to one of his table mates.

"Frau Engel, would you mind snapping a few photos of me as we pass the famous statue? I'll be happy to do the same for you. This event has to be preserved for posterity. What a day!"

"Of course, I will. Show me how to use your camera."

Hektor enlightened her on how to use the Leica and commented, "That must be Ellis Island. I have seen pictures of it. Aren't we lucky not to be subjected to immigration processing in that infamous edifice?"

"You got that right. My husband told me it will be permanently shut down on November 12. More than twelve million immigrants passed through its doors after they were opened to them sixty-two years ago. But look! Just get a load of those tugboats greeting us with water spouts! Isn't it the most beautiful welcoming gesture?"

Soon the drama of the Statue of Liberty and the skyline of Manhattan were behind them.

"What's all that crap floating in the water?" Hektor asked.

An officer overheard his question. "There's a protracted strike by the longshoremen. Many freighters abandoned their cargo. Rather than returning with their loads, they chose to dump the stuff in the Hudson River. We have to refuel and restock in Halifax. We were lucky they allowed us to disembark you passengers."

Hektor was full of questions. "What are those strange-looking oranges floating all around us?"

"Those aren't oranges; they are grapefruit."

"What's a grapefruit? I've never heard of or seen such a thing."

"They belong to the citrus family. Many Americans eat them for breakfast."

Hektor guessed he would become more closely acquainted with grapefruit when he lived with the von Unselms. There were more important things that needed his attention at the moment.

Waiting in line with hundreds of disembarking passengers, Hektor was confronted with his cabin mates. He just nodded at Ulrich and Delbert; he didn't feel like shaking their hands. Delbert stood right next to him. For a moment, Hektor thought he was trying to touch him. Hektor leaned toward Delbert and spoke quietly.

"Good luck, guys. Be careful where you fool around in the future. I didn't breathe a word about my observations of you two gentlemen."

"Thanks for telling no one about us. We appreciate your discretion," Delbert responded.

Hektor's suitcase was taken by the cabin steward; the other luggage would be handled by the freight crew. He made sure he had his important papers handy in his jacket pocket. *I certainly don't need this heavy overcoat. It's becoming downright stifling without the fans and the AC.* He pulled off the heavy herringbone coat. It had done its job on deck during the Atlantic crossing. First- and second-class passengers were relatively few in number. They were the first group allowed to disembark.

Hektor's table mates were huddled in a small group with other passengers. He felt like making small talk. "Have any of you discovered the people meeting you among those crowding the pier?"

None of them had, except Hiltrud Engel; she spotted her husband almost immediately. Hektor didn't see Werner. He had no idea what Hannah looked like. Passengers in tourist class were admitted in alphabetical order. Having a surname starting with "B" helped—soon it was Hektor's turn.

A friendly face looked up at him. "Let me see your visa. How much money did you bring with you?"

How much money did I bring with me? It was a good thing I left the remains of my marks with Doretta. "I have *kein Geld* with me. *Mein* sponsors are meeting me," Hektor said, half in English and half in German. While he wrote and read English fairly well, he didn't like to speak it, as he feared he would make a fool of himself. The INS officer was satisfied with the answer regarding the money.

"Do you want to change your name?"

"No!" Hektor replied emphatically.

He wasn't sure what the man's question meant. No one had explained this possibility to him. He didn't really understand what he declined. Hektor thought it was better to refuse than to accept a condition he might later regret. Actually, he had just missed a perfect opportunity to change his much-hated name.

"Your papers are OK. You will be notified in a few weeks. Your chest x-ray needs to be repeated. Otherwise, you are good to go. Move on to the next table. That man over there will ask you a bunch of questions. Your sponsors are allowed to join you. They can interpret for you, when needed. Good luck! Welcome to the good old USA."

The first hurdle of American bureaucracy was behind him. As clearly instructed, Hektor trotted over to the designated spot, the customs station. He had to have all his possessions with him before the check-in process could begin. At last, he spotted Werner and motioned to him. He and a rather heavy-set woman with a slight limp made their way toward him.

Werner stuck out his hand to greet Hektor and immediately introduced him to Hannah.

"Guten Tag; willkommen bei uns in Amerika," said Hannah. "Perhaps we should refrain from speaking German; this way you will speak English faster. Welcome to America." She took Hektor's hand but then gave him a welcoming hug. He needed that.

"Let's get the rest of your luggage and try to get through customs," Werner suggested. "I watched the guy to whom you are assigned. He seems to take his job seriously." Werner used a pushcart to move Hektor's heavier pieces into position.

The customs inspector barked out his orders. "Line up all this stuff of yours on this table. I refuse to bend over to do my inspections. My aching back is killing me as it is." His grimace was one for the books. "Unlock all these trunks and suitcases, and stand back."

The grump in his snazzy green uniform went to work. He reached in at the extremes of the first suitcase until his fingers struck bottom. Then he tossed everything in the air. It looked like someone tossing a salad.

So much for neatness. Hektor couldn't believe what he was witnessing. After performing the same action numerous times, the efficient US representative slapped down the lid of the first suitcase and moved on to the next.

They were all prepared for what was to follow. The "gentleman" seemed to delight in turning Hektor's suitcases into a shambles.

In all my travels in Europe, I have never seen anything like it. Hektor didn't dare say anything, but his facial expressions must have spoken volumes.

"Don't give me any lip. This is the USA, and we do things very thoroughly here," the mean bastard commented.

Werner spoke up in Hektor's defense. "He doesn't know what is happening; he hasn't said a word."

"He doesn't have to say anything. I can read what is going on in that head of his. It's the most efficient way of getting to the bottom of things. We have too many people to process to worry about messing up a few shirts and socks." Finishing with the last of Hektor's suitcases, the inspector spotted the Leica hanging around Hektor's neck. "Is that your camera?"

Werner was too quick to respond. "Actually, he brought the camera for us as a way of showing his appreciation. We advanced him the money for his passage."

Where did he get that idea? I never wrote anything about bringing a new camera with me—for them or anybody else.

"Is that so?" replied the "charming" representative of the United States government. "Take that thing off your neck, and hand it to me." The customs officer stared at the ground. Then he rummaged through his desk drawer. He beamed when he found the object of his diligent search.

They were all perplexed. No one knew what was happening. To their surprise, the customs officer held a large, rusty nail in his hand. He looked at Hektor and Werner.

"As long as it is a gift, you won't mind if I give it more of a 'used' look, right? This way, neither of you will be able to turn it into cold cash by selling it as a new piece of equipment. Furthermore, if I don't 'engrave' it, one of you would have to pay a pretty hefty duty on this item. I know you are not happy with my proposed demolition act, but it will save one of you big bucks."

Hektor was puzzled. He didn't see any bucks around. *What does the guy mean by big bucks?* He elected not to question what the man was talking about.

The customs inspector proceeded to scratch Hektor's treasured camera, mutilating the manufacturer's name, *Leitz,* and the serial number. A few seconds later, he handed the camera to Werner. "Here we are—it's almost like new. Hope you enjoy using it for many years. It's a wonderful present this young man brought for you. You would probably have to pay six hundred dollars in any store in this country. I would say you made a pretty good return on your investment."

It wasn't he who had invested in anything, but Hannah. Hektor swallowed hard but didn't say a word. He kept staring at the customs clerk and at Werner, who had slung the Leica around his neck.

"That's all folks. Close your bags, and clear out. Welcome to America! Next!" The miserable man practically screamed his order to the next victims in line.

None of them could accept what they had seen and heard. Dismissed and stunned by what just happened, they were left speechless but moved on. As soon as they were out of earshot of the inspector, Hektor questioned Werner in half German and English.

"What was he talking about, calling the camera 'big bucks'? I didn't understand. Why did you let him scratch up my camera?"

"'Big bucks' means lots of money. He didn't want the camera to look like new. This way, it prevents you or me from selling it for heaps of money. He's a regular fox."

Hektor only understood half of what Werner was trying to tell him.

𝕏

They stashed all of Hektor's belongings in the huge but dirty trunk of the old blue Hudson. The bottom of the trunk was covered with all kinds of dried weeds and grass clippings. Aside from all the crud, the trunk stank badly. Hektor held the passenger door open for Hannah. Werner was already slouched halfway into the driver's seat.

"Come on; sit with me in front. You'll see a bit more of the city and the scenery along the way. It's a good five to six hours before we'll get home to Birchtown. Hannah won't mind riding in the back seat."

Hektor was fascinated by all the bustle in the streets of lower Manhattan as they traveled close to the Hudson River, heading for the George Washington Bridge. Werner didn't like confining spaces. He avoided taking the Lincoln Tunnel. Hektor couldn't get over all the honking cars and taxicabs and the multitude of people of all colors.

"What an interesting city," he said in German. He had never seen anything like it. Crossing the bridge and having to pay tolls was another new experience.

"How was your voyage?" inquired Hannah in her heavily accented English. "Did you have good weather? We hope you didn't become seasick."

Hektor responded to all the questions in German. He chose not to say a word about his unusual cabin mates.

While riding in the car, Hannah appeared fidgety and agitated. Hektor wondered if he had said something that didn't sit well with her. As the traffic became less frantic, she looked at Hektor in an apologetic manner and said, "Werner and I have to tell you something. We didn't have the heart to share this with you in writing. After we agreed to sponsor you, and I paid for your passage, we decided to divorce; that is, I decided to part company with Werner. We realized you might have changed your mind about coming to the States if we told you about our resolution. I won't trouble you with the details now. We'll talk about it later in Birchtown. Then you will understand why this has happened. I want you to know you are still welcome to stay with either of us."

After Hannah dropped that bombshell, Hektor kept staring out the window, trying to digest their revelation. *What are they talking about? It has to be something bad. Do they not want to live together anymore? I wish they had explained the circumstances a little better and would speak German. They are right; I never would have made the journey knowing this. Too late now. I am here. I'll have to deal with it from day to day.* He could just imagine what his mother would say, had she been aware of what happened to her son on his first day in that "damned foreign country."

They stopped at the Red Apple for lunch before they headed toward Liberty. Friends of his sponsors, two old maids, ran a milk farm in the so-called Jewish Alps. Frieda and Wilhelmine were of German stock. They had owned the old farmhouse and numerous cottages for years. In the summer, hordes of city people would stay with them to vacation or just come for long weekends. It was a great location to get away from the heat of New York.

When they arrived at the old farm, Hektor heard something blaring. *Perhaps a radio?* Whatever it was, people were talking in English. While introductions were made, Hektor noticed a huge, strange-looking box with a small, flickering screen near the top. Focusing on the images on display, he realized he was looking at pictures of talking heads. They seemed to bounce back and forth between certain persons. There were questions asked and answers given with machine-gun speed and precision. Without wanting to appear too ignorant, while looking at Frieda, he couldn't resist asking, "What's that?"

"Oh, you haven't seen a television before. We call it a TV, short for television. Didn't you ever see one in Germany?"

"I've heard of them and read about them in magazines and newspapers. No, I've never seen the real thing."

"We are watching the inquiries by the House Un-American Activities Committee, held in Washington, DC."

"I have no idea what you are talking about," Hektor said in German.

Before they left later that afternoon, he had a pretty good understanding of the issue. It was explained to him half in German and half in English.

"Don't you think, Frieda, his English is good? I'm sure he lived in an English-speaking country in one of his former lives. I just know he must have," said Hannah.

Another crazy notion. Where did that idea originate?

Before they made their goodbyes, Frieda extended an invitation for all to come back and visit on Memorial Day weekend. The sisters knew of the von Unselms' resolve to divorce and the reasons why they had to call it quits. Obviously, they knew more than Hektor. The invitation was accepted, and they were on their way to Birchtown.

Once they were by themselves, Hannah wanted to share some of her beliefs with Hektor. Her two sons from a previous marriage, slightly older than Hektor, were away at college and preferred to stay with their father somewhere in Massachusetts when not attending school. Perhaps the empty-nest syndrome persuaded Hannah to extend the invitation to Hektor in the first place.

"I consider myself to be a good Christian, but I don't belong to any conventional church. I know we are surrounded by spirits of persons who have gone before us. Quite often, ghosts pay us a visit in our homes. I also believe that after we die, we return to this world again and again. We may appear as an animal or as another human being." She droned on and on while von Unselm just nodded his head and kept on driving.

What the hell did I get myself into? Mother is nuts with her Protestantism and reading the Bible or her prayer books every morning and night. I often told her it didn't necessarily make her a good Christian or a good person, for that matter. I'm not so sure how to handle Hannah's perceptions. Reincarnation? I know what that means, but is she suggesting that I'm reincarnated?

They arrived at dusk at their rented apartment on the outskirts of Birchtown. It was a relatively new two-story frame structure. The house was extremely warm as they entered. Actually, the place was beastly hot, and his room was stifling. Hektor was given the quarters of Hannah's older son, Walter. He was a senior at Ithaca College.

Over the bed hung a large map of the United States. It was fashioned from parchment paper and covered with photographs of various species of fish and wildlife indigenous to different states.

Son Walter was an avid hunter and fisherman. Hannah walked into the room, wanting to make sure all was in order.

"Oh, we can open these windows and let in some of that cool night air. We will do the same in our bedroom. Let's keep our bedroom doors open. This way we will have cross ventilation. You will be comfortable in no time. Sorry there is no AC in this house. It's still pretty expensive. The open windows will have to do for now. The windows have nice screens. You won't have to worry about bugs," she said, using the German word for mosquitoes. "We have lots of *Mücken* this time of year. It's great to have the screens. This will be your bathroom. There are towels right there."

He'd never seen such fluffy big towels at home. Hektor briefly glanced at the fancy contraptions in the bathroom and decided he would shower in the morning, when he was fully aware what he was doing and able to figure out how all the handles and buttons worked.

"Thanks for everything," was all he dared to say.

She gave him another hug. "Have a good first night in the States. *Willkommen in Amerika.* I hope you sleep well in Walter's bed. It's comfortable. Tomorrow, after breakfast, we will have a long talk and discuss your future in this country. I also want you to know why I have opted to leave Werner. For now, don't worry about anything."

That was easier said than done. Right now, he couldn't help thinking about all the implications. After he brushed his teeth, he put on his fancy new pajamas and slid under the sheets covered with a lightweight blanket. Another new experience since he was used to sleeping with featherbeds. When he closed his eyes, the impressions of his first day in the New World flashed through his mind. He thought about Doretta and felt alone in the strange bed. What a day it had been. He was exhausted! It didn't take long, and he was out. All one could hear were the echoes of snoring.

About two o'clock in the morning, a severe thunderstorm moved through the area. Hektor was dreaming he was making love to Doretta. He had turned on his back. His own snoring awakened him.

Gosh, that was an unbelievably loud snort. Now and then his eyes popped open and caught a brief glimpse of the lightning display. He listened to the wind and thunder.

Suddenly, something moved above his head in the dark. Hektor let out a bloodcurdling scream. *What the heck is happening? Am I being visited by one of Hannah's damn ghosts?* Hannah and Werner appeared promptly. They turned on the lights in his bedroom. He noticed them standing in front of the bed. Their images seemed as if he was looking through a photographic filter. *Did something happen to my vision? Did I have a stroke?*

"We are so sorry this had to occur the first night you are with us." Hannah removed the giant parchment map that fully covered his face and chest. It had blown off the wall and draped itself over Hektor. "Apparently, the cross ventilation caused by the wind blowing was too strong for the scotch tape," said Hannah.

"Wow! I am relieved. I was beginning to believe one of your ghosts was welcoming me back to earth. You know, one of those acquaintances from one of my previous lives, Hannah." He smiled and winked at her.

He wanted them to leave. He was dead tired; there had been too many new impressions in a single day. He couldn't help thinking about Doretta. Sleep wasn't distracting his thoughts. He began counting the years backward in English, starting with 1954. He was hoping the approach taken would make him fall asleep and divert his attention from his personal needs and desires.

Chapter 11

HEKTOR was facing the fancy faucet in the shower. He turned it to red and got icy water.

Shucks, I'm naked! I've got to figure this out for myself. Let me try the blue dot. Sure enough, he got hot water on the cold setting. *Must be a faulty installation.* Shaved and showered, he joined Hannah at the breakfast table.

"There is something wrong with the faucet in the shower."

"Oh, *yes!* We are so sorry. We forgot to tell you about it. The plumber made a mistake. Our landlord never got around to having it fixed. Glad you figured it out for yourself. You didn't get a cold shower, did you?"

"Well, I did for a second. It woke me up after that exciting interlude with your ghost."

"Weren't you glad it wasn't one?"

"That's for sure!"

"Werner is off to sign a contract with a well-to-do couple, Mr. and Mrs. Carolina. He's expecting to land a big job with them. Unpack your things this morning. We'll store your luggage in the attic."

"Yes, that's a good idea. My shirts are badly wrinkled after that wonderful and welcoming treatment by the customs officer. The pants and suits look like I slept in them. Do you want me to take them someplace?"

"No, no. I will iron anything that needs it. I enjoy pressing things."

Hektor unpacked all of his suitcases, hanging anything that could be put on hangers in his closet. He didn't know where the time went. Hannah was calling.

"Lunchtime! Come and get it. I hope you like German potato salad; that's what Americans call it."

He took one look and got a whiff off the bowl. "This is a change from my mother's."

Hannah handed him a spoon, wanting him to taste the salad.

"It tastes different; I've never eaten warm potato salad. I must say, I like it."

Hannah couldn't wait to enlighten her guest. "Let's talk about our situation here. When Werner planned his trip to Europe last year, I paid for it. His business was not doing very well. He was lonesome for his family and friends, and I determined it was important for him to make the journey. My generosity was sadly rewarded. Upon his return, Werner spoke to me. 'I fell in love with a distant cousin. She bears the same last name. How about the three of us just living together?'

"My reply to him was, 'You mean like a ménage à trois? You must think I'm out of my mind. No way. This is where I draw the line!' I resolved to divorce him after he brings Waltraute to this country. Supposedly, she will live in Boston as an au pair. Again, I'm so sorry to bring you into this mess."

Hektor sat there quietly, not knowing how to react to these revelations. *What have I gotten myself into? Divorce? What is that? Some kind of scandal? I don't know anyone who has gotten divided? And a ménage à trois? If I had only known!* Hektor was in his own mind as Hannah muttered on.

"When the time comes, Werner will have to move out of this

house. You may stay with me. But you may choose to go with Werner. He is the person who talked you into coming here. You met him first. Your allegiance to Werner may be stronger because of the link to your mother. No matter what you decide, I hope we'll remain friends."

𝗫

Werner got the Carolina contract. He approached Hektor.

"I hope you will consider working for me, at least through the next two big jobs. By then, you'll feel more comfortable speaking English. The going rate for unskilled labor is seventy-five cents an hour; I'll pay you a buck and a half to start."

There's that reference to bucks again. It just doesn't make any sense.

"What's a buck and a half?" Hektor hadn't encountered that expression in any of his classes.

"I'm sorry, Hektor. I'll pay you one dollar and fifty cents an hour."

That sounded OK. Hektor's first job in the US was as a ditch digger, and he was paid in bucks. He enjoyed making reference to such experiences in his daily diary.

Arriving at the Carolinas, he discovered how the other half lived. It was a sprawling ranch house with huge gardens in front as well as in back and was situated on a sizable acreage. Mrs. Carolina knew how to spend money.

"I love my backyard. I need that large flagstone terrace laid in time for my first garden party this season. That new hedge on the north side will give the terrace a more intimate feel. Be sure to pick plants that are mature enough. I don't want it to look like it was just done. Those two big trees need to be moved. They just don't work there."

A few days later she wasn't happy with the new location of the trees.

"You need to bring back that tree lift. Those trees can't stay where they are now. Let me find a location that works better." Mrs. Carolina moved trees and bushes like pieces on a chessboard. Money was no object.

The first day on the Carolinas' job, Hektor met Patrick Swansong. Just discharged from the Navy, Patrick signed on with Werner. He was recently married. He and his wife, Estelle, lived upstairs from Patrick's mother. Mrs. Swansong was quite the lady; some might have called her a dowager who ruled the roost with an iron fist.

On one of their errands for Werner, Patrick stopped by his home, wanting to introduce Hektor to his mother and his wife. Mrs. Swansong Sr. was first-generation Swedish. She spoke with a thick but charming accent. What a character!

As Hektor was looking over her shoulder, he noted a large building across the street. An elegant sign read "Tortelli Funeral Parlor." Hektor looked at Patrick and his mother, a puzzled expression on his face. "What's a *fun*-eral parlor?"

Patrick couldn't resist jumping on that question. "Hektor, anyone who is in one of those homes has had all the *fun* he or she will ever have."

"How is that?" queried Hektor.

"It's a house where people are taken when they are dead. They dress you up and put you in a fancy box on display. Don't you have that in Germany?" Patrick wanted to know.

Hektor finally understood and told him the dead were handled very differently in the Old Country. He had never heard of or seen a funeral parlor in Germany.

Two days after arriving in Birchtown, Hektor wrote to Doretta. He related all the exciting events that had occurred during the Atlantic crossing, including the extraordinary treatment he experienced upon his arrival in Manhattan. Describing the revelations by Hannah and Werner made him chuckle. His first day in America was anything but what he had envisioned. He was surprised that there wasn't a letter from his mother upon his arrival. Hektor looked forward to Doretta's first news. He truly missed her.

Doretta was pleased to receive his first detailed letter. She was stunned by his revelations, particularly remembering what had happened after his arrival. She assured him not to worry about the Leica and paying her back, now that their well-conceived plan had gone somewhat awry. Doretta was pleased to learn of his jobs and the friends he had made in such a short time. She was looking forward to future installments of Hektor's saga.

When Hektor heard from his mother, he could tell she was angry with him. The letter was so wrinkled; she must have debated a few times whether to toss it in the trashcan. She didn't care for the fact she was getting secondhand information through Doretta. When he sent her a terse note, he let her know he didn't have that much time to write the same thing twice. Helena got the idea that Doretta had become more important to him than his family.

The von Unselms and Hektor determined to take a much-needed break over Memorial Day weekend. They headed for Sunny Side Farms. The parking areas were jammed with cars. Most visitors were from Manhattan. The main house was fully occupied by paying guests. Hektor was asked to stay in one of the "rustic" cottages.

"The holiday was upon us before we knew it; the house was cleaned, but the cottages have not been spruced up since they were closed last fall. The linens were changed and are clean. Hope you are not afraid of a few creepy crawlies," said Frieda.

When everyone retired, he made his way with a flashlight to his very private little house. The bed was OK; the linens were indeed clean, and the mattress was firm but comfortable, although a bit damp. He brushed his teeth over the washbowl provided, with a matching pitcher filled with clear water. *I guess piss and poop will be at the outhouse. My God, it's shades of Köndringen, the little village near the Black Forest where Albert and I were sent during wartime.*

He took a closer look around, with every bare light bulb in the cottage turned on. *Get a load of those giant cobwebs and their busy tenants. What are some of those other vermin crawling everywhere? I better keep the lights on, read instead of sleep, and smoke to keep the critters away. This will not be one of my better nights.*

Hektor beheld his image in the slightly fogged-over mirror. He gladly would have shed his fancy pajamas and gotten into bed naked with Doretta. His imagination ran rampant. He could feel her hands running all over his body, touching his most erogenous zones. The sounds of the rain resembled those made by a percussion instrument as the hefty drops bounced off the tin roof. *Perhaps the steady dousing might encourage some of the guests at the main house to consider an early departure.* He finally succumbed to sleep.

Frieda greeted Hektor at breakfast.

"One of the rooms on the second floor became vacant. It might be more comfortable for you. You don't have to use the outhouse. There is a shared indoor bathroom for the guests down some steps from your room."

"That sounds great. I'll move my stuff, including the bedding, when the rain slows down."

"That's considerate of you. Your mother trained you good!"

Hektor shuddered; he knew the difference between the use of *good* and *well*.

Hektor slept OK and woke about six o'clock on Memorial Day. He needed to take a leak. *Did Frieda say the loo was downstairs from my room?* He opened his bedroom door. *Holy shit!* The light from his bedroom struck the lower steps that led to the third floor. Two beady eyes looked at him. Then he saw that unmistakable tail. Hektor thought he wasn't seeing right. He was staring into the face of the biggest rat with the longest tail he ever saw. The beast was the size of a cat.

He backed into the room and slammed the door as hard as he could. He grabbed himself. After a few minutes, he had sufficiently recovered from the initial shock. *Shall I try this again? I'm about to wet my pajamas.* He finally dared to open the door. The intruder had vanished.

Hektor opted not to say anything about his discovery to his hosts. However, when the next planned visit for the Fourth of July was discussed, he was honest.

"No way am I going back to that place. I don't sleep too well in the company of rats." He told Werner and Hannah the whole story of his encounter. There would be no return engagements at Sunny Side Farms for Hektor!

He told Doretta in great detail what had transpired during the holiday visit to Sunny Side Farms. He could just imagine what she felt when she read his note. He didn't hold back when he wrote of his need for her.

The following week, they finished the job at the Carolinas'. Mrs. Carolina had noticed how hard a worker Hektor was.

"It looks like we are experiencing an unusually hot and dry summer. How would you like to come every evening during the remaining weeks of this hot season and water our garden? We will pay you well. How about three dollars an hour to start?"

Hektor saw the expression on Werner's face. That bastard was ready to claim the job for himself. Werner swallowed and took a deep breath. Hektor was quick to respond and accepted the generous offer before Werner could flap his lips.

"Of course, Mrs. Carolina. When would you like me to start?"

"How about tonight? You can stay when Mr. von Unselm and the others leave. George, my husband's chauffeur, will take you home when you are done. It may take you three to four hours to do the job well. As dry as it has been, you will probably have to come every night for now. George will pick you up and take you home. Don't worry about eating; you will eat dinner with us."

Hektor was pleased with his amazing good fortune and noticed Werner's balled fists shoved into the pockets of his jeans. Werner was angry he didn't land the watering job for himself. He needed the money more than Hektor, who couldn't wait to share the news of his good fortune with Doretta.

※

Werner's next landscaping job was on the northeast side of town. The Leonardis built on a corner lot in an otherwise well-established neighborhood. Whereas the Carolinas were referred to as "old money," the Leonardis were viewed as "new money." Werner didn't care where the money came from or what kind of money his clients had, as long as they had the dough to pay him when the job was finished. Halfway through the project, a piece of equipment broke.

"No problem. Send the young man to the German folks at the end of the cul-de-sac. That guy has everything. They will be more than happy to loan us one of their mowers," said Mr. Leonardi.

Hektor went as told. He rang the doorbell at the gate. The garden was a splendor of roses in every imaginable color; the lawns were neat. Mrs. Schiefer came to the door. Hektor looked at the kind face greeting him.

"Mr. Leonardi, your *Nachbar* [neighbor] in the house at the corner sent me. May we borrow a lawnmower from you just for a couple of hours?"

"Certainly! From where in Germany did you come?" Gertrude could hear right away that Hektor hailed from the *Vaterland*.

"I was born in Düsseldorf and later lived in Essen."

"As you can see, I'm up to my elbows in cleaning shrimp. I would ask you to come in for a spell. We are having a large garden party tonight. I'm sure my husband, Knut, would like to meet you. Please write your name and telephone number on this pad. We'll call you tomorrow night. Maybe you could have dinner with us on Saturday."

"I wish I could. You are too kind. I have an evening job at the Carolinas' house, watering their gardens. I am pretty certain I'm expected to be there on Saturday night, with as hot and dry as it has been."

Gertrude Schiefer was not to be put off. "My husband will reach you somehow; if not this Saturday, then we will see you in the near future. Good luck with the mower, Hektor. The garage is open. *Auf-wiedersehen!*"

As it turned out, it rained all day that Saturday. Gertrude Schiefer was happy to greet her newly found "son" that night. She and Knut had no children; her elderly mother was living with them. Grandma spoke little English; she always welcomed any German-speaking guests in the house. And thus, a remarkable friendship began.

When he heard from his mother, she commented on all the traumatic adventures he had reported via his letters to Doretta. She reminded him had he stayed in Germany, he would never have been subjected to hard labor and the kind of work he was forced to do in America. She urged him to consider a prompt return to his homeland.

The Leonardi job was the last contract von Unselm had lined up. His lawyer insisted on his moving into an apartment of his own. Hektor opted to stick with Werner. They found a two-bedroom furnished flat in the heart of town. The best part was that the bedrooms had window air conditioners.

With no clients in sight, Werner laid off his workers, among them Patrick Swansong. He and his wife, Estelle, had become good and caring friends to Hektor. Hektor found a job in one of the shoe factories. He was paid a minimum wage of seventy-five cents an hour. It was better than no job. The dump was hot and dirty but within walking distance of the apartment. Every morning, as he walked by a huge hospital, Hektor would admonish himself. *Don't complain. Do not feel sorry for yourself. You have no one but yourself to blame for your situation. Be thankful you have your health. It's your most treasured heritage. Always remember that!*

He dragged himself to the factory. While he did not understand much of the slang, he understood "fuck" and "shit" and variations thereof used by his coworkers hundreds of times in a given day. He acted dumb and did his job, sorting shoe soles according to size and shape. The stench in the place was unbearable. He could not wait to tell Gertrude and Knut about his new and "stimulating" job when he saw them the next Saturday night. Thank goodness he was still being paid well by Mrs. Carolina for the watering job. He earned four times as much money watering trees and bushes in the evenings as on his forty-hour job at the factory. *Remember that when Mrs. Carolina pays you on Friday nights, you always receive a five-dollar tip to boot. You better be thankful for what you have.*

Werner couldn't find work but wasn't really trying. Their roles became reversed. Instead of Werner taking care of his young charge, Hektor found himself taking care of his sponsor.

"I should have gotten that watering job. You little prick, you have all the luck in the world. Why the hell did I ask you to come over here?"

"Listen, mister, don't feed me that crap. Yes, you planted the seed, but it was your loving wife who made it all possible. It was she who paid for my passage, not you. How dare you calling me a prick? If it wasn't for this 'little prick,' you'd be lying in the gutter or under a bridge with the homeless people. I'm the one who is keeping this ship afloat, not you, you miserable liar!" Hektor walked out of the apartment, needing to catch a breath of fresh air.

The next time he visited the Schiefers, he shared his dilemma with them. Gertrude was appalled by Hektor's current job and even more by von Unselm's behavior.

"Knut, you just have to help Hektor find something different. Don't you have an opening at the plant?"

"Things are kind of tight at the moment. I will contact Bill; he might be able to use Hektor."

During his third week at the Golan Shoe Factory, he received a phone call from Knut's friend. The interview went well. Being offered a job, he gave no consideration of a notice to his boss man at the snake pit of shoes. He had seen people come and go on a daily basis. Hektor saw no need for extending any sort of courtesies; he merely finished his third week. When he was handed his pay envelope by the foreman on Friday afternoon, he didn't breathe a word about not returning on Monday morning. He would just be another "no show."

He started working for Ozon on Monday. He was paid two dollars and twenty-five cents an hour; piecework was an incentive that increased his pay even further. His job was wrapping sensitized paper. The plant was super-clean and air conditioned. Just about all the people there were German. Hektor considered himself a lucky young man. While the job was not stimulating intellectually, it gave him a relatively good and steady income.

Hektor wrote to his mother in time for her birthday. He shared with his parents the positive sides of his visit to the United States. He never as much as hinted at the disastrous encounters and ups and downs he experienced. He knew it would add fuel to his mother's fire of condemning his adventure. He often wanted to tell her what a useless person her long-ago boyfriend had turned out to be.

The first day on his new job, Hektor had another encounter with his sponsor when he arrived at their apartment late in the afternoon. As he turned the key at the door, he was greeted by Werner, who apparently had just gotten out of the shower. Werner had torn open the door before Hektor could let himself in. He was standing in front of Hektor, stark naked. With his dripping hands, he grabbed Hektor by the scruff of his shirt and pulled him right up to his chest and face.

"You miserable bastard; you goddamn immigrant. You've got all the fucking luck. How come you get jobs that I should have gotten?"

Hektor hauled off with his right leg, and his foot hit Werner where it would hurt him the most. He didn't want to rearrange Werner's set of false teeth. Werner landed flat on his ass. The landing was relatively soft on the thickly carpeted floor.

Werner was stunned, not having expected Hektor to defend himself. Still on the floor, he was holding on to his "Glockenspiel," wincing in pain.

Hektor kicked the front door shut behind him before he screamed at Werner. "I hope you miserable prick learned your lesson. Don't you ever touch me again. If you do, you'll be sorry. As soon as I help Hannah get rid of you, I want you out of my life. I don't need you. Hannah is more than willing to be my sole sponsor. Got that, buster?"

Werner was amazed how quickly Hektor had learned to express himself effectively in the English language. Hektor walked away and got into a hot shower. He couldn't believe what had transpired.

In August, von Unselm and Hannah approached him about being a witness on her behalf in the divorce suit.

"I want you to testify that you caught me in bed with Waltraute, kind of like in flagrante delicto," said Werner.

"Are you out of your ever-loving mind? How dumb do you think I am? No way. I'm familiar with the concept of perjury. I certainly won't commit it for you. If you want to screw around with Waltraute and have me stipulate to that fact, you better plan on flying her into town and shack up with her for a weekend. All I need is to hear you bouncing on her in that squeaky bed, and I'll be happy to tell all in front of any judge. I certainly won't go to jail for your peccadilloes."

The following weekend, they welcomed the visitor from Boston. After some brief introductions, Werner and Waltraute disappeared. They took him at his word. They spent the entire weekend in Werner's bedroom. Hektor took care of "room service"; that is, they even ate in the bedroom. Hektor became jealous when he heard Werner and Waltraute screaming in ecstasy. He was amazed how often Werner was capable of ravishing his mistress. When Waltraute departed for the airport on Monday morning, Hektor was perfectly willing to go to court. By now, he was doing Hannah a favor. Werner's behavior confirmed that Hektor truly had chosen the wrong person in this bargain.

Werner arranged a meeting with his attorney. Hektor was supposed to be coached on what he should or should not say in court. He had none of it.

"No one tells me what to say in court. I am quite capable of speaking for myself. You just wait until I share in court how often you got laid. Let me know when I need to be there so I will be able to arrange my work schedule accordingly. I have no intention of losing money over this deal. It's costing me enough to keep you from living on the streets. It's a good thing we didn't sign a lease. After the divorce is final, I will find myself a room. I don't need an apartment and will be able to save myself a lot of money."

The court date came up faster than expected. The presiding judge was a handsome older gentleman. "Please call your witness."

They stuck a Bible in front of Hektor and asked him to tell the truth and nothing but the truth. He had every intention of doing so.

"How do you know Werner and Hannah von Unselm?"

"They are my sponsors and made it possible for me to come to the US."

"Please tell the court what happened on the weekend of August 10."

"Mr. von Unselm had his girlfriend fly in from Boston. I met Waltraute von Unselm when she first arrived. They retired immediately to the bedroom. I never spoke with her again until she left Monday morning. They came out of the room only to use the bathroom. They even ate in that room.

"It's an old wooden bedstead; it made plenty of noise. I could not help hearing what went on. The sounds coming from their bedroom didn't leave much to the imagination. I could hear them scream with pleasure when he got her hot and bothered. I stopped counting how often Mr. von Unselm *bumste* Waltraute von Unselm. Sorry for the language, Your Honor."

"Say that again. What is her name?"

"Her name is Waltraute von Unselm. She's a third cousin of his. He proposed to his present *Frau* that they could just live together, since they all have the same last *Namen*. He thought a ménage à trois would work just fine for all. Mrs. Hannah didn't go for that arrangement."

The judge looked at Hektor. "What do you mean by *bumste*, young man? Remember you are testifying under oath."

"I believe you call it 'f-u-c-k'; for a moment, I lapsed into German. Excuse me again, Your Honor." Hektor went on. "I'm experienced enough to know what was happening. I guess the *maîtresse*—I meant, the mattress—got a good workout. Is there anything else you want me to describe?"

"No, Mr. Birken, that is all we need to hear. You are excused."

"Excuse me, sir. How long will it take until Hannah and Werner are divided for good? Herr von Unselm is anxious to hump Waltraute regularly."

The judge, recorder, and the attorney practically were rolling on the floor with laughter. They had enjoyed Hektor's entertaining testimony.

"I believe, with your testimony, we can take care of the matter today."

They signed a great many documents. When all was said and done, Hannah and Werner apparently had parted company.

⋈

Hektor studied the local paper. He walked two miles out of town. Leonie and Hartwick Shelve rented a couple of their rooms to gentlemen. Hektor took one on the spot and told Leonie he would move in at the end of the month. He wanted to give his landlord two weeks' notice. That evening, he had a little chat with his sponsor.

"I have notified our landlady. I found myself a nice room on State Street. It's not too far for me to walk to the Ozon plant. The Shelves made an excellent impression on me. I suggest you start looking for a home of your own. I am tired of supporting you and paying for lodging, etc., etc.. We'll have to be out of here in two weeks." He was dumb enough to tell Werner where he was moving. Hektor thought his sponsor hit him over the head the next night.

"I got news for you. I rented the other room at the Shelves' home. Leonie was only too happy to accommodate me. You know me; I can be charming with the ladies. At first, she thought you and I were linked, if you know what I mean? I assured her I didn't do it with boys."

"Well, I'm glad for that. I wonder what kind of schmaltz you pawned off on her. You better not let me find out you bad-mouthed Hannah. I'm tired of your attempts at making yourself look great while defaming your ex-wife."

Hektor had a talk with Leonie the evening he moved into her home. He learned that Werner indeed had run true to form. Hektor cornered him. "How can you tell those terrible lies about Hannah? You are lucky the woman let you off as easily as she did. I have news for you: I set Leonie straight on what actually happened. As far as I'm concerned, I wish you would find yourself a different place to live. I don't particularly care to be associated with you. I happen to like the Shelves and do not want you to jeopardize my staying here. To be honest with you, I want you to get out of my life. I despise nothing more than a liar."

Within a week, Werner was gone. Hektor never saw him again.

⋊

Walking to Ozon two weeks later, Hektor learned a good lesson. A man who was probably twice—perhaps three times—Hektor's age honked at him. He gestured for Hektor to get into his car. He rolled down his window. "Where you headed, buddy?"

Hektor didn't know what possessed him to answer. "I'm on my way to the Ozon plant."

"I'm going that way. Hop in. I'll give you a lift."

The man had a full head of curly gray hair and wore a full beard. He looked almost like Santa Claus and friendly enough. Hektor didn't think anything of it and got in the car.

"I'm George; what's your handle?"

He wasn't sure what the guy meant. "I don't have a handle." He looked at the man, a puzzled expression flashing across his face.

George kept steering the car with his left hand. His right reached over and grabbed Hektor's thigh—hard. He tried unzipping Hektor's fly. "I told ya you had a handle."

Hektor was stunned. He didn't dare hit the man, fearing he might cause an accident. He grabbed George's hand firmly and pushed it away from him.

"Pull over before I roll down this window and yell."

George got scared and followed Hektor's orders. Hektor got out of the car, coughed up some phlegm, and ejected it in the direction of George's face.

"Serves you right, you bastard." Hektor slammed the car door behind him. He made up his mind to be more circumspect in the future before accepting rides from strangers.

Chapter 12

HEKTOR'S correspondence with his mother became guarded and even more infrequent. Mother Birken wrote often; Hektor's responses were largely channeled through Doretta. It saved time and much aggravation. He was always pleased when he recognized Doretta's handwriting.

Your mother read me her letters to you over the phone. She is annoyed with you, to put it mildly. I was surprised that she didn't breathe a word about Albert and Margarethe's engagement party. I was pleased they invited me for the festivities. It was a nice affair. I enjoyed meeting Margarethe's family. Her parents are delightful people. I'm glad I will never be in that poor girl's shoes. The way your mother talks about Margarethe's family being Catholic is just a bit too extreme for my taste. Albert and Margarethe are hoping to get married after you return to Germany—whenever that might be.

Thank you for the money order; it wasn't that critical for you to be in such a hurry to reimburse me for the Leica. I'm also glad you could settle up with Hannah von Unselm.

I don't know what your mother's problem is with your

jobs. Doesn't she understand why you are not working in merchandising? She clearly thinks you could jump right into that kind of job without ever having spoken the language of the country. Personally, I believe you have done well for yourself between being a ditch digger and a water boy, sorting shoe soles, and wrapping packages of paper. You are earning an honest living, and you and I know the time will come when you are ready for better opportunities.

You have no idea how much I miss being with you. Oh, I miss making love with you, but even more, I miss being able to hold you and talk about things and our future. It's much harder than I imagined. I keep busy with my work and am thankful for my secretarial skills. My nights and weekends are very lonely. I touch you in spirit and reciprocate your kisses.

Forever,
Doretta

On the Friday before Labor Day, Mrs. Carolina paid Hektor for the last time. She and her husband were very supportive of their water boy.

"Let's have a drink before dinner. Tonight is special. We have been very pleased with your work. Lately, we've had rain here and there, and the days are getting cooler. Mr. Carolina and I believe the time has come for your summer job to end. Your faithful care of our garden certainly saved the day. Here are the ninety dollars for this week's work. I had a chat with my husband earlier; he agreed you've done a wonderful job all summer long!" With that she pressed an additional hundred-dollar bill into Hektor's hand.

His jaw dropped. "You are too kind to me!" He could just imagine how Werner would have reacted.

Mrs. Carolina stepped close to Hektor and tried hugging and kissing him. Hektor wasn't quite sure what to make of the frontal attack he was experiencing. There had been a few other occasions when he felt he was being sexually pursued. Hektor just smiled and winked at Mr. Carolina, who had observed his wife's odd behavior from his wheelchair.

Hektor remembered a time, while doing the landscaping job, when Mrs. Carolina had given Patrick and him an unwanted shower, using a watering hose at full force, aimed at their crotches. She just stood there on the lawn, laughing in hysterics, as Patrick and he recovered from their initial shock. Patrick had said it all—"That lady is frustrated and is looking to get laid."

But this was the end of the hot summer of 1954. Hektor would run into Mrs. Carolina in town now and then, but he never again worked for them.

ᚸ

After Labor Day, he became more selective about which photos he would send home. Lately he noticed his clothes were just hanging on him; he had to punch extra holes in his belts. Gertrude Schiefer questioned his health at the Labor Day picnic.

"Are you eating enough, young man?" She then turned to Knut. "I wonder if Hektor should see our doctor."

"I don't feel sick in any way. My appetite just wasn't what it used to be. Frankly, when it was so hot, I did not feel like eating. I just drank a lot of cold water since I don't care much for soda."

He stepped on a scale at the Shelves' house; Hektor knew he lost weight but had no idea he lost more than fifty pounds since his arrival in May. *No wonder Gertrude was alarmed about my health.* He took another look at his emaciated visage in his bedroom mirror, something he didn't do very often. His stomach was flat and hard, but he could easily count all twenty-four of his ribs. *No more photos to the family for a while. I look like I've been in a concentration camp.* In the evenings, Leonie or Hartwick would knock on his door.

"Join us in the parlor and watch some TV." There were always snacks. Leonie would walk in with her special treats. Hektor looked at these mystery concoctions quizzically.

"Tell me, what is that strange food?"

"I'm serving you peanut butter and jelly on my favorite crackers."

Hesitatingly, he would take one of the offerings. "I have never tasted or seen peanut butter before." At first, he thought it was pretty gross-looking stuff. In time, he developed a taste for peanut butter and jelly.

The best part of watching television was the exposure to English and the ability to discuss with the Shelves the contents of the shows. They never missed *The Hit Parade* or *The Loretta Young Show* on Saturday nights; the *Ed Sullivan Show* was a must on Sundays. He learned, perhaps, the most from watching the *GE Theater* on Tuesday evenings. And there were the shows on radio; they left so much to the imagination and stimulated his curiosity. Slowly but surely, he felt more comfortable using contractions and idiomatic language, aspects of learning any foreign tongue rarely taught in a classroom. Late in fall 1954, he discussed some of his educational options with Leonie.

"I read about this GED test. You have any idea if I'm ready to take it?"

"Well, you've little difficulty reading or writing the language, and we certainly have no problems understanding you. If it was I, there wouldn't be anything stopping me from taking the test."

"Thanks, Leonie. That's encouraging. I'll make the arrangements in short order."

Three weeks later, he had taken the test and passed it to his satisfaction.

Shortly thereafter, Hektor went to a jeweler and bought a set of wedding bands; they were engraved with the date of their engagement and Doretta's birthday: October 27, 1954. The ring was sent by airmail in time for the event. The letter stated not to open the package until she received further instructions. On Doretta's birthday, Hektor made his first transatlantic phone call. The phone kept ringing. Hektor fingered Greta's silver Madonna.

"Osrams'. Gisela speaking!"

"Hallo, Frau Osram; this is Hektor. May I speak with Doretta, please?"

"Oh, she is right here."

"Hi, darling. Happy birthday! I hope you have that little package handy."

"Hi, sweetheart; I do!"

"Well, open it!" There was a pregnant pause.

"Oh, my God! Are you out of your mind?"

"Well, will you do me the honor of marrying me one of these days? You better say yes quickly before I run out of coins. This machine eats up quarters faster than I can blink an eye."

"Yes, yes—I will! I'll write as soon as we hang up. I'm sending you long-distance kisses. Love you, my *Bräutigam* [fiancé]."

The connection was gone. Hektor indeed used up his allotment of forty quarters.

He succeeded in totally surprising Doretta. No one was more shocked and pleased than his mother. Her patience and persistence had paid off. Nothing would stop her son from returning to the family fold; indeed he would leave that damnable country.

)X(

Hektor became anxious about testing his linguistic accomplishments in the business world and finally spoke with Leonie regarding the matter.

"I would like to try my hand at retailing at Christmastime. What about these part-time jobs they advertise in the papers? Do you think they would hire me for the holidays? What about my accent? Do you think it might be detrimental to getting a job?"

"Don't worry about your accent. You are doing just fine. I suggest you put in applications at both Simon Brothers and Folder's Department Stores and perhaps at Sears. You will like Folder's the best. It's an upscale store. They hire a lot of people before Thanksgiving. Folder's will even pay you for the training sessions in which you must participate."

Right after election day, he made an appointment with the personnel director at Folder's. He checked out his closet and wondered out loud how to dress for the event.

"Should I wear a suit and tie for the interview?" He reached for one of his suits and slipped on the pants. They practically fell off him and onto the floor. *My God, I better punch some more holes in my belt to hold up these pants.* He tried on the jacket and discovered that the double-breasted style covered a multitude of sins.

"This will have to do," was his final assessment.

He hadn't worn anything dressy in six months. As he walked through the Men's Furnishings Department, his heart skipped a couple of beats. The store was most attractive, and the merchandise he glimpsed in passing looked appealing.

When Miss Jones asked him to step into her office, he was pretty confident he would land the job. *What's the big deal? All I'm looking for is a part-time job. I'm not interviewing for a buyer's position or that of a department manager.*

"Please come in, Mr. Birken. I see from your application that you trained in Germany for three years. Have you had any experience in this country?"

"None in retailing or merchandising. I do have a full-time job with Ozon Corporation. If you have an opening, I would appreciate having the opportunity to work in your store. Do you think people will have difficulty understanding me with my accent?"

"I don't believe so; it's charming and kind of cute. You will do just fine."

That was the first of many times he was told that his accent was "cute." Sometimes, he wasn't so sure he liked that.

"Could you be here on Thursday at five in the afternoon? We have a training session scheduled for prospective part-time personnel. You will be assigned to the Men's Furnishings Department. We have senior sales staff designated as mentors; they can and will help you if you run into any sort of questions. Your mentor will be Molly Brown. She has been in her present position for better than ten years."

When he made his first appearance on the sales floor that Friday evening, Hektor was a little nervous. He did well with several customers who wanted to buy shirts, pajamas, sweaters, and ties. His first true challenge was an elderly lady who inquired about and wanted to look at suspenders. He had not encountered that term. So he decided to show the lady some attractive men's scarves.

"Did you not hear me correctly, young man? I asked you to show me suspenders!" yelled the impertinent old woman.

Hektor almost called her an old biddy. Molly Brown came to his rescue, having heard the raised voice of the irate customer. She apologized to the lady and then winked at Hektor as she showed her suspenders. His baptism by fire continued that first evening when, shortly before closing, a gentleman inquired about mittens.

"Ms. Brown, do we have gloves with mittens?"

"No, we don't, Mr. Birken. We have gloves, and we have mittens; let me show you the difference."

Naturally, Hektor knew the difference between the objects in question once he saw them. He just never was taught the English word for "fingerless" hand coverings.

One of the first purchases he made was that of a pair of suspenders. Hektor no longer had to worry about dropping his pants on the sales floor at Folder's. By the time the post-Thanksgiving madness began, he was a seasoned salesperson in Molly Brown's department. Saying farewell to the staff on Christmas Eve, Molly Brown encouraged Hektor to consider future employment with the company.

"We've enjoyed having you work for us and would like to see you again. Don't be a stranger. Have a merry Christmas!"

This would be his first Christmas away from Germany. As he and Knut were walking into the house, Gertrude was lighting beeswax candles on the fresh, noble pine tree. German Christmas carols were heard softly in the background. Gertrude welcomed him to their home and made it a most memorable evening. Drinks and food were a mix of German and American traditional cuisines.

Knut served homemade eggnog from a large silver punch bowl. Hektor realized quickly it was generously laced with bourbon and rum. He knew it was best to take it easy with the liquid refreshments to avoid making a fool of himself. There was *Hasenpfeffer* for the first course and a delectably roasted goose for the entrée. Gertrude's apple strudel was the grand finale. After dinner, they sat by the Christmas tree and reminisced about memorable holidays experienced in the homeland.

Knut Schiefer drove him home close to midnight. When Hektor closed the door to his bedroom, he began to sob. The Shelves were gone; he had the house to himself. No one could hear his cries in the night. He felt all alone and longed for Doretta. He wanted to be close to her, wishing she had immigrated with him. *Why haven't I thought of asking Hannah if she would consider sponsoring Doretta as well? I could afford to pay for her passage. I wouldn't have to be alone in this world.* He screamed, wanting the world to hear how he felt on this first Christmas in the New World.

He tore his clothes from his body, throwing his nakedness under the soft sheets covered with Leonie's precious chenille bedspread. He wanted Doretta to touch him; he wanted her to lie down with him. He fantasized until he finally gained relief from his sexual desires and passed out.

On Christmas Day, he sat at his desk and shared with Doretta how he experienced Christmas Eve. He knew she would understand. They needed each other and were both lost in loneliness.

For New Year's Eve, Hektor was invited to a party at Estelle and Patrick Swansong's home. They wanted to make sure he greeted the New Year in style and in the company of young friends. As Hektor joined them in a toast and the singing of "Auld Lang Syne," none of them realized what a momentous year lay ahead.

Chapter 13

Late in March 1955, Hektor received disturbing news. Kurt Beerenbaum had become deathly ill while skiing in Oberstdorf. He lost his vision completely. After an initial examination by a village doctor, it was recommended Kurt be taken back to Essen by ambulance. Further studies revealed Kurt had a large glioblastoma in the occipital area of his brain. The tumor was malignant and termed inoperable. Nevertheless, drastic intervention was undertaken by one of Germany's top neurosurgical teams in Bonn. Doretta called with the sad news early on the morning of May 4. Kurt had died the day before.

Hektor sent a telegram to Greta:

It is with great sadness I learned of Kurt's untimely death when Doretta called me. I feel badly I didn't call more often. Do you want me to come back at this time to be with you? Nothing holding me here. With you in thought and prayer. Touching my silver Madonna. I pray. In deepest sympathy and love,

Hektor

Greta appreciated his concern for the well-being of the children and her but encouraged Hektor not to make any hasty decisions. Hektor thought of Kurt as a second father, and his death cemented Hektor's resolve to return to Germany permanently within the next year. He became a slave to saving his money, spending only what was absolutely necessary.

In late summer, Hektor began contacting different shipping lines to Europe. There were many choices open to him for his return trans-atlantic crossing. He booked a one-way passage on the MS *Saturnia*, leaving New York on February 10, 1956. Hektor resolved to take advantage of the protracted crossing through the southern Atlantic at that time of year. He looked forward to the voyage that would take him via the Azores, Lisbon, Gibraltar, Tangiers, and Palermo to Naples, Italy. After touring Italy and Switzerland, he was to meet with the Beerenbaum family and Doretta in Oberstdorf before finally returning to his family in Essen.

As soon as he booked the passage, Hektor began having the same nightmare. He found himself utterly out of place in Germany and would waken from the torturous exercise bathed in perspiration. *Is my subconscious trying to tell me something?* Hektor took the hint. He considered getting in touch with the INS. Perhaps he should obtain a Permit to Reenter the US.

At the end of August, Hektor wrote to Doretta:

Thank you for calling me yesterday. Perhaps I am too frugal and should call you more often, but I am trying to hold on to my savings and keep our independence after my return home. The last thing I want to do is ask my parents to support me. As you mentioned, Mother was thrilled when I let her know of the future plans in my birthday message.

I'm not sure if I told you before about some distant rela-tions I have in Long Island. Floyd Unkovsky is the brother of my father's brother-in-law, Moritz, who is married to Aunt

Marianne. *Wir sind durch sieben Kellerlöcher verwandt.* [We are related through a string of seven basement windows.]

I contacted them by phone, and they invited me to visit over the upcoming three-day Labor Day weekend. I'll let you know how that went after I get back to Birchtown. More important, I'm getting truly excited about my return trip to Europe. I'm not sure you got it all when I spoke so rapidly on the phone, but I will be sailing on the MS *Saturnia* out of Manhattan to Naples, Italy, on February 10. Happy days! Details to follow. I miss you and love you. My body misses you too! I want to hold you in my arms and make passionate love to you. I'm horny!

Hugs and kisses,
Your Hektor

Chapter 14

DORETTA believed it was high time for her to visit with Helena and Alex after she learned of the firm date for Hektor's return to Germany. Helena greeted her with open arms.

"How nice of you to come and see us. It's simply been too long."

"I knew you would be thrilled by the good news."

"I can't wait for our son to get out of New York. I think that city is evil."

"But *Frau* Birken, Hektor lives in Birchtown in upstate New York. That is hours away from New York City. Please don't condemn the whole state."

"Well, let's forget about New York for a moment. How do you feel about his traveling through several countries before arriving in Essen? I would have thought he'd be more than anxious to see you— never mind you, but his family."

Doretta swallowed hard. "True, but I want him to take advantage of these travel opportunities before he becomes involved again with day-to-day living in *Deutschland*."

"Alex, what do you think of Hektor's plans? Personally, I'm not too happy about all this traveling before he gets here. I guess there is little I can do about it now. Hopefully, he will be here for Albert and Margarethe's wedding. I believe they are to be married on March 22—not that it is any of my concern since I have absolutely no intention of being a part of the affair."

Alex countered, "Can't you be a bit more civil and mature for once? I hate to inform you, but among other things, Hektor left for the New World because he simply couldn't stand our constant bickering about the lack of wealth, your persistent antagonism and hatred of anything Catholic, and your periodic threats of leaving me—or, even worse, of killing yourself. You should discuss these matters with Dr. Hamson one of these days. I know you like that homeopath next door, but he doesn't seem to help you with your mental issues. I don't think that guy knows his arse from his elbow."

"Are you suggesting that I have mental problems? Last I knew, my mind was pretty sound. Our customers like me. I handle all the books and financial matters. I run a pretty efficient household. What more do you want?"

"How about a normal life? Do you realize I have been living like a monk for almost fifteen years? Maybe we should close this damn business, get a divorce, and I could join an order and be a real monk. At least I would have someone to talk to about things other than not turning enough of a profit. Helena, you tell me you are sick of living. Let me tell you how I feel; I'm sick of living with you and your crazy ideas about sex."

Doretta became increasingly uncomfortable, being forced to listen to Hektor's parents' very personal squabbles. For once, Alex was unwilling to defer to Helena.

"Deep down in my heart, I didn't blame Hektor for wanting to get out of this house. At the Beerenbaums and Weldenfeldts, he discovered that there are better ways of living. It's not all about money but also about civility and joy in life." He turned to look directly at Doretta. "I wouldn't blame you and Hektor if you moved to another part of this world after you are married."

Doretta was stunned; she didn't respond, but her facial expression said it all.

Helena couldn't leave it there. "I pray that won't happen. Yes, Hektor and I had our differences during the last few years, but he is still my son, and I miss seeing him. There was a time when he couldn't be separated from me for a single night. You share his love of classical music and opera; when it comes to the love of language and writing, he is my son. In that respect, he is like Alphons. I don't know what I would do if that friendship were to come to an end."

"Screw fucking Alphons! In your mind, you've been doing it with him for years while you locked me out of your bed!"

Doretta couldn't wait for the visit to be over. She hadn't planned on stepping into a hornet's nest. She went home and detailed her experience for Hektor.

Chapter 15

HEKTOR took the Lackawanna Railroad to New York City. Eventually, the Long Island Railroad brought him to Garden City, where the Unkovskys met him.

Floyd and Flora Unkovsky had three daughters. The oldest, Ingrid, was Flora's child from a previous relationship. Ingrid was married and had a little boy. The younger daughters, Georgia and Ursula, lived with their parents.

Moritz and Marianne Unkovsky in Düsseldorf were the family branch that frequently suffered the wrath of Helena Birken. Just the name had given her fits.

"How could Marianne marry someone with a name that sounds so Polish?"

Her sister-in-law tried to set Helena straight by telling her the name was Russian and not Polish, but her words fell on deaf ears.

The Unkovsky family was anxious to meet their distant cousin—or whatever—who had been living in upstate New York for over a year. Floyd Unkovsky owned and operated a bakery and was successful in his business. Flora had not worked outside the home since they were married. She raised her three little princesses. Before she immigrated to the United States, she was a domestic for a family belonging to former German nobility.

Hektor learned Georgia was working at an exclusive shoe salon in Garden City. Previously, she flirted briefly with employment as a clerk at a high-end department store on the island. After that, she worked for a short while at an establishment that sold musical instruments. Georgia never did finish high school. Floyd finally agreed with Flora, and Georgia was no longer subjected to the whims of teachers who failed to appreciate the multifaceted artistic talents of their daughter. The cavalier attitude toward finishing her basic education struck Hektor in an odd way. He had obtained his high school equivalency diploma during his first year in the States.

Ursula was another story. She had finished high school and found a good position in a real estate office. She was successful and enjoyed it. Furthermore, she had aspirations of going to college, although Flora had different ideas. She thought the pursuit of the "MRS" degree was far more important for her princesses.

Hektor and Georgia attended a dance in Garden City. They had fun, since he enjoyed dancing. Hektor interpreted Georgia's clinging behavior as typical American slow dancing. He was headed for his twenty-second birthday, while Georgia would turn twenty-three in December. Georgia felt Hektor was rather naïve, as he didn't realize she was aggressively pursuing him. While they were dancing, she reached down to his crotch.

"Nice, very nice. You got any action lately? I'll be more than happy to help you in that department. I love to fuck."

Did I hear correctly? Did she say what I think she said? My God, what am I getting myself into? Hektor tripped and stepped on her feet. He suddenly began to cough. For a second, he thought his dinner would be all over Georgia's shoulders. He almost lost it right there on the dance floor. What he had initially interpreted as seductive dancing turned into something very different. This had become more than a friendly dance with a distant cousin.

What on earth am I doing? Why didn't I haul off and put an end to her unbelievable pursuit of me? How can I let this happen? What will I tell Doretta about my experiences in New York?

When he left Long Island late in the afternoon on Labor Day, the Unkovskys insisted he return over Christmas and spend a week with them to usher in the New Year. He was certain Georgia played a major role in engineering the early return engagement. Georgia's first of many letters, doused in White Shoulders perfume, arrived two days after his return from Long Island.

"What the heck is that smell?" Closing the front door, Hektor almost said *hell.*

Upon entering the Shelves' house, he knew instantly the strong fragrance and that it had its origin with Georgia. Just for a second, the thought crossed his mind she followed him to Birchtown. The odor practically knocked him out when he got to his room. He couldn't fail to see the pink stationery displayed on the white chenille bedspread.

Leonie got into the act. "That must have been some weekend you spent with your cousins. I couldn't help reading the return address. Isn't that the name you mentioned to me? Some cousin! If you ask me, that letter spells trouble!"

"What do you mean? It's just a letter."

"Wait a minute, young man. Letters dripping in White Shoulders are not your typical garden-variety letter from a distant cousin. You just wait until you read it. I would love to peek over your shoulder." With that, she left the room.

Let's see what this is all about! He slit the envelope and took another whiff of the perfumed pink epistle. He sat at the edge of his bed and began to read. The letter began, "My *very dear* Hektor." *Just a very friendly cousin. Of course, I know better after that experience on the dance floor in Garden City. Shucks, she threatened to masturbate me or give me a blow-job right there and then.* The letter was dated September 6, 1955. Hektor's eyes got bigger by the minute. As he read, he became fully aroused. *Have I lost my mind? Did I allow my brain to slide down a few feet? Holy shit, I better get a hold of myself. I'm engaged to a wonderful girl waiting for me in Germany.*

It was sublime meeting you over the weekend. My family and I truly enjoyed getting acquainted with you. It's just too bad that we didn't meet earlier. I truly enjoyed dancing with you. Perhaps I shouldn't have danced as closely as I did, but I felt a certain chemistry between the two of us as soon as our eyes met. It felt just great having your dick so close to me. You were lucky I didn't do what I wanted to do. Of course, I wouldn't do it on a dance floor. I could've waited at least until we were in the back seat of the cab.

Forgive my horny talk. I was so happy to meet someone who appreciates my artistic talents, particularly my love for the violin. Didn't you just adore that Bruch Violin Concerto No. 1 in G minor? Let me know if you have access to a record player. I would love for you to have your own copy. Like my letters doused in my favorite perfume, listening to the Bruch will keep you in close touch with me. I miss you fiercely. Aren't you getting a hard-on reading my letter? I hope you like the scent of White Shoulders. I find it seductive. I can see us making love to the sound of the Bruch in the not-so-distant future. I hope I'm not too forward, but I believe you are my destiny. I have the hots for you! I can't wait to be screwed by you.

Your *dearest* Georgia

There were a few whimsical drawings interspersed with poetic quotations scribbled on the sides of her note. As he got up, he couldn't help seeing his reflection in the mirror.

Look at me; my face is flushed. I feel like I've been verbally raped.

That letter was the opening blow. Against his better judgment, Hektor responded promptly.

You wicked woman. You sure know how to turn on a guy. My landlady had a ball commenting on my friendly letter from a distant cousin. She would have loved reading your message. Good thing she wasn't in the room when I read it. She probably never would have let me forget getting aroused while reading your recollection of what you wanted me to experience at the dance.

It is truly too bad that we didn't meet earlier. As you know, I am engaged to be married to a great girl in Germany. I believe we should let this whole thing cool down a bit. Perhaps I have become tired of being alone and being horny. Please think about how my fiancée might feel about this hot, heavy, and steamy exchange via the postal service. I feel flattered being pursued by a seductress, but both of us need to be concerned about continuing this affair. It just isn't right.

Your distant cousin, Hektor

The White Shoulders-doused epistles kept coming. Georgia became more aggressive and blatantly suggestive in her writings. Hektor should have realized what kind of person she was; he didn't. Georgia totally blindsided him and was as successful as Delilah ensnaring Samson. Hektor's closest friends—Hannah, the Swansongs, and the Schiefers, as well as Leonie and Hartwick—reminded Hektor constantly.

"What's wrong with you? Did you break up with your fiancée, Doretta? All this talk about Georgia. What's she trying to do to you? Have you lost your mind? This is totally out of character for you. You're a nice guy!"

But their words were to no avail. The affair moved full steam ahead. Totally euphoric at the moment, they both looked forward to their week together at Christmastime.

Between his nightmares and Georgia's persuasive powers, Hektor took some action. He contacted the INS and applied for a Permit to Reenter the United States. Next, he contacted the Italian line regarding the return passage to New York from Genoa. The agency urged him to consider their newest vessel, the MS *Andrea Doria*; she would sail out of Genoa and arrive in New York on July 26, 1956. Before Hektor could finalize booking his return trip, he heard from Georgia.

"My family and I believe a five-and-a-half-month stay in Europe is far too long."

What's it to them how long I stay in Europe? Why am I allowing them to manipulate me and control my life? He kept staring at the pile of unopened letters from Doretta and his mother. Reluctantly, he booked passage on the MS *Kungsholm*, sailing under the Swedish flag out of Copenhagen on May 5 and slated to arrive in New York on May 12.

In late November, Hektor couldn't stand it any longer. *I have to write to Doretta. I've made a total mess of my life. Never mind my life, but what about Doretta's life? How could I fall for another woman, knowing my first love was pining for me so far away?* He was guilt-ridden every night when he went to bed. He was thankful for the physical work. Being dead tired made him finally forget his shameful feelings as he passed out and slept.

At last, he sat down to write that long-overdue letter.

Dear Doretta,

You and the family probably have wondered why I have not written in such a long time. Something happened while I was visiting the Unkovskys and their three daughters in Long Island over Labor Day weekend. Their second daughter, Georgia, is a charming redhead and artistically talented. She paints and is an accomplished violinist.

I don't know how it happened, but she pursued me from

the moment we laid eyes on each other. When I say "pursued me," I mean she tried to seduce me right on the dance floor. The letter she wrote to me on the night we parted company can only be described as steamy. Obviously, she took advantage of my loneliness. I hate to confess, but I did fall for her. Perhaps it was falling in lust. She discovered my weaknesses.

My actions are totally unfair, but I believe at this time I need to come clean and confess to you. I feel terrible but believe we should call off our engagement. I don't blame you and your family for hating me after what I just told you. Someday, you may forgive me, although you will never forget what I did to you.

Hektor

His hand was shaking as he posted his letter at the neighborhood mailbox. Walking back to the house, he touched Greta's silver Madonna. *Dear God, forgive me for what I have done.* In a way, it was a blessing that an ocean separated him from Doretta and especially from his parents. Helena's first letter arrived a few days later. He dreaded opening it. As expected, his mother let him have it.

Hektor,

How dare you forsake Doretta for that hussy in New York? I cannot believe my son would do something as despicable as what you did to that poor girl. She is beside herself, and Lord knows what she might do. I don't blame the Osrams for being angry with you and us and expressing their fury through nasty telephone calls at all times of the day and night. Do you have any idea what you have done to Doretta and to us?

And what about your commitments to attend the Institute in Nagold and your planned return to Germany, etc.? It distresses me to think I raised such an irresponsible son as you have turned out to be. Now you will never leave that damnable country; you'll be lost to us forever. And how can you even think about marrying into that Polish family? I feel like disowning you. You are no son of mine.

The letter wasn't signed. Hektor got the message loud and clear.

Chapter 16

HEKTOR was thankful that no one in Germany was aware of what was happening to him across the Atlantic. *Dammit! What a stupid ass I am. What am I letting myself be roped into?* He was not even engaged yet. However, there were already some hints in Georgia's letters before he arrived for the Christmas holidays. Hektor was urged to consider a fashionable June wedding. Of course, they would live in Long Island. He would have no difficulty finding suitable employment on the island or in Manhattan. His fate was sealed. Once the Unkovskys had Hektor back in their circle (Or was it their *claws*?) the future plans for Georgia and Hektor would be solidified. The wedding was to be held the following year.

What's the rush? Why not get better acquainted with Georgia and her family? I'm beginning to have serious doubts.

There would be at least six bridesmaids and escorts. German trinkets would make some suitable gifts for members of the wedding party. How would he feel about 250 invited guests at the reception?

Do they think she's marrying a millionaire? I wish they would stop asking for these things and telling me what I have to do.

They would spend their two-week honeymoon on Martha's Vineyard. There were direct flights to the island every day. Hektor might give some thought to buying jewelry for his intended while in Europe. Of course, it would be practical to bring back all sorts of things from there. It would be much cheaper to haul it on board ship as part of his return passage. Perhaps his mother might part company with some of the precious things she managed to protect during the war, etc., etc., etc.

He tossed the letter in a drawer and slammed it shut. Leonie could hear him scream in his room. His euphoria began to evaporate. As strong-willed and determined as he had become since his early teens, he couldn't believe what was happening.

How can I let the Unkovskys steer my life? Where did all these ideas come from? I feel like a sailor who has lost his compass. Until now, I was the captain. What is happening to me? Hektor was convinced he was losing control.

The Christmas visit was sheer torture. He was sick and tired of Flora's and Georgia's tactics and couldn't wait to get away from them. His days and nights were filled with a multitude of questions to which he failed to find acceptable answers. He should have told Georgia and her mother to get lost and put an end to the living hell they had created.

Chapter 17

February 10, 1956, was an overcast and gray day in New York, perhaps reflecting the mood of a certain individual embarking on a journey to Europe. Flora Unkovsky and daughter, Georgia, had tears in their eyes and smiles on their faces.

"Stop crying, Mother. He'll be back for more. I made sure to set the trap. He wants more of me and my body. The dancing, the Bruch concerto, my checking out his healthy-feeling prick, and the perfume did the trick. I assure you there will be a June wedding."

Had Hektor known what Georgia was telling her mother, he would have realized he was being caught in a rat trap and played for a sucker. No way would he have made a return trip to the US. Even without that knowledge, he felt like he was riding a roller coaster without a braking system.

He was relieved when the MS *Saturnia* pulled away from the pier on the west side of Manhattan. The ship moved slowly down the Hudson River toward the open sea. The next few months of distancing himself from the situation would perhaps allow him to make the right choices. He looked forward to his journey.

What he dreaded was the whole uncertainty of the Unkovsky affair; the reunion with his dearest friends, the Beerenbaums, whom he would see for the first time since Kurt's untimely death; and facing the wrath of his mother.

Sailing out of New York on a late afternoon in February afforded a traveler magnificent views of lower Manhattan. The city's millions of office windows were lighted, giving the departing sojourners a spectacular visual treat. Hektor stood on the deck of the MS *Saturnia* as she passed the Statue of Liberty. Like fellow travelers, he waved at the famous landmark. Inwardly, he was glad Lady Liberty would greet him again in a few months. At this very moment, he was glad to be leaving; he looked forward to an exciting trip.

Although he was booked in tourist class, he was happy to note he was sharing the cabin with just one other guy. He seemed to be OK. One never was sure in such close quarters. Hektor had become cautious in male-to-male encounters.

After he changed, he went to the dining room. His table companions were Demura Finkel, an attractive bleached blonde, perhaps in her late thirties, and Syd Blumenstrauss, a cigar-smoking gent, probably in his mid-forties. He sported an impressive, almost-black mustache.

Hektor was intrigued by the man's surname; it was identical to that of the German gentleman whose given name, Hektor, had been bestowed on him twenty-two years earlier. Hektor Blumenstrauss was the man who had the highest score at bowling the night Helena gave birth to her second son. Hektor's mother never did understand how she let her husband persuade her to name her son after the winner of a bowling match.

Syd Blumenstrauss was obviously Jewish. Was Hektor's namesake perhaps Jewish as well? Not only was he his namesake, but supposedly he was his godfather. Hektor wondered why he had never seen or spoken with his godfather at any time in his life.

Perhaps his mother would have an answer to his questions and solve the mystery.

Following dinner, Hektor strolled into one of the lounges that served both tourist- and cabin-class passengers. After a few drinks and dances, Hektor had an opportunity to introduce himself to a couple in the lounge who were old enough to be parents or grandparents to most of the others who were there. He learned they were Edna and Andy from New Jersey. They were traveling in the company of a young priest, Father Anthony, who spoke fluent Italian.

Their cabins were in first class, but they preferred socializing with the younger folks in the tourist- and cabin-class lounge. At Andy's suggestion, Hektor approached the purser. For a token up-charge, he moved into cabin class and had the cabin to himself. Later, he often wondered if Andy had a hand in his getting such a reasonable upgrade in his accommodation.

Their first brief stop was in the Azores. A few travelers left the ship, but no new passengers were taken on. Lisbon greeted the visitors with blue skies. Andy, Edna, and Father Anthony arranged for a city tour by bus. All were game to live dangerously and did the screeching ride on the number twenty-eight tram. Hektor wasn't so sure he liked the driver looking everywhere but where his eyes should have been. They were all happy to get off the thing alive.

On their way to Palermo, they experienced Gibraltar and Tangiers. Who wouldn't enjoy the azure skies vaulting over the Mediterranean? The ship turned into the harbor of Palermo under a bright blue sky, but there was a distinct nip in the air. As they came closer to land, they noticed oranges and lemons still on the trees, covered with little white caps. The natives of Palermo had experienced a climatic trauma during the previous night—a cold wind off Mount Etna had brought snow into the capital of Sicily. The visit to the Byzantine cathedral and the colorful beaches of Monreale left them with indelible impressions.

Sunny Naples also did not present itself in its most favorable light. Hektor purposely booked lodging at a small private hotel at the outskirts of town. He was fully aware of many undesirable situations for which the inner city of Napoli was well known. Before he disembarked, he exchanged itineraries with Edna and Andy; they wanted to stay in touch with Hektor, since they were visiting several Italian cities at the same time. Hektor negotiated the ride to his hotel with a cabby. The fast-talking fellow, in his broken English, convinced Hektor to consider lodging in the heart of the city.

"It-a-be so much-a-more fun if-a you stay in hotel in de city." Before long, he convinced Hektor to cancel his lodging as planned. They were off to "dis exciting place in de city."

As the cabby pulled up to the "hotel," Hektor began to have his doubts. They walked with his luggage through a dingy archway and rang a doorbell. Once ushered in, they rode an ancient wire-caged elevator to the fourth floor. Riding up, Hektor noticed numerous lines of assorted laundry fluttering in the breeze.

"Dis-a here is-a your hotel," the helpful cabby exclaimed and stuck out his hand for a tip.

Hektor handed the guy a bunch of lire, just to get rid of him.

Madame had him fill out the necessary documents.

"Sorry, you may copy the information; the papers stay with me," Hektor insisted.

Madame wasn't happy with Hektor but didn't want to lose a customer.

Once he became accustomed to the dim light in his room, he noted all walls, ceilings, and the floor were covered with ceramic tile; the room was cold and damp. There were no heat sources in the room. He hated the musty smell in the air. Exhausted from the disembarkation and the journey to his hotel, he wanted to lie down for a while. He made sure the safety chain on his door was up; anything of value was safely tucked away on his body.

He awoke from his fitful nap freezing with his teeth chattering. Then he discovered he had to use a public bathroom across from his "cell." It turned out both sexes used the same facility. As he looked around, he saw a guy having sex with a woman, leaning against one of the urinals. Hektor soon put two and two together and realized he had checked into one of Napoli's finest—he had landed in a whorehouse.

Taking everything of value and importance with him, he walked over to the Hotel Continental and looked up Edna and Andy. When Hektor described his lodging to them, Andy inquired of the concierge what kind of an establishment it might be.

The man raised his eyebrows and quietly stated, "I believe the young man was dropped off at one of the local brothels."

"Did you get that, Hektor? You are staying at a not-so-fancy whorehouse," said Andy. "I suggest you hightail it over there and retrieve your luggage. In the meantime, Edna and I will arrange lodging for you at this hotel. Would you like Father Anthony to go with you? He could handle any situation, language-wise."

Andy wasn't telling him anything new. Hektor had come to that realization when he observed the sex scene in the restroom shared by both sexes.

"No, thank you. I got myself into this mess; I'll get myself out of it."

With that, Hektor headed back to his action-packed lodging. He rang the bell, trying to let someone know he was checking out. The little sidekick of Madame appeared. She tried to inform him the lady was sleeping. At first, he didn't understand until she mimed the meaning of her attempted communications by tilting her head against her folded hands and then pointing to the office door.

Hektor got the message and headed for his room. As he approached the elevator, suitcases in hand, the sidekick grasped what Hektor intended to do. Momentarily, Madame arose from the depth of sleep.

Among the shower of Italian terms of endearment, he recognized *vaffanculo* (fuck off). He hadn't come for that; he just wanted to sleep for a couple of nights. Eventually, they agreed on some ridiculous amount of lire, which allowed him to exit from his close call with destiny. *What an auspicious beginning to my tour of Italy.*

After Hektor's debacle in Napoli, Andy insisted that Hektor stay at the Hotel Flora on the Via Veneto, where they were lodging for a week in Rome. Father Anthony was a fantastic tour guide. Hektor was part of Andy and Edna's entourage, exploring the wonders of Rome, except for their private audience with Pope Pius XII.

Next, they traveled by express train to Venice. The canals were frozen. One pictures lovers being serenaded by gondoliers, not children skating on its canals. Under a cloud of sadness, it was here that Hektor made his goodbyes with Andy and Edna.

Milan was the next stop for Hektor. He went on from there to Locarno, Lugano, St. Moritz, and finally, Oberstdorf, Germany. Snow conditions had been splendid all through the alpine territory. Two days before his arrival, *Der Föhn* [a warm, dry wind] descended upon the little ski resort. Mountains of snow melted quickly and gave the village a Venice-like appearance. It was depressing. It was almost like everywhere he went—some ill omen befell his venue of choice.

Greta greeted Hektor lovingly. "I see you are still wearing my silver Madonna. May she always protect and guide you." Although she smiled, tears filled her eyes.

Hektor, Greta, and Nicklaus drowned their sorrows in alcoholic refreshments. They met in Oberstdorf to celebrate Kurt's memory. Instead of celebrating the joys of life, the event turned into a cabal, trying to forget Kurt's death.

Nick couldn't resist asking what had happened to Hektor. "Would you mind sharing with me what possessed you to ditch Doretta? That poor girl almost did herself in. I still cannot believe you did such a thing; it's totally out of character for you. We need to talk after Mom goes to bed."

Hektor came clean with his closest friend. Nick just kept shaking his head. "She must be some broad!" was all he would say.

After three days of binging, they took a sleeper back to Essen. Hektor's brother, Albert, drove to the railway station to pick up Hektor and his friends. At first, Albert thought his vision betrayed him. Hektor had a bottle of J&B sticking out of one of his overcoat pockets—that was startling enough. What Albert could not believe was how much weight Hektor had lost.

"Don't they feed you in America?" was his greeting. "You just wait until Mother sees you. She'll have a fit."

Helena took one look, and in a matter of minutes, she was on the phone discussing Hektor's condition with her friendly homeopathic physician. The thorough checkup revealed nothing to be concerned about. Hektor had lost fifty-some pounds since he left home. Helena was assured, however, that he didn't have TB.

"You just wait. My cooking will take care of that sickly look. Come into the living room. We have a surprise for you." They were all snickering as they pointed to an enlarged photograph of Georgia in an ornate silver frame, placed prominently atop the tiled oven in the family room.

"The picture was sent to me. The poorly scribbled note was written by Flora Unkovsky. Her German is terrible; I believe she is illiterate. She and her daughter wanted to make sure you had constant reminders of her. How can you even consider marrying into such a family? And then that pink letter of Georgia's, heavily doused in that awful perfume—our whole place stinks like a whorehouse. How could you even think of marrying a redheaded Polack?"

Georgia had made sure the picture was taken shortly after enhancing her fading red locks with dashes of cinnamon coloring by Lilly Daché.

"Is that hair really her color? You know how I feel about red hair. That means I could have grandchildren with *red shingles*. How could you do this to me?"

"Now, now, Mother. We are not married yet, and you certainly don't have to worry about grandchildren at this point in time, red haired or otherwise."

"You just wait and see. The way this thing is developing, you will be married in no time flat. I have a real problem with women who send perfumed letters!"

Helena had an uncanny ability to predict the future, not that it was too difficult in this particular instance. As it were, the concerns about Hektor's appearance and Georgia's little ploys of ensnarement were excellent deflectors of the real issues Helena was dying to discuss with her prodigal son. For the moment, she was happy to have him in her midst. Doretta could be discussed tomorrow. After all tomorrow was another day!

Chapter 18

HEKTOR opened his eyes after the first night in his former bedroom. His view drifted to the new windows on his left and to the sink located directly in front of him. Only hesitatingly did he gaze to his right.

I can't believe this dump. Why haven't they done anything about the old wallpaper? It's still working itself away from the walls. The clammy air in here feels awful. The smell of must and mold almost makes me ill. Why haven't they done anything to improve the situation?

Of course, after Hektor left, there was no urgency to do anything about the former children's bedroom. Mother Birken didn't dream of spending a mark to improve the scene should Albert and Margarethe have to stay with them until they found housing of their own after they married.

Hektor couldn't help thinking back to those horrible nights and his encounters with Uncle Lothar. By the same token, he fondly remembered making love to Doretta in the same bed where he now found himself stewing about Georgia. The living room, kitchen, and bath had experienced major remodeling. As he stood by the sink and contemplated his face in the old mirror, he could not help hearing his mother and father arguing. Helena's shouting piqued his interest, and he opened the bedroom door slightly.

"As much as I hate the thought of his returning to the United States, I almost wish he wouldn't stay this long. Where are Albert and Margarethe going to sleep after they marry?"

Alex fired right back. "I guess they will have to spend time with her folks. I'm sure they will be happy to accommodate them for a few weeks. Last I heard, they are only getting married in the required civil service. Neither of them mentioned anything about planning a church ceremony. Since you are so adamant about not attending a wedding at the Catholic church, they may skip that part altogether. You remember our own wedding at your parents' home, don't you? There was no church service because you could not deal with the Catholic/Protestant issue. I believe little has changed." Alex walked away from Helena. He knew it was safest to retreat to the butcher kitchen. Meat and sausages didn't talk back to him.

Hektor dressed quickly. He was ready to face the inevitable discussion with his mother. As he sat down at the old round table in the small parlor, directly adjacent to the store, he noted through the one-way glass that his mother was finishing with the last of the early shoppers. The sliding door was pushed back, and Helena faced him. She took a peek at her coffee cup and dumped the dregs down the kitchen sink before pouring herself another hot cup. Hektor knew what was first on his mother's agenda.

"You realize your decision to break up with Doretta and return to the States caused all of us much emotional stress. How could you do such a thing? As I wrote to you in December, the poor girl was absolutely beside herself. You should have heard the barrage of insults visited upon us by her mother and siblings. For days, the telephone calls kept coming at any time of the day.

"In one of my last conversations with Doretta, she told me she was leaving Germany and seeking a position in Zurich, Switzerland. I concurred it was perhaps a good idea for her to get a fresh start elsewhere. She has no desire to see you or speak with you. You can forget about getting in touch with her family to find out where she is."

Hektor put down the newspaper; he'd been glancing at the headlines and used the paper to partially shield his face from his mother. "I have no intention of calling the Osrams at this time, but I thought facing Doretta was the honorable thing to do. While it wouldn't make any difference, I want her to know what actually triggered my initial decision to return to New York. It wasn't just because of Georgia. Perhaps it will be more appropriate at a later point, when she is not as upset with me."

"You know how I feel about Moritz Unkovsky and your father's sister. And now this talk about marrying their niece in New York. I just don't know what you see in that girl. She strikes me as an opportunistic wench who is trying to get her claws into you."

"Mother, you do not know anything about the girl. You only saw her photograph and were annoyed by the perfumed letters she is sending. That does not make her opportunistic."

Hektor felt he needed to defend Georgia. But he had to be honest with himself; some of Georgia's and her mother's pushiness had given him cause to share his own mother's suspicions. Deep in his gut, he knew his mother was absolutely right. He just didn't have the nerve to admit to himself that he was about to make one of the biggest mistakes of his life.

"Are we finished with this conversation?" he asked.

"Yes! Don't be glib with me. I'm still your mother. I just cannot figure you out. I thought I had raised you to be a more responsible person. Doesn't your conscience bother you when you put your head down at night? Obviously, my daily prayers didn't help. I notice you are still wearing that darn Catholic emblem on your chest. Guess the silver Madonna didn't do a very good job of guiding you either."

"I will never understand your hatred of anything Catholic."

Hektor thought this was as good a time as any to broach a totally different subject. Ever since he had disembarked the MS *Saturnia* in Naples, he wondered about the serendipitous encounter with Syd Blumenstrauss.

"Mother, I'm curious about something. On my transatlantic crossing, I made the acquaintance of a Syd Blumenstrauss; he was seated at my dining table. During our conversations, I learned that both he and his travel companion were Jewish. Was my godfather, by any chance, Jewish?"

"Yes, Hektor and Henriette Blumenstrauss were Jewish. Sometime early in 1937, before we left Düsseldorf, they were incarcerated by the Nazis. Never again did we hear anything from them. I presume they perished in one of the concentration camps. We believed it was safest to never mention his name or what might have become of him and his wife when you were so young. While I was never particularly close to Herr and Frau Blumenstrauss, I was deeply concerned what might have been done to them by the ruling powers."

"Thanks for clearing up the puzzle. As I grew up and especially when I was confirmed, the thought crossed my mind that I'd never known my godfather. Well, that answers my questions."

Having dealt with the first brunt of his mother's wrath, Hektor opted to go for a walk and have a change of scenery. As he peeked out the living room window, he noted the lilac bush he'd planted as a young boy. It was starting to set buds. He had dug it up years ago in the yard of a neighborhood home destroyed during the war.

"Looks to me like that lilac bush I planted will soon be in bloom."

"It burst forth the year you left us; it has bloomed for the last two years."

"Well, that's a nice reminder of me!"

"I don't need blooming lilacs to be reminders of you!"

"I need to get some fresh air!" He walked away from his mother. He clenched his right fist, punching his left palm repeatedly with vehemence. He had to get the hell out of the house.

Walking the familiar streets, his feet turned toward his old school. He wondered if Rektor Nagelmann might be in his office. As he approached the secretary's desk, she looked up and recognized him.

"Herr Birken, what are you doing in Germany?" As she extended her hand, Hektor laughed.

"You may still call me Hektor; it isn't that long since I pranced around this school in short pants. Might Rektor Nagelmann be in?"

"Yes, of course. He will be delighted to see you. He'll be shocked!" She turned toward the heavy oak door and gave a hefty knock.

"Come in, please."

As Frau Meyer opened the door, his former principal saw Hektor looking over his secretary's shoulders.

"What a nice surprise! Come in, Hektor, come in." He got out of his comfortable leather chair and made his way around the large desk. He extended his right hand toward Hektor to greet him. When he was close enough, he gave Hektor half a hug with his left arm as he guided him toward a chair across from his desk.

The gesture touched Hektor; he'd always felt a special bond with his mentor.

"Sit down; I want to hear all about your adventures in America. I stop in the butcher shop now and then. Your mother is always more than willing to keep me informed about you and your life in the States. I know she is not happy about the changes in your plans, but you are not a child any longer. You are quite capable of making your own decisions. Your parents have to accept that you have been living on your own in another world—a world away—for the last two years."

"You are right about my mother's state of mind, but I've learned to deal with it. As I've said before, I have my own doubts about some of the judgments I made that changed the course of my future, but for now, I have to live with them. It sure was great chatting with you."

At first, they shook hands; then Rektor Nagelmann gave Hektor a brotherly hug.

He left the office of his former mentor and traced his steps home. He knew in his own mind he made the right decision to seek the Permit to Reenter the United States. He wasn't certain of what the immediate future would bring or how the Unkovsky affair would unfold. One thing he knew for certain, though, was that he no longer fit into the scheme of things in Germany.

The afternoon brought another White Shoulders surprise. The mailman was laughing sardonically as he handed the odoriferous pink letter to Helena. She could tell by the smirk on his face that he clearly disdained delivering Georgia's pink epistles.

"You might as well get used to it. My son is visiting from America. There will be more of these gems every few days while he is here. Apparently, it's the signature of his girlfriend." What Helena didn't know was that Georgia already had talked about a wedding date in a previous letter.

Hektor began to open Georgia's diatribes with distaste.

I almost didn't want to write today, since it is the Ides of March. I want nothing to interfere with our plans. Mother and I believe we will be able to reserve the church for June 24. Have you considered surprising me with a diamond ring fashioned in Germany? Of course, it would be wonderful if you also could purchase china and crystal while you are there. Things are so much nicer and more reasonable in Germany. Perhaps your mother will be willing to part with some of her precious linens that survived the war. It would make so much sense to transport these things as part of your passage back to New York. Obviously, Hektor, you need to decide all these things. These are just some suggestions Mother and I thought of.

We hope you have a wonderful time with your family. Think of me when you behold the photo we sent. Even better, think of me being stark naked. I wish you had a way of playing the Bruch concerto.

"Bullshit!" he screamed. He was getting sick of all their demands and suggestions. "Do they think I'm dense?" *I got your damn messages the first time. You and your mother are beginning to sound like buzz saws.* Hektor questioned his conduct and judgment in becoming serious about Georgia. *What have I done to myself?* Georgia and her mother had turned into royal pains in his ass. The next barrage arrived a few days later.

"I haven't gotten any mail from you," Georgia wrote. "Are you perhaps having second thoughts about our wedding?"

Why don't I sit right down and write a letter, telling her how I feel, and call off the whole damn affair? She gave me the perfect opening. But he didn't.

He glared at Georgia's letter. "Or is your family keeping you that busy that you cannot find the time to write to me? Frankly, I am a bit disturbed by your lack of responsiveness."

The more he read, the more he wished he could have spoken to her, right then and there.

You are goddamned right. I have second thoughts about this nightmare. It's not my family that's keeping me busy. It's all the shopping for the stuff you want me to buy. He probably would have called her a bitch at this point. He was seething with anger. His face was flushed. His blood pressure had risen a few points.

I am listening to our beloved Bruch violin concerto as I am planning the wedding. Mother bought yards and yards of material, and we settled on the pattern for the dress. You will just love it. There will be six bridesmaids, and my eldest sister will be the matron of honor. You may think about buying some nice little presents for everyone involved in the wedding party.

By the way, you need to plan on paying for the flowers for the church. My folks, of course, will be responsible for the hall and the reception. Paying the minister, organist, and soloists will be your responsibility. The party will be held at a fashionable venue on the island. They have a fountain spouting Manhattans; that's part of the deal. I arranged for us to use my Aunt Bella's cottage on Martha's Vineyard for the honeymoon.

I can't wait to screw with you on the beach. You can ravish me all you want; no one lives anywhere near Aunt Bella's cottage. (Please note, I'm refraining from using the f-word and using nicer language these days, since my outspokenness seemed to bother you.)

Hardly anyone walks the beach in her area. Now and then, a fast motorboat zips by. Otherwise, it is totally private and quiet. We'll be staying there for two weeks. If at all possible, we should consider flying there. Here's hoping that you are getting excited about everything Mother and I are planning. I would appreciate hearing from you real soon.

Hektor was already "flying high," without ever having been on a plane. His head was spinning. He felt like he'd stepped onto a careening carousel from which there was no escape. He felt utterly helpless, as his life was being manipulated by Georgia and Flora Unkovsky in New York. These were no longer suggestions but accomplished facts.

He truly felt like he was being railroaded into situations over which he had no control. The romance had clearly gone out of the upcoming event. At night, he would toss and turn. He was hoping to come up with a rationale to get out of the whole damn mess, but he was too young and too much of a gentleman to let Georgia and her family know how he felt about the whole sordid affair.

Hektor responded to her letters and made lame excuses for not having written more often. He wished he had the gumption to lay his cards on the table and tell the whole Unkovsky clan to go to hell. Hektor was getting tired of being constantly bombarded with what he had to do and what was expected of him. He had become a marionette whose strings were pulled from across the Atlantic. He began hating Georgia's letters.

Thank you for your letter. Mother and I were somewhat perturbed by your note. We thought we were doing all of these things with your approval and to make it easier for you in your absence from the scene. Guess we were wrong. We shouldn't have assumed that our proposals had your blessings.

There is another matter I want to bring to your attention. My parents do not want us to live so far away in Birchtown. When you return in May, you should look for work in Long Island. You won't have any difficulty finding some kind of job here. We have contacts and intend to put you in touch with these people.

Can't wait to see you and all the wonderful things you have purchased in Europe. So glad you are returning on the MS *Kungsholm* in May instead of taking the MS *Andrea Doria* out of Genoa in July. Had you chosen to travel in July, we would not have the experience of a June wedding, etc.

He screamed bloody murder when he put down her latest epistle. "What the hell will they want next?" Hektor was glad his parents didn't understand English. He let out a barrage of endearing Anglo-Saxon words that would have made a sailor blush.

What's the big deal about a frigging June wedding? A fall nuptial would have made a hell of a lot more sense. It would give me a chance to find another job in a strange location. I also could play an active role in the wedding plans. As it now stands, all is planned without any input on my part.

"Fuck it!" he screamed and was glad no one understood or heard him.

⋈

Hektor wished for a day when he didn't have to deal with thoughts of Georgia and her scheming mother. He was thankful when his brother asked him to be a witness at his and Margarethe's marriage ceremony. For Hektor, it turned into a delightful celebration, although his mother's absence was once again a reminder of his dysfunctional family.

Helena hounded him about visiting his Grandfather Krämer. He was the last person Hektor cared to see. She finally convinced him to visit the ailing patriarch. While Grandfather had a difficult time saying it, he somehow conveyed to his second grandson that he was proud that Hektor stood on his own feet in a foreign country. Grandpa thought Hektor had done well for himself. Listening to the old man, Hektor believed he was listening to someone else.

"Your journey to America brings back memories of the events when your grandmother and I left our home in Swabia to settle in this part of Germany in 1906. My parents questioned the wisdom of that decision. Later, they were happy for us and our success in an alien place called Essen. For them, it might as well have been the moon to which we traveled. Of course, all they had to do was hop on a train to visit us. Your undertaking was far more daring. I admire you for taking the risk. It shows you have some of that Swabian blood in you."

A greater compliment the old buzzard could not have paid his grandson. It was the last time Hektor would see his grandfather; four years later, Grandfather was dead.

Hektor purchased the wedding bands and the diamond ring at Deiter's. He bought china and crystal at Michelle's; everything was crated expertly and shipped to the receiving dock in Copenhagen.

Reluctantly, Helena selected some of her linens as personal gifts for the bride. Hektor chose appropriate tokens of appreciation for the bridal party. Soon, there were the goodbyes at the train station, and Hektor headed north to Copenhagen on May 2, 1956. The MS *Kungsholm* sailed just before midnight on May 5. She was built in Holland and put into service crossing the Atlantic just three years earlier; she was the pride of the Swedish American Line.

The MS *Kungsholm* accommodated 802 passengers; the majority were in tourist class. There was no cabin class on this new vessel. Hektor shared cabin U50 with three other young men. As their proud vessel departed the safe waters of the Copenhagen harbor, none of them knew what a wild ride across the Atlantic lay ahead of them.

Once in the open sea, the ship and its passengers and crew first faced wind forces of five to nine knots; high swells and rough seas were the order for each day. The captain made a decision to take the vessel four hundred miles north and perhaps out of harm's way. Nevertheless, the MS *Kungsholm* and its travelers experienced wind forces of seven to twelve knots for almost three days.

Waves were thirty to forty feet high. Hektor was one of nine passengers not suffering from the curse of seasickness. He got up to the captain's bridge at the height of the storm.

"Young man, you better hold on to this railing while you attempt taking photographs. Stand with your feet spread apart and bend your knees. You'll be perfectly safe. You are watching the drama of man against the forces of nature."

"Thanks, Captain, for allowing me on the bridge. It's a real honor."

The bow of the ship dipped into the swirling waters of the Atlantic. It seemed like the ocean was ready to swallow the *Kungsholm* in her entirety.

After seven days on the high seas, they experienced their first sunshine, albeit ever so briefly. Wind forces subsided, and the swells of the ocean became moderate for the rest of the journey. Detouring delayed their arrival by three full days. They sailed into New York in rain and fog; visibility was very poor. *Was the mood of the day a sign of things to come?*

Chapter 19

WITH the assistance of tugboats, the MS *Kungsholm* sailed up the fog-shrouded Hudson River. The date was the fifteenth of May. The *Kungsholm* had safely concluded her twenty-second transatlantic crossing. After a hair-raising journey through the North Atlantic, the vessel was finally docked at her pier on the west side of Midtown Manhattan. Hektor didn't realize it then, but he had just experienced the twilight of an era. Regularly scheduled transatlantic crossings by ocean liners would soon become a thing of the past. His next journey across the Atlantic would be by jetliner.

The crew tied the last ropes. Hektor spotted Georgia's cinnamon-red hair; she was in the company of her mother. They were frantically waving a large white sheet and an oversized umbrella. Hektor could hear them yelling.

"Hektor! We are here!" They were so blatant in their exuberance he was almost embarrassed. He moved his right hand up and down.

"I see you. I see you. Calm down." He felt like screaming: *"Don't make such asses of yourselves."*

Disembarkation with his Permit to Reenter was a cinch, quite a contrast to his first arrival two years earlier. Less than thirty minutes later, Hektor found himself in the embraces of his future wife and mother-in-law.

"Were you able to buy all the things we wrote about?" was Georgia's first utterance. So much for what he expected them to say. *Welcome back. How was your trip. How was your family?*

He should have tackled her without any hesitation, but he didn't. As outspoken as he had become (learned from the master, Helena), for some reason, he didn't have what it took to confront Georgia and her mother. He would soon come to regret his docile behavior, which was totally out of character for him in most situations. He was in a complete state of upheaval. Georgia kept staring at him, looking for answers to her questions.

"Yes, yes! We need to wait for the crates to be unloaded that contain all the stuff you asked me to buy. The trinkets for members of the bridal party are in this suitcase. They were small enough to be stuck in corners."

He didn't mention the ring he'd purchased. *Georgia and Flora won't be brazen enough to ask about it—or will they?* He would deal with that on his terms and in good time. Georgia and her mother must have sensed the disdain in Hektor's responses and weren't so unabashed as to ask about the ring. As they were still pressing Hektor about his purchases in Germany, loudspeakers from the dock blared important information to the disembarking travelers.

"Due to the delayed arrival, all luggage and parcels of freight held in the bulkhead of the ship will not be available for pickup until tomorrow. Free deliveries will start in the morning to addresses in the New York metropolitan area and Long Island."

"That means us. I'm glad we heard that. I have a dumb question. Where is your father, Georgia? How did you and your family expect to get the crates to your home, never mind my luggage? No cab would have transported those things to the Long Island Railroad and beyond. As it turns out, your dad saved himself some money by not coming with you." He shook his head energetically. *The old man should have been here to greet me.*

Carrying just one suitcase and a small valise, Hektor stuck his right middle and index fingers between his teeth and hailed a cab. They made it to the Long Island Railroad. As soon as they found their seats, the discussion turned to finding a suitable job for Hektor and the completion of wedding plans. Looking for a job was foremost on Hektor's mind; the remainder was clearly a case of fait accompli.

"Tomorrow morning, I will take you to see so-and-so and so-and-so, etc.; you will have a job before the day is over. You just wait and see," said Georgia. "The arrangements for the church, the hall, and even our wedding night are all complete. We are staying at the Garden City Hotel; it's a present from my parents. I checked out flights to Martha's Vineyard, but I have not booked ours yet since we are not 100 percent sure where we will live after our honeymoon. That, of course, will depend on what happens with you finding employment."

"Right!" Hektor blasted. "Let's keep everything in perspective." He could tell by their facial expressions that wasn't what they wanted to hear.

The cab dropped them off at the Unkovsky house. Both of Georgia's sisters, Ursula and Ingrid, were waiting. The house was all abuzz with female voices, each trying to outdo the other with their excitement over the upcoming wedding.

Hektor needed to get away from all the questions fired at him. He went up to the guest room. *Perhaps this is a good time to present Georgia with her ring. If I don't give her the darn thing soon, she'll probably ask for it. I'll spare her the embarrassment.*

He called down the stairway. "Georgia, come upstairs for a moment."

She rushed up the steps. He caught her at the top of the landing.

It was their first moment alone. He took her in his arms and kissed her but obviously didn't do a very convincing job. She reached for his fly and unzipped it.

"This is what I've been waiting for."

"Hold on, hold on. Just wait a minute. Your sisters and your mother are less than thirty feet from us. They are waiting for you to get back down there. Just tuck my dick back in my pants." She didn't. Hektor stared at his future wife. "Isn't this what you were looking for?" He handed her the red velvet box from Deiter's. She didn't hesitate to snap it open. Her disappointment was written all over her face. The stone was not quite half a karat and was set in a European style.

"You don't like it? Are you disappointed?" Those were dumb questions to ask. He shoved his prick back into his pants.

She caught herself as Hektor faced his acting star. "Oh, no, my darling Hektor. I love it; it's beautiful. It's so different!"

And of course it was. Hektor was too practical to spend a greater fortune than he had on an engagement ring. He had worked too hard for his money. He knew there would be far more important things to purchase in establishing their household. Besides, he spent a goodly sum of money on the china and crystal. Furthermore, he didn't know yet what his future income prospects were. He had no idea what was in store for them—period.

He slipped the ring on her finger. Georgia rushed down the steep and straight stairway; she almost took a spill, losing one of her Springolators. After dead silence, oohing and aahing emanated from the living room. Hektor could tell that the size and style of the ring decidedly did not meet with anyone's approval. C'est la vie!

She was lucky he'd adhered at all to the American custom of buying an engagement ring. In Europe, she would have gotten a gold band to wear on her left hand, to be switched to the right during the marriage ceremony. He could have acted dumb and done just that. He didn't care at the moment.

George and Floyd were much more sympathetic to the cause, especially Floyd, who was a hardworking man. Hektor soon discovered the reason for his long days at work. Being busy was good. It was his antidote to spending lengthy and chatty evenings with his womenfolk at home. Actually, he looked forward to the male companionship he might enjoy with his sons-in-law. All gathered around the Unkovsky dining table. They toasted Hektor's safe return to the States.

"How is my brother, Moritz, and his family?" asked Floyd.

"Did you, by any chance, get to see my sister, Edwina, and her new husband? I'm not sure if you are aware that her first husband escaped from a Russian prison camp just ahead of the troops moving west during the last days of the war. He made it back to Magdeburg and kept running toward the west with Edwina and their ten-year-old daughter, Hedwig. He was emaciated and suffering with an extreme case of dysentery. He never made it. My sister and her daughter scraped a shallow grave next to the road with their bare hands and buried him in the snow."

"No, I had not heard that story. I'm so sorry to learn your brother-in-law met such a terrible end after enduring those years of imprisonment. I saw your brother, Moritz, and his family on one occasion when my parents and I visited them in Düsseldorf; they all seemed OK to me."

He didn't have the inclination to tell him how they'd fought with each other, especially Helena's telling her sister-in-law what she thought of her son marrying some damn redheaded Polack in New York, instead of the nice girl he'd deserted in Germany.

Floyd enlightened him further. "I met your parents on the occasion of my brother's marriage to Marianne in 1929. It was the only time I visited Germany since I immigrated to the States in 1924. How are your parents?"

"They are doing OK, although my mother is not at all happy that our impending marriage derailed my permanent return to Germany."

Flora was incensed. "That's too bad! She should be rejoicing that you are marrying one of our little princesses!" She used the German word. All the women smiled in agreement.

Hektor almost barfed. He kept quiet; he didn't want to open that Pandora's box. The women returned to discussing wedding plans. Floyd, George, and Hektor continued idle chitchat around the dining table. Hektor finally ascended the stairway and retired. He had to look for a job the next morning.

ж

Floyd dropped them off in Franklin Square. Georgia knew a Mr. Myrtle, who ran a haberdashery in town. Perhaps he might offer Hektor a job. The visit didn't last very long. While Mr. Myrtle did have a vacancy, even Georgia realized they could not live on forty dollars a week.

The next stop was at the R&S department store. It was a slow summer, and the personnel director didn't hire new people until later in the year. They were off to Garden City. Georgia thought that Mr. Moron, her former boss at the music store, might be inclined to offer Hektor a job.

Moron acted like he was surprised to see her. There was something strange about the way he looked her up and down. Georgia seemed to be fascinated with Moron, the way she kept staring at his crotch. Hektor could tell Mr. Moron was getting a hard-on. He had everything to offer but a job for Hektor. Things were not as rosy as Georgia and Flora had promised.

Before they returned empty-handed to the Unkovsky house, Hektor decided what to do about a job. Spotting a public telephone near the men's room at the restaurant where they were having a quick bite, he called Jack Holstein, the foreman at the Ozon Corporation in Birchtown.

"Nice to hear from you. How was your trip to Germany?"

"The trip was great, but I am happy to be back in the States. Any chance you can still use my services?"

"As a matter of fact, we are quite busy and would love to have you back at the plant. When could you be here?"

"How about tomorrow? I will catch the first Lackawanna in the morning. I'll give you a ring as soon as I get to Birchtown. Thanks a million for having a job for me. We'll talk tomorrow. Say hi to the gang!"

He was relieved when he hung up. It was the best news in two days. Hektor wasn't sure what the Unkovskys would think of the latest development, but he simply didn't care. They succeeded in pulling his strings, relative to the wedding. In no way would they interfere with where and how he earned his living. Hektor took pride in his ability to stand on his own two feet. He couldn't wait to spring his news on them.

"I got my old job back with Ozon, and I'll be leaving early in the morning. We'll talk about the implications over dinner tonight."

For once, Georgia and Flora were faced with a fait accompli. "There is nothing that will change my mind," Hektor told them. "The prospects of finding a halfway decent job here are dismal. If you want to proceed with your wedding plans, this is one issue where I will not give in to your silly notions. You can spare me the theatrics and crocodile tears."

Mother and daughter realized they had met their match. They had no intention of upsetting the apple cart at the last moment. Of course, they might have done Hektor a welcome favor.

"How will this affect all the parties and showers we have planned? Where will we live after we return from our honeymoon?"

"As far as your damn parties are concerned, I don't give a rat's ass. I guess you will have to enjoy them by yourselves. What I have learned about *showers* does not particularly appeal to me. I consider it a form of begging for things from one's friends and relatives. It is something we don't do in Germany. I have much difficulty accepting the custom. I would not dream of attending *any* of them.

"I guess it was a good thing you didn't book a round-trip from La Guardia to Martha's Vineyard. I suggest you book the return flight to Birchtown. I will try for a furnished apartment in the same building where Werner von Unselm and I rented for a while. We may have to spend a night or two with the Shelves. I'm sure Leonie would put us up if she has a room available. Speaking of available rooms, let me call Leonie right now. I will need a place to sleep tomorrow night."

Hektor reached Hartwick and Leonie.

"Good to hear from you. Yes, your room is still available. I'm dying to hear about your trip and the wedding plans. Oh my, my, my—and I will get to meet that femme fatale of yours." Leonie was the first to recognize the troubled waters in which Hektor would find himself. She never let him forget the arrival of that first letter doused in White Shoulders.

Floyd couldn't agree more with Hektor's choice. "Under the circumstances, I would have come to the same conclusion. You can't support a wife on forty dollars a week. If you can make two and a half times the money in Birchtown, that's where you should be. Furthermore, your money will go a lot farther in a smaller town. Rents are high in the metropolitan area of New York City. Smart decision, young man."

That settled it. After dinner, Hektor packed some of his things. He had enough with him to tide him over. Georgia promised to write; Hektor said he would when he could find the time. He might call now and then. He didn't give a damn about talking with her. The less, the better. Those negative feelings should have been red warning flags to him.

Sometime after midnight, Hektor was awakened. He realized it was Georgia, trying to rip off his pajama bottoms. He was fully aware of her nicotine-scented breath and the presence of White Shoulders.

"Stop it, Georgia. Can't you wait until we are married in a few weeks? What would your mother think of her princess, were she to know what you are really like? I didn't think I was marrying a hooker."

Georgia slapped his face and stormed out of the guest bedroom. Hektor did not go back to sleep and wondered for the umpteenth time what he was getting himself into.

The next morning, Georgia's father dropped her off earlier than usual at the shoe salon and took Hektor to the Long Island Railway station in Garden City. The six-hour trip gave him plenty of time to mull over the events of the last few days. He was happy to be alone with his thoughts. *What am I doing, and what can I do about it?* The answer was always, *nothing for now! Maybe in time, things will get better. Once we are on our own in Birchtown, I will change some of her way*s. He sure hoped so.

⚱

"Good to see you, Hektor. We have missed you," said Jack Holstein when he met Hektor at the train station.

"Would you mind dropping me off on State Street? I called the Shelves; they did have a room for me. I will be staying with them until my future wife, Georgia, and I return from our honeymoon on the ninth of July."

"Did I hear you say future wife? When did this happen? I thought you were marrying a girl called Doretta from Germany."

"It's a long and complicated story. I'll fill you in on the details when we have time to talk."

Jack was dumbfounded but did not push the issue any further. He wished Hektor well when they arrived at the Shelves' home. "See you bright and early in the morning. If we are not too busy, you can tell me a bit more over a cup of coffee."

A healthy drink would probably be a more appropriate potion to help Jack swallow the news I have to impart, Hektor thought.

Leonie greeted him with a friendly hug. She poured some fresh tea. Then she aimed those inquisitive eyes over her cheaters at Hektor. "Now, tell me all about the trip and what's happening with Georgia. What did I tell you when you got that first letter from her last September? I just knew she would be your undoing. Well, you are both young and malleable. I didn't realize until today that she is almost two years older than you. One might have thought her to be a bit more mature about certain things."

"Oh, Leonie. What are two years? No big deal. Besides that, the Birken men always married women who were slightly older than they. I'll pay for the room in advance through the fifteenth of July. I'm not sure when Mrs. Brown will have a furnished apartment available for us. Actually, Georgia and I might find ourselves staying with you after returning from our honeymoon on Martha's Vineyard."

"That will be fine. It'll give me a chance to get to know the young lady firsthand."

Hektor quickly fell asleep; he tossed and turned in fitful dreams. The shrill sound of the alarm clock waking him was welcome relief. In a few days, he was back in his routine at work.

Gertrude and Knut Schiefer wanted to see him on Saturday night; they were anxiously waiting to hear about Hektor's trip and his resolve to marry Georgia in June. Gertrude turned her beautiful brown eyes on Hektor.

"You are blundering into something, but you have no idea how it all will end. Don't enter into this relationship lightly. Always remember what Schiller said so many years ago. *'Drum prüfe, wer sich ewig bindet, Ob sich das Herz zum Herzen findet. Der Wahn ist kurz, die Reu' ist lang.'"* ["So test, therefore, who join forever, if heart to heart be found together. Delusion is short, remorse is long."]

Why didn't I listen to her? Hektor asked himself often in the days to come.

Hannah was stunned to hear of his sudden announcement to marry a girl he hardly knew. Estelle Swansong swallowed hard before responding to the bombshell Hektor had just dropped; she thought her eager ears were failing her.

However, none of their well-intentioned counsel fell on fertile soil. Hektor believed the affair had gone too far for him to back out at the last moment. Walking out of the house with Patrick, Hektor cussed.

"What the fuck am I going to do? I'm stuck!"

"Well, have you fucked her yet?" Neither Patrick nor Hektor had a problem with using appropriate four-letter words when they served their purpose. Patrick had done his stint in the Navy. *Fuck* didn't hurt his ears.

"No, I haven't but probably should have. From the day we met, she was asking for it!"

Patrick shook his head. "I don't know what else I can tell you. All I know is, if I felt the way you do about this affair, I would get out of it *now*! She'll take you for every fuckin' dollar you will earn and more!"

In his gut, Hektor knew Patrick was speaking the truth.

The forty days between his return from Europe and the wedding date seemed to fly by, on one hand, and represented an eternity on the other. He did succeed in renting a one-bedroom, furnished apartment from his former landlady. It was an open-ended lease; they could move easily if different arrangements were necessary. Having been a good tenant in the past afforded Hektor the favorable terms.

The long days at the plant were a welcome diversion. Falling into bed exhausted made it easier to shut out nagging doubts. He read and reread the contents of the odoriferous pink epistles. The more he read, the more disgusted he became with himself and his behavior toward Doretta. He began to realize he had sacrificed a precious jewel for a cheap imitation.

Why aren't you listening to your friends? Why aren't you listening to your own brain? You know what you are doing is wrong! Wake up, man, and act accordingly!

1956–1963

Chapter 20

THREE days before the wedding, Hektor boarded the Lackawanna for New York. He chose to make the best of the situation. In spite of his protestations, he had to suffer through one of the detestable bridal showers. As Georgia opened present after present, it turned out that all gifts were exclusively for her—lacy nightgowns, slips, sexy panties, and daring stockings.

Just what you desperately need to further your kinky sexual orientation! Hektor thought.

There was a bachelor party on Thursday night and the rehearsal dinner on Friday. *If I get myself stinking drunk during these damn dress rehearsals, I might have the chutzpah to pull the plug on opening night.* Too bad he didn't! On the wedding day, he wished they had the ever-flowing Manhattan fountain instead of a baptismal font at the church. He would have sampled it a few times before the infamous service. He might have pulled it off then.

All went as planned; that is, the way the Unkovskys envisioned it. It was a sunny day in June. The men looked resplendent in their rented white tuxedo jackets, as did the bridesmaids and matron of honor in their gowns fashioned by Flora Unkovsky. The bride was dazzling in the piece de resistance, also created by her mother.

Hektor suffered through the introductory musical offerings presented by his sister-in-law, Ursula. Finally, the organist intoned the inevitable bridal music from Wagner's *Lohengrin*, and Georgia made her grand entrance on her father's arm. Hektor couldn't help himself; he sought momentary consolation by touching Greta's silver Madonna. The service was a blur in Hektor's mind. He listened to the words of the minister. The man slowly began to read the passage.

"If anyone . . ."

Hektor was tempted to scream *yes* and flee the scene of the event. But he was too young and immature to take that drastic step. Thus, they were pronounced husband and wife. The organist began to blast the wedding recessional from Mendelsohn's *Midsummer Night's Dream*. Hektor put on his best Hollywood smile as he and Georgia walked out of the church to face the well-wishers.

After being sufficiently pelted with rice, they were rushed off to the wedding reception by limousine. Hektor chose to make several stops by the ever-flowing fountain of Manhattans; being slightly high made the rest of the day more tolerable. He did not intend to anesthetize himself, but taking off the edge was a desirable state. It allowed him to deal more adequately with the events that followed.

Georgia's father drove them to the Garden City Hotel and pressed an extra hundred dollars into Hektor's hand. "Enjoy your honeymoon and your future life." He winked at Hektor, who wondered if Georgia's father had any inkling of what a cheap and useless whore his daughter was.

They ascended to their room, and Georgia grinned broadly. She was obviously pleased that she had finally met her objective.

Hektor opened the doors to the bridal suite and discovered a bouquet of roses, heavily doused with White Shoulders. A chilled bottle of champagne stood by the bedside. The fragrance of the perfume was so overpowering that Hektor moved the vase into an adjacent reading room.

"Sorry! These have to be put elsewhere. That perfume is just too much for me. A little of it goes a long way. I don't know why you always have to use that stuff with such potency!"

"Speaking of potency, are you ready to fuck?"

Did I hear her correctly?

"I have been waiting for this since Labor Day last year." She unzipped the fly of his fancy tuxedo pants and freed his member. "My, my, my! This looks enticing. Get me out of this damn wedding dress before I rip it to shreds. I'll skip the bath and champagne. First things first."

Hektor helped Georgia out of her wedding gown since she was ready to tear it off with both hands. Flora would have had a hemorrhage, had she seen how Georgia treated her masterful creation. Hektor shed his jacket, tie, and cummerbund, tossing them on the closest chair. He kicked off his shoes.

Georgia did not unbutton his shirt; she literally ripped it off Hektor's torso. "Down with those damn suspenders. And let's get all of these rags off you. I want to behold you like Michelangelo's *David*. His cock has nothing on yours. Of course, he couldn't carve him with a hard-on. Wouldn't he have loved to do that? You know he was gay! Get rid of that goddamn thing hanging from your neck. I don't like things swinging in front of my face when I'm being screwed. Of course, I wouldn't mind having your gorgeous prick dangling in my face but not that damn thing."

He grabbed her hand as she reached for the silver Madonna. "You might as well get used to it; Greta's Madonna will never come off my neck! Are you quite finished? I never imagined seeing you act like this. And stop using profanities. Were you raised in the gutter? You are insulting me and my faith. I don't appreciate your kind of talk. You sound worse than any common hooker I might have encountered. What kind of a person have I married?"

"You'll find out real soon! Get a move on! I've been waiting for this moment too long."

Hektor was nervous as he broached the topic of marital bliss. "If you don't mind, I would prefer we not become pregnant on our wedding night. I brought plenty of condoms with me and intend to use them."

"Don't give me that pompous talk of yours. I don't want to make love to a piece of latex. I want to feel you in me. Look at you; has your skin ever been touched by the sun? You are white as marble; there isn't a blemish on you. Come here. Let me hold you. I want to touch and lick you all over." She went on her knees and wrapped her lips around his penis.

Hektor almost lost it right there. He freed himself of her and quickly slipped on the condom he held in his hand. Before Georgia realized it, he had gotten her on the bed and was about to enter her.

"All right! I will go along with this charade tonight, but I have every intention of getting myself pregnant on Martha's Vineyard."

He ravished her a couple of times. Hektor fell asleep, exhausted. Now, it was all water over the dam. Patrick's words hung in his ears. *"You'll pay fuckin' dearly for the fuckin' you got."*

By sunup, Georgia had taken a bath and put on her white satin negligee. Her cinnamon-red locks flowed over her shoulders. Hektor took a long, hot shower and put on the fancy pajamas he had planned to don on their wedding night. He called room service and ordered breakfast. He popped the champagne they hadn't drunk. He was thankful not all the ice in the bucket had melted. It all had gone differently than he had expected. No longer did he wonder; he realized what kind of a slut had become his wife.

"What's your hurry with getting pregnant? Don't you believe we should establish a decent home first before we bring children into the mix? Evidently, you have no intention of working and making any sort of contribution in this marriage."

"I went along with your idea of precluding my getting pregnant last night. I didn't want to spoil the moment. We have time to talk about this on Martha's Vineyard. Hopefully, you will see it my way after we get to know each other better. It is too bad we essentially carried on our relationship via the postal services."

Hektor couldn't have agreed more.

They dropped off Georgia's wedding dress with the concierge. Flora had made arrangements to have it picked up later that day. The cab took them to La Guardia, where the newlyweds boarded their first flight ever.

Riding in a cab to the remote part of the island to Aunt Bella's cottage, both of them commented on the rose-covered fences that framed the New England gray houses and cottages. Aunt Bella had stocked her refrigerator sufficiently for the arrival of the honeymooners. Hektor fixed a light lunch before they sat down and had a chat.

"Did you enjoy our wedding night as much as I did?" purred Georgia. As long as she raised the question, Hektor came right to the heart of the matter.

"I had the distinct impression it was not a totally new experience for you, or would you rather I said it wasn't the first time you got laid? Am I wrong in that assumption?"

The wedding band on her hand and the marriage license safely tucked in the breast pocket of Hektor's jacket gave Georgia much confidence. "No, you are not wrong. Contrary to your need for preventing an early pregnancy, I would really like to throw all caution to the wind. I want to have a baby as soon as possible. I have been a failure in many different ways. I was a failure in school. My art and musicianship were never appreciated by my teachers. I was never successful in my attempts at working. I feel I could be a very good mother. I have had this urge to create a child for some time.

"Yes, I have been with other men. I seduced Josh Moron on several occasions. He enjoyed sucking and licking me all over while I played the violin. When I was ready, he couldn't screw me fast enough. I presume you noticed Moron getting a hard-on when he was looking at me a few weeks ago. You were looking for a job; he was looking to fuck me in the backroom. Gosh, just think—if you'd gotten a job with him, both of you could have done me at the same time. Of course, he always wore those damn rubbers. Unfortunately—and perhaps now I can say, fortunately—he was clever enough to prevent me from achieving my goal."

Hektor was stunned by her revelations. "My God, you are depraved!"

She got up from the table and disappeared into the bedroom. When she emerged, she was wearing black thongs on her feet and nothing but a large black silk shawl depicting colorful flowers and birds.

"Don't bother with swim trunks, and let's fuck on the deserted beach; there is no one around for miles. Don't forget to bring that fancy camera of yours. I want you to take some photos of me in the buff! I might even dare to take some of you with your dick ready to let me have fun with your Glockenspiel—at last!"

Hektor's hormones kicked in; he wanted to take her up on the offer. The last thing he grabbed was the Leica and a couple of condoms, which he tucked in the pocket of his swim trunks. Contrary to his wife, he wasn't all that willing to parade stark naked on the beach. As Georgia made her way through the sand dunes and beach grasses, she draped the shawl around her waist, exposing her bare breasts. She encouraged Hektor to photograph her in numerous seductive poses.

"These will be fun to look at someday when we are old."

She turned toward Hektor and removed his swimsuit as she dropped her own wrap and spread it on the beach. Hektor could not resist the temptation. Reaching for his trunks, Georgia knew what his intentions were.

"Please don't. I want your child. Please do not deny me this ultimate pleasure. Take some photos of me before my hair gets all messed up. Show me how to use your treasure. I want some closeups of your dick."

"Where do you plan to have these developed? Most labs will not print anything bordering on pornography."

"Don't worry about developing your film. I have my sources. One of my former classmates is into pornography and has his own photo lab. He'll be delighted to look at my teats and your cock."

They made passionate love and lay on the warm sand until the sun's descent. Because they were caught up in their efforts of creating a baby, they forgot about the fairness of their skin. When the honeymooners returned to the cottage, they realized they resembled boiled lobsters.

"My God, look at you. I got it on my back, but you are burned to a crisp all over. Your mother would have a stroke if she saw you like this. Let me make some baking powder paste. It might help a little. We are off to a good start," said Hektor.

Georgia became untouchable. Hektor was confined to the living room sofa. The pain gave way to almost intolerable itching. Eventually, they creamed each other's sensitive new skin as they carefully removed the dead and sunburned tissue from one another's healing bodies. Their lovemaking resumed during the second week of their stay on Martha's Vineyard. They learned their lesson; never again would they do it on any beach.

Chapter 21

THE single-engine prop plane landed at the airport in Birchtown late in the afternoon of July 9, 1956. As they approached the landing, Georgia commented that the community appeared larger than she had expected.

"It looks like three distinct places."

"That's right. We're landing near Birchtown, the oldest of the three towns. Directly adjacent is Jamison City, the home of the Evers-Jamison City Shoe Factories. The newest of the towns is Evers."

"Why aren't we living in Evers, presumably the most modern of the three towns?"

"We are starting out in Birchtown because it is closest to my work. Remember, I don't drive, and we don't have a car. Eventually, I will have to get a driver's license and will need to buy a vehicle. There is relatively good public transportation in town and between the cities. Most of the time, I will walk to save money. As it stands, I see us having no other choice."

Leonie and Hartwick were kind enough to meet them at the airport.

"Welcome to Birchtown. Our best wishes for a good life," said

Leonie, speaking for both of them. Hartwick was quiet and reserved, almost shy, despite the fact he was in his sixties. Leonie was bubbly and exuberant. She would take Georgia under her wing for the six days they were under their roof. Hektor felt comfortable being with Leonie and Hartwick.

"Thanks, Leonie. That's a beautiful quilt. The fresh flowers are a nice touch," offered Hektor, walking into his former bedroom.

"My pleasure. Enjoy! I had nothing to do with the fragrance in the air. It must hail from your letters in that tightly closed dresser drawer."

Hektor could tell by Georgia's facial expression that she was clearly pleased her presence had been felt in her absence.

"Well, you fool, you can hide my letters, but you can't hide from me." She strutted around the bed, her Springolators clacking loudly on the hardwood floor.

At work, everyone wanted to know how married life was agreeing with Hektor. His answers were guarded. The guys joked and couldn't resist asking the same question.

"Must be a hell of a lot better than taking care of business by yourself!"

Hektor assured them it was. He was unwilling to share to what degree and certainly didn't want to advertise he had married a nymphomaniac.

Leonie took Georgia shopping in town and drove by the apartment building where they would be living.

"You mean to say he wants me to live in that ugly dump? He must be out of his gourd. Never!" Georgia caught herself, almost using some of her favorite colorful language.

They moved into the apartment on the fifteenth of July, with nothing but their toiletries and a few absolute essentials. Georgia was terribly upset when she discovered one of her bottles of perfume had popped during the flight from Martha's Vineyard. The orange-red lining of the luggage bled all over everything. She could not wait to show the damage to her mother—her parents were delivering all their wedding presents the next day.

Hektor couldn't resist. "The stains on your negligee almost match the color of your hair. It's a perfect costume in which you could parade around this place pretending to be Lucia di Lammermoor. I bet you would have no difficulty putting on a mad scene; it's right down your alley!"

"I don't know what the fuck you are talking about!" Hektor walked out of the room without giving her an answer.

Georgia had a convenient excuse not to prepare dinner for her family. "How the hell can you or the family expect me to put a meal on the table? I don't have a damn thing that allows me to cook. The old man better have planned to wine and dine me at a restaurant."

"What about me?" interrupted Hektor.

"Well, I suppose they'll feed you too. You look like you could use a good meal between those emaciated-looking ribs of yours. You need a decent dinner after all the nighttime activities you've enjoyed with me. Haven't you just loved all the wild rides I've been giving you? I can't wait for my folks to see this joke of a place you are calling our home. I'm only staying here as long as I absolutely have to."

Flora, like her daughter, had nothing but criticism of the apartment they were able to afford at the moment. "The kitchen and bath don't even have windows." Walking into the bedroom, she kept pushing down on the bed. "The bed seems to be comfortable and has a good mattress, but the room is so small. It's a good thing the living and dining rooms are good-sized. You would be climbing the walls otherwise."

Floyd couldn't resist adding some levity to the situation when he spoke to Flora. "I would like to remind you of the dumps you shared with your guy and how primitively we lived during our first few years of marriage. This is a palace by comparison. Furthermore, these kids have a beautiful yard, with trees to look at. We looked at laundry lines and almost could touch the ugly adjacent buildings when leaning out of our windows."

That made Flora shut up. She had a tendency to portray herself as being better than others. Hektor would later discover she thought some aspects of the nobility for whom she worked as a maid in Germany had rubbed off on her. *If I hear her calling their daughters "little princesses" just one more time, I'll scream.*

Flora helped Georgia arrange their things in various parts of the apartment. Pretty soon, it began to look homey.

"I don't like all the freckles you gained on your honeymoon. You are lucky you didn't do permanent damage to your skin. I have always taught you to wear hats and to be completely covered after coming out of the water when you are at a pool or at the beach."

Hektor had to bite his tongue. He almost blurted it out, *"You should have seen your princess whore screwing on the beach."* He decided to offer a more sanguine alternative. "Why don't you tell your mother that you and I cavorted split-naked on the shores of Martha's Vineyard and had lusty sex all afternoon in the blazing sun?"

Flora almost keeled over but then acted like she hadn't heard a word Hektor said.

"We need to tint your hair so you look presentable when Hektor introduces you to his friends in the next few weeks. Did you two take any precautions while you were on your honeymoon? I hope you won't get pregnant right away. You should wait with children until you have a more desirable home."

"Mother, I can't believe what you are saying. I had a hard enough time convincing Hektor not to use any protection. He did on our wedding night but not thereafter. I want to get pregnant right now. I will be twenty-four in December, and I think this is the time for me to start a family."

"Why don't you tell your parents what you shared with me the day after we were married?" Hektor said.

"What's that, Hektor?" Flora asked.

Floyd walked outside, not wanting to hear what Hektor was about to reveal; he felt he needed some fresh air and to gain distance between him and his womenfolk.

"Your 'virgin' little princess informed me that she's been humping every boss she ever had, trying to get pregnant. She thinks she could succeed at being a good mother. She hasn't succeeded at anything else—these are her own words. Sounds to me like she's had a very fine upbringing. You should have seen what she did with that fabulous wedding dress you created. She would have torn it to shreds if I hadn't stopped her from doing so. Your daughter was that frantic to be ravished by me. By the time we were on Martha's Vineyard, I was convinced I had married a first-class whore. You should have seen that Moron character she worked for. He was something else when we spoke to him about a job for me a few weeks ago. That guy couldn't take his eyes off your precious Georgia. He probably was recalling sucking her cunt while she played the violin for him. He got an obvious hard-on just looking at her. It was utterly embarrassing."

Her mother just stood there with her mouth agape, gasping for air like a beached whale. For once, she had nothing to say. When Floyd came inside, Flora offered advice to Georgia. "You better get the name of a good doctor from one of Hektor's friends. It sounds to me like you will need a consultation with an ob-gyn real soon."

Hektor was glad when the Unkovskys finally left. It had been a trying visit for all concerned. The "happy" couple lived from day to day.

ℳ

Hektor opened the evening newspaper on July 27. The shocking headline glared at him. The MS *Andrea Doria* had sunk the day before after a collision with the MS *Stockholm* off Nantucket Island. Forty-six persons, mostly on the lower decks, were unaccounted for. Georgia slapped down the evening paper.

"Count your blessings. If it hadn't been for Mother and I insisting you come back sooner, you might have been among those unlucky forty-six bastards. Just think of all the good fucking you might have missed."

Hektor walked out of the room. He was tired of listening to his "charming" wife.

ℳ

Within a few weeks, Georgia discovered she was pregnant. She had a miscarriage in late August. Georgia went into hysterics.

"I wanted this love child so badly. Maybe I won't have another chance at having a baby. Why did you let me get up on that ladder to hang those damn shower curtains? When I got off that thing, I could feel the blood running down my legs."

"Give me a break. I didn't ask you to hang those curtains. It was your and your mother's idea that the ones hanging there weren't good enough. Don't blame me for your stupidity and vanity. Do what the doctor told you. Lie on your back and rest. That's one thing you don't have any difficulty doing. Cut down on your damn java and cigarette consumption, and you'll be ready to make another baby real soon."

Hektor felt badly about the miscarriage. He accepted that Mother Nature sometimes knew best. After a week of recuperating, Georgia went home to her mother and remained under Flora's care for two weeks.

While Georgia was in Long Island, Hektor read an advertisement by Simon Brothers in the Sunday newspaper. They were searching for a buyer/manager for their Boys Department. Hektor applied and started the new job in early October. Georgia was delighted. First thing she checked was her clothes closet. She had to have some new dresses and shoes. The job paid better, and Hektor was no longer a factory worker. Somehow, her snobbishness and her behavior didn't add up; she would never be called a class act.

Morning sickness in late October was a clear signal Georgia probably was pregnant again. Dr. Schillenkamp confirmed the assumption. During her third visit with the good doctor, he advised Georgia to spend some of Hektor's hard-earned money.

"Young lady, it's time for you to go shopping for some maternity frocks. You'll need 'em in short order. From the way you carry this child and from the strong heartbeat, I predict it might be a boy. It looks like the baby will arrive in late June." Georgia hoped the child would be born on their first anniversary.

Estelle Swansong was always willing to help. No matter what, she couldn't instill any virtues of domesticity in Hektor's wife. What Georgia enjoyed was sipping coffee, smoking extra-long Tareyton cigarettes, and espousing her love for the arts and music; housework was clearly not her strong suit.

Children were not allowed in the furnished apartment; thus, they had to move. They were lucky to find a place they could afford. It was still close enough for Hektor to walk to work. Buying a car was out of the question.

After Georgia met with the new landlord, she told Hektor, "Since Jack told me the place needed painting, I asked him to do the whole place in pink. It's my favorite color of the moment. I can use it as a background. Jack said I could paint murals if I wanted to. Wouldn't that be fun? Lately, I've enjoyed using instant coffee instead of paint. That's why I've been going through the jar so quickly."

Chapter 22

Frank was born in late June. There was no room for a nursery; a comfortable crib stood at the foot of his parents' bed. Georgia loved the boy. To her, he was a living toy. She enjoyed playing with him but found the maternal responsibilities abhorrent and too much for her to handle.

"It may have been your mother's pleasure to nurse you boys. I refuse to do it. Lord knows what my figure would look like. You better buy a lot of bottles and Similac. He'll never suck on these teats. Who will bathe him and change his diapers? I can't; I refuse to do any of those shitty jobs," Georgia told Hektor on the day he brought her and the baby home from the hospital.

"Who the hell do you think will take care of Frank? We can't afford to hire a maid. These are your jobs. All you have done for the last year is sit on your ass, paint your damn nails, smoke your cigarettes, and drink your coffee. It's high time you make an effort toward becoming a wife and mother. Remember it was your brilliant idea to have kids so soon. If you didn't want to take care of them, why the hell did you want them in the first place? Did you believe they were living toys?"

Hektor wrote to his parents:

This is a special delivery to let you know your first grandchild was born last week. It's a boy. His name is Frank Hektor. The Birken name is safe! His name wasn't my choice, but Georgia insisted on making Hektor his middle name. As far as I was concerned, there wasn't going to be a Hektor the second or third. As you well know, I have not liked Hektor since I learned how the name was chosen for me. I missed the opportunity to change it when I entered the USA.

Both mother and child are well and thriving. Georgia tries, but motherhood, other than playing with the boy, is not exactly her thing. I am disappointed in her lack of interest in taking care of Frank. Much of it is left up to me. It's a good thing I don't mind dealing with dirty diapers.

Look forward to hearing from you again. My days are truly packed from dawn to dusk. When I hit the pillow at night, it doesn't take me long to nod off.

Love,

Hektor

Hektor walked home from the store at lunchtime. He bathed and changed Frank and made sure he had his bottle. Then he began the twenty-minute trek back to the store. Usually, when he arrived home late in the afternoon, he would find Georgia playing with the baby while smoking one of her extra-long cigarettes and having her umpteenth cup of Mocha Java.

"Can't you ever get up in the morning, clean yourself, and put on some clothes? How about putting the kid in the carriage and taking him for some fresh air? You think all that damn smoke in the place is good for him? This apartment stinks like an opium den. And if you do put on some clothes, why don't you get in the habit of hanging up what you take off your back. I'm not your maid and at your beck and call. The next time I come home and find your worn clothes piled up on that damn chair and your shoes all over the floor, I'll pick them up and put them in a garbage bag. Out they go. That ought to open your eyes and get you off that lazy ass of yours. I'm tired of dealing with that Tower of Babel of your worn clothes rising toward the ceiling."

"I wish you wouldn't speak that way to the mother of your precious son."

"What do you mean by speaking the way I do? You should listen to what comes out of your mouth most of the time. And you are right; he is my precious son. Why do you think I walk home every damn day during my lunch hour and take care of him? If it was up to you, the kid would be floating in piss and shit and probably have starved to death by now. You are one worthless, lazy bitch. I wish I had never met you. You'll be my undoing yet."

He made sure little Frank was clean, fed, and in his bed. Then he went for a long walk to get away from his useless wife for a while.

Chapter 23

Two months after Frank's birth, Hektor made an appointment with Georgia's physician, Dr. Schillenkamp.

"Would you mind telling me if there is any reason why Georgia and I cannot resume a normal sexual relationship at this time? I'm curious—is Georgia feeding me a line, or is she telling the truth? She claims she is still in far too much pain to even consider returning to a marital relationship."

"Hektor, let me set you straight. I'm talking to you as a man. That's a bunch of bull. When I examined Georgia two weeks ago, there was every indication she made an excellent recovery after giving birth. She never made any mention of being in pain. There is absolutely no reason whatsoever for Georgia and you not to resume normal sexual enjoyment. She certainly does not show any signs of postpartum depression and physically is healthy as an ox. So go for it."

Hektor thanked the doctor for his sound counsel and headed home with a certain bounce in his step. When he confronted Georgia with Dr. Schillenkamp's assessment of the situation, she became irate.

"How dare you question my wish not to resume having sex with you? I don't give a fuck what the good doctor told you. I had a spiritual awakening during my pregnancy and the birth of our son. To me, the act of sex became a divinely inspired happening. I have created a perfect human being."

"What about me? Didn't I have anything to do with it? It wasn't exactly an immaculate conception."

Georgia completely ignored him.

"Would you mind sharing with me where you got this crock of shit? Who the hell do you think you are dealing with? I should take my belt off and give you the whipping you should have gotten a long time ago from your parents. I'm so tired of this princess crap. Your mother raised one useless broad. If and when we resume a relationship, I'll make damn sure you won't get pregnant again. You don't know how to take care of one kid, never mind more than one."

Georgia glared at Hektor's raised fists; he was ready to let her have it. She backed away from him before enlightening him. "My sources of power have not spoken to me. I don't know if I will ever be able to create another child. I am studying my tarot cards and tea leaves. So far, I have not glimpsed an appropriate message. You have two healthy hands. Go fuck yourself!"

"Shocked" wasn't the word for which Hektor searched. *Where did those ideas come from? Messages from tarot cards and tea leaves granting permission to resume a normal sex life? Who has ever heard of such nonsense?* He knew of women developing strange ideas after giving birth. His hope was that Flora would eventually talk sense into his wife. For once, he was glad to welcome his mother-in-law. He looked forward to someone else helping with Frank's care.

He immersed himself in his work; he was embarrassed when their friends would inquire as to their happiness. It was blatantly obvious to the Schiefers, Swansongs, Hannah, and the Shelves, that all was not OK at the Birken home. When Georgia called him at the store, Doreen, his able assistant, would walk back into the stockroom, just shaking her head.

At times, Patrick would jokingly ask, "Are you back in the saddle again?"

He could be honest with Patrick. "The answer is no! Georgia has some real kooky ideas. I'm beginning to live like a monk, if you know what I mean."

Flora's current visit was a blessing. She planned to return to Long Island the day after Labor Day, before she lost her own happy home.

Hektor was fortunate to win the door prize of a television set at a local store. The treasured object of entertainment became a blessing and a curse. While he enjoyed watching *Tonight Starring Jack Paar*, Georgia became enslaved to the daytime soap operas and cared even less about assuming any domestic responsibilities. Georgia believed it was high time for them to find a larger apartment. A flat advertised by a Mrs. Greenholz was the answer.

Chapter 24

IRENE Greenholz had recently completed major renovations in her apartment downstairs. She loved what she had done to her place. For the first time in her life, she had worked with professional people, who helped her to pick colors and buy new furniture.

"Whenever you and Georgia are ready to do any painting upstairs, just let me know. I will open an account for you at Sherwin-Williams, and you may charge any supplies you wish. It's the labor you will do that is the most expensive part of the process. I will have the flat cleaned and spruced up. I look forward to having some young people in the house. It's been so long since my children married. They and my grandchildren are scattered all over the country. I don't see them often."

Hektor and Georgia signed a one-year lease and paid two months' rent in advance. They moved into the Greenholz flat on November 1, 1957.

Two days after Christmas, the Birkens made their second post-Christmas trek to Long Island. This time they extended their stay. They attended a few parties with Georgia's siblings and contemporaries. There was much oohing and aahing over the boy; Frank clearly was the star of the show. When Georgia and Ursula went shopping with their mother, Hektor broached the subject of Georgia's and his unnatural relationship with his father-in-law.

"Floyd, I'm beginning to wonder if there is some form of mental illness on either side of Georgia's family. Perhaps a generation or two in the past? I have no other explanation for Georgia's strange and unrealistic behavior. Flora may not have shared this with you. We had a chat about your daughter some time ago. Georgia informed me on the day after we were married that she'd had sex with several of her bosses, always trying to get pregnant. She hasn't had anything to do with me since Frank was born. I'm looking for an explanation for her strange outlook on things. Georgia's mood swings have taken her from being totally promiscuous to becoming celibate after the birth of our son. Don't you think there is something wrong with this picture?"

"Young man, I have no explanation for Georgia's actions. Have you consulted a doctor or a marriage counselor? We are sorry things are the way they are, but we do not want to get in the middle of this problem. You need to talk with Georgia and resolve this yourselves."

Hektor touched on the problem with his doctor.

"Why don't I arrange for the two of you to meet with a counselor?"

"I'm not sure if Georgia is even willing to do that. And personally, I'm not sure if I'm ready to wash our dirty linen in front of a stranger. I'm uncomfortable with that sort of thing. And, of course, how much does it cost? It's not covered by my insurance, and I don't make that kind of money." That was the end of exploring the alternative.

In late spring, they began the renovating job at the Greenholz flat. Flora agreed to be with them for two weeks to take care of Frank while Hektor and Georgia began the removal of the ugly layers of wallpaper. They started in their bedroom. The next morning, Georgia and Hektor were covered with red welts all over their bodies. Flora and the baby were unscathed—they had slept in the bedroom where none of the wall covering had been disturbed.

Flora took one look at the bites and yelled, "Oh my God, you were bitten by bedbugs! I remember what those bites look like. I encountered bedbugs in an apartment when I first lived in New York."

"How can we be sure they are bedbugs? I have never seen one before. What's so unusual about their appearance?" Hektor asked.

"They are ugly brown creatures, resembling an irregular lentil, with many legs extending from their bodies."

The next evening, Hektor went to bed equipped with a vial and a flashlight. As soon as he felt the first nip on his legs, he threw back the covers and flashed his light.

"Good Lord! Look at that army of bedbugs ready to attack us again." He caught several of the creatures and put them in the medicine vial. Their good night was over. He stopped at an exterminator's office in the morning.

"What are these?"

"No question about it; these are prime bedbugs. Looks like they really got to you."

"Yes, they sure liked my wife and me. What can you do about it?"

"We will need to exterminate the entire house. Wherever there is wallpaper in the apartment, it needs to come down, or we can saturate the walls with hypodermic-like injections and get at the buggers that way."

"I will have the landlady get in touch with you."

When Hektor came home for lunch, he rang Mrs. Greenholz's doorbell, armed with the dead bedbugs inside the vial. "I have bad news. Do you see these bites on my face and arms? We have bedbugs upstairs. I saw the exterminator this morning; he confirmed what my mother-in-law suspected. He said all of us and your birds and cat will have to be out of the house for at least forty-eight hours. They need to exterminate the entire house. It will be easier down here since you no longer have wallpaper anywhere. They'll just use some kind of a gas bomb. Upstairs, the problem is greater and much more costly. He told me no one could live up there unless they treat the entire house."

"*Oy vey! Oy gevalt!* That's terrible. I had no idea what was going on behind all that damn wallpaper upstairs. Luckily, none of it was down here when we bought the house years ago. The previous owners liked all that wall covering in the rental unit, and other tenants were too lazy to do anything about it. Of course, I will abide by the exterminator's recommendations. You kids cannot live with that."

Mrs. Greenholz and her menagerie stayed with a good friend. Flora packed up the baby, and Hektor walked all of them over to the Swansongs' home. Three days later, they returned to the apartment. The house was a total mess, but the bedbugs were apparently gone. Flora chose to leave them to their own devices the day after Easter. She had fun playing Easter Bunny for her young grandson, but she could sense the tension that existed between Hektor and Georgia, who rarely spoke to one another. They coexisted and did their own thing.

Hektor worked hard at the store and at home. Most nights, he fell into bed totally done in. There was one benefit; he forgot his unhappy and unnatural relationship with Georgia. His life centered around his son, the precious towhead who had begun speaking in short utterances. Frank was indeed the sunshine in his life.

※

Shortly after Frank's first birthday, a family with two young children moved into the house next door. They met at a neighborhood party on Labor Day weekend. Hektor was glad to become acquainted with some different people.

Percy Masterton was a man in his late thirties, perhaps early forties. On Sundays, Hektor saw him bike and work out regularly in their backyard. Percy was in great physical shape and flaunted his masculinity to the whole neighborhood. He was presently unemployed, but his wife had a good position with the power company. Both their children were of school age. Hektor needed to socialize with people other than customers or colleagues at the store. He was anxious to get to know the new neighbors better.

"Why don't you and the family have dinner with us some night? I'm pretty good at whipping up a meal on the grill. Bring the kids and a bottle of wine. I'll do the rest."

♈

When Hektor arrived home on October 3, he didn't know what hit him. Georgia apparently had heard Hektor coming up the stairway. As he reached for his key to unlock the apartment, she opened the door. Hektor's long-lost wife was standing in front of him—stark naked. Frank was safely playing in his nursery with the door to his room just slightly ajar.

"Close your mouth, or do something useful with it. As you can see, I'm ready to be fucked. Don't worry about Frank. He is playing with his own toys. I'm ready to play with yours. Get those fucking clothes off, and give me the works."

"I'll be damned. You must be kidding. Did you get a message from your infamous tarot cards and tea leaves?"

"You're darn right; they have been sending me the right messages for weeks."

"This is so funny. I could crap in my pants."

Hektor didn't know what hit him. *Maybe I'm always trying too hard to be a gentleman.* Words like fucking, pissing, and shitting were not in his everyday vocabulary. He felt his member hardening inside his tight pants. He didn't grasp what was happening. *Perhaps Georgia finally saw the light; perhaps there is hope on the horizon.*

He ripped off his clothes. Georgia already was lying on the bed, her legs spread wide apart. Touching her, he could feel her anticipation. She was ready to be ravished by Hektor, but he chose against entering her for the moment. It had been so long; he wanted to prolong the agony and the ecstasy. He kissed Georgia. First on her lips, then the nipples of her taut breasts and worked his way down the length of her body. For the moment, he forgot how long it had been since their bodies had touched.

Hektor was about to take his estranged wife. Somehow, his sixth sense struck him like a bolt of lightning. He stopped in mid-action before entering into the first union with Georgia in well over a year. He turned on the overhead lights and looked Georgia straight in the eyes.

"What brought about your change of heart? Don't give me that crap with your tarot cards and tea leaves. Are you protecting yourself? Have you been with another man? Are you trying to make me your cuckold? You probably don't even know what that means, you dumb bitch. Let me help you. Have you been shagging another man?"

She sat up straight in her pillows and glared at Hektor. Her face turned ugly, resembling that of an angry and cornered bitch. "Yes, yes, yes. I have been fucking Percy Masterton at every opportunity we've had since first meeting at the neighborhood party. I'm getting hot just reliving the moment of our first encounter. He kept an eye on that Greenholz bitch. When he saw her leave for her weekly mah-jongg session, he came to see me after you had extended that silly invitation to have them join us for dinner. He knew I had been watching him when he was flaunting his manhood while exercising in their backyard. Percy wasn't in this apartment for five minutes before both of us were naked. He knew what I wanted.

"That afternoon he fucked me three times in succession. I have enjoyed every minute of it; I like being fucked by an older and experienced man. He even fucked me in the bedroom closet while you were grilling and entertaining his wife and kids. I was thrilled when you invited that handsome dog practically into my bed. I had dreamed of getting reamed by that cock of his when I kept watching him doing all those damn exercises."

"Fuck you, bitch! This is the final straw! If you think I will continue this farce of a marriage, you have another thing coming."

Hektor's prick deflated; he got out of bed. He threw on a pair of jeans and a shirt and walked over to Estelle and Patrick's home. He made sure Greta's silver Madonna was still hanging from his neck. In her anger, Georgia had reached for the medallion, wishing to tear it off his neck.

Estelle came to the door. She took one look at Hektor. "Come in. What's wrong with you? You look like hell."

"You'll never believe what just happened. You know how that bitch of mine has been treating me since Frank was born. Maybe Patrick didn't share my whole sorry tale of misery with you. You might as well be clued in as well. You two are my longest-standing and best friends in this country. She never did have relations with me after Frank's birth. As Patrick knows, I had to do the job to myself now and then. Sometimes, I even had wet dreams, taking me back to my teen years.

"When I got home tonight, she greeted me at the door. She stood there, stark naked, telling me she was ready to be had. Of course, that isn't exactly what she said. Can you imagine my surprise? She had made sure Frank was playing in his nursery. She practically attacked me, and I was out of my clothes in no time flat. She said her damn tarot cards and tea leaves had given her the OK to get into the sack with me. I was stunned. I was getting ready to let her have what she wanted. Believe you me, I was ready!

"Then a light went off in my head. I stopped dead in my tracks before I considered entering her. When I asked her if she was trying to cover up an affair with another man, she wanted to punch me. She told me how much she had enjoyed being screwed by our new neighbor since she'd first seen him earlier in the fall. To quote her directly, 'I like being fucked by an older and experienced man. He even fucked me in the bedroom closet while you were grilling and entertaining his wife and kids.'"

Patrick walked in and caught the tail end of Hektor's story. When Estelle told him what had happened, he was floored.

"What will you do?" Estelle asked. "You know we will always be here for you. You sure didn't deserve that. When I think of all you did for Frank, and she being so damn lazy and useless. I told you from the start; you stepped right into it."

These were indeed his trusted friends; they were astonished.

✕

Within two weeks, Georgia once again suffered every morning with the telltale signs of pregnancy; Dr. Schillenkamp confirmed the obvious. Hektor called the Unkovskys in Long Island from work and clued them in on what had transpired in Birchtown during the past months. With them, he remained a gentleman. He didn't share the gory details of his encounter with their daughter. He advised them he was filing for divorce.

There was momentary dead silence on the other end of the line. Floyd caught his breath before he said, "Let me talk this over with Mother. We will call you back later."

Within the hour, they returned Hektor's call.

Doreen handed him the phone. "It sounds like long distance. I'll busy myself in the stock area; I believe you will need some privacy."

Doreen knew of some of the tensions between the Birkens, but Hektor never discussed his private problems with coworkers.

He picked up the receiver. "Hektor Birken speaking."

"This is Floyd. Here is what we would like to suggest. We assume you have not renewed your lease with Irene Greenholz in view of these latest developments."

"What kind of a fool do you take me for?" Hektor spoke quietly into the receiver. "I would have preferred to have had this conversation at home."

"Let your landlady know right away that you will be moving to Long Island; she will be able to find new tenants in the next couple of weeks. Mother and I will be up on Saturday with a U-Haul and bring your family and belongings down here. You come and live with us for a while until you think about this more clearly. A change of scenery will be good for all of you."

"Just a moment. Not so fast. I don't need a change of scenery. I need a normal life. Obviously, that has become impossible with your daughter. How is a change of scenery going to undo the damage in our relationship that Georgia clinched by becoming pregnant with another man's child? Explain that one to me! You don't know the half of it. You haven't got a clue the kind of slut your 'little princess' has turned out to be. She is nothing but a first-class whore!"

"We realize a terrible wrong was done to you. But think of the innocent new life; it doesn't know who fathered it."

"You've got to be kidding? I'm no longer the naive dumb-ass who fell for your daughter's and your wife's histrionics two years ago. I never should have married the bitch when I had my first suspicions of being rooked into something I didn't want. I was a real bastard, ditching my fiancée, Doretta, in favor of your daughter. She is nothing but a prime-time hooker." Hektor could have gone on. He was pissed!

Floyd continued with his suggestions. "We want you to get yourselves on your feet while you are with us. Consider at least staying with Georgia until the child is born. Think about it. Regardless of what you decide, we will be there to pick up Georgia and Frank on Saturday." The phone clicked. The connection was gone.

Hektor's first concern was the job situation. At lunchtime, he perused the want ads in the trade papers. R&S in Long Island was searching for an assistant department manager in their Men's Furnishings Department. The department did in excess of two million dollars in business annually and had a sales staff of over one hundred in peak periods.

He was not inclined to wash his dirty linens in public; nevertheless, he needed to come clean with the president of Simon Brothers. Hektor was shown into Mr. Reeves's office and laid his cards on the table. Anyone in retailing knew that November and December were the most critical months of the year. No one wanted to be searching for new help during that period. Harold Reeves understood and offered any assistance he could give in helping Hektor land a job in New York; a letter of recommendation was on Hektor's desk within the hour.

Hektor still wasn't sure if he was doing the right thing. His father-in-law's comment about the innocent child made him ponder the situation. *Yeah, if I don't divorce the bitch, I'll be giving the child my name and legitimacy. I also will be financially responsible for a kid fathered by Percy Masterton. He won't be paying for the fucking he got; I will!*

Ж

The Unkovskys arrived by ten o'clock on Saturday morning, having left Long Island before the crack of dawn. Georgia's domestic lethargy was evident throughout the apartment; she was enjoying her third or fourth round of morning coffee and cigarettes at the kitchen table. Her mother and father walked in. They could not believe their eyes. She had done absolutely nothing in preparation for the move to Long Island.

Hektor was at the store, his last day with Simon Brothers. Late in the afternoon, he walked home to the apartment. He saw Floyd handling some of the furniture.

"Let me help you carry those bigger pieces. I'm a few years younger and in pretty good shape."

"Thanks, Hektor. At least someone in this family cares enough to give a helping hand. I'll tell you this: Flora nearly lost it when we got here this morning; she was ready to trounce your wife with a frying pan. Frank was still in his crib and screaming for attention. He had shit in his pants and was engaged in decorating the rods of his wooden crib with the crap. Flora gasped as she picked up little Frank. I've never seen her so angry. She lost it and screamed at your wife, 'Get off your bloomin' arse and help your father pack. I'll tend to Frank and give him a bath. Sometimes I don't believe that we raised you.'"

Hektor found that revelation surprising. Was his father-in-law trying to tell him that he and Flora finally understood his frustrations with their daughter? He didn't comment. He just worked silently side by side with Floyd. Hektor made last-minute phone calls to some of his closest friends.

Gertrude and Knut Schiefer were heartbroken over their leaving. Gertrude usually didn't mince words, but she didn't say, "I told you so." Hektor could read between the lines that they understood. They assured him they would always be there for him. Hannah and the Shelves were saddened as well by their sudden departure and wished them only the best in their new endeavors. Estelle and Patrick helped with the final loading of the van and the cleanup of the apartment. Unbeknownst to the Unkovskys, Hektor's closest friends and Harold Reeves were the only people who knew, at this point, what had precipitated the Birkens' unexpected exit from Birchtown.

Floyd hitched the U-Haul trailer to his car. Hektor, Georgia, and Frank; their belongings; and their troubled lives left Birchtown in total darkness that Saturday night. They stopped along Highway 17 for a late snack. Floyd needed to take it easy for a while since he was the only one driving. Once they were back on the road, the Packard blew a rear tire. Floyd, being an experienced driver, had little difficulty keeping the conveyance under control. He unhitched the van, replaced the tire with the spare he always carried, and an hour later, they were back on the road. Georgia, the boy, and Flora were finally sleeping soundly in the back seat of the car. Floyd broke the pervasive silence.

"I want you to know that Mother and I appreciate your decency. We will do anything in our power to help you get started in Long Island. Don't worry about taking care of your family. We are in a position to get you back on your feet. I will have a talk with my daughter after you are settled in with us. Most of your things can be stored in the basement. There will be room to put up your bed as well as the crib for Frank in Georgia's former room. If the job at R&S doesn't materialize, there will be other opportunities. This is probably the best time of year for you to find employment in your field of expertise."

Hektor just sat and listened. None of Floyd's commentary impressed him sufficiently. He was numb. His mind was racing as he berated himself. *You dumb ass. You are making the biggest mistake of your life. Correction—second biggest mistake! You never should have married that bitch. Why did you forsake Doretta for that worthless piece of cunt? Be still, my mind; don't do anything rash!* It was that esoteric strain in his blood that stopped him from following through with his original plan of divorcing Georgia. He had all the right ammunition on his side.

The sun came up just as they crossed the George Washington Bridge into Manhattan. As the large orange-red ball of the rising sun tinged the deep purple clouds in the distance, heralding the arrival of the new day, Hektor squinted, trying to envision what might lie beyond that magical horizon.

Chapter 25

HEKTOR finally needed to communicate with his family and wrote to his parents.

Thank goodness for short telephone conversations here and there. Otherwise, none of us would have any idea what's going on in our lives. I know the overseas calls aren't cheap; they are worth every nickel, or should I say, every hard-earned dollar. I was so happy to know that Alberti is thriving. Perhaps it is better that Margarethe found employment elsewhere. This way, it might be easier for all of you to get along.

Rather than telling you on the phone, I am writing to fill you in on the latest changes in our lives. Ten days ago, Georgia and I had a terrible fight. I finally had enough of her unreasonable behavior and demands and threatened to divorce her. The Unkovskys wanted us to cool down and seriously consider counseling before winding up in court. The upshot is that we have moved to Franklin Square. Floyd and Flora drove up with their car and a trailer. Our friends in Birchtown could not believe what was happening. We left the town by *Nacht und Nebel* [night and fog]. We moved with all our belongings into the Unkovsky home.

Georgia's parents think we should stay for a while with them and save enough money to allow us to buy our own home on the island. I'm not sure if this is the solution to our problems. This has been a trying and challenging marriage for me. Reluctantly, I agreed with them, especially since Georgia is pregnant again. The child is to be born next June.

Please make note of the Unkovskys' address; we'll be there for a while. I am going to look for work tomorrow. Unfortunately, tomorrow is October 13. As you used to say, thirteen is not a lucky number, but I have to try anyway. I'll give you a call in a few days to let you know how things went. Mutti, pray for your prodigal son.

Chapter 26

ON Monday morning, Hektor called corporate headquarters of R&S in Brooklyn. The company arranged for an interview with personnel and the division manager at the Long Island satellite store. Hektor wanted to approach his contacts with R&S strictly on his own merits. He refrained from making any reference to Georgia, who had been an employee at the store for only a brief period a few years earlier. He never understood why she quit her position; for all he knew, she was let go. Hektor certainly didn't want to jeopardize his own chances of landing a job with the company by bringing Georgia's employment record into the picture.

At the offices in Long Island, he completed a lengthy application document and presented letters of recommendation. Personnel acted favorably and set up an interview with the division manager, Mr. Westphalia. Hektor passed muster and was sent on to the department head, Burton Eppelrath, for a final grilling. Burton and Hektor hit it off right away. He appreciated Hektor's training in retailing/merchandising and schooling in Germany and the experiences gained with Simon Brothers in the US. He was hired on the spot.

Hektor reported for work on the morning of the last Tuesday in October 1958.

Burton put on his suit jacket. "Let me take you around the department and introduce you to some of the key employees. They have been with me for some time. You will enjoy working with them."

Once the introductions were over, Burton Eppelrath returned to his desk, taking off his jacket immediately, and advising Hektor to do the same at his assigned desk. Burton peered over his large horn-rimmed glasses, his hair slightly disheveled from yanking off his coat in a hurry. He spoke with a deep voice in a heavy Brooklyn accent.

"This is the heart of the operation. We always must have adequate stock and know what we have and what we need to order or reorder. Note: I never wear my suit coat when working behind the scenes. Also, I never step onto the sales floor without it and checking appropriateness of my tie. By the way, if you need any clothes, shirts, ties, etc., you let me know. When the sales reps come in, just give them your size and color preferences. They will send the stuff to the house. We always want you to be dressed in the latest fashions. The industry makes sure you represent them and us in a most favorable light." This was different from managing and buying for the Boys Department. These were perks of the trade that Hektor had not expected.

The week before Thanksgiving, Georgia, Flora, and little Frank waltzed into the store and paid Hektor a surprise visit. Some of the staff put their heads together when Hektor picked up his little boy and hugged him. They realized the redheaded femme fatale was Hektor's wife. He heard some whispers.

"Didn't that redhead work here for a short while a few years ago?"

Hektor tried ignoring what was going on. He shook hands with Flora but didn't make any kind of contact with Georgia. No one said anything derogatory, but he sensed a certain disdain. Marion, the gal in charge of the sport-shirt section, was the exception. She made no bones about it; she had little use for Georgia.

"Mr. Birken, I can't help myself. How could a nice guy like you marry that woman? I feel sorry for you! She's nothing but a tramp. I won't say more!" she whispered.

Hektor would have liked to agree with her, but for now, he said little, listened, watched, and kept his thoughts to himself. Clearly, Georgia's brief visit had made less than a favorable impression on the staff of the store.

⋈

Thanksgiving Day was a welcome break in Hektor's hectic schedule. It would be the last day off before the Christmas marathon. The last of the leaves blew off the trees. It was a crisp morning under bright blue skies. After breakfast, Hektor put Frank in the wool jacket Grandma Birken had mailed from Germany for his birthday. It was a colorful plaid coat with a white lamb's wool lining, including the warm hood. Listening, Hektor could hear the wind catching in the remaining oak leaves on the trees. They walked over to a nearby park and had fun playing in huge mounds of colorful memories of summertime past.

"Daddy, this is the best. Can we do this more? I love walk with you. I not see you much. Mommy not much outside. Mommy sick?"

Hektor loved listening to his precocious little boy, who was trying so hard to speak in complete sentences.

"No, Frank, Mommy is not sick. She will have another baby next year. Maybe you will have a little brother or sister, someone little to play with. Won't that be fun?" He tried to put as happy a spin on the situation as he could.

Frank giggled and laughed all morning. He loved rolling in the piles of leaves, tossing them about, and watching them as they floated away on wisps of gentle air.

Hektor looked at his watch. "Frank, we have been gone for more than two hours. It's time for us to head home for lunch." As they approached the house, Hektor noted a strange car in the driveway. *Must be a visitor. Perhaps Ursula has been dropped off.* She had been visiting a girlfriend the night before Thanksgiving.

They walked into the living room. The warmth of the house felt good on their ungloved hands. Hektor didn't know the middle-aged stranger talking to Flora and Floyd. As he looked toward the stairway, he saw Georgia lying on the floor at the bottom of the steep staircase, face up and apparently comatose. Hektor was carrying Frank and turned the boy's face away from the scene as he began to whimper. The child realized something was wrong with his mother.

"This is our family physician, Dr. Hancock. He would like to speak with you. Please take Frank upstairs and put him in his playpen, where he will be safe while you chat with the doctor," offered Floyd.

Hektor did as asked. He had to step over Georgia's motionless body. He shrugged his shoulders, not knowing what had transpired in his absence. As Hektor came down the steps rather quickly, he saw Dr. Hancock bent over Georgia, once again checking her eyes while he pushed her eyelids back. He motioned Hektor to follow him into the dining room. They sat down at the table after closing the door.

"I wanted privacy while discussing this delicate matter with you. It appears your wife threw herself down the stairway deliberately, an apparent attempt at aborting her child. She is quite healthy. Her effort certainly failed. I examined her. There is nothing wrong with her. As I explained to the Unkovskys, she is not comatose. She is merely pretending to be out. If she were indeed comatose, her pupils would convey her condition to me. You are married to quite an accomplished actress, young man. If she were my daughter or wife, I would tell her to her face the comedy is finished. That's all I have to say."

"What makes you say she was trying to abort the child she is carrying? Did her parents discuss our situation with you?"

"No, there was no discussion, other than our mutual observations of what apparently happened. Has she ever implied to you that she didn't want to have another child?"

"Not in so many words." Hektor apologized for the incident and let Dr. Hancock know he and the family appreciated his coming to the house on a holiday. "We are sorry to have inconvenienced you today."

"Oh, no inconvenience. I was glad to respond to your in-laws' call. They have been patients of mine for a long time. I delivered Georgia. I'm sorry she seems to be such a troubled soul these days. Perhaps we should talk about this in my office at some future time. Nice to meet you, Hektor, and good luck on the new job. I hope your stay with the Unkovskys won't be too long. Old and young just don't belong under the same roof for extended periods of time, especially people in your situation. Have a nice Thanksgiving, what's left of it. You'll be really busy for the next few weeks. Under the circumstances, perhaps it's not a bad thing. Take care." He picked up his little black bag, shook Flora's and Floyd's hands, and took off.

Troubled soul is an understatement, if I ever heard one. She's one screwed-up broad with major problems. She's lucky I fell for all those damn excuses her father made. I should have stuck to my original plan, sent them packing in Birchtown, and pursued the divorce. Giving the unborn she just tried to abort my name will cost me dearly. Big mistake!

Taking Dr. Hancock's suggestion, he walked over to Georgia's body, still lying on the floor. "Come on! Get up, Sarah Bernhardt, or is it Eleonora Duse? Calling you an actress is perhaps too generous. Why don't you end this masquerade and face reality? First you screw every guy with a stiff dick like a common whore. Now you want to destroy what you and your secret lover created. Did you want to get rid of the evidence?" He grabbed her by her shoulders and gave her a good shove. "Get up, you useless bitch. We all know you are just faking. The comedy is over! The good doctor just spelled out his assessment of the situation to all of us."

Floyd and Flora were aghast by Hektor's assertiveness but didn't say a word. When Hektor finally gave her another nudge, she started to move and opened her eyes slowly. *Sort of like the awakening of* "Sleeping Beauty," he thought. After a few minutes, she sat up and soon was ready for a cup of coffee and a cigarette. Realizing her stunt had failed, she chose to act innocent and as if nothing special had happened.

Floyd took charge of the situation. "If you weren't pregnant, I would have half a mind to give you the whipping you should have had years ago. How dare you put all of us and Dr. Hancock through this? It would have been bad enough if you'd fallen and hurt yourself, but to do this deliberately and then act as if you were comatose is the height of impudence, if you even know what that means. I agree with what your mother said a couple of weeks ago. I cannot believe we raised you!"

Flora busied herself in the kitchen; she was glad that Ursula had come home shortly after lunch and was able to assist her. Ingrid and her family joined them for the traditional Thanksgiving feast. Hektor looked forward to conversing with George and Floyd about things other than the confrontations engendering domestic hell. When Floyd suggested a beer with their light snack, he took him up on the offer. Perhaps it would numb his overtaxed brain; something stronger would have done an even better job.

No one enjoying the Thanksgiving feast mentioned the incident that shook the Unkovsky household earlier in the day. They were determined not to spread the news any further than was necessary. Nobody banked on Frank's sharing his observations.

"Mommy sick today. Mommy fell on stairs," he announced.

"What happened?" Ingrid knew that Georgia was pregnant again but not that Hektor wasn't the father of the child. Not even Ursula was clued in by her parents.

"Oh, your sister tripped over her nightgown near the bottom of the steps this morning. She fainted, and we thought it was best to have Dr. Hancock check her. Georgia came out of it when he used his smelling salts. She is just fine. There were no signs she might have had a miscarriage," commented Flora.

"Well, that's good. You better be a little more careful in the future," Ingrid admonished her younger sister. "Do you know how long I have tried to get pregnant again? You have all the luck in the world. Just don't endanger your unborn child by being so careless. Sometimes I wonder how good all your smoking and coffee-drinking can be for your baby. I wouldn't, if I were you." She was the only one of the Unkovsky women who was not addicted to smoking.

The tables were cleared and the dishes done. The men enjoyed an after-dinner brandy while the women discussed Christmas shopping in the offing. Ingrid couldn't let go of her concern for her younger sister and her unfortunate incident on the stairway. Hektor finally had enough of the hogwash being passed around the table.

"Let me set all of you straight. It's high time for this charade to be over. The only reason I am sitting with you at this Thanksgiving table is because I let myself be bamboozled by your parents, especially by your nice father. I have every right and reason to divorce your sister. She's nothing but a damn whore. The child she is carrying isn't mine. She screwed around with one of our neighbors in Birchtown while she denied me certain marital rights. I had to jerk off for more than a year.

"Your sister was waiting for important messages from her damn tarot cards and tea leaves, advising her of the proper time for me to resume a normal sexual relationship with her. She apparently got that message when she found out she was impregnated by the neighbor. I was smart enough to realize what had happened. Your sister confirmed what she had done and how much she had enjoyed fucking the other man. The father of this unborn child is Percy Masterton. She didn't trip over her nightgown. She threw herself down those damn stairs, trying to abort the child in an apparent attempt at getting rid of the evidence. There—you have the unvarnished truth about your princess. Happy Thanksgiving."

He pushed back his chair with vehemence and walked upstairs, leaving the clan in shock. He was glad to be alone. Hektor was thinking about the frantic weeks ahead as he lay down on the pillow. Listening to the soft breathing of his sleeping son, he went off to neverland.

Ingrid and her family left; all but Georgia had retired. She had her last cigarette for the day downstairs, contemplating her own life.

The weeks between Thanksgiving and Christmas passed quickly. Hektor and Burton shared a great working relationship. The staff took to Hektor easily. He looked forward to going to work in the morning and dreaded returning home at night. The only meal he ate at home was a quick breakfast in the morning. Flora saw to it he had juice and coffee and a slice or two of toast, heavily buttered. He did like her homemade preserves. Lunch and dinner, he grabbed at the employees' canteen. Sometimes, he and Burton had dinner at the elegant restaurant on the second floor of the store. It gave them a chance to talk about things other than business. Occasionally, Marietta, Burton's wife, would join them. Marietta was a social psychologist, working on her PhD.

"OK, what gives with you and Georgia? I just know you are all screwed up. You can fool some people, but you can't fool me. Let's hear it."

Hektor was flabbergasted. Never had he encountered anyone so blunt. "How did you know all is not well on my home front? What makes you think there is anything wrong?" Hektor tried to avoid any invasion of his very personal and private space.

"Listen, buddy, it's my training and my work that allows me to be sensitive to such things. I don't want to pry; rather, I want to be of help. Burt and I talked about it. He cares, and so do I. We both believe you are way over your head into something you can't control. Whenever you are ready to talk, we want you to know we are here to listen. You need someone to talk to."

Hektor thanked them for their honesty and willingness to listen when he was ready to share his problems with them. He wasn't quite prepared to lay his cards on the table—yet, but it was great to know there were outsiders willing to help when needed. When the store closed on Christmas Eve, he almost dreaded going home. Some of the part-timers said goodbye. They were hoping to return in time for the Easter business.

)(

The highlight of Christmas morning was seeing Frank as he came downstairs in his little red-plaid robe. He immediately spotted the child-sized race car under the tree.

"Can I ride?"

Floyd and Hektor carefully pulled the toy from among the other presents under the tree. They put a white cowboy hat, another present, on his head and put him inside the toy vehicle. He looked like hot stuff, and he knew how adorable he was. The rest of the day was a genuine challenge for the "happy" parents, who exchanged neither presents nor words with one another.

Hektor and Georgia's relationship had become a total sham. They had to sleep in a common bed out of necessity, unless Hektor wanted to sleep on a small sofa in the living room. He refused to do that. Hektor did need a halfway decent night of sleep. They shared their bedroom with little Frank. There was no longer any communication between his parents; they only spoke to him. Hektor thought disgusting terms in German, spelling out his negative attitude toward Georgia. He was careful not to show his feelings for Georgia in front of their little boy. Frank was a perceptive youngster.

In February, Hektor and Burt were in Manhattan, finalizing their commitments to the fall line. At day's end, they stopped for a drink at the Biltmore. Hektor went to the men's room and was washing his hands when someone put a hand on his left shoulder. Hektor almost lost it. He swerved around to face his attacker. His hands were still dripping wet.

"I know you; you are Hektor. I met you five years ago on the MS *Italia*. My brother Ulrich and I were cabin mates of yours. Don't you remember me? One night I tried to screw you, but you weren't interested."

Hektor backed away from the guy and took another look. "Is that you, Delbert? I can hardly recognize you with that full beard, and you've put on a few pounds. Where is Ulrich? And what are you two doing these days?"

"We are both doing OK. Ulrich has become a designer and is doing well in his own business. We got tired of each other and have our own lovers these days. He sleeps with a guy on his staff, and I bum around with a fellow in the beer business. I'm into selling the stuff and can't complain. Business is good, and so is my sex life. What about you? What are you doing in Manhattan?"

"I'm with R&S and am on a buying spree with my boss. I've

got to get back to the bar. Good seeing you doing so well, Delbert. I never would have recognized you. Say hi to Ulrich."

As Hektor turned to walk out of the men's room, Delbert stuck his business card in Hektor's suit pocket. "Give me a call next time you're in town. Let's go for a drink and talk. Maybe Ulrich could join us."

Hektor wasn't sure if he was interested in pursuing the offer. He waved goodbye as he headed for the bar. He didn't mention his encounter to Burt.

Chapter 27

ON his mother's birthday, Hektor received a call at the store. Georgia had gone into labor. He took a cab to the house and picked her up. Her water broke on the way to the hospital.

"This will cost you," said the cabbie. "There's a fifty-dollar charge for cleaning the cab!"

"Sorry, buddy. Not from this guy. I'm sure it's not the first time that happened. I'll take it up with your company." Hektor looked at the meter and paid the guy, plus a ten-dollar tip. He took down the driver's name and license number, and he made note of the company name.

"Let's get you in a wheelchair," he said to Georgia. He turned his back to the cabdriver—not another word was said—and pushed Georgia toward the hospital's emergency entrance.

They hadn't talked about a name for the child until this very moment. They decided on *Karen* if it was a girl; Georgia refused to call her Helena. They couldn't agree on a boy's name. Their answer came shortly after arrival at the hospital. Georgia gave birth to a tiny girl within minutes of entering the facility. Her ob-gyn, Dr. Schweikert, wasn't even present for the delivery. Everything happened so fast.

Karen barely weighed five pounds. She wasn't considered premature. The little girl was a full-term baby but rather petite.

Dr. Schweikert examined mother and child the next day and pronounced them both in good health. He attributed Karen's small size to Georgia's heavy smoking and poor dietary regime during her pregnancy.

Georgia let the doctor have it. "What's your problem with my drinking coffee and smoking? What the fuck did you want me to look like? Two-Ton Tessie? I wasn't about to lose my figure again after giving birth to Frank just two years ago."

Dr. Schweikert walked away from her. He had a tough time dealing with Georgia's attitude and use of foul language.

Hektor felt guilty; he opted to spend money on a telephone call. "Hallo, Mutti, I'm sorry to be a day late with my birthday wishes."

"No problem. I understand you have your hands full. I'm happy to hear your voice, even a day late."

"Yesterday was one heck of a day. Georgia had her baby. Her water broke in the cab."

"Oh, what is it? Another boy?"

"No, Mutti. You have a little granddaughter. We named her Karen Helena. I know you don't like red hair, but she looks just like Georgia. On first blush, I don't see any Birken in her at all. They often change as they grow up." He had to smile at his own duplicity.

"Well, that's good news. I'm thrilled to have a granddaughter. How is your new job going?"

"I still like it. My boss and my coworkers have been wonderful."

"That's good. I'm happy to hear someone likes you."

"Sorry, I need to hang up. I'm running out of quarters. Happy birthday again."

"Thanks for the call and the good news."

"Talk to you soon. Love to Dad."

"Aufwiedersehen!" She was gone; she had hardly gotten a word in edgewise. In a way, that might have been good. He was glad she didn't ask too many questions he would have had to answer with more lies.

⋈

When the cloak of darkness finally enveloped the hospital room, Georgia apparently rose from her bed and pretended to be a cross between La Sonnambula and Lucia di Lammermoor. She walked the hallways of the hospital in a sleep-walking–type trance while howling like a banshee, disturbing other patients and staff alike.

Early the next morning, Dr. Schweikert called Hektor at the house. "Hello, Mr. Birken, Harris Schweikert here. I hate to do this to you, but you must go to the hospital immediately and check out your wife and baby."

"Why? What's the matter with Georgia and the baby?"

"They are both in good health, but Mrs. Birken has been acting like an absolute fool and is disturbing other patients and the staff. I would have preferred to keep her and the baby in the hospital for a few more days, but I believe being in her parents' home might be a better solution for your wife under the circumstances."

"I'd hoped to have them at the hospital for a few more days. It's a good thing Georgia's mother is available to help with the newborn. I'm so busy with my job."

"I'm confident your mother-in-law can handle the baby, and certainly she should be able to deal with your wife's histrionics better than the hospital staff. On another note, I would like to speak to you very soon. We need to have a man-to-man chat at my office. Congratulations to you and Georgia on the new baby."

It was obvious to Hektor that the doctor was very much challenged by Georgia and her behavior. He made up his mind to talk with Harris Schweikert as soon as possible.

On his way home the following week, he stopped at the obste-

236

trician's office. The receptionist promptly showed him into Dr. Schweikert's office. The physician closed the door and sat across from Hektor.

"Originally, I had no intention of having this conversation with you. What I want to share with you may be viewed, legally, as a violation of doctor/client privilege. However, in view of the events that transpired at the hospital after Karen's birth and issues of a different nature, I feel compelled to share my observations with you. I'm not speaking with you as your wife's physician but as a man. I believe it is my moral duty to apprise you of my impressions.

"In the course of attending your wife during her pregnancy, she actually propositioned me and attempted to seduce me. She didn't just attempt to seduce me. She became physical and even *ordinaire*, or should I say vulgar. She reached under my coat and touched my crotch, wanting to unzip my fly. 'Come on, Doc; let's fuck,' she said. 'I'm hot for that rod of yours.' I thought I wasn't in my office but in some cheap bordello. When I declined her overtures, she informed me I needn't be concerned about you. She let me know you were not responsible for the child she was carrying. Furthermore, she shared with me how much pleasure she experienced in the process of conceiving Karen with a man named Percy Masterton. Obviously, with reference to what happened, I didn't couch my telling you in the same colorful language your wife used. I believe she was trying to get a rise out of me."

Hektor's jaw dropped. "I can't believe how Georgia behaved with you. I hate to admit to utter stupidity and naïveté, but I questioned her character the day after we first met. This tops it all."

Dr. Schweikert then said, "In the face of these events, let me give you my advice; take it or leave it. If I were in your position, Hektor, I would seek a divorce from this woman as fast as possible. Georgia told me about your irreconcilable problems and the total lack of communication between you. It sounds to me like a completely intolerable situation. She will ruin the rest of your life if you remain with her for whatever reason. You realize I will not be able to testify in a divorce case. The laws of New York being what they are, a simple blood test is all you need to confirm that you are not Karen's father. I do not believe I am violating any medical ethics, and Georgia would certainly deny anything I felt compelled to share with you."

Hektor took a deep breath. "I'm not sure if I should thank you for the enlightenment. I had no clue as to Georgia's actions while you were attending her. I'm very sorry for the whole mess. As I told you earlier, I had my doubts from the start, but my eyes were opened wide the day after I married her. I was convinced I had just been duped into marrying a whore. Worse, I jilted my fiancée in Germany, an honorable girl, to marry this bitch. One liveth, and one learneth. As one of my best friends told me three years ago, 'You'll get the fuckin' for the fuckin' you got.' Excuse my language. But it is the truth. See you around, Doc. Thanks again for the sound advice."

Doctor Schweikert felt for him. He put a hand on Hektor's shoulder. "Please feel free to call me anytime. I hope things work out for you. You surely deserve better than this."

"Thank you."

It took Hektor quite a while to walk the mile and a half home. He took a circuitous route as he digested the information Dr. Schweikert had presented to him. Hektor decided to confide in Burt and Marietta the next time they talked.

Burton exploded. "Ditch that bitch—*now!*"

Marietta was less emotional. "Let me ask you something. Have you started the process of becoming a US citizen? And if so, when do you expect to receive your citizenship? In my opinion, you would be much safer to hold off any proceedings until you are no longer subject to the whims of the INS."

Hektor listened closely to Marietta. "That's sound advice." He called the INS regarding the matter. The woman with whom he spoke checked on his application.

"Upon completion of course work, citizenship will be conferred in February 1960."

That's all Hektor needed to know. He took the classes under the guise of attending informative workshops presented after-hours at the store. No way did he want the Unkovskys to know about it. Georgia's behavior had become a real challenge to her mother. Flora could not believe how lazy her daughter was.

"Frankly, I am getting tired of feeding, bathing, changing, and caring for your baby and looking after Frank. I think it's time for you and Hektor to find your own home. You need to learn how to take care of your family."

After the first of the year, Floyd approached Hektor as well. "I think Mother and I are in need of some peace and quiet again. This arrangement has gone on long enough."

Hektor was irate. "Wait a minute. Whose idea was this whole bloody arrangement anyway? It certainly wasn't mine! Moving out of here might give you much-deserved peace and quiet. That still doesn't address my problems. I'm not sure I want to buy a house way out on the island. It's the only place we could afford right now. How would I get to work every day? By train? I suppose that could be done. Buying a house in Brentwood is just a matter of geography. It doesn't change a damn thing about how I feel about the situation your daughter created for us."

Floyd tucked his fat belly into his flannel robe and stood up. He shrugged his shoulders and walked out to the kitchen without saying another word. He poured himself a healthy glass of bourbon. "You figure it out. She's your wife!"

"And your fucking daughter—and I mean that literally!"

Hektor charged up the stairs and slammed the bedroom door.

Chapter 28

AGAINST Hektor's better judgment, he and his family moved into a tiny two-bedroom house during the first week of February. Frank was nesting in Georgia's bedroom. Because Hektor was the lighter sleeper, Karen's crib was moved into Hektor's bedroom. So much for getting needed rest.

Hektor was lucky; Georgia was too lazy to walk out to the mailbox. She didn't see the letter arrive from the INS. His citizenship would be conferred at the Mineola Courthouse on February 19, 1960.

Burton and Marietta made sure they accompanied him to the event. They were thrilled for him and celebrated with a special lunch afterward.

"Now that you are a citizen, let's talk about finding you a good attorney," Burton said. "This whole thing will need careful planning and orchestrating. Let's not jump into anything, but the time has come for you to deal with this impossible situation in earnest. You must put a stop to this farce and start a new life. You can't continue living this way indefinitely. So, go for it, Citizen Birken!"

The Unkovsky clan paid a visit to the Birkens at the end of February. It was a belated get-together for Hektor's twenty-sixth birthday. He couldn't wait to tell them. Hektor felt almost smug.

"I have a bit of news for you. You are looking at one of the newest citizens of the United States of America. I am independent of any sponsorships and may do anything permissible within the law. The only thing I can't do is run for president or vice president of the United States." A hush fell over the house. The only thing audible was Karen's cooing from her crib.

Floyd was the first to speak. His forehead was wrinkled, underscoring his question. "Why didn't you tell us you were seeking citizenship? At least one of us would have gone with you to the courthouse. We remember how big an event that step was for us. Congratulations! Let's have a toast to Hektor."

Flora and Ursula joined in the best wishes, as did Ingrid and George. Georgia was dumbfounded; she didn't raise her glass in the toast and said absolutely nothing. Frank was too young to understand what was going on.

Jeanette, a buyer in Women's Ready-to-Wear, had given Hektor a ride to and from the store since his family's move to Brentwood. He couldn't wait to get into the car and share with her how his announcement was accepted. Aside from the Eppelraths, Jeanette had become his confidant.

Jeanette laughed out loud. "I knew it would blow their minds. Good for you. I'm glad you kept it under wraps until it was behind you. What's your next step?"

"I need to find a pleasant and inexpensive room in a neighborhood close to the store. When I do, I will make my next move."

"Why not keep an eye on the employee bulletin board? Sometimes people post notices, wishing to find someone to room with them. You could even put up a card yourself; just put down the department telephone number to contact you."

"That might be too risky. I think I will just keep looking at the board periodically. But thanks anyway for the suggestion." Hektor knew he needed to speak with his mother and placed the call.

"Hallo, Mother. It's Hektor calling."

"As if I didn't know. How are things in the new house? I have a hard time keeping track of your address changes. You have become a regular vagabond!"

"Perhaps, Mother. The reason I am calling is to tell you that I became a US *Bürger* [citizen] on February 19. Isn't that exciting?"

"That's debatable!"

"Extra, extra—here comes bigger news! I am leaving Georgia as soon as the opportunity presents itself."

"Are you serious?"

"There are too many things to tell on the phone. As soon as I know more, I will write. Before I forget, thanks for my birthday gifts."

"Write soon. I'll be waiting anxiously to hear from you."

"Give hugs to all. Love you!"

"Love you too, but I'm truly concerned."

"Don't be, Mother. In time, it will all be just fine. Bye for now."

"Auf Wiedersehen."

Life at home became more unbearable. Hektor began to feel like a Trappist monk, although he never took a vow of silence. The Monday after Karen's first birthday, he spotted a card on the bulletin board. He called Pauline Singer, who had posted the notice.

"This is Hektor Birken. I am the assistant manager in Men's Furnishings. I would like to rent the room you are advertising. Is it still available? How much is it? Exactly where is it located?"

Mrs. Singer was more than happy to answer all of Hektor's questions. "The room is twelve dollars per week and is located in a pleasant residential neighborhood, ten minutes walking distance from the store, and will be available July first."

"Thanks, Mrs. Singer. I'll make arrangements to move in on or shortly after the Fourth. I need to line up someone to transport my things."

Hektor called his brother-in-law. George was fully aware of Hektor's predicament since he had revealed all at last year's Thanksgiving dinner. He was more than willing to help.

"I can give you and your things a lift on the afternoon of the Fourth. Plan on being ready by one thirty."

"That will work. I will let my landlady know when to expect me. Thanks a million for sticking with me. See you on the Fourth."

That night, while the TV was blaring in the living room, he started moving and organizing his things. He would have to retrieve the things from the attic later.

The next morning, both children were playing outside in the backyard after Hektor fed them breakfast. Karen had just begun to walk. He retrieved two suitcases from his closet and started packing. The one thing he did not want to leave behind was his portable typewriter. Somehow, Georgia became aware of the unusual activity in the bedroom. She pushed the door open in her inimitable fashion. Hektor knew exactly what was coming as Georgia spoke to him directly for the first time in months.

"What the fuck do you think you are doing?"

"What do you think it looks like? If you can't figure it out, let me help you. I am leaving you, you goddamn bitch. I've had just about all I can handle! I don't know how or why I continued this farce for four years. I should never have married you in the first place when I realized what a cheap tramp and conniving bitch you were. How did I ever leave an honorable woman like Doretta for a whore like you? It's high time I end it all before something happens that both of us might regret!"

"You don't have the balls to leave me and the children!"

She was within inches of his face now, spitting out her words in her classic dramatic manner. Her face was as contorted as it was the night when she told Hektor how greatly she enjoyed screwing Percy Masterton.

"Just try me!" Hektor slammed down the lid on the second suitcase he had packed. "I am taking these things and my typewriter. I'll retrieve my other stuff when I come to see the children."

"What makes you think I will ever let you back into this house? Once you leave, you will never see another fucking thing you leave behind. And you certainly won't see the children again."

"I'll let the lawyers worry about the children, even if I have to force you. Remember, I am the one who will keep this show on the road!"

With that, he picked up his things. The kids had come inside. They heard their parents yelling at each other. Frank and Karen climbed on the sofa, which was covered in an ugly large print on a navy background. The kids had some color from playing outside in the sun. Frank seemed to sense what was happening. His freckled, somewhat dirty face was streaked by tears as he looked up at Hektor. He was a sensitive child and fully aware that his parents didn't like each other. Karen's face was dirty as well. She was smiling at her daddy. Karen was too young to grasp the implications of their father's departure.

Hektor walked out the front door. His eyes squinted in the bright sunlight. He wiped away a few tears. Almost compulsively, he reached for Greta's silver Madonna. Who knew what lay ahead of them? It was a symbolic day. He embarked on a venture that would give him his independence someday, and he hoped it would be the start of a new life, a life with meaning, satisfaction, and dignity. Hektor didn't look back. If he had, he would've seen a mad woman cussing at him in a barrage of four-letter words. He was glad he couldn't see her. Their neighbors were astounded.

George and he made a quick getaway, with Hektor's things loaded on the truck.

Oscar Singer came to the door to greet Hektor. "Are you the

Birken guy? I *unnerstand* you work at R&S, and my wife is renting you a room upstairs."

Hektor realized immediately the man was drunk—not particularly what he had hoped to find.

"Can you point me in the right direction?" he inquired of Oscar Singer.

"It's the first door on your left when you get to the top of the steps. The john you can use is right next to your room. I don't know what the old lady told you when she rented to you. Just listen to me and what I've got to tell you. Keep your cotton-picking hands off my wife. You *unnerstand* me?"

"Sir, I believe your wife is old enough to be my mother!"

"You SOB, that makes no difference."

Hektor then realized he'd walked into a hornet's nest. But no matter what, he wouldn't return to the silent treatment in Brentwood.

When he came home that evening, Oscar was polite and acted like nothing happened that might have put Hektor out of sorts. Hektor rationalized, *Perhaps Oscar had just a little too much Fourth of July celebrating by the time I arrived on the scene.*

A few days later, Flora Unkovsky stopped by the department. She politely asked to speak with Mr. Birken. He had no clue what that was about.

Flora greeted him. "How are you, son?"

Hektor thought he wasn't hearing correctly. "I'm OK, under the circumstances. What brings you here? Is anything wrong with the children?"

"No, they're fine. I stopped by to invite you over for dinner on Friday night. Dad and I want to have a talk with you." Hektor never had addressed the Unkovskys as Mom and Dad. "If you can see your way clear, we would like to see you at six."

Hektor shook his head in disbelief but agreed to show up for the command performance. Arriving in time for dinner, he learned the reason for the invite.

"You must be wondering what prompted our invitation. Dad and I believe your leaving Georgia is actually a good thing. It's a lesson she needs to be taught. We think a separation will give both of you a chance to cool off and to think about what you are doing to those children."

Hektor didn't comment. He was not about to enlighten them. He had absolutely no intention of returning to the life he'd experienced with Georgia, if one could call it a life. The last four years had been sheer hell on earth. He got up from the table shortly after dessert was served.

"Thanks for feeding me. No need to bother. I'll catch a cab on the corner. Take care."

He was glad to be out of the house. A walk and catching some fresh air would do him good. In no way did he want them to know where he lived.

"Call Dave Mandelbaum of Mandelbaum and Mandelbaum; they are attorneys in Manhattan," said Burton as he handed him Dave's business card. Hektor had an appointment with the junior Mandelbaum within ten days. Dave Mandelbaum advised Hektor to take the first step toward separation from Georgia.

"First thing you need to do is place an ad in the paper. Here is a sample. It will announce your separation from Georgia and disclaim any responsibilities for any and all debts incurred by her."

Flora spotted the announcement in the evening paper. Floyd read it as well.

"I guess Hektor means business," Flora said. "There won't be a reconciliation after all. What now?"

Floyd took the initiative. "Sorry to tell you this, Flora. I really don't blame the man. Georgia gave him the shaft. Or, as I should have said, Karen's father gave our daughter the shaft. She is lucky he stayed with her this long. I wouldn't have. You ask, what now? We have to find an attorney for her and help her and the kids. Let's face it; she is our daughter. We have to stick together and fight fire with fire. There will be no happy ending to this drama."

A couple of weeks before Labor Day, Hektor made his first trip out to the island to see the children. Georgia barely allowed him to step into the house.

"I can't prevent you from seeing the children. However, you will never again be allowed to enter this place."

"Actually, I also stopped by to pick up my things I left behind."

"You bastard! You must be joking. You are one unbelievable idiot! Whatever you didn't take with you on the Fourth, I threw into the dumpster; your books, your diaries, and your photo albums I burned. How blasted stupid do you think I am? I looked at some of your meticulous recordkeeping in your daily diaries. Do you believe me to be ignorant enough to provide you with that kind of ammunition? I made one mistake—I should have held on to those pages detailing your conversation with Harris Schweikert. I could have sued that SOB. What he didn't tell you was that I almost succeeded in giving him a blow-job; his rod certainly was ready for my action."

"You are a real bitch. First of all, how could you say and do the things you did to Dr. Schweikert? The word is getting around; you are nothing but a two-bit whore. As far as my things are concerned, I shouldn't have expected anything other than what you did. You knew how much those things meant to me, especially my detailed records of my first years in the US. Don't worry about my ammunition. A simple blood test will prove that Karen isn't my child. That doesn't take a Philadelphia lawyer to figure out. But for Karen's sake, I might not seek to go that route. Much of it will depend on you. You are really a piece of work!"

Sadly, he never got to see the children that day. He walked away from her. *It's a done deal. How could I be so naïve? How could I believe she would let me retrieve my personal belongings? I should have taken everything with me on the Fourth. Chalk it up as big mistake number three!*

Chapter 29

Within days, Georgia received her first letter from Mandelbaum & Mandelbaum in the matter of Hektor Birken seeking legal separation. Floyd and Flora engaged an attorney. The attorneys were to meet the first time in late September. Perhaps a reconciliation was still possible.

Hektor's hopes for having found a pleasant and quiet situation were shattered all too soon. After an outing with the children on Labor Day, he was greeted by Pauline Singer. She stood on unsteady feet. One eye was bloodshot. Hektor saw bruises wherever the poor woman was not covered.

"You have to move out tonight. My husband has been on one of his drinking binges since Friday evening. He believes you and I are carrying on an affair. Perhaps you can call a friend or colleague."

He called Burton and Marietta. He was packed in no time. Burton was there within the hour. By the time they arrived at the Eppelrath apartment, Marietta already had searched the Long Island papers.

"There is a furnished studio apartment in a private home east of where you were. It would still be within walking distance to the store. It says no lease is required. Why don't you call them? It's a holiday weekend, and they might not have rented the flat yet." Marietta dialed the number and handed him the receiver.

"Kojak speaking," a man answered.

"Is your studio apartment still available?" inquired Hektor, trying to use his very best English.

"I let you speak to my wife; that is her territory."

"This is Alice Kojak. Yes, the studio is still available. It rents for eighty dollars a month, all utilities included. I often rent to R&S employees. I don't require a lease. You are not American; I can tell by your accent. My husband's and my parents emigrated from Poland. I talk too much. When could you look at the place?"

"Would it be OK if I saw you tomorrow evening? Will it still be available?" He explained briefly that he had to work the next day. Alice understood. She would hold the studio apartment for him.

The Kojak home was everything Hektor could have asked for. When he saw it, there was no question he would take it. He moved in that very evening. It was his tenth address in the United States since his arrival on May 5, 1954.

When he informed his mother of the latest news in his life, she came right back.

"Son, you must be always one step ahead of the sheriff. People in Germany are not that nomadic."

※

Getting a couple of suits ready for the cleaners, Hektor checked all of his pockets and discovered Delbert's business card. His first reaction was to toss it in the trashcan, but he picked up the phone and dialed the private number. Delbert answered on the first ring.

"Delbert Braun speaking."

"Hi, it's Hektor Birken. How are things going in Manhattan? Still selling a lot of beer?"

"Things are going just fine in Manhattan. You are lucky to catch me. I just walked in from my favorite hangout, a gay steam bath. It's always a great place for checking what's out there. How are things going with you?"

"Sorry to say, not so good. I've recently left my wife and kids and am in the process of legalizing the separation."

"That's too bad. Care to meet with us next time you are in town and see what's it all about? We do enjoy ourselves a lot in Manhattan. Sounds like you are in need of friends."

"Thanks for the offer. I just had to talk to someone. I'm really down in the dumps. If I make it into the city by myself, I may give you a call. In the meantime, thanks for listening. Good night."

"You take care, Hektor. No reason for feeling down. Ulrich and I can take care of you. You might discover having fun with a bunch of guys—or should I say, having sex with men—isn't so bad. Keep us in mind when you get too horny! Good night for now."

"Thanks again for listening and your generous offer." Hektor hung up the phone and threw Delbert's business card in the trash. They never spoke again.

Ж

That week, Hektor and Burt started interviewing temporary help. They hired a young man to be in charge of the stock areas. His name was Harry Rundstadt. Harry was short and stocky and sported a severe butch haircut; a full crop of hair would have been snow white. He was a college graduate, having studied civil engineering. Harry had recently completed his annual two-week stint in the Reserves. He started working the day after meeting with Burt and Hektor.

A couple nights later, Hektor was deep in thought as he was walking home. A dilapidated green Plymouth pulled up next to him.

Actually, it was more brown than green, showing much evidence of rust. Harry reached over to roll down the window. He pushed open the door.

"Get in. I'll drive you home. You live in the neighborhood? Don't you have a car? How about having a bite with me? Looks to me like you could use a drink. Want to talk? I sure could use some friendly company!" It was the beginning of a beautiful and enduring friendship.

Hektor and Harry sat down at the bar and nursed their first drinks. Harry kept looking at Hektor quizzically.

"I know you don't know me from Adam. Let's have another drink; then I'll tell you my miserable tale. You probably wonder why I took this crummy job at R&S. I'm totally broke. I need the dough. Worse, I need to keep busy. My kid was three years old a few days ago. Carl is a smart little fellow. When I came home from the Reserves, our home had been ransacked. My beautiful wife of four years apparently pulled up with a moving van. She took everything except the curtain rods. She threw those on the floor. Madonna left a note taped to the bedroom door. She would be filing for divorce. If I wanted to see Carl again, I'd better not try anything to interfere with her plans. There you have it in a nutshell. I think I could use a little bit more scotch. Bartender, pour me another double J&B and fill her up with milk; it's easier on my ulcer."

Hektor held his breath. "Scotch and milk? What a drink! Tell me more about your beautiful wife. I'm beginning to see certain parallels in our miserable stories."

"How's that?" Harry became curious and peered over his strange drink at Hektor.

"My son Frank is about the same age as your Carl. I was married to my wife, Georgia, in 1956 as well. She is a redhead, quite artistic, and rather temperamental. Wait a second; let's roll that film back. We need another look at that last statement. There's something wrong with what I just said. I could use another drink myself, bartender. Make mine straight scotch and without that white stuff." Hektor lifted his glass toward Harry. "She is a whore. I found out for certain what kind of a person she is the day after we walked down the aisle. I'm not shitting you, Harry. I knew I was making a mistake before I tied the knot. What I didn't realize was what an immoral and promiscuous bitch I was getting hitched to." *Brrrup!* "Excuse the burp. I left her after four years of misery this past Fourth of July. You get the similarity? I have an idea we both have plenty of fodder for many a conversation on evenings to come."

"That's eye-opening. Madonna is a redhead too. Of course, she helps it along with the bottle. It's not unusual in her profession. She is a model for a top-flight fashion house in Manhattan. I guess my family and I were simply too ordinary for her. By the way, do you drive? I think I'm getting tanked. It's my way of dealing with that bitch and what she has done to me and my kid."

"Sorry, Harry, I never learned to drive. I wasn't old enough to get a license in Germany when I left. In the US, I never had a real need for it—certainly not now, with all the public transportation at my disposal."

"That's OK, Hektor. We'll manage somehow. Bartender, get us another round. Don't worry about the tab; it's on me. I just love these little plastic suckers!" He reached for his wallet and let a string of credit cards spill down like a harmonica to the top of the bar.

Hektor didn't own a single one; all his transactions were by cash or check. He wasn't that Americanized yet.

They finally left the bar. Harry was not too steady on his feet. With Hektor's help, he managed to get behind the wheel of the car. He dropped Hektor off in front of the Kojaks' house. Thank goodness it wasn't a long drive. Before he pulled away from the curb, he yelled at Hektor, "Don't make any plans for Saturday night. I want you to meet my folks. They live in Freeport."

Harry made his way home to his empty house on Meadowbrook Lane. He had thrown a mattress on the floor and had a bridge table and four chairs in the kitchen. His folks had a washer and dryer as well as a refrigerator installed after Madonna took everything.

The Bobbsey Twins, as Harry started to refer to himself and Hektor, left right after work on Saturday night. Harry felt he needed to talk about his folks.

"Adelaide Gertrude—that's my mom—is looking forward to meeting you. My dad's name is Harry as well. You'll like him. The two of them are a hoot. Banker, my maternal grandma, will be with us tonight. I'm an only child; my family has always doted on me. Sometimes they can be a royal pain in the ass, but I have learned to appreciate the whole bunch of them in the last few weeks."

As they walked into the elegantly appointed condominium, Adelaide walked up to greet the boys. She put her arms around Harry's neck and gave him a smacker on the cheek. Then she started to extend her hand to greet Hektor but apparently changed her mind instantly. "I think you need a hug as well. Sounds like you and my son have a lot in common. Harry fixed a pitcher of old-fashioneds, my favorite poison for 'tini time. He makes the best. I'm on my second one. How about you, Banker? You need another drink? Turn up your hearing aids; this is Hektor Birken. He is one of Harry's new bosses at R&S. I have an idea you'll get to see him often. These boys face similar dilemmas."

With that introduction, she grabbed Hektor's hand and walked him over to Banker to establish a proper connection. Adelaide got Harry Sr.'s attention. "Harry, get off the phone. Your son and his buddy Hektor are here. It looks like we are almost ready for another pitcher of your old-fashioneds."

When Harry's father walked into the room, he gave his son an affectionate, fatherly hug and shook Hektor's hand. Harry's dad was a tall, handsome man; his snow-white hair was full and professionally styled and cut. He was the epitome of a successful businessman. Adelaide was rather petite; she sported a blond crop of hair and wore attractive spectacles. Harry had clued in Hektor that his mother almost always wore something deep purple. It was her favorite color. She was born, raised, and educated in New York. She had a New York accent without the Brooklyn inflection.

Hektor took to Harry's parents immediately. They became a vital link in a support system he greatly needed in his disjointed life.

Subsequently, Harry and Hektor scheduled the same day off during the week. It allowed them to be with their children on alternate weeks. In late September, they drove up to the house to pick up Frank and Karen. Hektor saw the mailbox by the street was open. An airmail letter was almost falling out of the box.

He turned toward Harry. "You think that letter from overseas might be for me?"

"Just grab it, and take a look-see."

He stared at the return address; it was Else Gunders' handwriting. Her son, Knut Gunders, was a mutual friend of his schoolmate, Nicklaus Beerenbaum. The Gunders were in New York City that very instant. They were staying at the Hotel Roosevelt in Midtown Manhattan and were anxious to see him, if at all possible.

"After we take the children home this afternoon, I want you to get on the horn and call these folks. We'll stop by the house. It will be a local call from Meadowbrook Lane."

Else and Walter were elated to hear from Hektor. They couldn't believe their good fortune. Helena hadn't been sure where they might reach Hektor; he seemed to be constantly moving. She trusted Georgia to forward their communication to him.

She must be kidding. Hasn't that woman understood a thing I've told her?

Else was so excited about their plans with Hektor. "We look forward to seeing you Sunday morning. We hope it won't be quite as warm and humid as it has been. We have been taking cold baths and soaking our lower arms in cold water with ice in the sink to bring down our body temperatures. We are just not used to such heat. The sunshine is lovely, but this heat and humidity are something else."

"I am happy you are here. We'll have lots to see and lots to talk about."

On Sunday morning, Harry dropped Hektor off at the subway station in Jamaica. It was on his way to St. Albans, where he would pick up Carl for the day. Hektor got off the train and walked over to the Hotel Roosevelt. He had learned his way around Manhattan in the last two years.

Else and Walter greeted him with "How are you?" in German. The two familiar friendly faces welcoming him in his mother tongue were indeed a pleasant experience for his eyes and ears. None of them tried to hide their emotions; they shed tears of joy. It was a most wonderful reunion and the right tonic for Hektor. Else and Walter could not believe what transpired since they'd last seen him in Germany.

They exchanged news of each other's lives over an elegant brunch served in the dining room of the hotel. After finishing their meal, Walter leaned over and said, "Let's take a cab to Lower Manhattan. We'll see more of the city. The subway is faster, but you don't see much. I want to ride the Staten Island ferry and stop at the Statue of Liberty. Let's take a quick peek at Wall Street on the way back. We'll grab another cab to the Empire State Building. It's a perfect day for taking in the views from the 102nd floor."

"I hope you can handle fast elevators," Hektor said. "Some people feel nauseous from the rapid acceleration."

"Don't worry; we'll be just fine. We are looking forward to dinner at the Gate of Cleve. The concierge told us that's supposed to be a good German restaurant. I want to catch the Rockettes at Radio City Music Hall before we call it a day. You know me; I've always had a thing for pretty girls with pretty legs."

Else not only had beautiful legs, she also had a brilliant mind and still was a stunning woman in her early fifties. They skipped the movie, always part of an evening at Radio City Music Hall, because of the language barrier and finished the day with drinks at the Biltmore. Sitting with Else and Walter at the bar, Hektor spotted Delbert and Ulrich at the other end. They were deeply engrossed in conversation with two young men. Neither saw Hektor before he left the Biltmore with his friends.

Hektor hugged Else. "Thanks for a wonderful day. I'm so glad I found that letter of yours just in time. I hope you have a great experience visiting this country."

Walter patted him on the back. "Good luck with all that lies ahead for you. Come and see us in the old country when you can." He winked at Hektor as he shook his hand.

Having said goodbye to Else and Walter, Hektor was tempted—just for a split second—to return to the Biltmore bar, but he changed his mind and caught the train at Grand Central Station. He looked upon his future with hope. He could see some light at the end of a dismal tunnel. There had to be better days ahead. He was grateful for his friends. For the rest of his days, he would tell others that true friends were perhaps the most important people one encountered in one's journey through life. He never failed to make the point.

"You choose your friends. With family, one often is stuck. It's like playing a game of Russian roulette."

Harry's parents had refurbished the house on Meadowbrook Lane. For now, it was a fairly comfortable site, where young Harry and his buddy Hektor could hang their hats, although Hektor still had his studio apartment at the Kojaks'. Their boys were a lot of fun since they began to communicate. Unwittingly, they shared stories that involved their respective mothers. Frank started talking about "uncles" visiting who sometimes were there for the whole night; one of them was now sharing Daddy's bedroom with Karen.

"When are you coming to stay with us again, Daddy?" was a question both boys asked regularly. Harry and Hektor were often hard put to provide a satisfactory answer.

"I really miss you!" was the tough one. At moments like these, volatile Harry would explode.

"I need a drink!" or "I need to get laid!" Of course, what he wanted to do was strangle Madonna.

On election day, they stopped at the polls. It was Hektor's first time to cast a vote for a president. Both he and Harry had determined several weeks earlier that they would vote for John F. Kennedy. Somehow, he was more appealing than Richard Nixon. Neither was married to a particular party, especially not Hektor.

As they pulled up to Harry's house after having voted, they noted right away that none of the lamps on timers in the living room were on. The house was pitch dark. They walked up to the side door. It was ajar, and its window was smashed in. Harry turned on the lights. "Fuck that bitch. She's done it again!" Madonna had cleaned him out a second time.

This time she bit off more than she could chew. Harry Sr. called the police and reported his daughter-in-law as the responsible thief of their property; none of the things belonged to Harry Jr. Madonna's home was searched within an hour by the St. Albans police. They found all the evidence they needed. It gave Harry and his folks the leverage they had been looking for.

She had to return, at her expense, anything she had removed from the house during the break-in and had to pay for any repairs. Furthermore, she signed papers relinquishing her share in the equity of the house on Meadowbrook Lane. Mr. and Mrs. Rundstadt Sr. ultimately bought the house from Harry.

Harry loved his parents dearly, but he believed it would be best for him to find a place of his own. It was Adelaide's idea for Harry and Hektor to find an apartment that could accommodate them both. She located a furnished apartment in Long Beach, available for six months starting December first. They would enjoy the quiet and the soothing sounds of the sea. It would give them time to get to know each other and to search for more permanent housing in the interim.

The house on Meadowbrook Lane was transformed to Adelaide's personal and elegant taste by the time she served the traditional November feast, with her immediate family and Hektor gracing the table. The "grandsons" were not there. They were supposed to spend Christmas Eve and Christmas Day with them and their fathers. It took a lot of haggling for Georgia to consent to the arrangement. Since Madonna's close call with the law, she was more inclined to let Harry have his son without casting obstacles in his way.

Harry and Hektor drove to St. Albans and got little Carl. As they pulled up in front of the Unkovsky home to get Frank, they saw a curtain being pulled back. Floyd came to the door.

"Sorry, but we are not letting our grandson spend Christmas with people about whom we know nothing."

"Wait a minute," Hektor said, "your daughter and I had an understanding that Frank would spend Thanksgiving with you and Christmas with me. I thought you would be decent enough to honor that agreement."

"Hardly, buddy. As long as you and our daughter aren't legally separated, we operate under the rules of this house." With that, he slammed the door in Hektor's face.

"Merry Christmas to you too," Hektor said loudly as he turned on the balls of his feet. What he felt like saying was, "Fuck you!"

"What was that all about?" Harry wanted to know.

"That bastard denied me my kid, and there isn't a blasted thing I can do about it until that b—" Hektor caught himself at the last second and didn't call her a bitch in front of little Carl. "Until she has signed her name to a legal separation."

"Bitch is right! Fucking bitch is damn right!" said Harry. It wasn't the first time his son had heard his father use those endearing terms. He looked at Carl. "Those kinds of words are among us men. Don't blabber to Nana and Papa what I just said."

They drove to Meadowbrook Lane and were greeted with open arms by Adelaide. She loved all of her "boys" and was sorry and hurt that she was being deprived of Hektor's son.

"Someday, this will all lie behind you; it will be like a nightmare. When you wake up, it will be over! Let's make the best of the situation. How about one of Harry's very best old-fashioneds? That ought to settle you boys down." She winked at them and nudged Harry Sr. to get moving and pour them a drink. "It looks like we all could use a little Christmas cheer!"

Harry and Hektor adored her. She was exactly what they needed. After dinner, Carl was tucked into bed by his grandmother. The gentlemen sampled one too many of Harry Sr.'s old-fashioneds. No one suffered from the lack of sleepiness on this Christmas Eve.

Carl woke them about seven o'clock. "Daddy, Daddy, the cookies and milk are gone from the window sill. Santa was here for sure."

Adelaide knew this would happen and was all prepared for her grandson. As soon as she heard voices upstairs, she flicked on the record player. The sound of Mitch Miller's "Must be Santa, must be Santa, must be Santa, Santa Claus"—the hit of the season—filled the house at above-average decibel levels. It was the signal for Carl to come downstairs to see what wonderful things Santa had left for him.

"Grandpa, Grandpa, look at this truck. Where are the 'constrictions'? Will you help me put it together?"

All were smiling; it was enjoyable to see such enthusiasm, although it would have been even more fun with a playmate. When Harry and Hektor took Carl home late on Christmas Day, he insisted Uncle Hektor tell him the story of *The Three Little Pigs* once more. He loved it when Uncle Hektor talked about the wolf.

"He hoooofed, and he poooofed, and he blew de house down."

"No, Uncle Hektor, he huffed, and he puffed, and he blew the house down. You know what, Uncle Hektor? You sound funny!"

Harry would sometimes split his gut and finally make some smarty comment. "What do you expect from a foreigner? I told you he is nothing but a goddamn immigrant!"

Carl didn't know then what that meant, but he could tell from his father's voice that it wasn't very nice what he called Uncle Hektor. "Daddy, I like Uncle Hektor. Don't call him bad names."

"You know what? I like him too. I'm just teasing him!"

These humorous conversations with a three-year-old added levity to a sad situation. It made the rides to return him to his mother more tolerable for all concerned. At least Harry got to see his boy regularly. Madonna had done him a huge favor by breaking into his house the second time.

On New Year's Eve, Harry and Hektor were invited to cousin Josef's house in Freeport. Josef thought Harry and his roommate needed to spend the evening in the company of some younger people. What they needed was to get drunk, perhaps even get laid. That was Josef's assessment of the situation. Everyone, including Hektor, stuck with scotch and water. Harry's ulcer was acting up. He thought it best to continue drinking his double-scotches laced with milk. Once the New Year arrived, Harry switched to straight gin.

They finally stumbled to the old rusty Plymouth at four in the morning, and Harry mumbled into the handkerchief he was holding to his mouth, "I can't drive home. I'll get us killed. You'll learn how to drive this piece of shit right now. It's automatic shift and nothing to it. Here, let me show you." He pressed the keys into Hektor's hands, encouraging him to test the waters and drive. The only con-solation was there would be next to no traffic. Harry slumped into the back seat while Hektor got behind the wheel.

"I can't do this. If you think you'd get us killed, what do you think will happen when I drive?"

"Nothing to it! Turn the key while you keep your foot on the brake. It's the pedal to the left. Then you put that thing on D, and give a little gas by stepping on the pedal to the right while holding onto the steering wheel. Just stay on the right side of the road. You know the way; we have driven it a few times from that Italian joint you like so much. It's right up the street. Come on; get going before there is more traffic on these damn roads."

And so Hektor drove a car for the first time in his life. Once he recognized where they were, he followed Harry's advice and stayed on the right side of the road. Periodically, Harry would bob up in the back seat and belch.

"Attaboy! We are almost there. See, I told you so; nothing to it!"

Clearly, drunks and children had more luck than anyone else.

As Hektor helped Harry up the stairs to their apartment, they could hear their housemates downstairs still celebrating. They shared the building with four barmaids. Apparently, the girls had not ushered in 1961 sufficiently at work.

Hektor heard from his mother on New Year's Day. "Hallo, Hektor, I have sad news for you."

"What else is new? Whenever you call, it's always bad or sad news!"

"Your grandfather died peacefully on the thirtieth of December. He will be laid to rest on the second of January. What a way to start the New Year. My father was in so much pain in the end that I am glad he is no longer suffering. Sorry that you didn't get to see him again."

"It sounds like it was a good thing for him, but I know it's hard for you."

"Yes and no. What's happening with you? Didn't you get my Christmas package?"

"Sorry, Mutti. I didn't get it yet. Did you make sure to address it to Long Beach, Long Island, New York? There is a Long Beach in California. If you didn't, it might have gone out there."

"I'm not sure any longer. Would they forward the package to you in case it went to California?"

"I believe they would. Let's just see what happens. By the way, I am moving forward with the divorce and don't have it easy with Georgia and her family. They have become very nasty. I'm glad to share my misery with my good friend, Harry, and his family."

"Although I never liked this situation, I am sorry for you."

"Don't feel sorry for me. I'm pleased that I finally made the break. Georgia would have killed my spirit and me. Mutti, please give my love to all. This is expensive for you. Next time, I'll call you. Auf Wiedersehen, Mutti."

"Auf Wiedersehen, Hektor. Let me know if and when you get the Christmas package. Happy New Year!"

Helena's Christmas goodies had indeed been sent to California and arrived six weeks after the holidays in Long Island. All of the illegally sent meat products were totally spoiled, but the cookies and marzipan had survived the long journey and were edible. He was surprised that the post office delivered it; it stank to high heaven. He let Helena know of the late arrival but did not upset her by revealing the truth pertaining to the contraband contents.

Chapter 30

THE New Year brought a decided change in the weather. Long Island experienced heavy snowfalls, the likes of which had not been seen in years. By mid-January, temperatures dipped way below the zero mark. New York was in a rare deep freeze.

In early February, Hektor and his attorney, Dave Mandelbaum, met with Georgia and the first in a string of attorneys representing her. Her demands were totally unreasonable. Her legal counsel threw up his arms. "I refuse to represent you. You are an impossible person. The invoice for my services will be in the mail!"

As they walked out, Dave turned to Hektor. "Just give it time. We will get this settled yet."

That Saturday night, Harry thought he and Hektor needed to go out for dinner and forget about their marital problems. "Let's eat at your favorite joint. Your birthday celebration is on me." They were greeted like regulars when they walked into the Italian restaurant.

"I need to take a leak. Order the usual for both of us as far as drinks are concerned," Harry said as he rushed away to the men's room.

They got around to dinner after the fourth or fifth round of drinks. Harry enjoyed the excellent food, but Hektor was feeling queasy from drinking so much on an empty stomach. Harry paid the bill and excused himself. He kept talking as he walked away. Their waiter was all eyes and ears. "I have to piss again. I wonder if my prostate is acting up. Am I getting old?"

Hektor knew he was going to throw up. Luckily, he was quick enough to grab the gigantic red napkin. He folded his vomit neatly into the napkin and set it carefully on the table. He placed a hefty tip adjacent to the dubious souvenir left for the waiter, who watched the whole maneuver. Open-mouthed, he glared at Hektor, noticing him stagger out of the restaurant.

When Harry returned to their table, Hektor was gone. The waiter gave Harry a dirty look. His vision swept from the folded red napkin to the front of the restaurant. He shrugged his shoulders, motioning to the exit door. Hektor was standing in the middle of a busy intersection, heaving and blocking traffic in both directions. Harry retrieved his housemate and hauled him off for a sobering walk along the shores of Long Beach.

Blubbering about the miserable experience with the attorneys and being sick of it all, Hektor wanted to go for a swim in the ocean. When Harry realized what was happening, he went charging after Hektor.

"Come back here, you goddamn fool. No fucking bitch is worth your even thinking about doing such a stupid thing." He threw off his own coat and barely caught up with Hektor before he went under. Harry dragged him by the collar, eventually gaining his own footing on the slippery sand, all the time shouting his famous litany of four-letter zingers. Harry was pissed at Hektor and the woman who was responsible for his depressed state of mind.

He grabbed his coat off the sandy beach, wildly shaking off any sand that might have clung to it. His jacket had only barely been missed by the incoming tide. Harry dumped Hektor in the back seat of the old Plymouth and got him to the apartment as fast as he could without getting a ticket. Hektor stripped off his wet and freezing clothes. Harry ran a hot tub and fixed strong, hot coffee for both of them. Hektor's unsuccessful rendezvous with death sobered them both.

"No matter what happens with that fucking whore, don't you ever try anything so stupid again. She isn't worth it. Remember you do have to live for those children."

In late February, Hektor was promoted. The buyer/manager of the Men's Shoe Department left the company. Burt recommended Hektor for the job. The department handled shoes, hats, umbrellas, and sundry accessories. After more than two years in the Men's Furnishings Department, Hektor's departure for greener pastures wasn't easy on anyone. Nevertheless, it was a step in the right direction. Hektor needed a boost to his morale and especially a boost to his pocketbook. Furthermore, his leaving the department allowed Burton to give Harry additional responsibilities and an increase in pay.

In March, Madonna obtained her divorce from Harry in Reno. Shared custody was stipulated. Harry was confident he eventually would gain full custody of Carl. Madonna couldn't have cared less about her child. Carl had been just a pawn and a tool in negotiating the most advantageous financial terms.

Harry was seriously considering finding a different and better-paying job commensurate with his educational background. He and Hektor signed a one-year lease for a new one-bedroom apartment in Rego Park near Flushing Meadows. On June first, they took occupancy on the seventeenth floor of the brand-new high-rise complex. Their new apartment came unfurnished. Adelaide and Harry made sure the young men didn't have to spend any unnecessary funds on decorating their apartment. There was enough furniture stored in the lower level at Meadowbrook Lane to furnish another house.

The location was an excellent solution for both Harry and Hektor. Hektor was closer to company headquarters in Brooklyn and the markets in Manhattan. At the same time, he could take a train to work if Harry wasn't driving in the same direction. Harry was closer to his son and could see him more frequently during the week. The only drawback was the distance between Hektor and his children. Visiting them became a regular excursion on his days off.

In July, Hektor and Dave Mandelbaum made an attempt at meeting with Georgia and attorney number two. Although not quite as explosive as their earlier confrontation, essentially nothing was resolved. Further meetings were not scheduled until Georgia's attorney had an opportunity to consult with his client in private.

As he so often did these days, Hektor stepped out onto the balcony of their apartment on the seventeenth floor. He hated to admit it, but there were times like this when he felt like Maxim de Winter in *Rebecca*, standing at the precipice in Monte Carlo, and he was tempted to take a leap over the railing and end it all. He was glad Harry rarely left him alone. Hektor didn't know how often he felt as bitter about Georgia as de Winter did about his infamous wife.

One night in September, Harry had good news for Hektor. His hunt for a new job resulted in an offer by Reynolds International, a construction firm specializing in the building of roads, bridges, railroads, etc. His initial assignments kept him in the New York/ Newark area. Eventually, he expected an overseas appointment. The news was a mixed blessing for Hektor. Nevertheless, they had reason to celebrate. They went into town.

"Let's check out the Biltmore. That used to be a great place to meet interesting people."

"Harry, what did you have in mind by meeting interesting people? Did you mean members of the opposite sex?"

"I didn't think I needed to draw you pictures. We've both been a bit horny, if you get my drift. I know you are not separated yet, but who gives a fuck? Speaking of fuck, that's what I need. So don't give me any drivel. Don't you want to find out if you can still do it with a beautiful broad? I see a couple of good-looking unattached dames right over there. Get cracking, and let's check 'em out."

They strolled over to the bar and sat down next to the two women who were carrying on a lively conversation. Harry took the lead. "What ya drinking? May we buy you a cocktail?"

"Sure, why not? This is Sheila; I'm Brenda. We are in port for the night. Just flew in on Braniff. As you can see, we are in love with scotch and water. What are you boys up to?"

"We are not so sure about *boys*; what about men?"

"OK, guys. Let's not be so sensitive."

Harry raised his hand and ordered three J&Bs with water on the side. His, of course, was a double-scotch with the inimitable white stuff. Sheila started to burp when she heard the word *milk*. Harry explained why he drank what he had ordered.

They chitchatted over a drink or two and were surprised when the two ladies invited them for a nightcap to their respective rooms at the Biltmore. Brenda had taken Harry's hand, and Sheila took Hektor's as they guided them to the elevator. Harry winked at Hektor. Both were pleasantly surprised by the apparent progress they were making. Neither thought it would be that easy to get laid.

Before they parted company, Harry insisted on shaking Hektor's right hand to wish him a good night. No one noticed Harry had reached for his favorite condoms in his right pants pocket. Hektor realized immediately what Harry was trying to share with him. He smiled at Harry and wished him pleasant dreams. Harry reciprocated with the same wish for him and Sheila. Both knew it wasn't dreaming they had in mind.

The rooms were adjacent and connecting. Hektor could hear Harry belch.

Hektor tossed his Dobbs hat on a chair. Sheila helped him out of his suit, tie, and shirt. He kicked off his shoes. He didn't bother taking off his socks.

"Your sock garters are sexy. They turn me on." She drew down his Jockey shorts and beheld his nakedness. He unwrapped one of the condoms. He let Sheila check him out.

"Pretty nice. I like a healthy-looking dick. Here—let me slip on your handy little hood." She took the condom out of his hand and slipped it easily over his penis.

Hektor bent down to kiss Sheila. He knew she wasn't a hooker—they never kissed on the mouth. Unlike with Georgia, this sex scene was civilized. No one tore each other's clothes off. Hektor undressed her with some respect. It had been so long since he'd held a naked woman in his embrace, he wanted to make it last.

Sheila seemed to appreciate the care with which he treated her uniform. When he had finally unveiled Sheila's naked body, he carried her to the bed. He easily stripped the bed of its fancy covering and laid her gently on the soft, cool sheets.

He whispered in her ear after he had kissed it. "How did you know what Harry and I wanted? Did we look that horny? It's been a long time since I have been with a woman. I'll spare you the details for now. Thank you for sharing yourself with me."

Sheila responded demandingly to his soft kisses. He let his tongue travel down to her breasts and nipples. He could tell she was responding to his languid foreplay. His tongue had Sheila writhing with pleasure. Her moaning and shivering became more pronounced.

"Enough, enough! Come and take me. I want to feel you in me. Enough of the gentle foreplay. I loved it, but now I want to be had hard by that weapon of yours."

"I'm only too happy to oblige. Believe me, it's been years since I've enjoyed being with a woman."

They rushed to orgasm in concert; both were screaming as they came. Hektor was sure their friendly neighbors knew what went down. Sheila got on top of Hektor, wanting to get a second ride. He was ready.

Harry needed to use the john. He pressed down the handle on the

French door to the bathroom, but it wasn't the bathroom he opened. It was the connecting door to Sheila's room. Hektor, stunned, looked around Sheila and faced Harry.

Brenda was sitting in bed, naked, ready for another round.

All Harry could say was *oops*, and he closed the door after slowly taking in the whole scene. Hektor knew he would hear his descriptions the next day. Before Sheila and Hektor enjoyed holding each other once more, they locked the connecting door. The guys stayed for the night. There was no one waiting for them at Rego Park. Hektor gave Sheila their telephone number before they parted company in the morning. He was hoping for return engagements.

Chapter 31

EXACTLY one week later, Dave Mandelbaum was on the phone.

"Can you meet me on Friday at the courthouse in Mineola? Georgia is supposed to be there with attorney number three. Judge Appletree has been assigned to the case and agreed to be mediator. I'm hopeful something will come of this meeting."

They met on September 15, 1961. Georgia was warned by her attorney to be more cooperative and reasonable; her financial demands were still totally out of line. Judge Appletree summoned Hektor and Georgia into his chambers.

"Young lady, you are completely unreasonable. Let's look at your situation as if we were dividing a pie. You want the whole pie, but he needs to have a certain portion of that pie in order to work, live, and earn that pie to be distributed between you, your children, and him. I believe a reasonable amount to be awarded to you will be 50 percent of his present net earnings, constituting child support. He will need to maintain health insurance coverage for the children." Judge Appletree took a healthy drink of water before he continued, always looking straight at Georgia, who tried to evade his eyes.

"I want you to understand these obligations are based on present and not future earnings. Payments will cease when the younger of the children attains the age of eighteen or is emancipated, if that occurs sooner. You are awarded custody of the children with visitation rights for your husband, as spelled out in the agreement. Do you understand what I just told you?"

Georgia nodded.

"You need to say it for the record!"

"Yes," was Georgia's reluctant response.

"This final recommendation is based on my personal philosophy that even a bad mother is better than no mother." He had been clued in as to the reasons why Hektor was seeking the divorce. Had she balked, he would have ordered a blood test to prove paternity. Proving that Karen wasn't Hektor's child, Georgia's financial future might have been impacted even more drastically.

The judge continued. "Last but not least, I hold each of you responsible for the expenses incurred with your respective legal counsel. If these conditions are acceptable to both parties, I suggest that you proceed with the signing of the documents after they are amended to reflect my recommendations."

All through the discussion with Judge Appletree, Hektor was silently praying Georgia wouldn't open her foul mouth. He must have had an exceptional long-distance connection, as the Man upstairs had clearly understood his fervent pleas. Dave winked at Hektor and nodded affirmatively.

"We accept your ruling, Judge Appletree."

After a brief conference between Georgia and her counsel, the two attorneys amended the prepared documents. Hektor and Georgia signed and initialed where changes were made in accordance with the judge's recommendations. The whole thing was over in a matter of minutes. Everyone shook hands with Judge Appletree. The document was duly notarized. Walking down the steps of the courthouse, Dave gave Hektor the victory sign.

"I'm glad you got my hint. I didn't want you to object to the 50 percent recommendation. I know it's a hardship for now, but remember it will remain a stable amount for years to come. It is an ironclad agreement. She signed her name to it after the judge reiterated and clarified his recommendations. Did you also notice it's all child support? She wasn't awarded any alimony.

"I'm glad we finally have this settled. You are a free man. You may do as you please. It's perfectly safe for you to start seeing other women. When you are ready to proceed with a divorce, get in touch with me. It's been a pleasure working with you. Don't worry right now about your financial obligations to our firm. We will work out a suitable arrangement. Celebrate the day!"

Hektor smiled as he made contact with the silver Madonna tucked under his shirt. Hektor elected not to share with Dave Mandelbaum the tryst he had recently enjoyed with Sheila at the Biltmore.

Dave Mandelbaum got in his car, heading off to another court date. Hektor took a cab back to the store. Marietta met Burton, Hektor, and Harry for lunch at one of their favorite watering holes. They had good reason for celebrating. Hektor was a free man, and Harry had found a new job. Harry and Hektor picked up their drinks.

"Here's to us; here's to new shores!"

Hektor called the Biltmore and left a message for Sheila.

In accordance with the separation agreement, Georgia was awarded all common property and the contents of the house, but the house itself was to be sold as soon as feasible. Of course, Georgia refused to leave the house. Hektor stopped paying the bank officially. While the money was deposited in an escrow account, it gave the institution leverage to proceed with foreclosure. Georgia called him at the store.

"How dare you let them foreclose on the house and put me and the children on the street? You are nothing but a fucking bastard!"

"Bastards are really more your specialty. Last I remember, I was of legitimate birth."

"I don't know how I let that damn attorney talk me into signing that separation agreement. The whole fucking thing is stacked against me."

"Actually, you are lucky that I didn't pursue divorcing you on adultery grounds. You never would have gotten anything but child support for Frank. Put that in your tea leaves and your damn tarot cards. Enjoy the reading!" He hung up, not giving her a chance to respond.

That night, Harry picked up the Long Island paper.

"Hektor, here is the answer why Georgia refuses to get out of that dream house of hers. In one of her more creative moments, she apparently painted a large mural on one of the pink living room walls. It was a depiction of a mythical scene, painted entirely with different strengths of instant coffee. The photo shows her with her creation. In her words, she simply could not leave the house and abandon such a personal statement of her artistic abilities."

Hektor took a look at the photo. "Hogwash."

Harry had an even better comment. "She should have called *Playboy* and had them do some nude shots of her in front of that ridiculous mural. Hefner might have titled it *Instant Fuck on Pink*."

Just before the Christmas holiday, Hektor had a most unsettling experience with his former wife and mother-in-law. It was on a Friday evening. The store was bustling with holiday shoppers when one of the salesmen summoned Hektor to the floor of the department.

"Your wife wishes to speak with you; she is waiting downstairs."

"She is my former wife, just to set the record straight. I'm no longer married to her. I'll be right down."

When Hektor appeared on the sales floor, Flora Unkovsky started spouting profanities and tried to strike Hektor with her purse. "You and that kike, Dave Mandelbaum, screwed our daughter out of everything. He's nothing but a shyster. I still cannot understand why our attorney went along with Judge Appletree's recommendations. I'm absolutely pissed that our shmok accepted those terms, especially sticking us with Georgia's legal bills and not even awarding her any alimony."

Apparently, mother and daughter concocted the idea of causing this horrendous ruckus in the store to intimidate Hektor. Before Georgia attempted to join in the fracas her mother had caused, Hektor winked at one of his sales people who wasn't with a customer and asked him to dial security.

The office of the head of security was close to the Shoe Department. Momentarily, Adam Bierbaum, resembling a bouncer, made his appearance. Right away, he knew with whom he was dealing. He recognized Georgia from her short stint with the company a few years earlier.

"Young lady, I presume this is your mother? If you two don't leave the premises of this store immediately, I'll personally throw you out. Do you understand what I'm telling you? Further, if you ever come into this building again and cause any kind of disturbance, we will take legal action against you!"

Georgia and her mother caught on instantly and left at once, never again to be seen in the establishment as long as Hektor worked there.

In March 1962, Harry received a notice from Reynolds International.

"Look at this, Hektor. I got my first overseas assignment. I'm flying to Liberia on May first. The company is building a railroad from some mine to the closest port."

"That sounds challenging, and you know what? I'm ready for a challenge myself. I believe the time has come for me to make a major change in my life as well. I saw an interesting ad in the trade papers. International Stores is opening a chain of discount stores all over the country. They are looking for qualified people and are talking top dollar. I'm not sure about this discount-store business, but nothing ventured, nothing gained. I'll arrange for an interview."

Things turned out even better than Hektor had imagined. He resolved to take the job. Getting out of New York would be a good move at this time. He reported to their offices in Bridgeport, Connecticut, for a follow-up appointment. Hektor would train at their Fairfield facility for six weeks, starting in early May.

The phone rang. It was Sheila calling.

May I come up to Rego Park and see you?"

"Are you kidding me? Of course! Love it!"

He met her at the subway station.

Sheila walked in and admired the views from their seventeenth-floor balcony.

"Harry is visiting his folks for the weekend. He'll be leaving for his new job in Liberia real soon. There's no problem getting out of the lease, and we're giving it up by the end of the month. For tonight, we've got the place to ourselves. Care for a drink, or is it too early in the day?"

"No, not at all. I need something to relax me a bit."

"How about a J&B with water."

"That suits me just fine."

"I have a couple of suggestions."

"Dare I ask what they might be?"

"After we get reacquainted in my comfortable bed, we could shower and hop on the subway. Dinner at the Tower Suite is fun.

Would you care to see *A Touch of Mink* with Day and Grant at Radio City Music Hall? It's supposed to be a lot of fun and the hit of the season. What do you say?"

"I'm impressed. Here I thought you were just ready to let me enjoy your wonderful manhood and nothing else. Dinner and the movie sound delightful. I'll make you a deal. As long as Harry is not coming home, I'll come back with you and stay the night. I don't have to be back at Idlewild until late tomorrow afternoon. Can you spend the time with me?"

"I've actually resigned. I'm leaving R&S and start in Bridgeport, Connecticut, on May first on a new adventure. I can think of nothing better than to use up one of my accumulated sick days. This man is all yours for the next twenty-four hours." He walked Sheila into Harry's and his bedroom. They had two full-sized beds that were ample in size for lovemaking.

"Isn't it nice that we discovered each other earlier? Now we can skip the seduction scene and get right down to business. You have no idea how great you made me feel the first time I made love to you at the Biltmore. At the time, I wasn't quite legal. I'm free of that bitch at last. I'll share some of my background over dinner. Right now, I want to embrace your nakedness and bring both of us to fulfillment."

Hektor wasn't as formally dressed as he had been at their first tryst. Taking off his T-shirt and shorts was done in a jiffy. The sock-garters and socks were missing. She pulled his Jockey shorts down with her teeth. She knew how to please a man. Sheila drove him almost out of his gourd.

"Easy, girl, easy. It's been a while. Give me a chance to pleasure you." He bedded her on the silky sheets. He explored her face, breasts, and nipples and let his tongue discover the mysteries of all of her. Sheila began to moan.

"Please, please, let me have all of you with vigor. I've so longed for you since the last time we met. I was fantasizing about being with you all across the Pacific. I don't know how I will handle your moving away from Manhattan."

They rhapsodized in culminating orgasms; they simultaneously howled with delight. No one could hear or see them. Her fingernails had torn into the skin of his back. She caught the rivulets of his blood with a tissue. They shared their nakedness freely and enjoyed each other as if it was for the last time.

"Let's shower and then get dressed for dinner. The hot shower will feel great. I made the reservation at the Tower Suite for seven o'clock. We'll catch the late show at Radio City. You had a wonderful idea of taking the day off tomorrow. I deserve it. We deserve each other."

They had a perfect table with a view from the Tower Suite restaurant.

"Don't you love looking at the light display on the Empire State Building?"

Sheila smiled across the table. "Thanks for arranging this evening."

Hektor returned her smile. "Do you care for a glass of wine with dinner? I recommend one of their game dishes. Red wine would be great."

"Spoil me. You order the wine and order something special from the menu. I'll have anything but fish."

"Don't worry. It won't be fish." He ordered elk steaks, medium rare; a spinach soufflé; and wild rice. The waiter recommended an excellent Cabernet. They had cherries jubilee and freshly made vanilla ice cream for dessert. Over dinner, they shared some of their personal backgrounds. It was beyond Sheila's imagination why Georgia had treated Hektor the way she did. Sheila enjoyed being with him and loved the attention he showered on her.

"That was lovely. Now let's go for that *Touch of Mink*. Skip the cab; I'm ready for a little walking," said Sheila.

They loved the movie. It was late at night when they got on the subway at Fifty-First Street. They were all alone on the train. Sheila flirted mercilessly throughout the trip. When they got back to the apartment, they gave it their all for the rest of the night. Sleeping until late in the morning was a special treat for both. Sheila had her arms around Hektor's blotched neck. He looked into her eyes.

"I hate to kiss you goodbye. I have no idea how things will work out. I have your telephone number. Perhaps we could meet some other time, when and if I'm back in town on business."

He gave her a languid kiss before he put her in the cab that would take her to Idlewild. The last twenty-four hours had been a true celebration of life for both. For once, Hektor felt alive again. Sheila had succeeded in making him feel like a man.

Chapter 32

AT the very moment Harry stepped off the plane in Monrovia, the capital of Liberia, Hektor walked into the store in Fairfield, Connecticut. Neither of them knew what their destinies held. Harry was going to complete a railway connection between some obscure diamond mine and a seaport in Liberia. He would be gone for at least eighteen months. His work was fraught with danger to his health and general well-being.

The month before he left the United States, Harry was physically probed, examined, and inoculated against most known tropical diseases. His step into unknown territory was far riskier than Hektor's.

Hektor took a bus to Bridgeport and found adequate lodging in Irene Pearl's emporium of rented rooms. The rooming house, a well-kept older home, was ideally located. It afforded Hektor a comfortable site on weekends or on his days off when he wanted to escape his motel room in Fairfield. Irene and her invalid mother resided on the ground floor; all the upper rooms were rented to single men. Irene was a successful real-estate broker and ran her rooming house with a distinct flair for efficient business. She thought it was easiest not to deal with sexual dalliances among her roomers; for that reason, she thought it was best not to rent to women.

What Irene didn't realize was that a couple of her male tenants were an item. Some of their nighttime activities made for curious listening for the other guys with their windows wide open. The old house didn't have AC.

One sultry night, George, one of the renters, got fed up. He yelled loudly enough to garner the attention of the whole neighborhood. "Hey, Oscar, can't you hump Ben more discreetly? We can hear every fucking word you say. And that noise from your mattress! Why don't you guys get down on the floor?"

Harvey got into the act. "I don't know who you two guys invited. Whoever it is, tell 'im to keep down that damn moaning while he's getting a blow-job. You are making the rest of us horny."

A window was slammed down hard. It would have awakened Irene and her mother, had they worn their hearing aids to bed.

Hektor heard his immediate neighbor, Frank. "Shucks! I was just beginning to enjoy the entertainment." None of the guys had realized Frank was gay as well.

※

Entering the Tip-Top Store in Fairfield, Hektor knew immediately he would be exposed to a totally different kind of merchandising. The displays in the stores lacked a certain degree of glamour, flair, or appeal to the individual shopper. *So be it. They are paying me well for my expertise and previous experiences. I'll give it a whirl. It's a new adventure.*

The days were often extremely long. During his six-week indoctrination into the realm of discount merchandising, he often was on his feet from eight in the morning until closing time at ten at night. By the end of the week, he knew he had earned his money.

In July, he received his orders from company headquarters. He and Lew Simons, a fellow trainee, were assigned to the opening crew in the Cleveland area. Lew was a medium-built man in his early to mid-forties, with graying hair that showed signs of typical male balding. He had gone bankrupt in the haberdashery business a year earlier. It was tough for him to swallow his pride and start anew in a totally different milieu. As soon as Lew and Hektor got their marching orders to report in Cleveland, Lew approached Hektor.

"How are you planning on getting to Cleveland? Have you made any arrangements yet?"

"I don't have that much to move. I'll probably ship some things ahead and then take a bus and hope to see some of the country going out that way."

"That's foolish. I'm driving a big car, and you are more than welcome to join me. I would like to have company on the long drive. Before we venture on the trip to Cleveland, I want to spend the weekend with my family in Westchester. Since we are sharing living quarters for a while, I'd like you to meet my wife and daughter."

"Thanks for offering me a lift. That certainly will make the move much easier for me. I'd be delighted to meet your family."

"Leslie will start college in the fall. She wants to talk with me before I embark on this challenging turn in my professional life. Miriam isn't in the best of health. She isn't looking forward to this separation brought about by my new job. Let's go out to dinner and talk."

"I'm sure it's not easy for you to leave your wife under those circumstances. Hopefully, she'll be better very soon."

Hektor enjoyed being with Lew's wife and daughter. They made him most welcome and helped him to forget about his own issues.

He realized he wouldn't see his children very often once he was traveling farther and farther west and away from them.

Miriam and Leslie shed a few tears as the blue Oldsmobile rolled out of the driveway, heading toward Cleveland. Hektor's thoughts were: *Go west, young man. Go west!* He was glad they were driving. He admired the wide-open country as it passed them by.

Lew had the car radio on. No matter what station they turned to, sooner or later the song of the moment, "Stranger on the Shore," would play.

Hektor was thinking about Sheila. They had met as strangers on the shores of the Biltmore bar. The night to remember had turned into a special relationship. Hektor felt good about the sex both he and Sheila had craved and enjoyed. It was a part of his life that had gone so far astray. He thought about Doretta and what he had done to her. *How could I sacrifice that heartfelt relationship to marry a tramp like Georgia?* His heart and mind were still in a constant turmoil. He often wondered what had happened to Doretta. Having been rejected by Georgia and the various exposures to homosexuality along his life's journey, Hektor sometimes questioned his own sexuality. Having found complete relief in the arms of Sheila allowed him to reaffirm the belief that he thoroughly enjoyed being with women.

Lew interrupted his mental meandering. "What do you think of staying in Jamestown overnight? It won't be too bad a drive tomorrow morning. That way, we'll miss the rush-hour traffic when we get to Cleveland."

"Whatever you want to do is fine with me. You are the driver. If you've had enough, Jamestown it is. I'll keep an eye open for an appealing motel. I can't see you driving all the way. We are not expected in Mayfield Heights until early Wednesday morning anyway."

They stayed at a relatively new motel. The price was right and certainly within their per diem. They got a room with two double beds. Separate rooms were a waste of money. Hektor was certain Lew wasn't gay. Lew thought they ought to have a good steak dinner; so steaks it was. When they returned to the motel, Hektor noticed that Lew was suffering with indigestion.

"What's wrong with you? Are you not feeling well? Say something. You are not choking, Lew, are you?"

"No, it's nothing like that. I suffer with a lot of gas. That's why I take these pills. Don't worry. I'll be fine. I'll get you to Cleveland for sure."

He took some of the little pink suckers, which seemed to alleviate the discomfort. After Lew went to bed, Hektor scribbled down a few notes pertaining to his observations of their travels. It was a unique experience for him to see the countryside, heading west for the very first time. Hektor was impressed with the abundance of space between the smaller and larger towns as they left the densely populated areas of the East. He loved seeing the immensity of blue sky covering huge stretches of open land. The millions of black-eyed Susans nodding in the breeze were entertaining.

The rest of the trip to Cleveland was uneventful. The apartment in Shaker Heights, arranged for by the staff of International Stores, was sufficient in size, clean, and comfortable.

Early the next morning, they drove up Gates Mills Boulevard and headed to the new facility built by Tip-Top Stores in Mayfield Heights. It was a sunny summer morning. Hektor could not get over the huge homes along the broad boulevard. They were beautifully landscaped, and the immaculate lawns were kept green by hundreds of sprinklers, giving the appearance of graceful fountains along the way. Marveling at the lush lawns, he was taken back to his early days in the United States when he watered the gardens for the Carolinas. Much water had passed under the bridge since those adventures when he first lived in Birchtown.

Upon their arrival at the store, Lew and Hektor met Edward

Mortimer, Ida Lupine, and Georgette Plutino, the management crew in charge of setting up new Tip-Top Stores mushrooming all over the East and Midwest. Currently, three new stores were slated to open simultaneously in the Cleveland metropolitan area. Lew and Hektor were assigned to the Mayfield facility. Lew would coordinate Women's and Children's Wear, Hektor was in charge of the Men's and Boys Departments. By now, they were used to the long hours of being on their feet.

It was mid-August when Lew received a telephone call from Miriam, letting him know she needed surgery immediately. She was to undergo a radical hysterectomy. Lew was given permission to fly to New York to be with his wife before, during, and after the emergency procedure. He planned to drive himself to the airport and park the car in the garage for the days he would be gone. Hektor shook Lew's hand.

"Convey my best wishes for a speedy recovery to Miriam. Say *hi* to Leslie when you see her. Have a good and timely flight. See you when you get back. I'll keep an eye on your crew."

"Thanks for everything, Hektor. You are OK! See you real soon."

Hektor wanted to give Lew a friendly hug but opted against it. He didn't know what possessed him to show his caring for his roommate. *He wasn't saying goodbye forever. Lew was just leaving for a few days.* Hektor turned away from Lew and took off with his colleague, Sal, who was now residing in an adjacent apartment at the motel. They had left at seven thirty that morning. Miriam's surgery was scheduled for the following day.

After another full day at the store, Sal dropped Hektor off at his and Lew's apartment at close to eleven o'clock.

"Until tomorrow, Hektor. I'm starved. I'll grab a bite at one of the nearby fast-food joints."

"Enjoy! I can't believe you can eat another meal this late in the day. See you in the morning."

Hektor walked over to the bank of locked mailboxes. He thought he wasn't seeing right. There was Lew's blue Oldsmobile parked outside their apartment. Hektor quickly reached for the mail and headed straight for their place. His heart rate had slightly increased as soon as he spotted the car. He knew something had gone awry.

He turned the key with his left hand and pushed the door open with his right elbow, trying not to drop anything from his hands. He switched on the living room lights. There was Lew in front of him, lying face up in the middle of the floor. Lew's right hand was clutching his heart area; in his left, he held a roll of Tums; some of them had spilled on the carpeting. His vacant eyes were wide open, staring back at Hektor.

He touched Lew's forehead. "My God, you are as cold as ice." As the words escaped Hektor's lips, he realized immediately Lew was dead. *He must have died hours ago.* His first call was to Ed Mortimer.

"Don't touch anything, and don't try to move Lew. Call the Shaker Heights police. Georgette, Ida, and I will be over right away. If you feel up to it, call Lew's wife. It's already past midnight in New York."

Hektor made the calls in the order Ed Mortimer suggested. His phone call to Miriam was the most difficult thing he had to do. He let the phone ring for a long time. On the tenth ring, a strange voice answered the phone.

"Who is this calling?" said a woman, having that raspy and geriatric inflection and who was obviously awakened from deep sleep; she sounded most annoyed.

"This is Hektor Birken calling from Cleveland."

"Who did you say you are?" she asked, seeming alarmed.

"I said this is Hektor Birken. I'm Lew's roommate in Cleveland."

"This is Maryanne. I am Miriam's sister. My husband, Irwin, and I came to be with her. She had to have her surgery early yesterday morning. She was losing too much blood. They couldn't delay the operation any longer. Leslie stayed with her at the hospital. Miriam is still heavily sedated. She doesn't know about Lew's non-arrival at

New York International Airport. When my husband checked with the airline, he learned that most flights were rerouted because of the terrible storms. United Airlines told him Lew's flight was diverted to Atlanta. We thought it was strange he didn't call from his hotel. Perhaps he couldn't get through on the phone; too many people were trying to connect with others. No one answered when we tried calling the store, as well as your apartment. We went to bed, totally exhausted. Earlier this morning, we expected Lew to arrive from Atlanta. We still don't understand why he didn't get in touch with any of us when he was delayed. Why are you calling us in the middle of the night?"

Hektor exhaled. No way was he going to interrupt that lady's outpouring. He was stalling for time. *What would be the best way of breaking the bad news to Miriam's sister?* By now, Irwin had picked up an extension. Hektor felt relieved. He didn't have to share his bad tidings with Miriam directly. Irwin and Maryanne would have to inform Miriam of what had happened to Lew. Hektor took a deep breath.

"Ma'am…sir, I have sad news for you. Lew never got to the airport. When I arrived home from the store a few minutes ago, I found Lew lying on the floor in our apartment. He was dead."

Both Maryanne and Irwin spoke in one voice. "*Oy gevalt*; oh my God, I can't believe this."

"I'm so sad to give you this terribly disturbing news. The chief of operations and the police are on their way now. It looks to me like Lew had a massive heart attack. I will call you back as soon as I know more. I am sure there will be an inquiry since I was the last person to see Lew this morning at seven thirty."

"Whatever you do, don't let them perform an autopsy; it's against Lew's religion. We will wait to hear from someone there."

He heard the click of the phone and realized the connection to Westchester County was gone. As he hung up, there was a loud knock at the door. Three policemen charged in as he opened the door. He didn't have to show them the body. Lew was still in plain view, lying as Hektor had discovered him a few minutes earlier. They checked for a pulse. By the stiffness of Lew's body, evidence of rigor mortis, they knew immediately he had been dead for many hours.

"Are you the person who found him? When did you see him last? Did you touch him or move him?"

"He was to fly to New York earlier to be with his wife. She was having major surgery tomorrow. I saw him last at seven thirty this morning. I found him lying where he is when I returned from work shortly before eleven tonight. Yes, I did touch his forehead. From the looks of things and as cold as he felt, I realized he was dead."

Just then, Ed Mortimer and his assistants walked in.

"There will have to be an inquiry," one of the cops said, greeting the new arrivals.

"I spoke with Mr. Simons's sister- and brother-in-law a few minutes ago. His wife had emergency surgery early this morning. She is still heavily sedated. They told me he is not to be subjected to an autopsy. Lew was a practicing Jew. An autopsy is a violation of the body in his religion."

The phone rang. It was Maryanne and Irwin, calling back from New York.

"Sergeant Pfister, Cleveland Police, speaking. Yes, we have conducted a preliminary examination. It appears Mr. Simons died of a major heart attack. Under the circumstances, an autopsy must be conducted. An inquiry will be held to rule out homicide. We will proceed as rapidly as possible and have the body turned over to the family promptly. We realize the deceased is to be buried within twenty-four hours. Did you say you wish to speak with Mr. Birken? Here he is."

"Mr. Birken, may I call you Hektor?"

"Yes, certainly."

"Irwin and I believe you should accompany Lew's body to New

York when they release it. We realize there is no choice in the matter pertaining to the autopsy."

Hektor turned to his supervisor. "Ed, will you get in touch with company headquarters first thing in the morning and arrange for me to fly back to New York with Lew's body? Lew's sister-in-law thinks that Lew's wife would want to hear the whole sad story from me in person."

"Yes. That won't be a problem at all."

"Maryanne, I will definitely accompany Lew on his final journey home. As soon as I know any details, I'll get back to you. Be strong when you speak with Miriam and Leslie. I need to hang up. The police are ready to proceed with their interrogation."

"Please show us where you keep any medications," said Sergeant Pfister. "We have already taken samples of any food items in the refrigerator. Also, we need to confiscate any open bottles of liquor and/or other beverages."

"Wait a minute—before you take our J&B, I want to pour myself a drink. Believe me, I will need it if I want to catch any sleep after you are finished with me."

They put Lew in a body bag and were taking him out the door as Hektor took his first sip from a water glass filled with scotch. A different cop repeated the same questions Hektor had answered when they first arrived on the scene. Noting there were no changes in Hektor's responses, they were ready to depart.

"Don't leave the motel until Mr. Simons's cause of death is con-firmed by the coroner. Do you understand my instructions?"

"Yes, sir." Hektor almost felt like clicking his heels. *Does that cop believe I'm stupid or something?*

Georgette thought Hektor needed some Valium.

"Are you crazy? Are you trying to kill him as well? Just look how much of the scotch he guzzled down already!" intervened Ida.

"Oh, my God, I didn't even think about that. Good thing someone is paying attention to what's happening!"

Ed Mortimer got Hektor's attention. "Call me as soon as you hear from the coroner's office. It makes no difference what time of night it might be. I have an idea you will hear relatively soon since they are aware of the twenty-four-hour stipulation. Let's go, Ida and Georgette. Sal, I would appreciate your staying with Hektor for the night."

Georgette gave Hektor a motherly hug before she walked out of the apartment. With that, all cleared out except Sal.

"Isn't that the shits? I wish I'd filled my glass. I think I'll run next door and fetch myself a nightcap. The poor sucker never had a chance. I just can't forget that frightened expression on his face. How awful to die that way—all alone. I don't envy you the trip to New York. I hope her sister will be the one breaking the sad news to Lew's wife and daughter."

Hektor agreed with Sal; the expression on Lew's face was nightmarish. He almost didn't want to fall asleep. He was afraid he would relive the last couple of hours again and again. He passed out on the sofa in the living room. The phone awakened him at five thirty in the morning.

"Mr. Birken, this is the coroner's office. Your roommate's death was indeed the result of a massive coronary. We issued a death certificate stipulating to the cause. You are free to go. We understand Mr. Mortimer made tentative arrangements for Mr. Simons's body to be flown to New York posthaste. Have him get in touch with us ASAP regarding the arrangements."

Hektor replaced the receiver and then called Ed. "I just got the word from the coroner; it was a heart attack that took Lew. I am free to travel."

"I have been on the horn with United and the funeral parlor in Shaker Heights. They will move Lew's body in a plain pine box, as his sister-in-law requested. Be ready on a moment's notice. As soon as they have picked up the body, they will call you and take you directly to the airport. You and Lew's body will arrive on the same flight he was supposed to be on yesterday. Lew's daughter and her aunt and uncle are meeting you with a hearse at the airport. His body will be taken directly to Holy Sepulcher Cemetery in New Rochelle. If all goes as planned, he will be committed to the ground before the sun sets. The family plans a memorial service at a later date, when Miriam Simons has recovered from her surgery."

"Thanks, Ed, for making all the arrangements. Do me a favor and give a quick call to Lew's sister-in-law. Confirm what we learned from the police and what will need to happen at the airport. I'll call you tonight from New York."

Hektor hung up. He packed a small valise for the sad journey. Sal Schwartz would be visiting his own family in ten days. He offered to drive Lew's car and belongings back East.

The hearse pulled up in front of the apartment shortly before nine. Hektor was glad Ed made all the arrangements. The last twenty-four hours had been a nightmare. He glanced only briefly into the back of the hearse. "They were serious about just a simple pine box," Hektor commented to the driver. "You got it," was his reply.

By ten fifteen, Hektor and Lew's body were airborne. The pilot announced the plane would arrive on time. Hektor was deep in thought. He did not realize how fast the time had passed. He wondered about his own life and its many ups and downs. He thought about Doretta and Sheila and even Georgia. *Perhaps I should be more forgiving. Maybe there is a remote chance Georgia and I could make a go of it. Should I give her a call while in New York and share the events of the last day?* No matter how he wished to be euphemistic during the present attack of sentimentality, he could not bring himself to reverse the steps he had taken.

Leslie Simons, her aunt and uncle, and Rabbi Moyem met Hektor at the plane. The simple pine coffin was placed in the hearse. The motorcade proceeded to New Rochelle for the burial. Hektor stood in the background and observed the rabbi performing the keriah. He made a small rip in the blouses or shirts of family members. Leslie said the Mourner's Kaddish for her father. There were neither flowers nor music during the graveside service. The rabbi conducted the rite in Hebrew. Leslie delivered a brief eulogy, a traumatic experience for someone so young. The ceremony was over quickly. Everyone walked back to the limousine in total silence. Now they had to face Miriam at the hospital.

Leslie, Maryanne, and Irwin had shared their grief with Miriam earlier. Miriam was lying in bed and appeared to be coherent when Hektor walked into the room. She tried raising her arms as high as she could, wanting to embrace the messenger. Hektor bent down, allowing Miriam to put her arms around him. As she did, she spoke softly into Hektor's ear.

"Thank you for bringing my Lew home." Nothing else was said for what seemed an eternity. Hektor couldn't help shedding tears in his grief for Miriam and his dead colleague. Eventually, Miriam was ready to talk about the events that had transpired.

Leslie spoke for her family. "Thank you for bringing my father home. Thank you for being there and respecting our wishes." Even the rabbi had accepted that an autopsy had to be performed.

Hektor kissed Miriam on her forehead before she drifted off in response to a sedative. She was in terrible pain. Hektor spent the evening in the company of Lew's family and friends. There were many sitting Shiva at the house in Westchester. All mirrors were covered with black cloth. Irwin and other males who were part of the immediate family hadn't shaved. Those who were present for the first meal after the funeral service ate hard-boiled eggs and round pieces of matzo.

Irwin explained, "It is customary during Shiva to serve round foods such as eggs, symbols of eternal life and its cyclical nature."

Hektor took a cab to his hotel near the airport. While he hated to depart, he believed it was most appropriate to leave the family to mourn in private. He called Ed Mortimer, indicating he would return to Cleveland the next day. Hektor went to the bar and ordered a double-scotch on the rocks. He couldn't help thinking of Harry, but no way was he going to dilute the scotch with milk. By the time he retired to his room, Hektor had decided against calling Georgia. He wished Sheila was with him. He yearned for an affirmation of life.

Ed Mortimer picked him up at the airport. Hektor was surprised to see the chief of operations chauffeuring him to his motel.

"You probably are wondering why Ida or Georgette didn't pick you up," Ed said. "It was reported to me that you and Georgette were a bit too friendly with each other. In view of that and the tragic episode with Lew, I made an executive decision. I am transferring you to operations in Detroit, with the intent of keeping you on staff at the Schoolcraft store. The store is slated for opening in early November. You will be housed at a motel nearby. Your contract with us will remain in force, and expenses will be reimbursed on a per diem basis. Do you have any questions?"

"Whoa! You sure know how to hurt a guy! I'm not sure where you got this notion about Georgette and me. We just became good friends. Nothing illicit transpired between us. I know she is happily married. Did someone interpret our friendly hugs as a sexual expression on my part? I don't believe what I am hearing. However, under the circumstances, I accept your recommendation for my transfer to Detroit. Perhaps a change of scenery after Lew's untimely death and the events that ensued is a good idea. When do you expect me to leave for Detroit?"

"Pack your things tonight. I'll take you to the airport tomorrow. I'll inform the staff that the transfer was recommended by company headquarters because of what happened to Lew. Happy packing; I'll be here at one thirty in the afternoon."

There wasn't that much to pack for himself or Lew. *I still can't believe it; they are giving me the bum's rush.* Hektor didn't like that he wasn't allowed to say goodbye to his colleagues at the Cleveland store. He believed he didn't deserve to be treated like a pariah.

The plane for Detroit took off on time; it was a short flight. Robert Mitchell, the designated store manager for the Schoolcraft store, met Hektor at Metropolitan Airport. He was an affable fellow, perhaps ten years older than Hektor, and a long-time employee of International Stores. Bob had earned his promotion to store manager by coming up through the ranks.

"I am taking you directly to the Garden Motel. That's where all the staff is being housed until the store opens in a few weeks. It's close to the store and excellent restaurants. If you are staying on with us here in Detroit, you'll have to find your own housing within two weeks after the grand opening. At that time, your per diem arrangement will cease. Henceforth, you will be paid the salary stated in your original contract. I heard of the ordeal you encountered in Cleveland. I hope this will be a more positive and rewarding experience. Welcome to Detroit. Perhaps we can have dinner later and chat a bit about my ideas for running a discount store."

"That will be fine, Bob. Give me a chance to get settled. How about dinner at six o'clock?"

"I'll meet you in the lobby. I think you will like Topinka's

Country House. They serve great steaks. I'm a meat-and-potatoes man myself. How about you?"

"I like a good steak here and there but enjoy almost any kind of food."

Hektor thought he would say no more. He didn't believe in blowing his daily allowance on big steak dinners and drinks every night. However, this night he felt like celebrating the exodus from New York. Perhaps, at last, he had arrived in the land of milk and honey. Maybe his seven lean years were about to be over.

Chapter 33

THE three new Tip-Top Stores opened simultaneously during the last week in October 1962. The crowds were horrendous, and business was brisk. The public response to the venture in shopping was excellent. Anticipating his move to a more permanent address, Hektor started to read the rooms-for-rent columns in the Detroit newspapers.

He investigated a few of the available possibilities and came across a location that was a few miles from the store. Checking out the neighborhood, Hektor discovered the house was located at the dead end of a quiet street. The bare branches of huge old elm trees arched toward the sky, holding the promise of shade and coolness during the heat of future summers. When Hektor called to make an appointment, an elderly person answered the phone. The room was still available, and Hektor decided to check it out.

Agnes, a tiny old lady, answered the door. "Please come in. This is my husband, Walter. His speech and his gait have been slightly affected by a recent stroke. These days, we stay on the first floor. Walter can no longer maneuver the stairs. It's for this reason I can rent two rooms. I won't have more than two gentlemen at a time. For now, it would be just you using the upstairs. You would have to share the large bathroom with someone if I find another suitable renter. Go on and have a look."

Hektor noted that the house was spotless; the furnishings were mostly antiques. The woodwork throughout the house was marked by quality workmanship and obviously received excellent care. He called down to Agnes.

"Do I have a choice of the two rooms? I like the one toward the front of the house. It's brighter because of the two windows."

"It makes no difference to us. If you like it, it's yours. I made some tea. Come downstairs, and we can talk about the arrangements."

Hektor felt the smoothness of the banister as he made his way down to the living room. The fireplace took the chill off the air. Walter sat in a comfortable chair close to the fire. Pine cones were crackling in the fireplace, and the pleasant scent of evergreen hung in the air. Agnes served tea in pretty china cups and talked continually.

"There is a large refrigerator in the kitchen, actually much too large for us two old folks. We have no problem with you keeping something in the fridge for breakfast and lunch. Also, you may use my laundry facilities downstairs. I have a new Maytag washer and dryer. You may use a fresh towel every day, and I will change your bed linens twice a week. Right now, I am planning to charge fifteen dollars per week. If this isn't too much, we would love to have you. Of course, we frown on excessive drinking, loud music, and womenfolk taken upstairs. You understand, you may have women visit you in our living room, but I would not like women staying with you overnight."

Hektor got the message loud and clear. With those important matters settled, he decided to take the room. If he found the time to entertain a serious relationship, he would be able to make other arrangements. There always was the Garden Motel. As soon as things calmed down at the store after the grand opening, Hektor made the transfer to Agnes and Walter's home.

Although easily within walking distance to a convenient bus,

Hektor resolved the time had come for him to get a driver's license and a car. He looked in the Yellow Pages and found a driving school close to the store on Telegraph Road.

"How long will it take for you to teach a twenty-eight-year-old male how to drive? I want to do it as fast as possible. I would prefer to have lessons in the afternoon on Mondays, Tuesdays, and Wednesdays."

"When do you want to start? This Monday afternoon? If you are available on all three days for two to three hours, I could arrange for your driver's test on Thursday morning. How does that sound?"

"I'll see you in the parking lot of the new Tip-Top Store on Telegraph and Schoolcraft at one thirty this coming Monday. I need to be back by five o'clock to help with the changeover for the evening cashiers."

He had his three days of lessons, passed the driving test, and received his license on Thursday morning. He bought his first car, an ugly bluish-green 1963 Ford Falcon, on Friday night. The car was new, and the price was right. He got insurance and was thrilled to be totally independent. On Monday morning on his way to the store, he had his first accident. Hektor learned the most important driving lesson that day—one never pulls out into traffic unless one sees for oneself that the coast is clear.

Agnes introduced Hektor to her bachelor nephew, Robert Henkel. Bob and Hektor were close in age with similar interests. Bob held an excellent position with the Ford Motor Company. Once they discovered their likes and dislikes, they went out to dinner or caught a movie now and then or stopped after work at a bar to have a drink. Nothing was ever done to excess.

After Thanksgiving, the store made such hefty demands on Hektor's schedule he had absolutely no time for any socializing. There were no days off. As management, he was expected to be on board from eight in the morning until eleven at night, every day of the week.

Chapter 34

WITH the Christmas rush behind him, Hektor realized it was high time to see his family in Europe. He discussed the matter with Bob Mitchell. He and the district manager determined that Hektor should plan his trip for three weeks, starting in early February. In view of his performance since he joined International Stores and the trauma experienced in Cleveland, they believed he was ready for a change of scenery. His superiors were aware of the fact that Hektor was seriously considering a position with another company. International Stores didn't want to lose Hektor after investing heavily in his training and indoctrination.

In her Christmas letter, Mother Birken volunteered Doretta's current address. She was living and working in Zurich, Switzerland. Hektor contacted her without telling his mother and kept his impending journey a total secret.

When Hektor wrote to Doretta, he didn't hide behind platitudes, lame excuses, or justifications for his deplorable actions; he bared his soul. Hektor shared with her every sordid detail of his miserable years since he'd broken off their engagement seven years earlier.

"I need to speak with you in person. I have to look into your eyes and seek your forgiveness, if you can forgive this miserable bastard.

I want to wish you well in whatever lies in your future. I just cannot do it in a letter or over the phone. I must see you. I must be able to touch you!"

Doretta was prompt in her response. She was forgiving and agreeable to meet with him. Only two people were informed of his travel plans: Doretta and Greta Beerenbaum. Doretta would pick him up at the Zurich airport and Greta at the airport in Cologne.

⋈

Cocktails were served as soon as the plane was over international waters. Flying by jet was a brand-new experience for Hektor. He was amazed by the service provided. The food was excellent and abundant. Cigarettes and alcoholic beverages were freely offered repeatedly. He smoked some but was determined to get a good night's sleep before arriving in Europe after a relatively short night; the double-martinis had done their trick.

He awoke as the captain announced they were approaching Ireland. It was fascinating to observe from almost forty thousand feet how far streetlights could be seen as they clearly outlined boulevards and entire villages and cities. For the first time, Hektor truly understood the importance of the total blackouts mandated during the war.

His plane landed at Zurich International Airport early in the morning. The airport was heavily shrouded in fog, almost preventing the landing of the Suisse Air flight. Hektor couldn't believe the ease with which he was able to enter a foreign country with his American passport. Passport control was almost a joke. All the inspector saw was the navy-blue cover with its gold inscription, and he waved him on. The next guy just flipped the thing open to one of the blank visa pages and affixed the stamp that indicated port of entry. That was it—no fuss, no muss, no questions, and no demands for declarations.

Hektor peered in the direction of people obviously waiting for the arrival of friends or family. As much as he searched, he could not spot Doretta's face. He expected her to have changed but not to the degree that he wouldn't recognize her. As he walked past the cordon of greeters, he spotted a man about his own age, holding a sign that read "Hektor Birken." The gentleman, tanned and olive-complexioned, looked exotic—Spanish or South American, anything but German or Swiss.

Hektor walked over to him. "Are you looking for me? I am Hektor Birken."

The greeter stuck out his hand, addressing Hektor in part German and part English. "*Mein Freund*, Doretta Osram—she sick. She sent *mich* to airport—pick you here. *Komm* with mich to mein auto."

Hektor understood what the man was trying to say and followed him to his car.

"Oh, me sorry. Me forget tell you mine name. I'm Fernando de Lopez."

"Nice to meet you, Fernando. I'm so glad you could help Doretta and fetch me at the airport."

They got into his sporty Mercedes cabriolet and made a fast getaway. Fifteen minutes later, they pulled up in front of an apartment building in a relatively well-preserved but old section of Zurich. Fernando parked the car half on the road and half on the sidewalk, as everyone else did. He pulled out his keys and rang the doorbell, letting Doretta know they were on their way up to the fifth floor of the building. There was no elevator.

Huffing and puffing, they arrived at their destination. Doretta greeted them at the door. She was enormous in size and looked like she was ready to deliver her baby any second. Doretta gave Fernando a quick kiss on the lips and walked over to Hektor, giving him a friendly and welcoming hug.

"How nice of you to come to see me. You must excuse my appearance. Fernando and I are expecting our first child any day now. In view of all the steps in our building, we opted for him to meet you at the airport. Come in; we have a light champagne breakfast prepared for your arrival."

"You didn't have to go to that much trouble for me. I was a bit worried when Fernando told me you were *sick*. You are not sick; you're having a baby and look radiant. I'm so pleased that you agreed to see me."

"You don't need to feel embarrassed about anything. I forgave you for what you did many years ago. We just were not meant for each other; evidently, neither were you and Georgia. I hope someday you will meet the right person. You deserve to be happy."

"Again, thank you for seeing me. You and Fernando are truly kind."

"I made some strong coffee for you men; I'll have some pale tea. Please have some of the food I prepared. You notice from my ring"—she was wearing a simple gold band on her left ring finger—"that Fernando and I are not married yet. He will finish his studies at the university shortly. We hope his mother will finally give us her blessing to be married once we arrive in Santiago. My first baby will most likely be born in Switzerland. He or she will always be considered a citizen of this country, no matter where we ultimately live."

"Fernando, does your mother not wish for you to be married to Doretta for religious reasons? I don't quite understand."

"No, no. It's not religion. Doretta, *sprech mit* Hektor. Es easy for *Dich* in Deutsch *und* Englisch. I'm not very good in Sprachen anders als Spanisch." ["Doretta, speak to Hektor. It's easy for you in German and English. I'm not any good in languages other than Spanish.]

"Let me explain. I don't believe it's for religious reasons, although that might enter into the picture. Fernando is humble and feels awkward explaining to people why his family is rejecting me. They are from the old Spanish aristocracy and are very wealthy people. They expected him to marry a Chilean woman who met with their approval. He has lived in Switzerland for several years and met me three years ago. When he informed his parents he would be returning to Chile with a German wife, his family threatened to disown and disinherit him. Perhaps now that the birth of their first grandchild is imminent, his parents, especially his mother, may be more agreeable to our union. At least Fernando and I hope so. We are flying to Santiago shortly after the baby is born."

"Nothing is ever easy, is it?" said Hektor.

Doretta knew to what Hektor was referring. She had clued Fernando in on some things but not everything. When Doretta wanted to lie down for a while, Fernando took Hektor for a spin in his spiffy convertible to show him some of the sites of Zurich. The city was not particularly pretty in its mantle of gray on gray. Before they headed back to the apartment, they stopped at a stand-up café and ate a bratwurst on a bun.

"Boy, this tastes great," Hektor said. "Haven't had one of these wonderful morsels on a crusty roll in years. I forgot how good they are. Thanks for stopping, Fernando. While we have a few minutes by ourselves, let me say something to you. I hope you will understand me and take what I'm about to tell you in the right way. I'm sure you have discovered that Doretta is a very special young woman. If I would have had half a brain, she would be living with me in the States, perhaps even carrying my child instead of yours. It was one of the biggest mistakes I made in my life to sacrifice my love for Doretta for a tramp like my former wife, Georgia. Doretta deserved better than that. You are a fortunate man. Treasure her and love her the way she deserves to be loved." He gave Fernando a hug. Tears streamed down Hektor's face.

At the apartment, Doretta was busy, in spite of her advanced stage of pregnancy. She prepared a typical Swiss fondue, pulling out all the stops. She thought it would make a great meal, allowing them to share a national tradition while discussing personal concerns. Hektor was thankful he could see Doretta before she left Europe. The evening went by all too quickly. While Doretta refrained from drinking, they all had a joyous time of togetherness. Hektor stayed with them that evening. That way, no one had to be concerned about driving after drinking.

As Fernando was getting ready to take Hektor to the airport for his flight to Cologne, Doretta walked over to Hektor to say her goodbyes. She put her long, slender arms around his neck and kissed him on his forehead.

"Be well, my friend. I wish you much happiness. Have no regrets. What's done is done. Wish me the same. I hope all of us will be allowed to find happiness and joy in the New World. I know we will be hemispheres apart, but I will always remember you as a very special person. Be safe in your travels."

She had moved him to tears and left him speechless. He tried hiding his emotions as he hugged her affectionately. Not wearing a tie, it was easy for Hektor to grasp Greta's silver Madonna. Gently, he retrieved his treasured talisman. He took Doretta's hands, allowing them to make contact with his protector, and held her hands close to his chest. He looked into Doretta and Fernando's eyes. "Be blessed, and be safe—all of you!"

It would be the last time they would see each other. Worse, they never heard from one another again. On that cold and foggy morning in Zurich in February 1963, Hektor, Doretta, and Fernando didn't realize what the fates had in store for them.

)(

Greta Beerenbaum met Hektor at the airport in Cologne. It was a Saturday. He knew how much both of his parents were involved in their business. Aside from wanting to totally surprise his parents, imposing on them in any way was the furthest thing from his mind. Albert was still working for his father. They would all be busy in the butcher market; their customers were shopping for Sunday meals. Hektor had made up his mind. He would surprise them after business hours.

Greta was driving her new deep-red Mercedes convertible. They pulled into the driveway on Weidenweg less than forty minutes after leaving the airport.

"Let me fix you a drink. What would you like? You still don't like beer, right? How about a glass of champagne or a nice wine?"

"Let's celebrate. Champagne sounds great. Please let me help you." The pop of the cork was perfect. He poured Greta's glass first. "Here's to Kurt. I'm so sorry he is no longer with us."

Their eyes shone with sadness.

"I still don't believe you are actually sitting in my living room. Your mother will have a stroke when you call later. She'll probably be angry with me for not letting her know you were coming. I respected your wishes. I didn't even tell Judith or Nicklaus. Your parents and your brother were up here a few times over the last months. We discussed the possibility of their opening a branch of their butcher shop here. The market would be where my parents had their apartment. I believe they would do well here. It would give me a good tenant and some additional income from space now standing vacant."

"I haven't heard a word about it. I wonder if this will be a way for Albert and Margarethe to get into their own business. Have they said anything about it?"

"Not to my knowledge. It sounded to me like your mother would like to run this branch. She believes she could do a great job with the affluent clientele in this neighborhood."

"How do you feel about having my mother this close to you? I've often told you how jealous she is of my special relationship with all of you. Personally, I consider her attitude toward you completely out of line and immature. No matter what happens, it will never change how I feel about you and your family."

"I know that. I'm of the same opinion. Actually, I had hoped it would be Margarethe and Albert running the branch. I feel for Margarethe and the situation in which she found herself. That has to be tough on those kids. Well, let's see how things work out. I didn't want Judith and Nicklaus to accidentally spoil your surprise visit during one of those meetings, so I thought it was better not to let them know. You realize how Judith feels about you. She has had a crush on you forever and would have spoiled your surprise for sure. You won't believe how grown up she's become since you last saw her.

"She is a typical sixteen-year-old and full of ideas, mostly concerning boys. They will be here shortly—Judith from school and Nicklaus after the final deliveries. He and our old driver work well as a team. I usually don't see customers on Saturday and Sunday anymore. I spend much time in the business Monday through Friday. I took over many of Kurt's PR responsibilities. Nicklaus is better with other aspects of the enterprise."

Judith was the first to see Hektor. "Oh, my God! Nicklaus, you won't believe who's sitting in our living room!" She ran over to Hektor and hugged and kissed him fiercely. Judith was full of youthful exuberance; she almost took his breath away.

Judith had become a beautiful girl but was much too young for him. Thirteen years was a significant age difference, although not quite as noticeable as it had been seven years earlier. Judith no longer was a child; she was a young lady with a womanly figure. Hektor decided not to touch this one under any circumstances. The family relationship was too precious to spoil—ever.

He and Nicklaus gave each other a brotherly welcoming hug.

"Let me look at you!" Nicklaus said. "You don't look quite as skinny as you did seven years ago. They must feed you over there after all. Just wait until your mother gets hold of you. She'll make sure you'll get some more meat on you. You don't look like a typical German." He slapped his right upper thigh. "Well, I'll be damned. How could you do this to all of us, pulling such a stunt?"

"I thought it might liven things up a bit. You know me; I love nothing better than surprises. I can't wait to get on the phone and call my folks."

Nick felt he needed to be blunt. "You realize Margarethe and

Albert no longer live with your folks or with her family. They finally got their own apartment. It was high time. I understand they were getting on each other's nerves. Your sister-in-law isn't working for your parents these days. She and your mother had a major falling out. Your mother referred to your nephew just once too often as the 'Adenauer bastard,' making reference to the fact that little Albert is being raised Catholic. Margarethe has gone back to her former trade. She is altering clothes for some of the biggest department stores in town. This way, she can stay home and take care of her child and earn money when it is convenient. I don't know why I am telling you this. It can't be news to you."

"I'm completely in the dark on that one. Like you and your mother, I feel for Margarethe. That is no way to treat her or the boy. It's outrageous! If this arrangement comes to pass, it would be great if Albert and Margarethe were given half a chance at being on their own. Who knows? Under the circumstances, I have an idea it will be an extremely exciting three weeks."

"I didn't want to burst your bubble, but I believe my forewarning was merited. At least you will be somewhat prepared for what is waiting for you once you get home. You probably wonder how I know all this stuff. I bowl with Albert twice a month."

⚭

After seven o'clock, Hektor picked up the phone and dialed his parents' number.

"Birken Butchery," was his mother's response.

"Hallo, this is Hektor calling. How are you? What are you doing? Are you very busy tonight?"

"Why are you asking such silly questions? This is costing you a lot of money."

"For once, Mom, let's not worry about the money. If you are not too busy, maybe you would like some company?"

There was momentary hesitation in her response. "What do you mean?"

"How about if I come over tonight? Like maybe in half an hour?"

"My God, Alex! It's Hektor. He's in Germany. He must be in Essen. He says he will be here in a few minutes." She started to cry and then caught herself. "The table will be set when you get here. We were just ready to have our evening meal. Your brother has gone home to his family. It's just your dad and I."

"Well, that will be fine. I'll be there shortly."

Greta could hear and see how he had surprised his parents. She knew how she would have reacted, had she not known in advance he would be coming home after seven long years in a distant land. "Let's get you there," she said when he was off the phone. "They'll be anxious. There will be plenty of time for us to catch up on what's happening here."

Soon, they were on their way. Greta kissed him good night when she left him in front of the house on Kupferstrasse. She knew it was best not to wait around. She and Hektor's mother had learned to be civil to each other, but there never was any feeling of friendship. Hektor rang the doorbell, and he could hear someone rushing to open the door.

"*Willkommen, willkommen.* Take off your coat and sit right down. Your father is just getting your favorite kind of wieners from the cooling house. Let me look at you. I don't like that severe haircut. You look like some American soldier, but at least you are not as skinny as you were the last time. I can tell you are getting older. The hard times do show around your eyes."

"Mother, stop it. I am not looking older. I am twenty-nine years old."

"As if I didn't know. Remember, I gave birth to you." She hugged him then and gave him a big, wet smacker. "Happy birthday, even belatedly. Why didn't you come home for your birthday? It would have been fun to celebrate it here for once."

"Mother, I do have a job. I couldn't leave until the seventh of February. The other thing I did was to stop in Zurich before I flew to Cologne. I saw Doretta and her future husband. She is expecting his baby any moment. Doretta and her family will be living in Santiago, Chile, after the child is born. They hope to be married soon after they arrive in Santiago."

"Why so far away? Her mother will be sad too. I hope she'll find happiness at last. She is such a nice girl. You erred by not marrying her to begin with."

"I hate to say it, Mom. You are absolutely right and figured out Georgia long before I did. I was a damn fool for deserting Doretta and marrying Georgia. But that is all in the past. Please, let's not rehash it tonight. Let's enjoy the moment and be positive about the future. I came home to forget *sad*. I want to remember happy times when I return to the States in three weeks.

"Before you ask if I will get married again, I can't tell you right now, but it will be a cold day in hell if I do. For now, I'm footloose and fancy-free. I enjoy being with an Australian girl I met in New York. She flies for Braniff. I look forward to being with her whenever business takes me to New York and she is in town. We might even arrange a tryst wherever. I'm not saying I love this woman; we just enjoy each other in every respect. It's a lot better than living like a monk."

"I don't like you talking this way; it's blasphemous."

"Don't get on that self-righteous, religious, and puritanical horse with me and especially not on my first night home after being gone for all these years. I was deprived of a normal life for a long time and found happiness and self-respect in my relationship with this woman."

His mother shut up as his father walked into the room. She hadn't asked yet who had picked him up at the airport.

Hektor jumped out of the overstuffed chair and gave his father a great big hug. Both had tears in their eyes.

"How wonderful to have you home. Sit down, son. You need some food between your ribs. I know you like these. Good thing we didn't sell them all." He was delighted to see Hektor at his table.

Hektor felt like the returning prodigal son and Joseph wrapped into one. He could tell Helena was itching to ask her next questions.

"Would you mind telling us how you got here so fast? Who picked you up at the airport?"

"Greta met me in Cologne. I wanted my visit to be a total surprise. I guess I succeeded."

"I don't like this kind of a surprise. You should have let us know about your arrival. Why involve strangers instead of your family?"

"I beg your pardon? Greta Beerenbaum is not a stranger. She was and is one of the most important people in my life. Your reference to her in that way is totally out of line!" They were off to a running start, and Hektor was anxious to change the subject. His freezing feet gave him a perfect excuse. "Gosh, that floor is cold." He was so used to central heating. He rearranged one of the overstuffed chairs in such a way that he could put up his feet. Of course, he took off his shoes. Every time he left the room to use the WC or get something out of his luggage, he found the furniture put back.

After the meal and talking for half an hour, his dad got up to turn on the TV. Apparently, Alex could not miss the next episode of *Lassie*.

Hektor thought he wasn't seeing right. *Reruns of* Lassie, *poorly dubbed in German, are of greater interest than a conversation with me, having returned after seven long years?* He didn't say anything until the chair was turned away from him just once too often.

"If you are wondering why I want that chair facing me to put up my feet, I'll tell you. I'm not used to the cold and dampness in this house. Central heating has spoiled me in America. Sorry, but you will just have to put up with me for a few days here and there. I plan to spend some time with Albert and his family, as well as with Greta,

Nick, and Judith. I need to get to know my own brother. We never were close before I left."

"That wasn't our fault," his mother said. "You are just different. Maybe you can overlook such differences, now that you are older. I didn't always see eye-to-eye with my siblings either."

"What do you mean, you *didn't*? You still don't. You have fought like cats and dogs over your parents' estate ever since Grandpa died three years ago. Nothing was ever the same. I just don't get it. How can the world live in peace if a family can't learn to be civil with one another? And it is always about the *m-o-n-e-y*. I am so sick of it."

Time had lapsed but nothing had changed. Once again there was disagreement in the air. Right after the news broadcast, Hektor went to bed. Thank God the musty old wallpaper had finally been replaced. He crawled under the thick featherbed and was asleep in seconds. His mother probably came in to say a prayer and kiss him good night. If she did, he wasn't aware of her presence.

When he awoke in the morning, he looked around. His right hand reached over to the bed next to him. As he touched it, his mind took him back eighteen years. He didn't want to go there, but he saw Lothar lying next to him, naked and pleasuring himself. His fleshy hands reached out for Hektor. He pulled him toward his hardened penis and made him swallow his instrument of pleasure. Hektor once again felt the abuse of being sodomized by an old man who was howling with delight while crucifying the eleven-year-old boy. *Why can't I shake that encounter with the miserable bastard after all this time?* He jumped out of bed and went to the bathroom. There was no shower. He ran a hot bath. It calmed his nerves. He couldn't wait to get to the breakfast table.

"Are you by any chance still entertaining Lothar these days?"

Helena looked at Hektor in shock. She hadn't expected that question. "Actually, yes. He and Alphons visited us a few weeks ago. I was thrilled to see Alphons after all these years. They stayed with us. We let them sleep in your former bedroom. Alphons said he felt close to you, sleeping in your bed."

"I betcha he did, probably while Lothar was screwing him."

"I forbid you to use that language. They didn't do any such thing. How do you come up with these ideas? They are both mature men. I might even say older men."

"Mother, I'm twenty-nine years old. You aren't forbidding me anything. I cannot believe how blind you must be. What does *old* have to do with those guys enjoying sex? In my opinion, they have done it for many years. They loved nothing better than doing it in the beds where Lothar had his fun with me. Lothar was surely laughing in Alphons's ears, reliving the ecstasy he experienced with abusing me. They are still going down memory lane while I continue to be haunted by what that prick did to me. I've got to get the hell out of this damn place. It blows my mind that you still haven't learned your lesson. Remember what I told you seven years ago? I didn't even want his name mentioned in this house, never mind inviting him back into my bed. Why the hell did I ever come home?"

"Remember, it was you who brought up Lothar's name, not I. I just don't understand why you cannot forgive and forget that long-ago event in your life."

"Because you have no idea how often I am traumatized by reliving those days. It's like it was branded onto my brain; it's indelibly immersed in my psyche."

Helena was left speechless.

That afternoon, Hektor walked to Mörikestrasse. Albert, Margarethe, and their five-year-old boy, Alberti, were just as greatly surprised as his parents had been, but Hektor felt far more welcomed.

"Uncle Hektor, Uncle Hektor, come and see my room. My daddy built me a track for my electric trains. I can play with them anytime

I want to. You like to play with electric trains? Do you have them in America? Why don't you stay with us tonight?"

"As a matter of fact, I will. You and I will have to share a room."

"No, you won't. While you are here and want to stay, Alberti will sleep with us. There is plenty of room in our big bed. That's settled," said his sister-in-law.

Albert grabbed a bottle of wine and some Kirschwasser. Soon, there was a party going. One thing those two understood was to celebrate the moment. They had to; otherwise, they would have gone stark-raving mad.

Hektor never understood how his brother could tolerate the way their mother treated his wife and child—and all because she was Catholic. *Give me a break.*

During the week, Hektor made it a point not to interfere with the business. He went to visit uncles and aunts who didn't speak to his mother. He visited with numerous friends but spent much of his time at the Beerenbaum home. He hoped that if this little business deal with his parents came to pass, it wouldn't spoil his close relationship with Greta, Nicklaus, and Judith. He didn't need to worry. There was no cause for alarm. Greta knew how to handle Helena.

However, Helena resented the time Hektor spent with his brother's family and friends. Toward the end of his second week in Germany, they came to another impasse. Hektor's mother never was happy unless some witch's brew was boiling all over damnation. She didn't like peace and contentment. It was almost like she thrived on emotional turmoil.

Hektor had enough of it. He was seeking peace and quiet, and peace and quiet he found, especially when he succeeded in anesthetizing himself with alcohol.

He spent the last night in Germany at his brother's home. Nicklaus Beerenbaum came over to have a drink with them. They all got sloshed, remembering the happy days when his father was alive. Nicklaus offered to drive Hektor and his brother and family to the airport in Cologne the next morning. That would make things easier, since Hektor wasn't speaking to his parents and had no plans for saying goodbye. Their last confrontation regarding his frequent absences from his parents' home was the crowning touch.

"You want to know why I'm staying away from you? I can't sleep in that room any longer. It gives me nightmares. Every night I sleep in that damn bed, I feel like I'm being raped all over again by that bastard friend of yours. For once in my life, I want to forget that episode. I wonder if I ever will be completely free of the trauma!"

⋈

The brothers had been experimenting with a reel-to-reel tape recorder that Albert had bought as a gift for Hektor.

"You should have no problems using it in the States. You probably won't recognize your own voice when you listen to the playback the first time."

"I know about that one. Kurt Beerenbaum bought one of the first recorders years ago. We had fun discovering the sound of our own voices at the time."

It would be only three years later that Hektor discovered the actual reason for sounding so different when listening to one's recorded voice; it is the voice that others perceive when listening to a given speaker.

Albert was truly taken by the ability to communicate without having to write or make expensive long-distance calls. "Now you have the same recorder as ours. Instead of letters, we can exchange tape recordings. Doesn't that sound like fun?" Albert stated again and again with pride.

"Yes, it sounds like a great idea. This way, I'll hear from you two more often."

They were waiting to be checked in at the airport. "Will you ever consider getting married again?" asked Albert.

"Like I told Mother, it will be a cold day in hell if I do. For now, let's forget about that idea. In the meantime, I am planning on seeing you again in two years. Let's be positive. I don't want to see any tears. It was great seeing all of you."

He put his arms around Margarethe, who was fighting back her tears. Then came Alberti's and Nicklaus's turns and finally, his brother's. Hektor waved goodbye with one of the large white handkerchiefs Greta had given him. He didn't look back. He didn't want them to see his eyes filled with sadness as well as happiness. It hadn't been a perfect trip, but he had gotten to know his brother at last.

1963–1965

Chapter 35

THE jet to New York took off on time. As the plane headed toward Amsterdam, Hektor spotted the twin spires of the famous Cologne Cathedral in the distance. Twenty years had passed since he had viewed the landmark but from a much closer perspective. No one had dreamed in 1943 of jets crossing the Atlantic.

The plane was flying high over the Atlantic, above the clouds, and soon would turn toward New York City. More than halfway across the "big lake," as Mother Birken referred to the Atlantic, the skies opened up, perhaps just in time for Hektor to gain a first view of Greenland and gigantic icebergs floating in the North Atlantic. It still seemed unbelievable to him that one could be in Europe in the morning and touch down in New York eight hours later.

"Welcome back to the USA," the INS representative greeted him and then advised him to proceed to customs. His plane to Detroit took off at three o'clock and landed at Metropolitan Airport at four thirty.

Bob Henkel met him at the gate. "How does it feel to be back? Was your trip all you had hoped it would be?"

"Yes, I had a meaningful reunion with an old friend in Zurich. Actually, she and I were engaged before I, like a fool, fell for my ex-wife. My visit with my parents went largely OK. I had the best time with my brother and his family and close friends. Yes, all in all, it was a good trip. I'm glad I went. It was high time. I couldn't get over all the changes in Germany. Parts of my hometown I hardly recognized. Some things rebuilt by 1956 were torn down and replaced with even more modern buildings. I was astounded by all the new and much-wider streets. Many of the trains and streetcars were put underground. There were next to no signs of all the destruction I remembered. It's almost unbelievable!"

"It sounds like the trip was good for you. I'm glad you got away for a few weeks. Agnes and Walter are looking forward to your return. I don't know how you feel about having a date, but I took the liberty of arranging a blind date for you. My girlfriend, Deena, called me a couple of days ago. You remember—she works at Henry Ford Hospital. A girl in the same office, Laura Prior, is supposed to be your date. I don't know the girl, but I understand from Deena that she comes from a nice family. The girls seem to like each other. If it's OK with you, I'll call Deena tonight and confirm the double date for this Saturday."

"That's a new one on me. I've never had a blind date. *Why not?* I need to think about starting a new life. Dating will be a different experience. I'm slightly out of practice. Tell me; how old is this girl?"

"I'm not certain, but I believe Deena said she was going on twenty-one. Is that a problem for you?"

"No, not at all. That's a pretty healthy age difference. How are we working the logistics? Are you driving?"

"*Oh, yes!*" He was well aware of Hektor's hesitancy to drive across town.

"I'll pick you up at Agnes and Walter's about six o'clock on my way home from the office. We can have a drink before I take you over to Deena's home. She and her folks are eager to meet you and hear about your trip to Germany."

Bob pulled into the driveway at Agnes and Walter's home and

helped Hektor with his luggage. "I won't come in; otherwise, I'll never get home tonight. You know how Agnes likes to talk, and talk, and talk. See you Saturday at six sharp."

After Hektor freshened up a bit, he presented Agnes and Walter with small souvenirs and a box of Swiss chocolates.

Agnes smiled at the presents. "Thank you. That was thoughtful of you. I love European chocolates. They are much smoother than our stuff."

They were delighted and wanted to hear all about his trip. He was happy to oblige and answered all of Agnes's questions. Walter largely smiled and nodded his head repeatedly. They were happy to have him under their roof again.

After getting to the store on Friday morning, he went first to Bob Mitchell's office to see if there were any changes in scheduling. He noted he was to start early on Saturday, meaning he could leave at five-thirty. While he had his doubts about this blind date, he didn't want to back out of it. Curiosity had gotten the better of him.

The date was March 2, 1963. Hektor chose to wear a blue suit and a fashionable tie to the office. While he preferred working in his shirtsleeves on the job, he would be ready to step out on the town when he said good night to his colleagues at five thirty. The little Falcon took him home. A few touch-ups here and there, and he was ready. He grabbed the beautiful new alligator wallet Greta had given him as another farewell present. The important papers were tucked away in his billfold, and he was ready to meet the total stranger.

She lived across town in a neighborhood called Grosse Pointe Farms. He had looked it up on the city map. The drive was about twenty-seven miles, using various expressways. He was glad Bob had volunteered to drive. Hektor had little difficulty maneuvering along the main drags and side streets in the neighborhood. Getting across town and switching back and forth between expressways was not one of his favorite things to do—yet.

Bob was prompt, as usual. It was only a short drive to Bob's house. As promised, Hektor was offered a healthy dash of J&B over ice while Bob put on a fresh shirt and tie. Fifteen minutes later, they were on their way to pick up Bob's girlfriend, Deena. When the introductions were over, Deena's father, being of German extraction, wanted to hear about the old country.

"Would you like to sample my homemade wine? Most people like it very much. I pride myself on my Cabernet."

What else could Hektor say? "Of course, I'd be delighted to try your wine."

It was pretty good stuff, but Hektor wasn't so sure when he didn't succeed in declining a refill. First scotch, then two glasses of wine on an empty stomach. *That might spell trouble ahead, but it might also make it easier to deal with this blind date.*

Hektor rode in the back seat as they departed for their journey across town to pick up "the blind date." They pulled up in front of the house on Kurtis Road.

Mr. Prior came to the door. "Hi, I'm Melvin Prior. Please come in. Laura will be ready momentarily. I'd like you to meet some of our lifelong friends. We usually get together on Saturday nights. Ask your friends to come in, please."

Hektor turned around, raising his shoulders and grimacing. They had no choice but to meet the family. Hektor assumed he was being checked out. He couldn't blame the Priors for wanting to do so. He was a total stranger to them and their daughter. Bob and Deena got out of the car and followed Hektor into the house.

Bob introduced himself to Mr. Prior and then looked at Deena. "This is my friend, Deena Hover, who is responsible for arranging this blind date with your daughter."

"Nice to meet you. Laura talks about you often. These are our friends, Grete and Herbert Woven and Mariah and Herbert Carlson.

We've known each other since we were kids. How about a drink? What's your poison? We probably have something you would like. Oh, here is Laura."

Hektor stepped up to the plate and introduced himself. Then Deena introduced her date, Bob Henkel, to Laura. Finally, those first few awkward moments were over. Everyone but Deena and Laura had scotch on the rocks. *Why not?* Hektor thought. All enjoyed the drink and conversation.

Laura was wearing an American-beauty–red wool dress with a jewel neckline. Hektor noted her nice figure in the well-fitting sheath. As they were leaving, Laura slipped on a cervical brace. She put on a black wool coat trimmed with a mink collar and placed the matching pillbox on her head. Jacqueline Kennedy clearly had made a worldwide fashion statement.

"I was in a bad car accident six months ago. I still need to wear one of these when riding in a vehicle. But let's not talk about it now; perhaps some other time."

She seemed to be OK; Hektor hadn't noticed anything unusual about her. As they were walking toward Bob's car, Hektor felt unsteady on his feet but still was looking forward to a fun evening. He was glad the ride to the Golden Lion wasn't too long.

They were ushered into the bar for—what else?—another drink. Deena and Laura ordered soft drinks; Bob, a beer; and Hektor, another J&B on the rocks. The bartender put the drinks in front of them, and Hektor reached for his impressive new wallet, intending to pay for the first round of drinks. He opened it, only to discover he had failed to switch the money from his old billfold. He took a deep breath and looked around for someone to rescue him. It turned out to be Deena who lent him fifty dollars. Thank goodness he was feeling so high that nothing fazed him. What an auspicious beginning! Had he been sober, he would have been embarrassed to death. Not so this evening.

They had a delightful dinner at the Gaslight in downtown

Detroit, went dancing, and listened to music of the day at the Mermaid's Cave, a real dive. At one in the morning, they landed in an English pub, where Hektor opted to entertain all guests by dancing on the tables. Their last stop was a pizza parlor in the vicinity of Laura's home.

They finally dropped her off shortly before three o'clock. Hektor walked her to the door and thanked her for a lovely evening as he shook her hand. Laura wished him a good night as she walked into the house. For a fleeting moment, he thought of Senta in *The Flying Dutchman*. Might Laura be the one who would save him from being forever a wanderer on the earth? He pondered if he should have tried to kiss her but was glad he'd decided against it. He felt he made enough of a fool of himself that evening.

He was sound asleep, slouched down in the back seat of the car, when Bob finally dropped him off at Agnes and Walter's house.

"Talk to you tomorrow, buddy."

"Thanks for the ride. Nice meeting you, Deena. And thanks for arranging the date."

Stumbling more than walking, he made his way to his room upstairs, thankful that Agnes and Walter were sound asleep. Hearing their snoring contest confirmed his assumption. *Sadly enough, I'll never see those girls again. No way!* He didn't even bother to brush his teeth. He didn't care; his clothes were strewn all over the room.

"You blew it, buddy!" he blurted out as he slumped under the heavy woolen blankets. He fell asleep instantly.

Hektor was pleased he didn't have to work that Sunday. After fixing himself a simple breakfast in Agnes's kitchen, he tried out his new tape recorder. With an adapter, he was able to use it with the standard US current. He read the instructions and began to make his first recording for the family in Germany. He thanked them for the great time, described the fascinating experiences of seeing Greenland and gigantic icebergs floating in the Atlantic from forty thousand feet in the air, and finally recounted, in great detail, his blind date with Laura. He didn't touch on the closing chapter of the evening.

Albert and Margarethe replied by tape in a matter of days. Albert came up with a poignant remark. "We believe things must be cooling off in hell. That day you referred to just before taking off from Cologne must be closer at hand than you assumed. We want to hear more about this Laura."

By Tuesday afternoon, he had worked up enough gumption to call Laura. As he dialed her office number at Henry Ford Hospital, he wasn't sure what would happen. Deena answered the phone.

"Hi, Deena. May I please speak with Laura."

She recognized his accented voice immediately. "Just a moment; let me see if she is still here."

"Laura Prior speaking. May I help you?"

"Hi, this is Hektor Birken. How are you today?"

"Well, thank you."

"Have you recovered from our disastrous date on Saturday?"

"What do you mean—recovered? Disastrous? Surprisingly, I had a lot of fun and didn't think there was anything wrong with our date. Actually, it was my first blind date ever."

"Mine as well. Would you be up for an encore? I'm calling to ask if you might care to see me again after that *exciting* first act. I have to work this Saturday night, but I would like to take you out to dinner at Topinka's Country House the following week. How does that sound? It might give us an opportunity to get to know each other a little better." He finally paused and gave her a chance to respond.

"Yes, I would like to see you again. Dinner on the sixteenth sounds fine. I will be at Ferris College in the meantime but plan to be home sometime on Friday, March 15. Since you are still so hesitant about driving on the expressways, I could call my Aunt Grete and Uncle Herbert. They live in your neighborhood. I'm sure I could stay with them overnight. I'll drive my father's car, and you can pick me up at my aunt and uncle's house. Would that work for you?"

"That would be great. Where do your uncle and aunt live?"

Laura gave him the address, and he scratched it out inside his left palm.

"Thanks. That will work for me. If you don't mind, I'd like to stop at my place and freshen up a bit before coming to meet you at your uncle and aunt's home. I will make a reservation for seven. What do you think?"

"Seven is fine. I look forward to seeing you in ten days. Perhaps we'll talk by phone in the meantime. Thank you for calling."

As he stepped out of the phone booth just outside the store, he ran into Bob Mitchell. Hektor's imagination had run wild while standing in the privacy of the phone booth.

"Boy, the way you are smiling, one might think you just lined up a hot date. What's happening?"

"I met this girl on Saturday night, and she caught my eye and my interest. We are meeting again a week from Saturday. Stay tuned, Robert."

A few days later, Hektor called Laura at Ferris.

"I think I should be forthright with you," he said. "Bob probably didn't tell Deena I am still married but legally separated from my wife. We parted company three years ago. There are two children—a boy, going on six, and a girl, almost four years old. I think you should know about this before you elect to see me again. Pardon the noise; I have to step outside this telephone booth. Someone took a crap in here; the stench is unbearable."

Laura cracked up. "You better step out. I don't mind the noise at all. We can talk more about this later. I look forward to seeing you next weekend."

On Saturday night, Hektor dashed out of the store promptly at five thirty. He got into the Falcon and stepped just a little harder on the gas than usual. When he got to Agnes and Walter's, he took the stairs to his room two at a time. He stripped off his clothes and jumped into the shower. Running his soapy hands over his body felt great. It had been so long since he'd been with Sheila for a last time.

He opted to wear a three-piece, navy-blue, pin-striped Kuppenheimer suit; a pale blue tie; and a matching fashionable Dobbs hat. He wasn't hurting for clothes; the manufacturers had always been more than generous in his R&S days. As he waved to Agnes and Walter and wished them a good evening, he heard Agnes say, "Boy, don't you look sharp. Have a great time. We hope we get to meet the young lady one of these days."

"You will, you will—soon," he said as he hurried out the door to his car. He drove to the Wovens' house, where Laura was waiting.

"Hi, come in. How nice to see you again," said Aunt Grete. "Laura is in the living room with Herbert."

As he walked in to greet her, he saw she was wearing a black shantung jacket dress. She seemed to favor that jewel neckline, very prim and proper. It underscored that nice-girl look.

They arrived at Topinka's just before seven.

"We are running a bit late with our reservations. How about having a drink at the bar? I'll seat you as soon as possible, Mr. Birken," said the headwaiter.

The bartender also knew Hektor and didn't ask Laura for identification. She appeared quite mature, and as she was with Hektor, he saw no need to ask her. He knew what Hektor would drink since he,

Robert Mitchell, and Toni Antorio often had stopped by for a drink after work when setting up the store, but he asked Laura, "Young lady, what's your preference?"

"I believe I would like J&B and water on the rocks with a twist, please."

"That's a sensible drink. Coming up, right away." He placed the drinks before them.

They silently looked at each other. Hektor picked up his glass.

"Here's to a happy reunion and a fun evening. I am glad you wanted to see me again, especially the way things went a couple of weeks ago and knowing what I told you about my past. When we spoke the other day, I failed to mention that Georgia and the children live in New York. I plan to seek a divorce ASAP, based on the separation agreement. Well, for now, that's enough about me. You may find my life is too complicated. On top of that, my crazy work schedule won't allow us to see each other more than every other weekend while you are away at school. By the way, my apologies again for commenting on that odoriferous condition of the phone booth when I called you the other day. Tell me a little about yourself."

"You don't have to apologize. I understood and thought it was terribly funny. I'm sure you didn't think so. Well, you know about my going back to college at Ferris. It was in Canada that I was involved in the accident last September. I am lucky not to be paralyzed; it was a pretty close call. A friend of mine was driving when we collided with a garbage truck. His mandible was crushed, and I sustained serious injury to three of my cervical vertebrae and deep lacerations and bruises from head to toe. Like I said, someone was looking over my shoulder. I have two sisters and no brothers. My sisters and I are each three years apart. Elaine, three years younger than I, will be graduating from high school and starting college this fall. Caitlin, the youngest, is just fifteen. My mom has a position with Goodwill Industries, and my dad is self-employed. And there is Jacques, our poodle—I should say, Caitlin's poodle. She is the animal lover in the family."

They sat at the bar for almost two hours. Time just got away from them. Hektor finally caught the headwaiter's eye; his body language and facial expression spoke volumes. He realized that Hektor was obviously annoyed at the unusual delay in being seated. Within seconds, a table in a dark, secluded corner was readied for them. For a moment, Hektor couldn't help thinking of Nancy Wilson's song "Guess Who I Saw Today?"

He helped Laura with her chair, seating himself across from her. He ordered an excellent Cabernet, since he knew they would have some kind of steak for the main course. There wasn't anything better to order at Topinka's. They knew how to prepare beef.

"May I suggest the filet mignon with the roasted potatoes. Their blue cheese dressing is excellent."

"That sounds fantastic. I'm starved."

"How do you like your meat prepared? I like mine medium rare."

"That's what I prefer; I don't care for it well done or rare."

"Both of us would like a shrimp cocktail with that wonderful sauce of yours to tide us over until the main course arrives; it was a pretty long wait!"

"We apologize for the prolonged delay, Mr. Birken. We had a busload of unexpected guests drop in on us, a tour bus from out East. Again, our apologies."

They enjoyed their shrimp and sipped the wine.

"Since we are eating so late, would you like to go out dancing later? There is a charming little bar down the street on Schoolcraft. They have a terrific combo that plays until two in the morning. I think you will like the *Night Light*."

"That sounds like fun; I'd almost rather dance than eat. I look forward to it."

The dinner was perfection; they couldn't resist the presentation of the desserts. For Hektor, no meal was complete without the crowning touch. They had a slice of New York cheesecake, one of Hektor's favorites. Laura had hers covered in raspberries; his was topped with blueberries and whipped cream.

"I agree that we need to dance off a few of these delectable calories," Laura said. "Dinner was wonderful. Thank you for asking me. But now, let's dance."

They were at the Night Light in a few minutes. As they walked in, the band was playing Duke Ellington's "Satin Doll." They checked their coats quickly and stepped onto the dance floor. Hektor realized instantly that Laura was an excellent dancer. She had a natural beat in her feet. When the combo took a well-deserved pause, they sat down to another J&B. At one thirty, they chose to call it a night. As they were walking out, they knew it was just the beginning. Hektor took Laura to her aunt and uncle's home. He kissed her good night; it was a gentle kiss on her lips.

"Thank you, Hektor. I had a wonderful time."

"In two weeks, let's try this little Italian dive called *Capraro's*. Afterward, let's go to the *Beef 'n' Bourbon* on Telegraph. They have a terrific piano player. You'll love him. We'll finish at the Night Light again."

Hektor never gave any thought to the possibility that Laura might be asked for identification regarding her age and having drinks with him. There never was any question about responsibly drinking as he grew up in Germany. And, of course, Laura acted very mature and would be of legal age in a matter of two months.

He blew Laura a kiss as he was backing out of the driveway.

He called her after ten the next morning.

She seemed happy to hear his voice. "I had a great time. I loved the dancing. Call me later at home, OK?"

"Great!"

That sure made his day. He hoped she liked more than the dancing. Well, obviously, she must have; otherwise, she would not be willing to continue seeing him after another lengthy discussion of his situation.

Their third date was decidedly a success. Laura wore a beige brocade dress, looking elegant with her blond hair. Of course, it also had a jewel neckline. Dancing to "Satin Doll," Hektor couldn't resist whispering in her ear, "Don't you ever wear anything a little bit more peek-a-boo?"

She almost broke up right there on the dance floor. He couldn't help joining her in her laughter. On their next date, she wore a dress with a slightly lower neck treatment. Whenever they walked into the Night Light thereafter, the combo switched to "Satin Doll." It became their song.

May brought a separation. Laura and her cousin took their long-planned vacation to Florida. They also visited her maternal grandparents for a few days. Hektor couldn't wait for her to come home. He'd lie in bed at night, undressing her in his mind.

While Laura was away, Hektor's colleague, John Krauter, lost his battle with cancer. His death was a great loss to Hektor. Both John and Marna Krauter had become good friends. After an initial unsuccessful search for John's replacement, Hektor was given temporary responsibility for running both the Ladies and Men's divisions; eventually, he was appointed manager of all departments in the women's area.

His responsibilities at work occupied most of his time. Laura was the bright spot in his life. She became his everything. When they were not dancing, they enjoyed Jerry Vale's renditions of the classic Russ Colombo songs. Bob Henkel had introduced them to the recording.

By Laura's twenty-first birthday, Hektor knew he wanted to marry her. When and how were questions to be answered later.

The basement at the house on Kurtis Road was cleared out and decorated. Her folks gave her quite a party. The next day, they continued the festivities at Bob Henkel's home. At the end of that weekend, Hektor made up his mind to pursue the divorce.

Chapter 36

THE week after Laura's twenty-first birthday, her mother confronted Hektor.

"Young man, you and I need to have a chat. I'd like to know what your intentions are with our daughter. I'm aware you are separated from your wife and are responsible for two children from that marriage."

Hektor looked Millie Prior straight into her questioning dark eyes. "So you think I'm serious about your daughter? Well, I am. I want to marry her. And the sooner the better. I can't get away from being responsible for the kids. I will proceed with the divorce ASAP. After Laura started that new job of hers with the doctors, we talked about a wedding next year. We are both leaning toward October. One thing neither one of us wants is a big production. Been there; done that. And look what it got me. I'm fully aware that it would be a first-time happening for Laura. But she is a sensible girl and agrees with me. Does that answer your questions?"

"Yes and no. However, I understand your situation. Melvin and I obviously have only Laura's best interests at heart. She's a very special girl. We don't want her to get hurt. We believe you are an honorable man and will do the right thing. Let's have a drink on that." Millie liked her scotch on the rocks with a water chaser on the side.

Hektor picked up his J&B. "I'll get right on it." The following week, Hektor went out for a drink with Tony Antorio.

"Tony, you need to put me in touch with that attorney who handled your divorce in Alabama. I remember you talking about it last year."

"You mean Dempsey F. Pennington III in Birmingham? You'll like him. I'll call you later when I get home and give you his telephone number. I think he'll charge you $350 for handling the case since you have a legal separation. If there are no complications, the whole thing will be over in a matter of days. He'll jump right on it."

Hektor called Mr. Pennington the next day and explained the whole rigmarole.

"Just send me the separation agreement and a check in the amount of $350 by registered mail. I'll process the papers for your former wife to sign. If she returns the documents without contesting anything, you will be free to remarry sixty days from the date the divorce is granted."

Within four days, Dempsey Pennington was on the phone.

"Good day, Mr. Birken. This is Dempsey F. Pennington III calling. I've heard from Mrs. Birken." There was a pregnant pause, and then he laughed in his high-pitched, heavily accented Southern voice. "She signed the documents the day she received them. She didn't argue about or question anything. It's unusual, but for your sake, I'm not complaining. Can you arrange to be down here in a couple of days and plan to stay over the weekend?"

Hektor couldn't believe that Georgia signed the release and the other documents without protesting any part of it. It was almost too good to be true. But she had, for whatever reason, and he wasn't about to question it. He had been prepared for lengthy phone conversations; in his imagination, he could hear his ears ringing with a barrage of four-letter words.

"I'll call you right back." He walked into Bob Mitchell's office. "That was Pennington calling from Birmingham. He would like me to fly down there ASAP. Are you OK with that, Bob?"

"Call the airlines and take the first flight you can get. Call Pennington back right now and have him book you a hotel room for the next three or four days—whatever it takes. Good luck! You deserve it!"

Hektor was on his way to Alabama that evening. He stayed in Birmingham until June 30. After signing the necessary documents, he shook Dempsey F. Pennington's enormous hand and thanked him for making the efficient divorce possible. On the fifth of July, Hektor received the letter dated July 3.

"Your final decree of divorce was issued on Monday, July 1, 1963, by Judge Horace Blackstone. Best wishes for your future."

After he read the letter a few times, he called Laura. "Guess what? I'm a free man. Just heard from Dempsey F. Pennington III. Don't you love that name? It just rolls off one's tongue. Wish you could have met him; he is a riot. When do you want to marry me? Of course, we have to wait at least until September 1."

Laura was elated. "How about celebrating at the Night Light tonight? I want to see you. It will be worth losing a little sleep. We just won't stay as late as usual. OK?"

Hektor liked that idea. "I'll meet you in the store parking lot at five thirty. We'll grab a quick bite and then go dancing."

When she got into his car, he gave her a lingering kiss, the kind she loved.

"Let's eat at Topinka's," he suggested. "They won't dare keep us waiting tonight."

Laura was anxiously fidgeting with her purse. "Let me see the letter, please." She studied it intently and finally handed it back to Hektor. "You better keep this one in a very safe place." She beamed from ear to ear.

Now her eyes were really laughing. He had told her on their

second date that if she had been an Indian maiden, she would have been called *Laughing Eyes*. They enjoyed their dinner but were looking forward to the dancing at the Night Light. Of course, as they strolled in, the combo switched immediately to "Satin Doll."

They finished the dance and sat at their favorite table close to the dance floor staring at each other. He had done it. They knew they would get married. At this moment, they weren't exactly sure when. Hektor knew his time had come; it was the dawning of Aquarius.

Chapter 37

IN early August, Hektor thought he wasn't seeing correctly as he flipped through a bunch of letters. He recognized his father's handwriting. This was a first. He had never received a letter from him. *My God, did she finally succeed in killing herself?* was the first thing to cross Hektor's mind.

Dear Hektor,

You were probably in shock when you realized it was your father writing to you. I have left the writing to your mother for all these years that you have been away from home. I'm sorry to tell you that your mother once again made an attempt at ending her life.

I have no idea what makes her do it. Every so often, she sinks into depths of depression and feels she cannot deal with life any longer. She simply disappeared. Luckily, I found her in time, curled up in your former bed. The ambulance took her to the Kruppsche Krankenhaus [Krupp Hospital], where they followed the usual procedure. After they pumped out her stomach, she eventually came to.

She feels guilty about putting all of us through this.

Mother continues to be extremely sad about your permanent absence from our lives. She has never quite forgiven you for leaving Germany. She did this after you called to let us know that your divorce went through and that you met this girl you intend to marry. She views this latest development as the final straw.

When you separated from Georgia, your mother thought you would return to Germany. Of course, after you explained the situation to us, we understood that you couldn't leave the country. You have to take care of Frank and Karen. I don't want to hold you responsible for your mother's behavior. That wouldn't be fair. She has attempted to end her life on several occasions, even long before you boys were in the picture—or I, for that matter. So please do not consider yourself to be the cause of her actions. We have to accept that this is the way she is and deal with it as best as we can.

Please stay in touch with us by means of the exchange of recordings established with your brother. While your mother is on a steady warpath with Margarethe, I visit with her and Alberti whenever I can.

Lovingly,

Your father

Of course, Hektor was overwhelmed and concerned when he recognized his father's handwriting. The latest news about his mother was disturbing. Hektor felt helpless and disconnected, particularly from his mother. While he had known of her several attempts at ending her life, he never considered the possibility he might be the cause for her strange behavior in recent years. *That's quite a trip she laid on me!* He decided he wasn't going to shoulder that burden.

After Helena recovered, she informed Alex she would leave him for good. First, she obtained a managing position in a large butchery in a neighboring city. After she found housing, she arrived on the scene with professional movers. The whole neighborhood knew that Frau Birken was moving out with all their possessions.

Alex was devastated. First, his older son and wife left the family business, largely due to the untenable conditions created by Helena's tirades and attitudes toward Margarethe. And now it was her turn to leave him. The business, destined to failure, was his least concern. Every Sunday, he would drive to Oberhausen and plead with Helena to return. Initially, it was to no avail. At last, she played her final trump card.

"I cannot return in defeat to the business on Kupferstrasse. What will people think? You must sell the store and find another apartment for us in a different part of the city."

Alex Birken obliged, and he and Helena entered into retirement temporarily. They were finally settled in their new abode—a pleasant, modern apartment in a distant suburb of Essen. Alex tried playing salesman again; of course, unsuccessfully. Eventually, Albert sprang into action and secured for his father a rewarding job with his corporation. The proper nod in the right direction landed his father the position of gatekeeper at one of the company stores. The employees and his employer loved him and vice versa. The job was ideal for Alex. Helena became head bookkeeper for a small but successful industrial plant. At last, both had guaranteed incomes, and it appeared Hektor's parents had found happiness for once.

Chapter 38

THE back-to-school business was in full swing. Racks in all the departments were bursting with the new fall merchandise. Rather than mass displaying some of the better dresses and coats, Hektor tried to feature them on mannequins or in boutique-like showings. He never quite got into the discount-store mold; he could not jump over his well-trained shadow.

On weekends when he worked, he usually was at the store on Saturday mornings by eleven and would close at ten, never getting home much before eleven. His dinner was usually a couple of hot dogs on the run at the store cafeteria. In between, he might munch on a doughnut or two—not particularly a stellar diet. Following the long weekends, he would be off on Thursdays and the following Sunday. The Saturday prior to his day off, he would be at the store from eight to five thirty. These were the times he and Laura savored.

As he left the store on Sunday, September 15, shortly after five thirty, he jumped into the Falcon and headed straight for the Lodge Expressway. Once he switched to the Edsel Ford Freeway, traffic wasn't too bad. His fears of maneuvering the Detroit expressways were a distant memory. He pulled into the driveway on Kurtis

Road after six. He gave Laura a bear hug and kissed her. Finally, he touched his lips to her laughing eyes and rubbed noses with her in the Eskimo way.

"Do you have a drink for your man?" he asked. "What am I smelling?"

"It's a surprise. No one is home. Elaine is with Charles, and Caitlin has a date with one of her many boyfriends. Mom and Dad are on the west side with the Wovens and Carlsons. I don't expect anyone back until much later. Anyway, I'm fixing you a nice American dinner. The table is set. Take off your shoes and sit down with the paper and enjoy your drink."

She was happy being very domestic and preparing a surprise meal for Hektor. He had a couple of tastes of his scotch and barely got past the front page of the *Detroit News* before he nodded off.

"How was your day? Did you sell a lot of pretties?" As Laura peeked around the kitchen door, she discovered he was sound asleep. She didn't wake him until it was time to cut the meat. Everything else was already on the table. "Come on, sleepyhead; it's time to eat. Would you mind cutting us each a nice piece off the standing rib roast I fixed? It looks like it's just the way we like it."

"Would I mind? No way; that's a real treat. You are an excellent cook. How did you ever learn to do these things so well?"

"Don't let the dinner get cold. I'll tell you later; it's a rather long story."

He helped her with her chair. They toasted each other with a glass of red wine and partook of a wonderful meal.

"You are something else. How did I ever find you?" he asked.

"On a blind date! Don't ever knock them. Actually, as you say so often, we were 'in the right place at the right time.' I prefer to think that we were meant for one another. Someone looked over our shoulders."

After dinner, he helped Laura with the cleanup in the kitchen. She saved the rack of bones for Elaine. She was a devotee of bones.

Later, she would sit in the kitchen, gnawing on every single one to her heart's content.

"How would you feel about making a tape recording for Harry? I want him to be my best man when we marry next fall."

"Do you have that little recorder with you? If you do, we certainly can take an hour or so and let him in on our plans." Hektor got up and retrieved the recorder from the trunk of his car.

They went downstairs to the recreation room and made themselves comfortable. They stole a few kisses here and there since they were all alone in the house. Just for a split second, Hektor wasn't sure if he could control himself. He stuck to languid kisses and a bit of more daring foreplay. He resolved to save Laura for their wedding night. A whole year? He wasn't so sure that would work for him. He didn't want to check out the red-light district.

He spoke first on the recording. "Hi, buddy. I don't have to tell you who this is. You'll recognize that goddamn immigrant voice every time. I assume things are OK in Liberia. You should be done with that assignment pretty soon. I'm here with a young lady. Her name is Laura. Come here, sweetie. Say hi to my good friend."

"Hi, Harry. I feel like I know you. Hektor has shared so many of your stories with me. I'm hoping to meet you soon. I'll turn the mike back to him. He's anxious to speak with you. Bye; until soon." She walked away and gave Hektor privacy while speaking to Harry. She knew that the language might get a bit rough when these guys talked to each other.

"I found Laura on a blind date almost six months ago. When you meet her, you'll agree she is a winner. I flew to Alabama at the end of June and got my divorce. The bitch didn't fight me on anything. I still can't believe she was that agreeable. But we are not quibbling. I'm a free man and ready, willing, and able to marry Laura. And I mean ready. I'm sure you're getting the idea. How would you feel about coming to Detroit to be my best man? I can't think of any guy I'd rather have.

"At this stage, Laura's mom is talking about a wedding in October next year. Personally, I don't know why the hell we're waiting so long. She may not be a virgin in a year. I better watch out what I'm saying when Laura comes back downstairs. Give the idea some thought and call me when you are stateside. I presume you still have my number at Tip-Top. They can always page me. Safe journey home. Look forward to hearing from you." He stopped the recorder as Laura came down the stairs. Hektor looked at her and took her in his arms.

"Now that we have told him what will happen in a year, I wonder if we are being stupid about this whole affair. Why are we waiting this long? As much as I would like Harry to do me the honor, I'm sure I can find someone else to stand up for me. Lord knows when Harry will finally return. He might do some traveling when he completes his contract. He told me when we spoke a few months ago that he might want to visit my family in Germany. I don't even know for sure if this tape will get to him in time before he leaves Liberia. There are so many unanswered questions. His eighteen-month contract was up in August. How would you feel about getting married sooner? You know, I am legal at this point."

Laura's eyes became as big as saucers. "I wouldn't mind getting married sooner. That would be just fine with me."

"How about next Thursday on my day off? We could do it during your lunch hour. The doctors are usually in surgery on Thursday mornings. No one would have to know about it."

Laura almost fell off her chair. "You're kidding me, aren't you?"

Hektor looked dead serious. "No, I never was more earnest. Remember, after my fiasco with Georgia, the farthest thing from my mind is a huge, expensive wedding. Being with you and having you by my side as my wife as soon as possible is the most important thing to me."

Laura realized Hektor meant what he said. "Let's think this through. If you stay here overnight, we could go downtown together and have our blood tests done at one of the labs in the building. I know most of the technicians. Then you could go to city hall and take out the license and arrange for a judge to marry us. Call Bob Mitchell and tell him you'll be there later tomorrow. Ask him about standing up for you. I'm sure he would come downtown and be part of the ceremony. I'll call DB, a school chum of mine. She and her husband did the same thing a year ago. Come to think of it, my parents were secretly married for two years. They finally did it officially. Much of the family never knew about the two wedding dates until one of Mom's sisters blurted it out at a party thirty or so years later. This is crazy but terribly exciting. I love you! What will I wear?"

"How about that pretty pink jacket dress with the flowered hat? I always liked that outfit on you. You even have shoes to match. More important, what are we doing about wedding bands? I'm actually kind of short on cash right now. I'm still making my monthly payments to Mandelbaum and Mandelbaum as well as on the Falcon."

"I have an idea. My godparents gave me pieces of sterling silver for years. Just recently, I ordered some pieces to get an even number of soup spoons. If I cancel that order at Wright Kay, we could buy our wedding bands with the refund and have a little left over. Maybe you could meet me for lunch tomorrow after you have your chat with Bob. I'm sure he will let you have a little bit more time. It isn't like you watch the clock normally."

The gears were put into motion. On Monday morning, the first stop was Owens Lab for the blood tests. Hektor went to city hall for the license and arranged for the marriage ceremony to be performed in the same building at noon on Thursday. Hektor shifted from one foot to the other, almost like a little boy needing to pee. He wasn't sure how to broach the next subject with the license clerk.

"Be sure not to publish our intended marriage in the press."

"Sir, I can't do that; it is illegal. It's a public notice that must appear in the local papers."

Hektor had to do some quick thinking. "But ma'am, my intended bride is pregnant, and we don't want her parents to know about our elopement."

"Well, that is different. In that case, I'll slip it under the blotter. We won't put it in any papers. When is the lucky girl expecting?"

"I guess sometime next spring. Thanks for being a dear. How much did you say the license was?"

"Oh, just three dollars. It's a real bargain. It's a lot cheaper than a divorce. Of course, I don't have to tell you about that. Best of luck this time around."

He walked over to a public telephone and dialed Bob Mitchell's private line at the store. "Hi, Bob; it's Hektor. You'll never guess where I am. Laura and I are getting married at city hall this Thursday at noon. How about standing up for me? You think you can handle that?"

After a short pause to catch his breath, Bob said, "Sure can. Got yourself a nice girl there. I'm delighted to do this for both of you. I'll get the particulars this afternoon when you come in. Best of luck!"

"Wait, wait, before you hang up—one more thing. Is it OK if I take an extra hour for lunch? I want to meet Laura at Wright Kay to pick out our wedding bands."

"Sure enough. Can't get married without rings."

His missions completed, Hektor stopped by the David Whitney Building to check with Laura.

"We're all set. Bob is excited about our marriage. Let's go to the jewelry store after lunch and pick out our rings. Are you all set with DB? By the way, I got you pregnant at city hall. It's the second immaculate conception."

"What do you mean, you got me pregnant at city hall? And yes, we are on for Thursday at city hall with DB."

"I had to tell them you were pregnant. That was the only way they would keep the notice out of the papers. I hope they are not holding their breaths." He didn't say more. Hektor wished she had been pregnant; that would have meant they had tried it and succeeded in bed.

They went out for lunch and then to Wright Kay. There almost wasn't a wedding but a funeral. As Laura stepped off the curb to cross the street, a car coming from her left crashed through a red light. Hektor saved her from getting killed by pulling her back hard and just in the nick of time. They stared at each other.

"That was just a bit too close!"

Hektor and Laura were fitted for their Lohengrin golden wedding bands. He got her back to the office before anyone discovered she was out to lunch. He made a reservation at the new motel across the street from the Beef 'n' Bourbon on Telegraph.

Laura became pensive. "What are we going to tell my parents we're doing on Thursday night?"

Hektor smiled. "No problem. Got it covered. We'll say the Wasserglasses invited us for dinner. They wanted us to celebrate Rosh Hashanah with their family. Their New Year falls on Thursday, September 19. Your mother may wonder, but it's not unusual for secular Jews to invite Christian friends on many of their holidays, Yom Kippur being an exception."

Thursday rolled around sooner than expected. For the occasion, Hektor wore a dark-blue, three-piece suit and one of his many colorful ties. He picked Laura up at the David Whitney office. She looked him over.

"Boy, aren't you the fashion plate. I've never seen your shoes polished shinier. That hat goes perfectly with your suit. You must have been in a great hurry. Let me straighten your tie just a pinch. There; that's perfect."

"Thanks for noticing that. I wouldn't want to get married with a crooked tie. Let's hurry. We can't be late for our own wedding ceremony."

They met Bob Mitchell and DB in the lobby of the Detroit City Hall and were ushered into the judge's office at noon.

Judge Former was a handsome black man with a deep voice and a pleasant manner. "Please have a seat in these chairs. If you don't mind, I would like to conduct the ceremony with a touch of Christianity. It's not a substitute for a church wedding, but I'd like to make it just a little more meaningful for the two of you."

Both Laura and Hektor were very much touched by his thoughtfulness. When he reached their respective parts, intoning *until death do us part*, he got to both of them. Their eyes were filled with tears of joy and sincerity. There hardly was a dry eye in the room, including Judge Former's. When he presented them to their witnesses as husband and wife, the congratulations were heartfelt.

They walked out of city hall on a bright and sunny fall day. The canopy of blue sky took the place of a vaulted cathedral ceiling. They headed for the sandwich shop across the street from the David Whitney Building. The choices were tuna, egg, or ham salad. Laura just blurted out her response.

"I'll take it on rye."

"But which one, my dear?" the waitress wanted to know. Laura obviously was nervous.

At one thirty, she crossed Woodward Avenue, heading back to the office. Bob caught her walking across the street with his movie camera. These snippets of film turned out to be the only "wedding pictures." She quickly switched to her uniform. No one knew she was just married.

After thanking Bob and DB for standing up with them, Hektor went to the Fox Theater and saw *The Great Escape*. Seeing the film again many years later, he realized there wasn't a single female actress in the movie. The lengthy, exciting epic kept the new groom occupied until he went to pick up his bride at five thirty.

He helped Laura into the Falcon; it wasn't a fairy-tale coach, but he made sure the ugly car was sparkling clean for the event. They headed to Capraro's for one of their Italian specialties, veal parmigiana. It was a favorite of theirs. They checked into the motel as Mr. and Mrs. Hektor Birken. When Laura stepped out of the bathroom in her pink baby-doll pajamas, Hektor flipped on the tape recorder, playing Jerry Vale's rendition of "You're My Everything"—and she was.

Hektor threw all caution to the wind. He tore off his clothes and assisted Laura with undressing. He was fully aroused when he looked at his beloved wife. He reached out with his right hand to touch her breasts. His left hand wound up on his own chest. He couldn't help himself from wanting to touch Greta's silver Madonna. He had done so at every turning point in his life for the last nine years—but now, his chest was bare.

It had been there in the morning, before he and Laura had entered the judge's chambers. He picked up his clothes and shook everything frantically. Laura helped him in the search for the missing treasure. The broken chain and the medallion fell on the hardwood floor with a clanging noise. Hektor retrieved his protector and stuck her in a hidden place in Greta's priceless wallet. The silver Madonna would remain safely there for all of Hektor's days.

Was his talisman trying to convey a silent message? Had the silver Madonna served its purpose? Did the break of the chain symbolize a break with the miserable past? At this moment, they didn't care to know the answers. They were thrilled his treasured talisman wasn't lost.

He enfolded Laura in his arms and carried her over to the bed. She had turned it down as soon as they entered the room. At this point, Hektor had become a skilled lover. He knew how to prepare Laura for her first encounter with a man. His tongue and hands were vital instruments in leading the way to fulfillment. When he entered Laura, she experienced little pain. She was overjoyed in having him close to her at last. They enjoyed each other's bodies with abandon. Their lovemaking was passionate and the fulfillment of everything they had longed for during the past months.

Laura spoke softly. "I'm glad Georgia didn't really appreciate you. I feel sorry for Doretta and Sheila. I hope they find love in other lovers' arms."

Hektor nodded in agreement. He happily held Laura. "Let's shower and then get dressed. Keith will be delighted to hear he played an important part in our lives leading up to this day."

When they sat down at Keith's piano bar and ordered their favorite drinks, they told him what they had done. He shook their hands with his left as he continued playing with his right, never missing a beat. They left the piano bar shortly before ten o'clock and headed to the Night Light. Hektor had to dance with his "satin doll" on the evening of their wedding.

Ever-practical Hektor looked at his bride. "The room is paid for the whole night. Let's make love one more time. Who knows how long I will have to wait to get laid again?" *Harry would have said, "Spoken like a man!"* he thought and then said, "Let's not wait forever to tell your folks that we are legal. I want us together as soon as possible. I've waited too long for this."

They went back to the motel, giving each other pleasure one more time before they reluctantly headed for Kurtis Road. As it was, Laura didn't get there until after three in the morning.

Elaine heard the car pull into the driveway. She thought it was taking them an awfully long time to say good night. After Hektor kissed Laura for a last time, he got into the Falcon. Only momentarily did Georgia enter his mind; he couldn't believe the startling difference in the wedding nights he had experienced.

Elaine met Laura as she came into the house. She couldn't say anything; she and Charles, high school sweethearts, weren't much different. Laura glanced at her sister and motioned for her to come into her bedroom downstairs.

"What are you doing up so late?" Laura asked. "Why aren't you in bed? You're leaving for Lansing tomorrow with Mom and Dad. Aren't you excited about starting school at Michigan State?"

"Yes, I am, although I will miss Charles once he starts school at Michigan. My question is, where were you tonight? What did you do? Get married or some crazy thing? Who has heard of dinner invitations to Christians by Jewish people on Rosh Hashanah?"

Laura was dumbfounded. "What made you think Hektor and I got married?"

Elaine almost lost it. "You're kidding me, aren't you?"

"No, I'm not. We were married at noon at city hall. Whatever you do, don't you blow it tomorrow on your way up to Lansing. We will tell Mom and Dad sometime this weekend. Just don't give us away. Kiss me good night now and wish us well."

Elaine loved her sister; there were tears of joy in her eyes as she put her arms around Laura, wishing her only happiness with Hektor. They retired to their rooms, but neither slept for a long time as they thought about the event that had taken place.

On the way up to Lansing, Elaine had a hard time staying focused on the conversation. She was glad when they finally arrived. Her folks helped her get settled into the dorm. They went out to lunch, and then she was on her own. She was relieved not to be on her constant guard and wondered how Laura was doing at the office.

Hektor called Laura at Henry Ford Hospital about nine, when he knew she would be there for sure.

"Hi, love, how are you this fine morning? Did you sleep OK?"

"Not for quite a while. You won't believe what happened. Elaine was waiting up for me, and she was curious why I came home so late. She asked me out of the clear blue, 'You didn't, by any chance, get married or some dumb thing?' I fell for it and asked her how she knew or guessed. The cat was out of the bag. I swore her to secrecy as far as my parents are concerned. I can't wait to see you tomorrow night. Let's break the news to my folks after dinner. I agree with you and don't want to play games indefinitely."

"OK, let's do it right after dinner. I should be there shortly after six. I hope the traffic won't be too bad. Catch a kiss; I have to run. There is an LD call for me. I'm being paged. Love you bunches."

Friday and Saturday seemed to drag on forever. Hektor could never be accused of being a clock-watcher, but this day was an exception. As soon as the clock struck five thirty, he stepped off the tower at the front and handed the microphone to Joe.

"Good night! I'm out of here."

And he was; he had everything in the car that he needed. He didn't have to stop for gas; Hektor was on his way to see his bride. Laura was standing by the side door of the house as he pulled into the driveway. These days she had a pretty good idea how long it would take him to get there. They had a lingering kiss and then walked into the house.

"Hello, Mr. and Mrs. Prior. How are you tonight? Thank you for having me over for dinner again."

"Fix yourself a drink, Hektor, and take a load off your feet. Knowing you, you were on them for most of the day," said Laura's father.

They were both sitting in their favorite chairs. Hektor sat across from them on the antique sofa. This way he could converse with Laura's parents and peek into the kitchen, where Laura was busy finishing dinner. After the meal, he helped her with the dishes, wanting to be closer to her. Laura's mom was reading the evening paper.

"Laura, Hudson's is having a special on down pillows, two for seventeen dollars. I think you should get some."

Her normally soft-spoken father rose to his feet in anger. "Push, push, push! She'll be marrying soon enough!"

Hektor and Laura pinched themselves.

"What a perfect opening; let's tell them right now," said Laura.

But the moment passed, and they didn't. When they were finally done with kitchen chores, enjoying a kiss here and there, they walked into the living room and sat close together on the sofa. It was nine o'clock, and Mr. Prior had his hand on the knob, ready to turn on the TV. It was the first broadcast of the new *Danny Kaye Show*. Danny was one of Melvin's favorite comedians.

Hektor decided to take charge. "Mr. Prior, please don't turn on the TV. Laura and I have something we want to tell you."

Millie Prior put down the paper immediately. She took off her glasses and looked back and forth from Laura to Hektor. There were tears in those beautiful dark eyes. "You have something to tell us?"

Hektor chose not to prolong the agony and came right out with it. "Laura and I are married!"

"Wha…wha…what did you say? You didn't, you wouldn't, you couldn't, you shouldn't have!" Mrs. Prior sputtered.

"But we did."

Laura's father said nothing. He just shook his head and muttered to himself, not wanting to create further tension. "I told you so just minutes ago!"

"When did this happen?" Millie probed.

"Mrs. Prior, we were married on Thursday at noon at the city hall in Detroit."

"Well, is there any reason why you got married the way you did? Is there something we should know?"

Hektor had Millie Prior's full attention. "Yes, we just love each other and did it on the spur of the moment. We decided to get married on Sunday night after we made the tape for Harry. Both of us thought it was stupid to wait a whole year."

Mrs. Prior regained her composure. "Well, we'll just forget all about it. We'll speak to the minister tomorrow and arrange for a proper wedding. We'll send out invitations right away. A few weeks won't make that much of a difference now." Laura and Hekor spoke in one voice.

"Oh, no," they said. "We are married and don't want a fancy wedding."

"Obviously, the big production I was part of the first time around was a qualified nightmare," added Hektor.

Laura's mom realized they were firm in their resolve. She rose quickly from her comfortable chair. "Melvin, let's take Jacques for a walk. Let's leave these kids alone."

It was most uncharacteristic for her to go for a walk, never mind with the dog and then at night.

Laura and Hektor were glad they had broken the news. Once they were alone, they hugged each other and kissed. Laura couldn't resist. She touched Hektor all over. They heard the dog bark by the back door. Laura looked her most prim and proper when Millie Prior walked into the living room. Laura's mother insisted the newlyweds spend the night in her and Melvin's fourposter bed. Linens were changed and the room straightened for the honeymooners. After having a drink and toasting the bride and groom, the Priors bid them good night, and Laura and Hektor retired to the fourposter.

They turned off the last light and held each other. Hektor was ready to test the sound spectrum of the fancy bed. He loved lying on top of Laura. He was ready to make love to her when Caitlin entered the house and slammed the side door. They couldn't help hearing the commotion downstairs.

"So much for enjoying the fourposter," voiced the groom.

Caitlin was taken completely by surprise, seeing her parents sitting in the living room. "What gives? How come you are still up? You weren't waiting up for me, right? What's with the strange expressions on your faces? Is anything wrong?"

"Nothing is wrong. Your sister and Hektor ran off and got

married on Thursday. It's not wrong as far as they are concerned, but it surely took us by surprise. They seem to be very happy. They are upstairs in our bed as we speak."

"I have to check this one out for myself." She charged up the steps and knocked on the door. "Birken, get your butt out of bed. I want to see the rings and, more important, the marriage license. No sister of mine is sleeping with a guy without a license!"

Hektor could appreciate Caitlin's fifteen-year-old exuberance. He reached down the side of the bed for his Jockey shorts, slipped them on, and got the license out of his briefcase. Being aroused, he didn't want to face his young sister-in-law. Always acting quite mature for her age, it might not have shocked her to see a naked man.

Hektor slipped back under the covers and asked Caitlin to come in, wanting to show her their wedding bands and the license. Hektor didn't blame her for making sure they were legal. After she had studied the document sufficiently, she nodded her approval. She walked over to Laura and gave her a great big kiss and hug.

"I'm gonna miss you, Winnie Pooh, but I'm happy for you." Her big, brown eyes focused on Hektor. "You better be nice to my sister and love her the way she deserves to be loved." Departing for her room, she tossed over her shoulder, "OK, guys, sleep well. Sleep, my foot!" She walked out of the room, closing the door none too gently.

Sunday became moving day. Beds were moved from the attic into different rooms, trying to accommodate Hektor and Laura for a few weeks until they could establish their own home. When they finally settled on the temporary arrangements in the house on Kurtis Road, Laura's mom sat down with her address file to plan a party to celebrate the wedding. She still wasn't sure what she would tell people when asked to explain the unusual circumstance of their union.

A few days after they got married, Hektor and Laura thought they needed to let family and friends know what transpired. They sat down and composed a short note.

"We are busier than you can imagine. Nevertheless, Laura and I feel we owe you a brief explanation in this enclosure to our wedding announcement. A week ago, we were communicating with my friend, Harry, in Liberia. I asked him to be my witness in our wedding, tentatively planned for October 1964. Obviously, we changed our minds about the date and were married three days ago. No one in the family knew of the event. My boss and a friend of Laura's were our witnesses at the civil ceremony conducted at the Detroit City Hall. For now, we are staying with Laura's parents until we can locate suitable housing. We have no regrets about the unusual manner in which we were hitched. Laura's parents couldn't complain; as many of you know, they did the same thing many years ago. For now, wish us well in our latest adventure. Stay tuned for further announcements."

Eventually, the Prior phone stopped ringing. Friends and family members wanting to congratulate the happy couple were advised they could do so in person at a reception scheduled for the second of November. Millie Prior took charge of the situation. Hektor and Laura's marriage was to be blessed during a private service at the Grosse Pointe Methodist Church, followed by a reception at Laura's parents' home. Of course, the living room area needed to be painted, the carpeting replaced, and several pieces of furniture reupholstered prior to the event.

Chapter 39

AUDREY entered their lives on the thirtieth of September in 1963; that is, Laura met her on that day. She and her aunt Mariah had studied the vacancy columns in the *Detroit Free Press*. They found a second-floor apartment for seventy dollars a month on Marion Boulevard. Laura and her aunt checked out numerous other apartments. None of them seemed satisfactory. They contacted Audrey by phone and learned her offering was still for rent.

Aunt Mariah was well versed in searches for housing. She was the right person to assist Laura. After Audrey showed them the flat, Aunt Mariah began the negotiating process.

"The price is OK, but the place is badly in need of a paint job and updating. The wooden ice box in the kitchen has to go. Those gas-station blue and chocolate-brown walls in the dining room and the bedrooms must be painted."

After some haggling, Audrey consented to buying a modern refrigerator of reasonable size. They rented the unit, subject to the negotiated improvements and Hektor's final approval.

Hektor and Laura walked through the apartment. They could see all the possibilities of enhancing its appearance.

"Let's take it," said Hektor. "It's convenient to my job. If you have to, you can take the bus on Grand River to the office. We need to paint the whole darn place, especially that ugly fireplace—it could be improved by painting it white to match the walls. It will give us plenty of room for entertaining. And, of course, we need to buy some furniture. Let's go and see Audrey. She sounds like a character."

They made their way down to her flat and were excited about having found a suitable home so quickly. Hektor knocked on the door. The scene was somewhat reminiscent of Hänsel and Gretel knocking on the witch's door.

"Who is there?" came a scratchy, definitely elderly voice from behind the door.

"It's Laura and Hektor Birken."

"Just a moment, please. I have to find my keys to unlock all these locks."

"What does she mean by 'unlocking all these locks'?" said Hektor.

"You'll see; she is quite eccentric."

Hektor couldn't believe it as he listened to key after key being turned in the various locks. At last, the door slowly opened. There stood a tiny woman with long, straggly hair, tinted in shades of carrot-red. At the moment, she looked like she was in need of a color redo. Audrey peered over the top of her bifocals and looked Hektor over from top to bottom. *She has to be at least eighty*, he thought. Her face was marked by deep wrinkles. What appeared to be her breasts were slumped down to her waist. Audrey was wearing an unflattering house dress.

"Please come in. What do you think of the place? Do you believe you and your new bride could be happy upstairs? Yes, I concede it needs updating. I will pay for all the materials if you will do the work. I won't charge you a deposit or any rent until the fifteenth of October. This will give you time to make all the improvements and changes your wife and her aunt discussed with me. I ordered a new refrigerator. Montgomery Ward will deliver it after you paint the kitchen. I'm not changing the linoleum; it's not a pretty color, but the quality of the floor covering is still good."

Finally, Hektor could get in a word edgewise. "We can accept your conditions and will plan to move in sometime after the tenth of October. We are borrowing some furniture from my in-laws until we can find new things. Did you tell my wife you are leaving for Miami within a week? And did I understand you are renting your home to another young couple?"

"Yes, the Solomons are coming back on Wednesday night to finalize their arrangements with me. I would like it very much if you and your wife could join us for drinks and hors d'oeuvres. It would be a nice way for all of you to become acquainted."

They shook hands on the deal and assured Audrey they would be delighted to meet with the Solomons.

When leaving Audrey's apartment, Hektor counted six locks on the front door. They pinched themselves as they were walking out. Once in the little Falcon, they broke into bursts of laughter.

"Have you ever seen anything like it?" asked Laura.

"No, I surely have not. She must be paranoid about her safety. Well, to each his own. In a way, I am glad she is here for only a few months each summer and seems to like Miami and the warmer climate during the colder time of year. I am looking forward to meeting our winter housemates on Wednesday night."

Laura wore a nice dress to the office. These days, Hektor always sported some kind of suit and tie as his business attire. He picked her up at the bus stop, and they eagerly looked forward to the evening.

Audrey finally cracked open the door; both Hektor and Laura

almost keeled over. She had undergone a major "transfiguration" since Hektor first met her. While she still had her wrinkles, they had become secondary as a result of her new-and-improved appearance. She wore a stunning, stylish black dress over her sleek figure; that is, undergarments clearly gave her an attractive bust and waistline. An expensive strand of pearls with a large diamond clasp graced her neck. The diamonds on her hands and throat were definitely not of the paste variety. She was wearing four-inch-high heels and a shocking red bouffant wig that called attention to itself.

Wow, they thought and had a hard time controlling their facial muscles. Neither wanted to betray their utter shock. Audrey extended a graceful hand, welcoming Laura and Hektor to her little soirée and turned to introduce them to the Solomons.

"I would like you to meet Laura and Hektor Birken; these are Susan and Edmond Solomon."

The Solomons were in their late teens and also a newlywed couple. She was a waitress, and he worked at one of the automobile plants. With Audrey's shockingly beautiful reinvention and the introductions behind them, all settled down to enjoy a glass of wine and the hors d'oeuvres their hostess offered. The conversation became lively as their landlady shared some of her background with her new tenants. She kept winking at Hektor, since he was almost ten years older than the others. The young people sat there, all ears, listening to Audrey tell of her marital escapades.

"My second husband enjoyed kinky sex. I don't remember how often he ravished me on the kitchen table." When she came out with that corker, Hektor couldn't help himself from laughing out loud. "At present, I am widowed. Who knows? There may be a number-four husband somewhere in this universe."

Little did they realize on that evening that there *was* a number four in Audrey's future. He came along a few years later and turned out to be gay. He and a jealous lover would murder her by drowning Audrey in boiling-hot water in her fancy bathtub.

All of her stories were hilarious. Never in their wildest imaginations had they expected their landlady to be so eccentric. Hektor couldn't resist inquiring about the multiple locks.

"Mrs. A., why do you have so many locks on the doors? Are you afraid that someone might break in?"

"Exactly! My hearing is not the best. With so much riffraff in the cities these days, I feel safer behind all my locks."

"I can accept your rationale. Who knows what we might do as we get older?"

"Don't talk to me about getting older. Age is just a state of mind. Please don't consider me an old person. I still have what it takes. I hope you young folks get along well in my absence. It was fun to spend the evening with you."

𝄡

They had not heard from Harry for some time. As they learned later, he was between assignments. The contract in Liberia was fulfilled, and he was temporarily reassigned to the headquarters in Houston and was on a three-month furlough before starting a new job in Kingston, Jamaica. Harry left Liberia in mid-October and toured Europe for a month. While in Germany, he stopped to see Hektor's family.

Later, Albert talked for years about the amount of alcohol Harry could put away without ever showing any signs of inebriation.

Twenty days after Hektor and Laura's wedding reception, the nation was rocked by the assassination of President Kennedy. Harry was halfway across the Atlantic when the deadly bullets were fired in Dallas. He didn't learn of the violent act and the death of the president until his plane touched down at New York International Airport. He called the Birkens on Thanksgiving Day, and they made plans for him to visit right after the New Year.

✳

After the Christmas rush, Hektor and Laura looked forward to Harry's visit. They picked him up at Metropolitan Airport. Harry walked toward Hektor and Laura. Hektor almost didn't recognize Harry. He was sporting a full head of snow-white hair.

"How are you, you damned immigrant? Gosh, you are a sight for sore eyes. Better yet, is this the young thing you snatched for yourself? You are one lucky son of a gun. How did you ever convince her to marry you? You've got all the luck in the world. I hope you have a good supply of booze at home."

"Don't worry about a good supply of booze. Are you still drinking that awful stuff you used to put away?"

"What do you mean? My J&B and milk? Yup, I still consider it my favorite poison. Perhaps it's a little heavier on the scotch these days; otherwise, nothing has changed—other than my hair. I got tired of that butch look. What do you think?"

"You sure shocked me. I think it looks great! As far as your gorgeous mane is concerned, you are taking after your dad."

Laura fixed an Italian dish. Hektor had clued her in on Harry's culinary likes and dislikes. He loved her dinner; even more, he enjoyed being with Laura and Hektor. Jet lag and the J&B did their jobs as the evening wore on. Harry announced, "Douse der Glimmer"—his attempt at saying, "Turn off the lights," or "Let's call it a day" in his special version of German.

He was full of praise for Laura's domestic skills. Most of all, he admired her wholesome approach to issues at hand and the genuine affection she showered on both Hektor and him. Laura soon realized she was looking at a diamond in the rough. Harry's crusty exterior was more of a defense mechanism than anything else. While Laura was futzing around in the kitchen, they had a little bad-boy talk.

"Are you enjoying what you're getting? Laura has great teats. I betcha you love them. How's she in bed? Are you trying for some kids? She'd make a great mother. Not like that bitch you finally succeeded in ditching. Man, it was high time for that."

"Boy, you are a nosy, horny son of a gun. Laura and I are doing just fine. To this day, we can't believe Georgia didn't contest any part of the legal separation agreement. When Dempsey F. Pennington III, the attorney in Birmingham, called me with the good news, neither he nor we could believe how smoothly all of it went. But like I said on my tape, we didn't quibble about it. All I could say was good riddance. She was one goddamn bitch. Thanks again for saving my life. I would have never experienced Sheila or Laura if not for you. Sheila surely knew how to make my pecker sing. Don't get me wrong; Laura does a good job too. Sheila was just a bit more practiced. Remember that night at the Biltmore? I can still see you standing in that fancy French door. I thought you were going to piss on the floor. Your *oops* keeps ringing in my ears. That was one hell of a night. Boy, did both of us need that. I was so frigging tired of whipping my own dick."

Harry cracked up. "Where is that scotch? Is Laura hiding it from me?"

"No, it's right there. Are you sure you want to spoil it with milk?"

"Listen, my ulcers are damn bad. That was a pretty tough assignment in Liberia. I didn't do it with any of the beautiful black women, but I came close to it. I understand what you mean about whipping one's own boy into shape. I need a woman in my life. You don't know how lucky you two are. I am so envious of your relationship. I wish I could find a nice girl like Laura."

Hektor remembered a girl from their days in Long Island. "How about Carolina, the buyer in the Fur Department at R&S? She always struck me as a special person. Laura reminds me a lot of her.

I always thought she was sweet on you. When you get back home, a telephone call might not hurt. What do you have to lose?"

With that seed planted, Harry returned to New York. A few months later, Harry and Carolina were married.

Chapter 40

IN late February, Laura and Hektor made their first of many trips to upstate New York to visit Frank and Karen. The trip took them through Canada. On their way, they stopped at Niagara Falls, a fascinating sight during the winter months. Georgia and the children were now living in the Hudson Valley in the vicinity of West Point. Hektor drove on the New York Throughway from Buffalo to Newburgh, where they located a motel room that evening. The next morning, they searched out Georgia's address and eventually located the small house on a large lot outside town. Chickens scratched in the dirt that once had been a lawn surrounding the little abode. Hektor rang the doorbell, and a young lady, perhaps sixteen or seventeen, answered the door.

"We are looking for Georgia Birken. She is my former wife."

"Just a moment; let me call her. We received your letter, and she is expecting you."

With that, Georgia made her grand entrance, carrying a newborn infant like a football on her left hip.

Hektor's jaw dropped. "Hi. May I ask who this is?"

Georgia was only too happy to brag. "Of course you may. He is my newest toy. His name is Alexander Stratton. I gave birth to him on Valentine's Day. I jumped off a chair to induce labor; that way, he was born on a special day."

Laura and Hektor looked at each other and started counting. There was the answer to the question that had puzzled them since the previous July. Hektor winked at Laura; his facial expression conveying his thoughts. *That's the good reason why the bitch didn't contest anything. She was pregnant and only too anxious to tie the knot with Mr. Stratton, a divorcee with seven children of his own.*

Later, Hektor shook his head. "She didn't know how to take care of one, never mind ten children." Eventually, there would be eleven.

This was none of their business. Georgia and her new husband had to deal with their own problems. Nothing had changed as far as Hektor's responsibilities were concerned since Georgia only received child support. They spent a fun day with Frank and Karen, taking them to a petting zoo and out to lunch and dinner.

Karen was going on five. She was Georgia all over again in looks. She had the cutest haircut. Her hair was a pretty shade of red. She didn't need the help her mother always gave to her own hair. She had a sweet disposition and was pleased to see her daddy.

Now that Hektor and Laura had a better idea of the sizes the children were wearing, they could outfit both of them with the new clothing they seemed to desperately need. They took the kids shopping. Among other things, they got them swimsuits. Karen insisted on modeling hers for her daddy. She stood with one hand tucked in where there would be a breast in years to come. She was quite the model. Karen was sweet and had a soft voice. As far as she was concerned, Hektor was her daddy and not Mr. Stratton.

Frank was inquisitive and kept pushing about a trip to Detroit. "Daddy, when can we come and visit you?" he wanted to know.

"I will have to discuss that with your mother. Laura and I hope you will be able to come to Detroit sometime this summer."

At first, Georgia was opposed to letting the children out of state.

Eventually, Mr. Stratton convinced her that it might give them a break if Frank and Karen were gone for a week or two. Georgia was only too happy to return Don Stratton's children to his first wife periodically, especially the younger ones in the bunch. The two older girls were welcome household slaves. It was easier for the Stratton kids to spend time with their mother. They didn't have to travel quite as far as Frank and Karen did.

"We will look into the cost of flying Frank and Karen to Detroit. We'd like to have them for ten days in late August. I believe our agreement stipulates that I am entitled to have the children for longer than that. We will call you as soon as we know the details."

They left with that understanding. Laura was heartbroken to leave Hektor's children. For now, there was nothing that could be done about it. They headed northwest toward Birchtown, driving through the wintry landscape in silence on their way to see Estelle and Patrick Swansong. Their house in Evers sat on top of a steep hill, commanding a beautiful view of the entire valley.

Estelle and Patrick were just what they needed. They immediately fell in love with Laura and could not have made her more welcome. By now, the Swansongs had two children. They were of school age, and Estelle had gone back to work. She liked her position as a lab technician at one of the local hospitals. Patrick was in business for himself.

They went out to dinner. Patrick succeeded in swinging Laura around in a couple of polkas, a dance Hektor had never particularly enjoyed.

Estelle couldn't wait any longer. "When we get to the house, I want to hear all about how you met and why you chose to get married the way you did. I know you briefly touched on that in your Christmas letter. Now I want to get the lowdown. It all sounds so romantic," chimed Estelle.

The visit to Birchtown was a mix of joy and sadness for Hektor. The Shelves had not changed at all. They were delighted to meet

Hektor's new bride. Martina Parcells was happy living in her little shack out in the country. Knut Schiefer had moved to New Jersey and married Gertrude's sister after his dear wife succumbed to her long battle with cancer. Hannah von Unselm had moved to New England in order to be closer to her two married sons.

The next day, Hektor and Laura drove back to Detroit. It was a long trip, especially during the winter months. Laura was so glad to have met Hektor's children. She also was pleased to have met Estelle and Patrick, Hektor's longest-standing friends in the United States, people who clearly meant much to him. Martina fell in love with Laura during their all-too-brief first visit with her, and the Shelves approved of Hektor's choice of a second wife.

Hektor turned toward Laura. "Don't you think Estelle and Patrick are some of the dearest people one could know? I have no idea what I would have done without them in those dark days of 1958. Those two will always be special to me."

"Yes, they are very dear. I don't blame you at all for feeling that way. How lucky we are to have each other, to share the life we enjoy, and treasure the special relationships we built with our family and friends. Most of all, I am thankful our paths crossed," mused Laura.

"Yup, like I always tell you, it's all in the timing. We were at the right place at the right time."

"I still like to think it was meant to be," Laura said.

Just then, Tony Bennett was on the radio, singing, "Love is wonderful, the second time around . . ."

Hektor couldn't agree more with Mr. Bennett as they pulled into the driveway on Marion Boulevard.

As promised during their first visit to see the children in New York, Laura arranged a trip to Detroit for Frank and Karen. She learned the children had to fly first-class (a requirement in 1964 for children traveling unaccompanied by an adult). She bit into the sour financial apple and arranged for the visit.

The trip itself turned into a nightmare, due to Georgia's total unreliability. The kids—that is, Georgia—missed not one but two flights before they were finally on their way to Detroit. Laura drove back and forth between airports. She almost couldn't believe it when Frank and Karen at last emerged from the plane, but she could have sunk into the ground. The children were in rags—filthy rags to boot. They each carried a paper sack with one change of well-worn and dirty underwear and socks.

"Are these the children you have been looking for since this afternoon?" inquired the airline agent.

"Yes, ma'am, they are," Laura said. "They are a sight for sore eyes."

Standing behind the kids, the airline agent raised her eyebrows and rolled her eyes. She seemed to imply she understood the situation but did not want to embarrass the children by commenting on their appearance.

Laura gave them big hugs, dirt and all. She looked for a payphone at the airport and called Hektor. "You have no idea what your kids look like. When I saw them, I couldn't believe what I saw. The airline personnel couldn't wait to get rid of them. They are filthy dirty and smell to high heaven. I refuse to bring them into the store. You would die of embarrassment. We'll wait for you in the parking lot. I thought I would never say this, but your first wife truly is a piece of work. You were right in describing her as a real bitch. To do this to those children and to us is simply beyond belief."

They finally arrived at the Tip Top Store. The children jumped out of the car and flew into their daddy's arms, bringing tears to Hektor's and Laura's eyes.

Once they got home to their flat, the first order of business was a heavy-duty bath for each of them. At first, they cried and begged not to take baths, but when Frank stepped into the tub, he was pleas-antly surprised.

"It's not bad, Karen," Frank said. "This tub has warm water!"

After putting the kids in Hektor's T-shirts, they were fed and put to bed.

Hektor and Laura later learned from Karen that Georgia had deliberately sent them on this journey in their oldest clothes. Hektor and Laura were stunned, but Frank told them it was true.

"Mommy said, 'I know you don't want to travel in these rags to Detroit. Maybe when they see how poor you are, they will dip into their f-ing pockets and buy you some decent clothes. They can afford it!'"

Their first day in Detroit started with appointments at the dentist, followed by haircuts, and then a shopping spree for new clothes and shoes. Hektor and Laura opted to have the children visit with family and friends on the weekend. They toured the zoo, Greenfield Village, and downtown Detroit during the week. It was a fun time for all. By the time the children had to board the plane for New York, they had only one question: "When will we get to see you again?"

"We will see you in October for sure," promised Hektor.

Chapter 41

In January 1965, Hektor and Laura finalized their plans for a belated honeymoon. As they boarded the plane, neither had any idea of what an adventurous journey they had embarked upon. They arrived in London on the morning of February 5, six days after Sir Winston Churchill's funeral. It was a partly sunny but cool day. They checked into the Strand Hotel and were satisfied with their accommodations. Nothing was special, but the location was ideal. They took a hop-on/hop-off bus tour in the morning and then revisited some of the typical "musts" in the heart of London.

Laura loved it all, but Hektor hardly dared open his mouth. The tour guides were still espousing the evil deeds the Germans had visited upon them during the war. While Hektor couldn't help agreeing with the Brits, he believed that not all Germans, particularly those of his generation, should constantly be portrayed as evil.

In the evening, they had a typical English meal at *Simpson's*. Neither Hektor nor Laura were particularly impressed with the food. The next day, they went to lunch at *Rules of London* in the theater district. The restaurant had been in existence since 1798 and came highly recommended. First, they made sure that women were allowed in the establishment, since they had learned the day before that some restaurants only served men. They were seated and ordered Italian cuisine. The food was superb. Hektor couldn't resist the English trifle shown them on the dessert table.

"Would you care for coffee with your dessert, ma'am?" asked the waiter.

Laura declined and asked for black tea. Hektor elected to have coffee, which was placed next to his trifle promptly. After five minutes or so, Hektor wondered what had happened to Laura's tea. He motioned to the waiter.

"Did you forget about my wife's tea?"

The good man shook his head and stepped back to the spot where he'd stood like a statue.

Hektor turned toward the waiter again. "Sir, this is London, isn't it? I would have thought you would have tea."

This time the waiter stood closer to Hektor; he was going to put the foreigner in his place. "Yes, sir, we have tea, but we do not serve tea with meals. *It…just…isn't…done!*"

In no uncertain terms, Hektor and Laura were advised, albeit without discretion or courtesy, of their ignorance relative to English tea etiquette. That was it. Laura never did get a cup of tea in Rules of London (at least not until forty-one years later, when they paid a second visit to Rules).

Hektor settled the bill. Once outside, as soon as they passed the heavy, padded-leather wind catch, they had a good laugh. The lunch had been great, but the waiter was a stitch with his pompous English demeanor.

Later that afternoon, when they did have tea in an old English pub, they realized they had completely forgotten it was Hektor's birthday. Neither of them could believe they were that immersed in their discoveries of London. Before they flew to Germany, they stopped at the duty-free shop and bought two bottles of J&B, just in case they could not find it in Germany.

Albert picked them up at the Frankfurt airport. He made sure to take them straight to their parents' new apartment. Laura had no way of knowing how different the place was. All she knew from Hektor were his descriptions of the place on Kupferstrasse, where he'd grown up and had his traumatic experiences.

They rang the doorbell and were ushered in by Helena and Margarethe.

"Welcome, welcome," his mother said, extending her hand in greeting.

Laura thought she might get a hug. Not so. Helena wasn't quite sure how to receive this new woman in her son's life; in Helena's opinion, Laura was the second nemesis that prevented Hektor from returning to the familial fold. On top of all else, she had expected Laura to be a regular "Amazon or Brünhilde"—Hektor couldn't help overhearing an aside.

"But she is so little!"

The explanation came later. Shortly after they were married, Hektor and Laura had a formal photo taken and had sent it as a Christmas present. Laura did have a full bosom, and the dress she wore seemed to emphasize her physique. The photographer posed her in front of Hektor, almost dwarfing him in the background. The reel-to-reel recordings they exchanged with the family presented Laura's voice a full octave lower than her real voice, due to the difference in cycles of American versus European electrical current. Taking these facts together, the family surmised Hektor was married to "Superwoman."

Hektor's father welcomed his new daughter-in-law with a bear hug; he was pleased that Hektor had found and married a good woman. He just smiled a lot. "Sorry, I don't speak English," he kept apologizing.

Helena sounded like a broken record.

Laura could tell right away that she had upset many of Helena's plans for her son. She made up her mind she would deal with it in good time. She felt absolutely useless because of the language barrier. On one occasion, she convinced Mother Birken she could be of assistance, washing or drying the dishes after a family dinner. Of course, the very best china was used for eight or ten persons. Helena reluctantly agreed to have Laura help her in the very small kitchen. She demonstrated and instructed her in German.

"First, my dishes must be scraped and pre-rinsed. Then I will wash them in soapy water and rinse them twice before I hand them to you for drying."

Of course, she talked in her machine-gun speed of delivery and always finished a sentence by turning to Laura and saying, *"Hast Du wieder nicht verstanden?"* ["You didn't understand that again, did you?"] Both women were utterly frustrated.

After handing Laura the sixth dinner plate, one that wasn't properly rinsed, it slipped out of Laura's hands. It struck the stack of already dried dinner plates, which resulted in four broken plates. Helena glared at the damage done and then at Laura.

"How could you do such a stupid thing? With your young hands, you shouldn't have any difficulty holding onto a plate without dropping it. I knew I shouldn't have allowed you to help me. All you American women are good for is painting your nails and lounging around."

It was a good thing Laura didn't understand a word of what Helena had said, but she got the body language and knew she had arrived on the top of Helena's special list. Laura wanted to die on the spot.

Helena realized she had overreacted. Once she recovered from her initial shock, she faced her daughter-in-law and said, "That much less to be thrown on the inheritance heap." She dismissed the issue as if nothing earthshaking had happened.

When her last will and testament were read twenty-one years later, she revealed her true self: "I leave all my personal belongings to my favorite daughter-in-law, Laura, including my jewelry, linens, silver, and my very best china—that is, the pieces that survived the onslaught!" She never quite forgot the incident during Laura's first visit.

The honeymooners tried to be as diplomatic as possible, but Hektor insisted he show off his new bride to his uncles and aunts, despite the fact that none of them were on speaking terms with his mother. His brother, Albert, and his family had, at the moment, declared a truce with the senior Birkens. Albert had left his father's business and found a promising position running the meat department in a branch of a large department store. Ultimately, it proved to be one of the wisest commitments he ever made.

As far as the senior Birkens were concerned, losing their slave labor caused the demise of their business, forcing them into early retirement, for which they were not prepared—financially or otherwise. Helena never did own up to the fact that her irrational behavior and moving out of Alex's life after the most recent attempt on her life was the root cause of giving up their business on Kupferstrasse. Hektor and Laura tried to strike an acceptable balance between spending time with his parents, his brother and family, Greta Beerenbaum, and the "outcast" members of the family.

After ten days in Essen, they headed for a weekend in Worms, visiting the Weldenfeldts. Hektor was eager to introduce his bride to his friend Peter and his family. They spent a delightful afternoon with Peter and Gerda and their children. They were sipping champagne when it finally dawned on Hektor that Laura had been gone for quite a while.

"I wonder what happened to Laura. She had to use the lavatory," said Hektor.

Peter explained. "Oh, she probably fell victim to our temperamental lock. Sometimes when people don't turn the key just right, they can't get out. Let me go with you; maybe we can talk her out of the bathroom. You may have to translate the instructions."

Indeed, Laura was trapped in the WC. No one had heard her

pounding on the door to get someone's attention. Once they discovered what had happened, Hektor knew Laura wouldn't be too happy.

"OK, honey, if you put a washcloth around the key and turn it first to the left and then push it up before turning it to the right, the door should open." And indeed, it did.

Laura was furious. "This custom of locking the bathroom with a key is crazy. After your dad walked in on me a few times without knocking on the door, I figured I'd better follow the local custom and use the key. So much for that! I've had just about enough of Europe."

Peter and Gerda arranged for them to stay at a small pension hotel not far from their home. When they arrived at the pension during the wee hours of morning, Hektor dropped the huge key with its wooden block and heavy chain on the hardwood floor in front of their room. He thought he might have wakened every other guest in the hotel. Then they discovered they had to use the WC in the hallway—one for gentlemen and the other for ladies. Laura was in her slip as she headed for the bathroom. She cracked open their room door but closed it quickly.

"That was a close call. There is a huge naked man in the foyer, doing his exercises."

Hektor opened the door and took a peek. "Yes, the man is big, and he is doing bend-overs but he isn't naked. He is wearing very minuscule bikini briefs. And you're right, his ass is practically bare."

They waited a few minutes before they tried again. The man had disappeared.

"Let's head for the john; the coast is clear." As they were in their respective rooms, listening to the sound effects, they cracked up. So much for privacy.

The room had twin beds. They got naked; after all, they were on their honeymoon, although delayed. They wanted to sleep together in one of the small beds. Hektor got next to Laura.

"I love the feel of your body close to mine. That warmth of yours radiates all through me. You want to come on top of me?" Laura whispered.

As Hektor did, the bed collapsed. They deferred their lovemaking until their first night in Paris. They finally slept in the other bed for a few hours.

Later that morning, they boarded a trans-European express—or TEE—train for Paris. They took a cab to the Hotel Molière, located just off the Rue L'Opera. Madelyn, a good friend of Laura's, who studied at the Sorbonne, had recommended the hotel.

"Don't worry about your French. Their concierge always speaks English or German." Those were Madelyn's famous last words.

Hektor paid the cabby and held the door open for Laura. He stepped up to the desk and inquired in his best French if the concierge spoke either English or German.

"Regrettably not," was the reply.

Hektor negotiated in French for a room with one bed. The concierge smiled and was friendly enough. He handed Hektor the key and motioned for a maid to accompany them to the fourth floor.

They rode up in a rickety wire-caged elevator. Hektor thought this looked like shades of Naples. When the chambermaid opened the door to the room, they were amazed at the size. It was huge, with two single beds on opposite walls.

Hektor shook his head and tried his French again. "I asked for one bed, not two."

The maid laughed, closed the door, and pointed to the elevator. They soon began their descent in the wire cage for another round with the concierge. The man apologized for the mistake and handed the maid a different key. When they beheld their next chamber, they faced a single, huge bed in the center of the sizable room. She walked them into the bathroom, which held the longest bathtub either of them had ever seen. The room looked pleasant and clean.

Hektor inquired of the maid, "How much?"

She didn't grasp the meaning and assumed he was asking something about the fourposter. She took his right hand and walked him over to the side of the bed. She drew an invisible line in the center and then pointed to the left half—"Madame"—and then to the right side—"Monsieur"—slapping her hands together, while turning them quickly and repeatedly upside-down and saying, *"Uh-uh-uh!"* She was obviously trying to tell them what action she expected to occur in the bed.

Hektor looked her straight in the eye and said, "Honey, I know how it works, but how much?"

As he used the international gesture of rubbing his right thumb against his fingers, she finally understood what he was asking. She closed the door and pointed to a sign on the back, with the prices shown in francs. All three of them laughed heartily at their charming communication deficiencies.

It was the beginning of five wonderful days in the City of Lights. They delighted in experiencing most of the venues every visitor to Paris must see at least once and enjoyed venturing into neighborhood restaurants that tested their linguistic abilities—spoken along with the generous use of body language.

After their last breakfast, enjoying wonderful, fresh croissants, Hektor glanced at Laura. "Well, what did you think of Paris? Wasn't it fun? We'll have to come back someday."

"Next time, let's fly right to Paris and spend all the time we want. I just love the atmosphere. It's utterly charming and has so much to offer. Perhaps I could take some cooking classes."

"I'll keep it in mind."

They boarded the TEE for the return trip to Essen. The train seemed endlessly long. They found a first-class compartment and settled in with their luggage. They shed their winter coats and hats and made themselves comfortable. Soon, it was time to go to the dining car. Hektor selected a special meal from the menu in celebration of the successful conclusion of their first trip to France.

They were enjoying their Cabernet as the waiter skillfully served the medallions of veal with all the trimmings. He was holding the gravy boat, standing next to Hektor, as he asked Laura if she cared for some sauce on her potatoes and meat. The train hit an uneven connection between rails, causing a momentary shift in the otherwise steady hand of the waiter. The result was the gravy landed in Hektor's crotch rather than on Laura's plate.

The waiter apologized profusely, explaining in French that he would be right back. And so he was. With a white terry-cloth towel and a bowl filled with boiling-hot water, he proceeded to blot and rub the gravy out of Hektor's gray-flannel slacks in a strategic spot. Hektor wasn't quite sure how to respond to the attention he was receiving. He got up from his chair and looked at his soaked slacks.

"Merci, merci, merci beaucoup. Thank you very much. No more rubbing, please." He gestured to get his message across. Laura could see why he wanted to stop the treatment.

The waiter finally understood. He bowed from the waist repeatedly and kept waving a dry towel in the direction of Hektor's pants.

"Don't worry," Hektor said. "We'll have the slacks taken care of by a dry cleaner in Germany."

Obviously, the attentive waiter understood neither German nor English. Laura was almost in hysterics, laughing mostly at the expression on Hektor's face.

After being in the dining car for more than two hours, they headed back to their compartment. Many of the cars were totally empty. Now they wondered if they would find their belongings intact. No problem—everything was just as they had left it.

Laura took one look at his soaked slacks.

"Get out some dry underwear and a different pair of pants," Laura said. "We can put what you have on in this plastic bag. You can't travel in that condition all the way to Essen."

They pulled down the shades, and Hektor changed.

"Phew! That was some treatment I got from that guy. Between the heat and his attentive rubbing, he almost got a rise out of me."

"You aren't just kidding. I could see what was happening. I almost wet my pants from laughing so hard."

"I didn't think it was so funny!"

Eventually, they played a game with miniature cards. Shortly after the train pulled into the station in Liège, someone banged on the window and called out in a strange language, which turned out to be Walloon, a French dialect spoken in southern Belgium. Hektor raised the shade and looked at a conductor frantically waving his hands, trying to tell them they had to move ahead into another car.

It was then that Hektor realized he'd never looked at the sign on the outside of the wagon when they got on the train in Paris. This time, they made sure they entered a car that would stay with the train all the way to Essen and beyond. Had they turned off the lights in their compartment, they might have discovered the next morning that their railcar was uncoupled and dead-railed in Liège.

Shortly before Hektor and Laura's departure for Detroit, Albert and Margarethe gave a splendid party for their visitors. Margarethe decorated the living room with confetti, streamers, and the centerfolds of the *Playboy* magazines Hektor had brought for his brother. He never shared that the shady magazines almost got him in trouble. When checking in at the Detroit airport, the Pan Am agent inquired as to the contents of his weighty briefcase; he was satisfied with Hektor's reply that he carried much business correspondence. Hektor held his breath until the agent smiled, not asking to inspect the contents. Laura could have sunken into the ground.

Several of Albert's and Hektor's contemporaries and their spouses were invited to the celebration. Laura was seated in a corner spot, allowing her at least to make eye contact with the invited guests. Albert wanted to know how to fix "that whiskey stuff."

Hektor told him what to do. "Use one shot glass of J&B with two shots of water over ice."

Albert thought it sounded like a pretty lousy drink and reversed the specified quantities.

Laura commented, after sipping the first drink, "This drink is pretty healthy. What is he doing?"

Hektor told her the exact instructions he'd given Albert. "Let's not make a big deal of it; just sip slowly."

Laura sipped, smoked, and smiled a lot. When she had to use the lavatory a few hours later, she stood up and fell flat on her face. Hektor and Albert carried her to Alberti's room. He was spending the night with his maternal grandparents.

When Laura came to, she began to cry. "I'm ready to go home."

"We're going home in a little while," Hektor assured her.

"I don't want to go home to your mother's; I want to go home to America," she whined, using a voice Hektor never had heard before. Clearly, she was still in the soup; certainly a case of too much J&B and not enough water. Laura never lived down the fact that she was the star attraction of the party, surpassing by far the impact of the notorious *Playboy* centerfolds.

After bidding goodbye to the senior Birkens a few days later, they were off to Frankfurt with Albert and his family. Margarethe and Laura had become soul mates at first sight. They found it most difficult to part company, especially not knowing when they might see each other again.

The transatlantic flight was pleasant, but the journey from New York to Detroit turned into a nightmare. Due to terrible weather conditions, they wound up traveling by train. Millie and Melvin picked them up at the depot in Detroit. Laura was thrilled to be home with her family but even more so to be with people with whom she could communicate.

Chapter 42

HEKTOR and Laura had sufficiently recovered from their European sojourn and were both in their daily grooves of working hard. Easter 1965 was a thing of the past. One late afternoon in May, when Hektor came home, Laura greeted him with a glass of red wine in her hand. He looked at her, startled, and wasn't sure what to expect.

"Are you pregnant? What are we celebrating? Do you have some bad news for me? What gives with the wine?"

"Dinner is in the oven. We have a good hour to enjoy a glass or two. I have been meaning to have this chat for some time. It concerns you; it concerns me; it concerns both of us."

Uncharacteristically, she had caught Hektor completely off guard. "What's wrong?" he asked, "What have I done to deserve such a mysterious introduction? Please clue me in."

"You haven't done anything wrong. It's something that's been bothering me for some time. If there ever was a time to discuss it, it's now. It's not you; it's your work. You are doing a great job, and you are obviously appreciated by the management of the company. *But*...are you really in it with your heart and soul? Is this what you would like to do until you retire in thirty-five years or so? That is, if you are still alive at the rate you're going."

Hektor looked pensive. "Interesting questions. What choices do I have? I'm thirty-one years old and have two children and us to support. I suppose I could try getting a job in the automobile industry. I'm not sure if I would make a very good used-car salesman. I'm a pretty good actor, but that kind of job would be almost too much of an acting job for me. What ya got in mind, young lady?"

"I think you should consider going back to school and getting a degree in what was denied to you in Germany due to your screwed-up education." *Fucked-up education*—Laura would never use such words. "You are a bright man. You are well read and have mastered the English language to a degree that will allow you to study anything you wish. I watch you reading certain catalogs at times and can see those wheels turning. Don't deny yourself. Follow your dream. You might even consider acting school, if that's what you want to do. It might be a bit too risky in your financially conservative mindset, but dream big! I now have a good job at GM. The kids' and our health insurance are covered. I will make more money as time goes by. If we want to do this, the time is now."

"How did you ever figure out that I wasn't happy in what I'm doing? Being in business was always second choice. When the clan denied my attending the Folkwangschule, with a career in acting in mind, I wanted to study the humanities and eventually become a university professor. I felt teaching could almost be an acting job. I love being a ham in front of people. Having had some excellent teachers for a few years and also some not-so-good models, I think I could make it a successful and fulfilling career. Obviously, that wasn't meant to be either. If I had my choice, I would love to teach at a good but not necessarily large university. I would much rather teach and have an impact on young dreamers' lives than sit in some office or lab, working on some esoteric and boring research. That wouldn't be for me. I'm quite aware of 'publish or perish.' I wouldn't be a happy camper at such an institution."

Laura had poured them a second glass of wine. "I want you to take entrance exams at some of the Detroit and other Michigan universities that are convenient to where we live. We'll never find cheaper housing, and I do like my job. So keep that in mind. I mean business. I realize these are your most productive years as far as business is concerned. If you use these years to change tracks, we might live longer and much happier lives. A degree in whatever will allow us a totally different lifestyle. It won't be easy, but you can do it. Please do this for us. Dream! And dream *big!*"

Hektor took Laura in his arms and held her tightly. "Thank you for being so proactive. Thank you for understanding that deep in my heart, I would like to earn my living in a profession I truly love. I'm absolutely amazed that you are willing to sacrifice much in order to make my dreams come true. I had completely given up on any of those ideas. Have you discussed this with your parents, by any chance?"

"As a matter of fact, I have. My mother believes it's one of the smartest things you could do. She would stand behind us all the way, unlike your parents. When you mentioned looking for a different job in retailing, your mother almost had a stroke. She thought you should stay where you make the most money, not necessarily where you might find happiness and satisfaction in what you do."

"I'll look into it. Let's take it one day at a time."

The thought of returning to academic studies had never crossed his mind. *How will I handle studying in a language other than my mother tongue?* He had never had any kind of schooling in an English-speaking country. Although he felt tempted to pursue Laura's idea, he was scared to even think about it. Still, the more he dwelt on the subject, the more compelling became the dream that had eluded him so many years ago.

Chapter 43

LATE in spring, Hektor took entrance exams at Wayne State University, the University of Michigan, and the University of Detroit. He passed the exams easily. In the end, he opted for WSU because it was the most conveniently located institution. He had to be somewhat practical. Laura was thrilled that Hektor was finally embarking on a career of his choice. She knew he would be driven to do well, no matter what subject in academia he ultimately pursued.

On the first of June, Hektor arranged a conference with James Wasserglass, district manager, and his immediate boss, Bob Mitchell. The exchange of greetings was mutually respectful and cordial. Hektor sensed immediately that both gentlemen had an inkling of what he was about to say.

"Please don't get up," Hektor said as he entered Bob's office. "I would like to keep this as informal as possible. Rather than my writing you a letter of resignation, I wanted to discuss, in person, my reasons for wanting to leave International Stores. I know this comes as a surprise. Laura and I gave much thought to our decision.

She encouraged me to return to school with a definite career change in mind. My resignation is effective August 31. I was accepted at Wayne State University, and my studies are to commence in early September. I believe a three-month notice will give you adequate opportunity to hire my replacement."

"Not so fast, young man," James Wasserglass responded. "We have three years invested in you. The company has big plans for Hektor Birken. Think about the significant financial gains in your immediate future and the prestige that goes along with a promotion. We are talking a starting salary of twenty thousand dollars as district manager. Of course, it would involve a lot of traveling. You might even have to move to another location. You can't be serious about giving up all I am prepared to offer you."

"Jim is right," Bob said. "You should discuss his offer with Laura. You are thirty-one years old and have to think about the responsibility for two children. Just think what you are blowing in exchange for going back to school."

"You sound just like my parents in Germany. When we told them of our plans, my mother thought we had lost our minds. She said, 'How can a grown man with responsibilities even think about returning to a school bench? The idea is preposterous and unheard of.'"

James Wasserglass and Bob Mitchell realized they were fighting a losing battle.

Hektor stuck to his guns. "I never have been more serious about anything. We are aware of the sacrifices we'll be making; it will be a struggle initially, but we believe it is the right option for us at this time. Sixteen years ago, when an acting career was totally unacceptable to my family, going to business college was the lesser of the evils open to me. If I couldn't act on a stage, I wanted a classroom to be my platform. I believed then, and still do, that teaching is an honorable profession. The individuals I admired most in my life were some of my teachers. I didn't have that choice then. German pedagogical rules precluded me from pursuing an eventual academic career in

1949. Now that this opportunity presents itself to me, I want to take advantage of it. There is no position with International Stores and no amount of money that would persuade me to change my mind."

"I can see your mind is made up," James Wasserglass conceded. "I admire your gumption, and I am all in favor of people pursuing their educational dreams. Two of my sons are in academia; I would never want to stand in your way of realizing your professional goals. I agree; if there ever was a time for you to undertake such a step, that time is now. You are still young enough to hazard this drastic change in direction in your professional life and for you two to enjoy the fruits of your labor and investment of time and effort. If you need any kind of recommendations in the future, please do not hesitate to call on me. I accept your resignation reluctantly but want to wish you well. Don't become a stranger after you leave the company."

All shook hands before Hektor stepped out of Bob's office. He was relieved he hadn't wavered in spite of all the temptations dangled in front of him.

Chapter 44

HEKTOR finally heard from his mother. He could have predicted her reaction to the drastic changes Laura and he proposed to make in their lives. None of what she espoused in her letter surprised him.

After your phone call the other day, I feel that I must write to you. Your father and I have talked about your wish to quit your present position. We realize that you are doing this for a reason; you hope to achieve something you were denied as a result of your botched education during World War II. All of us have to learn in life that we must relinquish certain dreams. I had to learn that bitter lesson myself so many years ago. You are thirty-one years old and have the responsibility of caring for two children and a young wife. We find it admirable that Laura is willing to work in order to make this dream a reality, but we find it utterly irresponsible on your part to pursue a career in academia at this stage in your life. Actually, I view your resolution to give up a substantial income as pure selfishness. I know my son and realize that it is futile to try to change your mind. Nevertheless, I feel compelled to share my views with you.

The transition from a profession in merchandising and retailing to one in academia played out over the next nine years. Hektor was awarded his PhD on December 10, 1974.

Hektor and Laura walked out of Cobo Hall. He was clutching his doctoral diploma in his left hand. Laura clung to his right. She held firmly to him as she looked up at him. There were tears of joy in her laughing eyes.

"Were all those sacrifices we made through the years worth it? Was the price that we paid too high? You are standing on the threshold of realizing your dreams. Are you speechless?"

Still clad in his doctoral regalia, he stepped in front of Laura. They were surrounded by hundreds of other graduates and their families. He didn't care. He took her in his arms and kissed her deeply.

"Thank you for making my dreams possible. The sacrifices are in the past. Let's look to the future." As he looked into Laura's eyes, he couldn't help recalling one of his favorite songs by the incomparable Edith Piaf. "Non, je ne regrette rien" echoed through is mind.

"No! No regrets.
No! I will have no regrets."

The Birken Saga
Book 3

The Born-Again Phoenix

1965–1974

Chapter 1

THE third week of the fall quarter of 1965 at Wayne State University, Hektor walked into his classroom at seven forty-five and sat down in the front row. He was about to write his very first exam in an English-speaking country. Hektor had never attended school in the United States, nor had he taken any exams, other than getting his GED, passing the citizenship tests in 1960, and taking the recent college entrance exams.

He opened his blank blue book and made sure all his pencils were sharpened. The course in question dealt with ancient history; the anticipated topics for the test were aspects of the Law Code of Hammurabi. He'd read and studied extensively in preparation for this first major event in the new direction he had chosen. Hektor felt confident as he waited for the start of the test. His professor walked in promptly at eight o'clock and passed out the feared questions.

Hektor took one look at the query and panicked. *What's this all about? Who is Hammurabi? Where did I see that name before?*

It was like a curtain had been drawn, wiping away all that was stored in his thirty-one-year-old brain. Everyone around him was frantically writing, but Hektor sat quietly staring into space, at the blue book in front of him, or at his teacher. After twenty minutes, the professor walked over to speak to him.

"Why aren't you writing? I am quite aware of what you know and what you should be able to write. Aren't you feeling well, Mr. Birken?"

"I feel just fine; the only problem is that I can't remember a thing about the subject at hand. I've drawn a complete blank. Sorry to disappoint you."

The teacher returned to his desk, his body language conveying total disbelief of what he was observing. He kept glancing at Hektor every few minutes, hoping that Hektor would attempt to answer a question or two. He waited in vain; it didn't happen. After fifty minutes, Hektor turned in a blank blue book.

His professor opened the exam and just shook his head and shrugged his shoulders. "Now I've seen it all," he mumbled as he tucked the exam papers into his briefcase.

Hektor walked to his next lecture like a zombie. He was half tempted to head straight for the garage and drive home. He was convinced his American college career was short-lived.

Mr. Late Bloomer couldn't help seeing a public telephone and was ready to call Bob Mitchell and ask for reinstatement to his job at the Tip-Top store. But then, he knew better than to do anything rash, and he first wanted to discuss his testing debacle with Laura.

After his last lecture, he walked up to the GM building and stopped by her office. They sat down in one of the conference rooms, and Laura looked at him in complete disbelief. Uncharacteristically, Hektor was totally deflated. He finally spoke up.

"I can tell by your eyes; you don't have to say a word. You keep asking me what happened. I drew a total blank and didn't write a single word. It was almost like I had a stroke—and it wasn't a stroke of genius. Talk about making a big mistake; talk about feeling like a complete ass. I'm tempted to call Bob and beg him to take me back. This just isn't going to work for me."

"*Oh, no!* We are not giving up this easily. I remember you often telling me that you've never started anything in life that you haven't finished. This is one of those starts—and you will finish it. You have spoken of talking to me like a Dutch uncle? Well, let me tell you something, mister; I'm talking to you like a Dutch aunt. You make an appointment with that Hammurabi professor and see if he will give you a make-up exam. And if not, you'll just plan on doing a heck of a lot better for the remainder of the quarter. This is one time that I'll insist on you trying harder and doing well in the end. And don't give me that nonsense about being too old to learn new things. Put that in your pipe and smoke it."

He could tell Laura was angry. Hektor saw a side of her he had never encountered before. It was clearly a case of a strong woman behind every successful man.

Subsequently, Hektor did well on all exams and ended with a 3.65 GPA for the three classes he took during his first quarter. A professor in the Humanities Center became his adviser. He encouraged Hektor to pursue a degree in comparative literature, English/ German, allowing him to take advantage of his extensive knowledge of German and the works of Germany's many well-known literary greats.

After the successful completion of the first quarter, Hektor believed it was high time for him to find some sort of part-time employment. He felt guilty letting Laura shoulder all of their financial responsibilities. She wasn't sure, however, if this was the right time for him to find work.

"I'm not certain you should spread yourself so thin at this point. Just because you managed to come out on top during the first quarter doesn't mean things will be easier from now on. I believe you are making a mistake."

"Well, let me make my own mistakes. I just cannot allow you to be the only breadwinner in this family. I need to make some contribution toward keeping this ship afloat. It can't all rest on your shoulders alone."

A search in the want ads of the *Detroit Free Press* was the first step. He found exactly what he was looking for. The small company was conveniently located halfway between home and school. "Laura, this job sounds perfect for what I want. I have to put in twenty hours a week but can work anytime—day or night. There's total flexibility in my being there. I'm going to call and make an appointment."

Mrs. Dorato was a charming and efficient businesswoman. She and her husband and one other employee basically ran the entire operation. During the interview, Hektor realized that Mrs. Dorato was not exactly a spring chicken. While she had flawless skin and was attractively made up, he could tell that her dark hair had been helped by a dose from a bottle of dye. He liked her smile and the light in her eyes.

"You have excellent recommendations, and I do admire your efforts at returning to studies at this stage in your life. That took guts. More power to you. If you decide to take the job, you will have keys to this place and access to the alarm codes. You may come early in the morning before anyone is here and work as many hours as you choose before heading out to your first class and/or return in the afternoon when it is convenient. There may be days when you have too many classes and cannot come at all. You pick the days and times that fit your schedule best. What do you say?"

"Sounds like a winner to me. You are pretty trusting to hand me keys and security codes right from the start."

"Mr. Birken, you are not some irresponsible kid. You have impeccable credentials and are obviously overqualified for the job. Nevertheless, I appreciate your interest in working and wanting to make a contribution to the well-being of your family. My husband and I are hardworking people and are impressed with what you are trying to do."

"When would you like me to start?"

"How about right now? I'll take you into the stock area and show you what some of your responsibilities might be. There will be crates and boxes that need unpacking and breakable items that require proper storage in specific sections. I hope you are not afraid to use ladders."

"No problem; ladders are fine."

They walked into a room filled with jars and little boxes, a tiny scale, and shipping materials.

"There may be times when you will need to fill orders in this room, where we keep all our china paints. Other times, you will work in the front and help us to get catalogs and mailings out to our many customers. On occasion, you might even wait on a customer in the store. I'm glad the hourly wage was acceptable to you. My husband and I look forward to having you with us."

※

Hektor started working and quickly picked up what was expected of him. While he got along well with the owners, eventually there would be occasional tense moments between the one and only other employee, Ludovico, and him. For some idiotic reason, the Oriental gentleman appeared to be threatened by the newcomer.

One Friday morning, after six months on the job, the store was brimming with chattering women, all excited about the latest china blanks advertised in the most recent mailing of the catalog. Mrs. Dorato stepped into the stockroom and asked Hektor to serve some of the anxious clients waiting to be helped in the store. Ludovico was great, laying on his schmaltz in that syrupy voice of his, when he could take all the time in the world and tend to a single customer. However, crowd control was clearly not his forté.

Hektor had gotten to know some of the regulars by taking their orders over the phone; these ladies were pleased to make the acquaintance of that unknown face at last. He could tell that Ludovico was not exactly thrilled with the reception Hektor received. *It's great to be exposed to some daylight and mingle with people,* Hektor thought. *I enjoy helping out in a pinch.*

As soon as things settled down, Hektor and Ludovico had their first showdown. The Doratos had gone out to lunch, and Ludovico was brazen enough to confront Hektor.

"I believe it is high time for you to return to the jobs for which you were hired. Put your apron back on and disappear to the stockroom where you belong. I don't need you in the store. This is my domain, and I intend to keep it that way!"

Hektor was ready to give the guy a fat lip. "Whoa! Whoa! You remember who summoned me to work in the store this morning. Let me set you straight, buster. You may have worked here for a few years, but I will not take that kind of crap from you. You are not talking to some kid you can bamboozle. I have absolutely no interest in usurping your precious territory. I have bigger fish to fry! If you make another remark like that, I'll discuss the matter with Mr. and Mrs. Dorato."

Hektor walked away, giving him the finger; he had no intention of taking the matter any further—for now. He could tell by Ludovico's demeanor and facial expressions that he understood what Hektor had tried to make perfectly clear. In the course of the almost three years that Hektor worked for the Doratos, he and Ludovico had occasional spats, but Ludovico had learned his lesson well and never again addressed Hektor in such a demeaning tone.

To Hektor, it was a convenient means of supplementing their weekly income. He succeeded in doing so and did it on his own terms. He and Ludovico learned to coexist peacefully and did their respective jobs.

At the end of his first year at WSU, he received a Wayne State

University Board of Governors scholarship for his entire undergraduate work; even his tuition for his first year was refunded. It was found money. He opted for a very special surprise.

On her next buying trip to Germany, Mrs. Dorato bought an exceptionally beautiful Hutschenreuther service for six and all serving dishes. The factory shipped the order directly to the store. Hektor carefully unpacked his treasure and smuggled his surprise into their home. It was fully on display in their china cabinet when Laura first laid eyes on it.

"What's this? Where did you get it? Where did you get the money to pay for all this?"

"No, I didn't rob the Doratos. I used the money I was refunded from WSU; they gave me back my tuition for the first year. I wanted us to have something beautiful to reward us for what we have achieved during this challenging year. Let's consider it an early Christmas present to each other. Just think; I might have spent the money on a huge artificial Christmas tree."

"Oh, let's not even go there. I still have the events associated with our first two natural Christmas trees in front of my eyes. How could I forget you bending the tree stand to straighten out the crooked tree we bought in the darkness of night in 1963 or the whole tree taking flight off the balcony when you became angry at not being able to fit its trunk into the stand? I was thrilled when you gave up on the idea of natural trees after that unforgettable episode last year and bought that beautiful artificial tree at a bargain price right after Christmas. Thanks, but no thanks, one tree will do us for now! And … thank you. I love what you have done; these dishes are priceless. I didn't think we'd have anything this beautiful so soon."

His studies in the humanities opened his eyes to the worlds of art and music that would enhance his life for the rest of his days. As hard as he tried, he couldn't avoid having to suffer through a science sequence. Eventually, he settled on geology, the least invasive and challenging. By testing out of many general education courses, Hektor was able to save one year and received his BA in June 1968.

One of the unexpected perks of being a humanities major was the ease of access for reasonable tickets to many cultural events in the city. The highlight of the spring 1967 quarter was the week-long appearance of the Metropolitan Opera at the Masonic Temple in Detroit. Hektor thought he had died and gone to heaven. Through his professor of music appreciation, he garnered tickets for all seven performances. It was Laura's baptism by fire into the world of opera. Prior to that week, her only exposure to opera had been a performance of *Carmen* when she attended college, the lead having been sung by none other than Beverly Sills.

Opening night was *Un Ballo in Maschera*, with Leontyne Price as Amelia. The evening began with a humorous event in the auditorium. Just before the lights were dimmed, an elderly gentleman and a lady in white walked down the aisle to take their seats in the expensive orchestra section. The lady called attention to herself with her tightly fitted dress that flared out dramatically at the hem. It was the fit of the dress that caught the attention of many a gentleman, who trained his opera glasses on the appearance of the latecomer.

Laura had learned a few phrases from a self-study book in beginning German. During the first intermission, friends of theirs and Laura and Hektor couldn't believe their good fortune when the lady and gentleman in question walked toward them.

Laura took a deep breath and uttered distinctly—and to everyone's surprise—*"Aber die Blonde ist hässlich!"* ["But the blonde is so ugly!"]

On close inspection, they saw that the lady was at least seventy and perhaps older but was trying to look twenty-seven or younger. Her makeup appeared to have been applied with a spatula; the woman looked almost grotesque. It was indeed comic relief from the seriousness of the operatic plot.

Elisabeth Grümmer sang Elsa in *Lohengrin* the next night. The high points for Laura were the performances by Birgit Nilsson, Franco Corelli, and Renata Scotto in *Turandot* and Franco Corelli and Mirella Freni in *Romeo and Juliet*. For Laura, it was indeed a tour de force, working all day at her job and then looking perky and appreciative of seven performances in a row. Nevertheless, she showed enthusiasm for an art form to which she'd had little prior exposure. For Hektor, it was glorious from start to finish.

Hektor pursued his Master of Arts in German and French nineteenth- and twentieth-century literature and obtained his degree in June 1969. His graduate assistantship allowed him to teach various sections of German. The interactions with students in his classes gave him the pleasure he had always dreamed about as a young man. The classroom had indeed become his stage at last. His MA adviser encouraged him to go for his PhD in modern languages; he was accepted into the Department of Germanic Languages and Literatures at the University of Michigan, with studies to commence in the fall of 1970.

But this was Fall 1969. Hektor's teaching contract at WSU commenced in September. He believed he needed a break from the intense studies he'd pursued for the last four years. Teaching his three classes in beginning and intermediate German was pure joy for the new man among the established faculty. Many of his former professors were only too willing to provide helpful hints to make the process productive, meaningful, and pleasurable for his students and him.

It had been four years since the Birkens had benefitted from two regular incomes, and Hektor wanted to show Laura his appreciation for all she had done.

"Have you taken a close look at that 'good' winter coat of yours lately?"

Laura looked quizzically at Hektor. "What do you mean? Don't you like my black coat any more, or have I outgrown it?"

"Neither. It just looks tired and is in need of replacing. I want to take you shopping on Saturday. And I don't want any arguments or talk of frivolity. You deserve it."

She had no idea he had bought her a beautiful diamond that he intended to present to her under the Christmas tree. He felt it was high time—they'd been married for going on seven years. She, on the other hand, was perfectly happy with her simple Lohengrin ring of fourteen-karat gold.

They parked the car and walked over to Woodward Ave. Having worked in downtown Detroit, Laura was familiar with most of the better stores and their locations.

"Aren't we going to Hudson's? It's in the opposite direction."

"No, honey. We are going to that little fur salon where I bought you that stole for the beautiful wedding we attended a few years ago."

"Are you nuts? I don't need a fur coat. A nice wool coat will do just fine."

"Let me be the judge of that. I know exactly what I want to get for you."

The friendly owner of the shop, Maurice, remembered Hektor and Laura. "How nice to see you again. What can we do for you today? You have anything in particular in mind?"

Hektor took over. "I have been eying that beauty of a black broadtail coat with the stunning mink collar in the window. I would like my wife to try it on."

"No problem." He took a quick glance at Laura and decided it might be just the right size for her. "Here we are. Let me slip it on you. Of course, if it isn't just perfect, the crew and I know how to make adjustments."

Laura held her breath and didn't say a word as she admired the coat, looking at her mirrored reflection. Tears crept down her cheeks. "It's beautiful but much too costly and precious for me. I never dreamed of having a fur coat. I can't get over how lightweight it feels. I always thought Persian lamb was heavier."

"Honey—if I may call you that—it's broadtail, which is much lighter. How does it feel to you otherwise? The only change necessary that I see is a slight adjustment in the length of the sleeves. I suggest we give it a pretty cufflike treatment, which would clearly add to the beauty of the coat," suggested Maurice.

"You have yourself a deal," Hektor said. "I would like Laura to try on one of those matching mink hats that I see in the cabinet over there."

Laura decided not to make any waves. She had learned over the years to accept her husband's spontaneity when it came to periodic splurges that involved her. He often encouraged her to learn to *"live, live, live!"*

"Laura, that hat looks great on you. My God, you look like Lara in *Dr. Zhivago*. We'll take it. When will you have the coat ready?"

"It's early enough in the day. We can have the coat ready for you in a couple of hours. You have any other shopping to do?"

"As a matter of fact, we do. After shopping for boots and a purse, we'll have lunch at Hudson's. They feature one of my favorite things. Their Maurice salad is outstanding. It isn't, by any chance, named after you, is it?"

"No, no. It must have been some other lucky Maurice. But I know what you mean about that salad; it's one of my favorites as well. See you at three thirty. It will all be ready for your pickup. It's been a pleasure doing business again." Maurice held the door open for them to leave.

They walked out onto Woodward Avenue, with Laura hanging tightly to Hektor's right arm and smiling like a Cheshire cat.

"You are something else. Thank you, thank you! I'll love wearing my new coat and hat to church on Sunday."

At Crowley's, Hektor couldn't resist buying Laura a stunning alligator bag and beautiful black boots at Hudson's.

"Let's go and enjoy our lunch." The Maurice salad was as enjoyable as ever.

Maurice kept his word; the coat and hat were ready when they stopped at the salon after lunch.

Laura decided it was time for her to plan a little surprise for Hektor. "Before we head home, I would like you to drive over to Grand Boulevard. There's a painting I've been admiring in that charming little boutique gallery near my office. It reminds me so much of the idyllic oil landscape in Greta's dining room. I know you've always admired it."

"So now you want to have your kind of shopping spree to get even with me, huh?"

"I won't get even with you. I don't believe its price will match anything you spent earlier in the day. But indulge me, and let's at least look at it."

The painting was still in the window, although Hektor didn't care at all for the framing. It didn't do anything for the beautifully executed work. "Well, let me find out what the damage might be."

They were greeted by a friendly gentleman, perhaps old enough to be their grandfather.

"We like the landscape featured in your window but don't care for the frame," Hektor said. "It just wouldn't work with the rest of our décor."

"That's no problem. It's a stretched canvas we can just pop out. I'll give you a good price without the frame. You can select a different frame or buy it without any frame. The price for the painting is two hundred dollars. What do you say?"

Laura was ready to jump at the offer, but Hektor hesitated, just for a pregnant moment. He had learned to deal in certain situations.

"Thanks for the offer; I would like to think about it. We'll stop in next week after I pick up my wife at GM. We drive by your gallery five days a week."

A friendly handshake, and they left the kind old gentleman standing there wondering. He didn't quite get it when Laura winked at him as she marched out of the gallery, clinging to Hektor's arm.

Hektor turned to Laura. "It's a nice painting, but let me see if I can get him to come down a few bucks. Some starving artist might accept a little less."

"Why do you need to dicker with the man? It's certainly something I would never have done. I thought his price was fair. You suit yourself."

"I will. I will. Don't give it another thought."

They drove home and enjoyed the rest of the fall weekend. Laura was a vision in her new duds when they went to church on Sunday.

As he drove her to the office on Monday morning, the landscape was back in the window. He had no time to stop back before Wednesday of that week and had the shock of his life as he walked up to the gallery on Wednesday afternoon after he had taught his last class.

"Sorry, sir. The painting is gone. A lady came in yesterday afternoon and bought it just the way it was, frame and all. May I show you some similar paintings by the artist?"

"No, thank you. The other one reminded us so much of a painting a dear friend in Germany has enjoyed for years. Perhaps some other time." He walked back to the car. When Laura joined him a few minutes later, he couldn't wait to tell her what happened.

"That's too bad. I wish you had let me buy it for you on Saturday." She just giggled to herself.

※

Come Thanksgiving, he couldn't stand to sit on his other surprise any longer. He decided to give Laura the long-overdue diamond at the traditional family feast at her parents' home. No one was more shocked than Laura.

"When did you do this? And it even fits perfectly." She kept holding it against the light, mesmerized by the sparkle on her left hand. "Boy, you know how to surprise a girl. Thanks! I love it!"

Caitlin smiled at Hektor; she had been in on the deal.

It was mid-December, and Hektor sat in his office reading final exams for his students. He had closed his office door. With his shoes kicked off, he propped up his stockinged feet on his desk. He was totally absorbed in reading his students' papers when the phone disrupted his train of thought. *Who the hell wants to break the spell of the moment?* There was a touch of annoyance in his voice as he lifted the phone off the cradle. "Hektor Birken. How may I help you?"

"Hi, Hektor, it's Evelyne at the office. I've got bad news. Laura wasn't feeling well and had to be taken to Harper Hospital. They are not sure but thought she might have had a mild stroke. Can you get away from the office and hightail it over there? After you see Laura and speak with the doctors, please call me—anytime. I'm really worried. Josef and I will keep her in our prayers." She hung up, realizing what must be running through Hektor's mind.

He was on his way to Harper Hospital within seconds, just briefly informing his next-door colleague where he was headed. He was glad to see Laura bedded in a private room, thanks to GM's generous health-care plan.

Laura smiled as he walked in the room. "Sorry, honey, I hadn't planned this as a last-minute Christmas surprise. I seem to be much better; they gave me some kind of injection. The doctors attending me here and Dr. Humburg want to speak with us ASAP. Right now, all I want to do is close my eyes and sleep. Sorry—I'm not great company."

Stepping out of Laura's hospital room, he was greeted by their family physician.

"Let's grab a cup of coffee in the cafeteria. I'll fill you in on what happened. From what the initial assessments show, Laura will be OK and make a full recovery."

Hektor walked next to Dr. Humburg without saying a word. He needed to digest all that had transpired in the last few hours.

"Apparently, Laura was totally disoriented when trying to get on the correct elevator. Most of the operators knew her and got her to the Gold Coast OK, because she had often worked on the floor where the financial staff executive offices were located. Once she arrived, she had no idea who she was or what she was supposed to do. One of the big bosses called her office and spoke with her cohort, Evelyne. She is the person who ordered the ambulance that took Laura to Harper. She's in good hands.

"It appears she had a mild stroke that primarily affected her occipital lobe, thus causing the disorientation and visual problems. The quick intervention precludes further damage. There are two things that I recommend: Laura should not continue with her birth control regimen, and she should give up smoking completely. The first might bring about a change in your family constellation; the second will be tough on her day-to-day well-being. I believe Laura should never again subject herself to any sort of hormone-related treatments."

"I agree. Giving up smoking will not be easy, but she'll do it. As far as going off the pill, she won't have a problem with that at all. She has wanted to have children for some time. We'll give it a whirl. Thanks for speaking with me."

They shook hands, and the good doctor was on his way to consult with other patients. Hektor called Evelyne to give her the news.

"Boy, giving up smoking will be tough on Laura. I remember the last time she tried that. She was hell on wheels. As much as I wanted her to quit, I reached the conclusion that she was better off smoking than being so traumatically impacted by the absence of her nicotine fixes. Gosh, I might become a godmother!" Evelyne let it rest there.

⋈

Hektor took Laura home two days before Christmas. Once she was settled comfortably in the Impala, Laura spoke up.

"I have a little surprise for you. It was supposed to work differently, but under the circumstances, you must claim the present yourself." As they passed the little gallery on Grand Boulevard, she gently nudged him with her left elbow. "Please stop and see the old gentleman. He's waiting for you with a Christmas present."

"You are kidding me, aren't you?"

"No, I was the lady who bought the painting. I asked the old gent to be in on the surprise and to tell you that it was sold just the way it was. I only bought the painting, not the frame you didn't like. It's all paid for. He'll have a good laugh when you walk in. I spoke with him on the phone from the hospital. He knows why I couldn't pick it up myself."

⋈

"Nice to see you, young man." He smiled from ear to ear. "Hope you will enjoy this lovely painting your wife bought. I was happy to be in on the little deceptive game she was playing with you."

They shook hands, and Hektor walked out with his treasure, all wrapped in beautiful Christmas foil. Laura laughed out loud as he got in next to her and planted a soft kiss on her lips.

"Thank you; that was sweet of you!"

"You are most welcome, Sir Hektor. And Merry Christmas!"

⋈

Hektor had put up their beautiful, although artificial, tree, and the house was completely decorated for Christmas. Nevertheless, the holiday spirit was somewhat subdued since Laura was still not completely herself. It took several weeks before she was ready to return to work. What they did enjoy were their moments of extreme closeness in their efforts to conceive a child.

For now, the oil painting was stored in their bedroom closet. Hektor had it appropriately framed and presented it to Laura for her twenty-eighth birthday the following June.

Acknowledgments

THE author wishes to express his sincere gratitude to Graham Schofield for his invaluable critical support and suggestions during the editorial process of this work. Expressions of great appreciation are extended to the staff of Wheatmark Publishing Services for their efforts in bringing the Birken Trilogy to fruition. Special recognition is accorded to Wheatmark's Senior Project Manager, Lori Conser, for her dedicated and diligent work leading to the publication of the author's writings. Many thanks are due those who have encouraged the author to write, in particular the members of the Green Valley Writers' Forum and family and friends. Last but not least, the author recognizes his wife, Lynne, with heartfelt thankfulness for her endless hours of reading and providing critical editorial commentary.